Uncle Clint & Aunt Tan,
I hope you
as much as I e

with love, your neice,
EC Moore

INCURABLE

by E.C. Moore

Booktrope Editions
Seattle WA 2015

Cover Design by E.C. Moore
Edited by Jennifer Farwell

This is a work of fiction. Names, characters, places, brands, media, and incidents are either the product of the author's imagination or are used fictitiously. Any resemblance to similarly named places or to persons living or deceased is unintentional.

Print ISBN 978-1-5137-0015-1
EPUB ISBN 978-1-5137-0046-5
Library of Congress Control Number: 2015909984

This book is dedicated to all the women who, for whatever reason, became *sporting girls* before and during WWII on Hotel Street in Honolulu.

Everyone's youth is a dream, a form of chemical madness. **F. Scott Fitzgerald**

Beauty is a short-lived tyranny. **Socrates**

ONE
1953

In the midst of those glitzy Hollywood days, before up-and-coming Las Vegas shoved a switchblade in the back of the Sunset Strip and killed the glamour dead, Marilyn Walsh met Gary Palmer at Ciro's nightclub. Lucille Ball and Desi Arnaz were cozy in a nearby booth. Not many stars could turn Marilyn's head the way Lucy did.

Lucy wasn't the only one turning heads that night. When Gary Palmer spotted Marilyn Walsh, sitting at a table with her co-worker Ginny Hartford and a few of her closest friends, he promptly abandoned his date to mosey over. He was acquainted with Ginny, but it was Marilyn he was interested in. Gary didn't bowl Marilyn over on the spot, although he was striking and confident, square-jawed, sandy-haired, and blue-eyed. She was out on the town with the girls—not on the prowl for male company. Besides, she couldn't ignore the way he had thoughtlessly abandoned his date.

He telephoned Ginny a few days later at the studio, and she supplied the anxious bachelor with Marilyn's number, without permission. Marilyn was not pleased; she expected friends to respect her privacy.

"Who are you, again?" Marilyn asked, but of course she remembered.

"Gary Palmer. I work at Huntington Memorial Hospital in Pasadena. I met Ginny through the Goldmans. I'll have you know, I'm a respectable guy. They say I'm a good catch."

"Did I give the impression I might be interested?"

"Come on…be nice. Since I laid eyes on you, I've come to believe in love at first sight."

If he'd only known how many times she'd heard that tired line, then he might have chosen a better one. Marilyn stood five-foot-seven in her stocking feet, sporting measurements that men noticed and women envied. Radiant, with auburn hair and large expressive green eyes, she was accustomed to flattery.

"You don't have to lay it on so thick," she said.

"Fine, I'll tone it down. But I really do want to get to know you. Tell me about yourself."

Beryl Quinn was her real name, but as with so many in Hollywood, that had changed. Marilyn Walsh was a very different person from Beryl Quinn, anyway. "I'm from Jacksonville, Florida. I was adopted by elderly parents. After they died, I made my way to California."

She had told a barefaced lie, and the gullible guy bought the fabricated history hook, line, and sinker, no questions asked.

"The land of milk and honey," was his reply.

"So, you're a doctor? My mother would love that." She corrected herself immediately. "I mean, she *would have*, but, as I told you, she's gone now."

He expressed his heartfelt sympathy for her fictional, dearly departed mother, then made a startling announcement. "I'm searching for a suitable wife."

Taken aback by his overly bold approach, she rolled her pretty eyes. "Is that so?"

"I wouldn't mind looking at you over the breakfast table for the next fifty years. How about I take you to dinner sometime soon? Sometime very soon."

Marilyn agreed to a date. The wife-seeking doctor picked her up the following Saturday at her house on Nepeta. They dined at Musso & Frank's, where they discovered their mutual adoration for thick steaks served rare.

Marilyn visited Gary's hometown of Pasadena on their sixth date. She accompanied him to a gala at the Annandale Country Club, a posh affair if there ever was one. She'd picked up a smart silk dress at Saks earlier in the week, a good move to be sure, as there were numerous fashionable ladies in attendance, all very chic, with gobs of sparkling ice hanging from swan necks and dainty wrists. She would have been mortified if she hadn't dressed fittingly. Gary was no Fred Astaire, and Marilyn knew for a fact that she was no Ginger Rogers, but they still had a good time on the dance floor.

They left the club after an hour or so because Gary seemed bored with the crowd, and he drove to his place—a knotty-pine-paneled ranch house with oodles of property, which backed up to a large pond. They lounged on the covered patio and shared a nightcap. Marilyn marveled at the quiet country feel of the backyard. She regretted the lie about being an orphan. As it turned out, she'd grown fond of the doctor, and now felt trapped by untruths.

Suddenly serious, he cleared his throat. "I'm a Freemason," he told her. "I belong to the Masonic Scottish Rite Temple."

"Really, Doc?" Marilyn said, using the pet name she'd recently given him. Perhaps he was falling for her, why else would he share such private information? Unsure how to respond, she said, "How enigmatic."

Gary frowned, and she could tell he meant for her to understand how important this Freemason business was. "It's a family thing— Palmers are Masons."

She didn't divulge her Catholic upbringing. She couldn't help but wonder if Masons were a club or a religion. Her knowledge of such things was virtually nonexistent. Marilyn wasn't particularly concerned about Gary's religious affiliations because she had long since given up on hers.

✢ ✢ ✢

Gary popped the question a few weeks later, and Marilyn accepted. She wasn't madly in love, but after all she'd been through, stability was more desirable than fireworks. She insisted they marry in Las Vegas. Celebrities had made tying the knot in quickie ceremonies on the strip all the rage. Plus, the Vegas plan eliminated all the nonsense his mother was cooking up, with guest lists and full-blown orchestras and such.

When Lillian Palmer discovered her son's fiancée was an orphaned girl from Florida, working in the costume department at a Hollywood studio, she balked. Marilyn's only saving grace, in Lillian's eyes anyway, was how she readily agreed to give up her career to have a baby right away. Lillian's son was finally ready to commit to someone, and his parents were looking forward to grandchildren. Marilyn would have to do.

Lillian was thrilled to learn that her fertile daughter-in-law was expecting so soon—just four months after the wedding—and swept her off for an extravagant shopping spree featuring proper maternity frocks and sensible shoes.

After twenty hours of grueling labor, Marilyn gave birth to a baby girl. They named her Lilly. It would have been preferable to name the child Nicole, after her own mother—a woman very much alive back in Michigan who could not know her daughter had just given birth to her first grandchild.

Bossy old Lillian fussed over Lilly, while Marilyn's own mother missed out. Marilyn hadn't seen or spoken with her in over fourteen long years, and she missed her more and more with each passing day. Memories of her long lost childhood crowded Marilyn's guilt-ridden thoughts.

✧ ✧ ✧

1928

Her birth name was Beryl Quinn. She struggled to keep her upbringing as a child of privilege in Detroit hidden, ever watchful to not speak of her father, Patrick Quinn, and never divulging the identity of her grandfather, James Quinn. Her grandfather had been a shrewd businessman and the founder of Quinn's Bottling Company. Shocking the family, he'd instigated a hostile takeover of the wildly successful conglomerate, Modern Engine Works, ripping it away from his very own brother. He had also snatched up Swifty's Drug Store for a song after Swifty Swartz suffered a crippling stroke. And James loved nothing more than acquiring prime real estate at bargain basement prices.

Yes, her Detroit childhood would remain hush-hush. People in her life did not know she'd grown up on River Road, in a grand house with a massive porch flanked by two stone lions imported from France. Despite Nicole's hesitation, James urged Patrick and Nicole to move into one of his luxuriously furnished homes as soon as they returned from a three-month long honeymoon in Europe.

An only child, Beryl became the center of attention. The entire third floor of the grand house was tailored to meet her every need. The Negro nanny slept in a nook adjacent to Beryl's bedroom, instead of the maid's quarters downstairs. Beryl was extremely fond of Opal and demanded the nanny remain close.

Her father was the youngest of nine children, and the only son. Beryl was twenty-second in a long line of grandchildren. Anne Quinn, her faultfinding grandmother, barely tolerated Beryl at best. But her grandfather frequently told her, "You, Beryl, are by far my favorite granddaughter." He showered her with attention and encouraged her to sit on his lap. Her grandfather gave her many treats and gifts and bestowed her with a colossal present for her sixth birthday. As one of James's employees led a fine-looking pony down the gravel driveway to where the family had been instructed to wait, Nicole's delicate hand flew straight up to her scarfed neck, and she let out a little gasp followed by a shrill squeak.

"What on Earth?" she declared.

Beryl jumped in place, clapping her hands together wildly. "Yippee!" she cried.

"Where will we ever house that creature?" Nicole exclaimed.

"Don't you fret, woman," James told Nicole, "Blossom will stay in my stables. Beryl will ride out at the country house."

James lifted his granddaughter, proudly set her atop the pretty pony, and proceeded to lead Blossom around the yard. Beryl remained keenly aware of her mother's scowl. Her somber, blue-eyed, dark-haired Papa leaned against a tree and watched the scene play out. Every now and then he took a nip from a silver flask. Patrick liked his whiskey. James did not approve of his son's propensity for liquor, and neither did Nicole. Patrick's folly was one issue the two agreed on.

It was November, and chilly. Nicole allowed Beryl to ride around the yard for a brief spell, then insisted they all return inside the warm house for cake and tea. Beryl threw a tizzy fit.

"Never you mind," Grandfather said, in an effort to console his distraught granddaughter. "I'll come for you next week and you can ride Blossom properly."

Beryl loved Grandfather almost as much as she loved Papa. She was only six years old, but she understood he was set to attain whatever his heart desired. Everyone said James was a man of power. Her Papa was cut from a different cloth: She'd heard Mama say often enough that Patrick was a sensitive sort and no match for the old man, or *the bully*, as she often referred to her father-in-law.

Beryl overheard Mama tell a friend how James had coldly refused to help Patrick launch the Continental-style restaurant he longed to open. Patrick felt Detroit was primed and ready for true European elegance. James was a meat and potatoes man, and he did not share his son's enthusiasm for exotic fare. James placed Patrick in charge of Swifty's downtown instead. If Patrick could make a go of the ice cream counter and soda fountain in the drug store, then someday he might be capable enough to manage a full-fledged restaurant.

⛨ ⛨ ⛨

It was difficult to understand why so many men were compelled to ingest great quantities of liquor, but most women viewed all manner of drink to be *demon rum*. Papa often reeked of whiskey when he came home at night, and Mama would say, "Patrick Quinn—you're corked. Sit down and eat before you pass out!"

Opal left the house every Saturday night, and she wouldn't return until first thing Monday morning. Beryl had no idea where her beloved nanny went, or what she did while she was away. She asked plenty of questions, but Nanny would not divulge details about her personal affairs. Enticing to her to talk about her life outside the house was harder than pulling teeth.

"You ever tasted whiskey, Nanny?" Beryl asked Opal one night, after Papa had come home again with a snoot full and Mama had thrown a pitcher of water in his face. Beryl was curious about her father's ardent fondness for what Mama termed *a social evil*.

"Now, why you ask that?" Opal's dark eyes opened wide and became encircled in white, a sure sign Beryl had gone too far.

"Papa likes whiskey, but Mama and Grandfather hate it. Hooch is against the law, but people drink it still. They go to speakeasies. I wondered if you've ever been, that's all."

"Uh-uh, oh no, not me," Opal replied, as she folded bedding. "I never."

"Why do you think Papa likes whiskey so much?"

Opal wagged her head from side to side in slow motion. "My Daddy, he drank like a fish," she said, sadly. "Moonshine, mostly." Her nanny's eyes took on a familiar look. It was as if she could see her father once more. He had died from snakebite, and her mother had died of tuberculosis not long after.

"What's moonshine?"

"Liquor cooked up out in the woods. Down home, that's what folks like best."

Opal had come to Detroit from the Deep South—a mysterious, hot place, which by all accounts was chock full of snakes and mean people. Not that there weren't mean people in Detroit.

✛ ✛ ✛

Aunt Francis came down with Bright's disease. The name didn't sound awful, but Beryl knew it must have been a terrible ailment, because Grandfather paid a fortune for his daughter to go to a special hospital called a sanitarium. It was far away in San Diego, California, and it was one where they would administer special baths and provide progressive medicines and treatments. Family members whispered whenever they spoke about the ailing spinster. Beryl's plainest aunt had never married. The poor thing was an old maid—a fate worse than death. "Any fool can see," Aunt Penny claimed, as she shuddered dramatically for emphasis, "a woman without a man is doomed to a solitary, unfulfilled existence. A woman without a man is to be pitied."

Her aunt's terrible ailment caused Beryl to fret about coming down with some kind of sickness too. But, she didn't come down with Bright's disease, as she feared. She contracted the measles instead. One afternoon her nose began to run like a faucet, and shortly thereafter she suffered a coughing fit at the dinner table. Mama ordered Opal to remove the ailing child from the dining room immediately.

When Nicole arrived upstairs to check on Beryl, the nanny told her she had come down with the measles. Nicole hurried out of the room. She had never had the measles and dreaded coming down with them. Everyone knew the stories about how terrible an adult case could prove to be.

Nanny cared for Beryl nonstop. The doctor visited. The drapes were kept shut, as per his instructions. Opal listened intently to his every word. Beryl did not leave the gloomy nursery for several days, and Nicole never entered the room.

Feverish, and in and out of a deep sleep, Beryl's eyes hurt. She was covered in red bumps. The itchy redness lived inside her ears, between her toes, and way up inside her tiny nostrils.

She recovered, and Beryl developed an even stronger empathy for Aunt Francis. How strange and lonesome her aunt's life must be in that sanitarium, sick, *day in and day out*, and so far away from family.

When Nicole believed her daughter had finally recovered, Grandfather was allowed to come and retrieve Beryl, so she could ride Blossom to her heart's content at last. Nicole had dressed Beryl head to toe in wool finery. She had also insisted Beryl use a muff. Outside, Opal—ever a practical influence—whispered in the child's ear, "You can't ride no horse with no muff." She then shoved Beryl's gloves in her pocket at the last minute when the lady of the house wasn't looking.

Beryl fell asleep on the ride out to the much-loved country house on Grosse Isle. Upon arrival, an Irish servant woman with a thick brogue greeted grandfather and granddaughter. They took a quick lunch of vegetable soup and warm bread, and then set out for the stables. To Beryl's delight, she was able to spend quite a good deal of time atop Blossom, and wished she could stay with her forever. The sky grew dark, though, and Grandfather feared snow. He turned Blossom over to the stable boy and suggested they head on home, as there was no point in causing her fretful mother undue concern. Before leaving the island, he turned down an unfamiliar side road, drove through a thick forest of trees, and pulled into a clearing.

Beryl asked why he stopped the car. If he answered, she had no recollection of his reply. He turned off the motor and sat still for a few moments. The quiet spell stretched on long enough to make Beryl's pulse quicken. All of a sudden, he reached over and drew her close. "You are a fine girl," he said. "The pulse of my heart." His voice sounded odd, and Beryl felt twitchy in his clench. "Does your Papa tell you how pretty you are?"

"He does," she replied. "Mama does, too. And Opal says she could eat me up." Maybe, if she talked fast, the icky hug would end, and they would start off for home again. She offered up a sweet smile to please him.

But Grandfather's mood darkened. "That nigger said that?" he snapped. His bloodshot eyes bugged out, he glared at Beryl, and a menacing grimace spread across his flabby face. He began to run his hands over her thick overcoat. "So many clothes. Your mother keeps you bundled, doesn't she?"

"It's winter," she replied, or something similar, as she wriggled in discomfort. She wore her scratchy liberty bodice—a long vest with suspenders attached to woolen stockings—and grew itchier and itchier by the minute. She wanted to get home so Opal could help pull them off.

"Beryl, remove your hat."

She followed his command. She set her favorite felt cloche down on the car seat. Grandfather ran his thick fingers across her cheek and fondled her curls. His labored breath made her wonder just what was the matter with him. He slipped his left hand inside his trousers and she instinctively looked away. "Tell me about your night clothes," he said, thickly. "Tell me what you wear to bed."

Beryl didn't understand what was he was up to, but still, she was more afraid than she had ever been. It was all she could do to whisper, "Nightgowns."

"White...soft?" he said, breathlessly. "You must look like an angel." *An angel?*

His left hand moved violently up and down inside the tent of his trousers, and he radiated warmth. His meaty face pinched. The crook of his right arm suddenly yanked her tight against his side. A pained grunt gave way to a series of spasms—a routine she would grow accustomed to—as he sought the same exact release over and over whilst in her company. Grandfather's grasp slackened, and a sickly odor affronted her nostrils. Beryl wriggled free and scooted across the seat to the opposite window. Her hat tumbled towards the floorboard. She left it be. He yanked his hand free and wiped it clean on his monogrammed handkerchief.

"Grandfather," she cried, from the other side of the car. Near the window it felt so much colder, but a great deal safer. "It's almost dark. Mama will be worried."

"That she will," he agreed. "We better get to getting." He started the car engine and left the clearing. They drove along, and Beryl vowed to stay awake. She no longer felt sheltered in Grandfather's company. His peculiar behavior had changed things between them forever.

"Are you hungry?" he asked, a short time later.

"No," she answered, her voice flat. Food was the furthest thing from her mind. She wanted to be safe again. She wanted to be home.

"Beryl, listen to me," he said coldly. "You must never tell your mama or papa about our time in the car. Don't say a word, or I'll send Blossom to the glue factory. Your pony will be killed. I won't let your Papa work for me anymore, and your family won't have any money. I'll be forced to take the house away. Do you understand me? Do you hear what I'm saying?"

She nodded. She understood. What he had done in his pants was wrong—so wrong she knew other grown-ups would be upset if they found out.

"You made me act that way," he insisted.

It was dark outside, by then. Beryl watched the fat wet snowflakes hit the windshield and stick. Without the windshield wipers, her grandfather would not have been able to make out the road ahead.

"Sweet, flirty girl, that's what you are. If you hadn't beguiled me, I wouldn't have behaved like a beast."

Had she made him behave like a beast?

"You ought to be ashamed of yourself, Granddaughter, but you can't help it, can you? Just as the flowers can't help but bloom and the fish can't help but swim. I can't help myself, either. We are all sinners, imperfect and flawed."

By the time they arrived in the city, the snow had turned to sleet. Nicole was distressed because James had kept Beryl out past dark and, as if that weren't bad enough, he had neglected to feed the child. Beryl went straight to the nursery with Nanny, as she was instructed to do. She wondered—if Mama was that angry because she hadn't eaten dinner, how would she feel if Beryl told her what Grandfather had done?

Nanny shoved a plate in front of her sad face. "Now eat," she said. It was all Beryl could do to nibble a bite of biscuit, and to take a few meager sips of warm milk.

"That all, little one?"

She avoided the question. Beryl had questions of her own. "What's 'beguiled' mean?"

"Not one a my words, I can't say," said Opal, her brow knit together so tight it formed a ropey V shape.

Beryl knew Nanny expected her to lick at the butter and make that flaky biscuit disappear lickity-split, and for her to drain the glass dry, the way she always did. But she pushed the plate away and let out a long sigh.

Nanny snatched up the plate and patted Beryl's head. "Don't seem right…" she muttered.

Beryl considered asking if Nanny was a sinner, but changed her mind. She washed at the dry sink and dressed for bed.

"My, my, but you wore down," Nanny said. "Get your little self under those covers."

"Will you sleep with me?" The feel of Beryl's white nightgown against her skin felt naughty. Grandfather's admonitions and remarks replayed through her troubled mind. How could she make him be a bad man, but still remain an angel in a nightgown?

Nanny scratched her head. "Should I stay?" she asked.

"I'm scared. *Please*?"

"Lordy mercy, girl," Nanny said, as she pulled the covers down briskly. "Jus' 'til you doze off, though." But, it was Nanny who dozed off right away. Beryl just couldn't. She tossed and turned. After she finally fell asleep, Grandfather came to her in a dream. He pulled down the covers and stroked her nightgown. Beryl bolted upright and let out several ear-piercing screams. Opal tried in vain to comfort her. The ruckus brought Papa and Mama to the third floor.

Beryl tore at her white nightgown. "Get it off me!" she cried repeatedly.

Mama tried to hug her tight to her bosom. "Now, now," Mama said. "It's all right."

Beryl resisted and ripped the nightgown in the struggle. "I can't wear this! Nanny, get my pajamas!"

"Get the damn pajamas," Papa hollered. Beryl wished she could tell her father why she was so upset about Grandfather's busy hands. But she couldn't. Swallowing her sobs, she said, "Mama, throw all my nightgowns away. I hate them."

"That must've been some dream," Papa whispered to Mama, after Beryl had changed and was tucked back in bed with Nanny.

Beryl heard their steps on the stairs and took hold of Nanny's arm. "Don't leave me," she told her. "I can't be alone."

"Shh," Nanny said softly, patting Beryl's hand. "I won't go."

The family labeled Beryl haughty and spoiled when she lost all interest in Blossom for no apparent reason. Grandfather gifted the pretty pony to one of his other granddaughters, which was fine by her. Beryl no longer sat on his lap. The only man she felt safe around was her papa.

Grandmother eyed her warily. The rift between Anne and Nicole widened. Anne had no problem voicing her opinion; she claimed Beryl was too isolated and indulged as an only child, Opal treated the girl like a princess, and Nicole overprotected her. Papa would laugh when his mother carried on, and then he'd say something along the lines of, "Bloody hell, Mother, leave Beryl be. You've got loads of other granddaughters to torment."

Grandfather next came for Beryl while Mama was out. He said they would meet Papa, but Beryl knew better. He wanted to be alone with her. She threw a fit and refused to leave the stoop. Grandfather blew his top and scolded Opal harshly when she attempted to stand up for the child. When at last Beryl gave in to his will (she knew he would get Opal fired if she didn't), they headed for his big ugly car, and she feared what would happen once they were alone again.

More of the same, that's exactly what James Quinn had in store for his six-year-old granddaughter. He parked in a shadowy alley behind one of his warehouses, where he proceeded to fondle her curly locks and touch himself *down there*. An exact repeat of his former transgression. After he wiped his hand with a handkerchief, he delivered yet another scary lecture. He provided a detailed account of precisely what would happen to Papa and Mama if Beryl told on him. Papa would be jobless. Mama would be forced to fire not only the maid, but the cook and the nanny as well.

"Did you know that nigger's an orphan?" he asked. "She's not but a child—barely seventeen, I hear. What would happen to Opal *if you told?* She'd be put out to live on the street, that's what. She would starve. Keep that in mind. Your nanny's welfare is in your hands."

Red-faced after the stern warning, James drove over to Swifty's. Papa sat Beryl down on a stool at the counter and asked the man behind the soda fountain to fix her a sundae. Her stomach felt off, so she requested a glass of Vernors instead. Father and son walked away. They stood behind a stack of boxes and talked business. Grandfather always harped at Papa about how to do his job, which caused Papa's ulcers to flare. Beryl's own tummy hurt something fierce. Maybe she had ulcers, too.

When Papa saw that she'd ordered Vernors ginger ale instead of ice cream, he winked. He got a kick out of his little daughter's fondness for Vernors. Younger kids didn't usually care for the fizzy drink. As a rule, when he was through with coffee for the day and not quite ready for a snoot full of whiskey from his trusty flask, Papa would drink Vernors.

Mama didn't let her drink soda but on rare occasions. Although she would usually gulp it down greedily, that afternoon her heart felt far too heavy for refreshment.

TWO

1956

Reg Hartman's pocket-sized office was located in a nondescript building in Hollywood, off Western, just south of Adams. Caravan Moving and Storage was the building's main tenant. His Western Detective Agency shared a stairwell and a narrow second floor hallway with a door-to-door encyclopedia sales outfit. For an extra seven bucks in rent, the moving company's secretary would act as if she were his secretary, and answer calls and jot down messages, and Doris brewed strong hot coffee to boot. Since Reg was out of the office a good deal of the time, and a major caffeine addict, both services came in handy.

Doris slipped a wad of messages into the detective's hand, as he asked his customary, "What's up, Toots?"

"Some woman called several times," Doris said. She seemed flustered. "Every one of those messages is from her. She's in a real flap. And, she's on her way over here from Pasadena."

Doris was normally the calm, cool, and collected type. Reg was startled to find her so rattled on that rainy afternoon.

"She wouldn't leave her number," Doris continued. "I made it clear. I told her I had no idea when you'd show. But she's on her way over anyway, said she'd sit right here and wait for your return. Her name's Marilyn."

"Sounds like a nervous wife," Reg said, before he dropped the messages in the trash can. "My bread and butter."

"Believe you me, this one's at her wit's end." A bony, middle-aged, single gal, Doris lived vicariously through Reg's cases and relished the intrigue. But Reg knew very well that she'd been interested in true crime, carnage, bloodshed, *and such*, long before she had ever met him.

Just as Reg poured his first cup of coffee, the bell on the door jingled, and he glanced up to see a huge bright red umbrella close. The shrinking umbrella revealed an unforgettable face. When he was in the service, *Yank Magazine* provided much-appreciated woman flesh in the form of pin-up girls. Most soldiers were nuts for Betty Grable and Rita Hayworth. To Reg's way of thinking, Gene Tierney stood head and shoulders above the rest. The beauty framed in the doorway was not the famous actress, and it seemed impossible, but Reg thought she might even be better looking—a real vision.

Doris took the umbrella from the woman's grasp, dropped it face-down to drip dry in the stand, and assisted with the removal of her soaked overcoat.

"You must be Marilyn," she said, shaking droplets of water from the woolen garment to the floor mat below. Then Doris turned to Reg. "Mr. Hartman, this is the woman I told you about."

Reg sent a slight nod in his prospective client's direction. "Good to meet you. Let's go upstairs to my office. How about a cup of hot coffee?"

"No coffee," Marilyn said. Her tone was icy—she was all business.

Reg led the way up the dark stairwell. He took a seat behind his desk. Marilyn did not sit—she stood at the window and watched the rain make a mess of traffic.

"You have a last name?" Reg asked.

"Sure," she said. "Who doesn't?"

Her eyes were green and definitely her best feature. He had to admit those gorgeous emerald pools held a huge claim to fame, because they were in competition with flawless skin, a perfect nose, and full lips, all framed with long silky auburn hair begging to be touched. Never had he laid eyes on such a lovely head so up close and personal. Reg did his best not to let his hungry eyes travel south. He recognized what was happening. He felt like a breathing cliché, a private eye in a seedy office facing a beautiful dame in need of his know-how.

"Palmer. My married name is Palmer."

"Call me Reg."

She lowered her gorgeous backside onto a side chair facing his desk, and crossed her long slender legs. Reg supposed she was doing her best to hide the anxiety Doris had detected over the phone. He pulled a pen and notebook from his drawer and printed out her name.

"Mind if I smoke?" the beauty asked.

"No," he fibbed. Reg loathed the odor of tobacco more than any other stench on the face of the earth, but he knew puffing cigarettes often put clients at ease. He retrieved an ashtray from atop the file cabinet and set the filthy thing down on the small table at her side.

"I'm being blackmailed."

Ah, so she was more than likely a cheat, and her cheating had backfired. He hadn't figured her for a two-timer.

She reached into her purse and pulled out an envelope. "This was in with the milk bottles on the stoop this morning. Luckily, my husband had already left for the hospital. He's a doctor."

Reg pulled out a small piece of paper and read five short words and two periods. *I know. You will pay.*

"Who knows *what*?" He refolded the note and stuffed it back into the envelope.

"That's just it," Marilyn Palmer said. "I can't say."

"No affairs?"

"I've only been married a short time, and if you knew my husband, you wouldn't ask that question."

Reg smiled. "I see," he said. "Look, from where I sit, I don't make assumptions. People even cheat on their honeymoons. Expect hard questions."

She cracked a cynical smile. "No—no affair."

"Old boyfriends?"

"A few."

Of course. A looker like Marilyn Palmer would be wined and dined up the yin-yang until some lucky well-heeled Mister walked her down the aisle. "Can't you give me a little input—any clues?"

"No, not a one," she answered, without pause. "What happens next?"

"I can question the milkman and the neighbors, see if any of them spotted someone lurking around."

"Not a good idea," she said, with a flip of her hand. "Not our neighbors. We don't want to cause alarm. It's a sleepy community. Safe. Quiet. I'm not sure it's a good idea to bother the milkman either."

"If your neighborhood's as quiet as you say, it doesn't sound as if I could stake out your place without drawing attention. Will you consider telling your husband about the note?"

"No. Never. He can't know."

"Sounds as if you're hiding something."

"I am hiding something. You see, I lied to him. I told him I'm an orphan, and I'm not."

"And why did you deceive him?"

Her lids lowered. "Do I have to tell you?"

"Look, you called my agency. You don't have to tell me a damn thing. You don't have to hire me. We can part ways right here and now. Maybe it was only a prank, huh? Is that what you think?" His patience was running short.

"Could be. Sure. Maybe I'm overreacting."

"Okay. Have it your way. Head on home and take it easy, wait around and see what happens next."

Marilyn Palmer sprang to her feet. "I will. That's exactly what I'll do." She extended her hand, and Reg gave the perfectly-manicured specimen a quick shake. "What do I owe you?"

"Forget it," he said, curtly. "No charge, I've done nothing."

"You made me feel better."

"I didn't mean to."

"No?"

"Personally, I think you're in a tight spot. But go ahead, just sit back, and let the writer of that note make the next move."

"That's exactly what I'll do. Goodbye, then."

She never did light up, and Reg didn't see Marilyn Palmer out. She'd be back. Her menacing past was on the loose and in close pursuit. The fear of the thing lived in her eyes, and trepidation sounded with each step her heels made as she fled out the door, through the dark hallway, down the steps, and out the building. It seemed to Reg as if she thought that placing enough real estate between her shapely body and the Western Detective Agency would cause the reality of what was surfacing to elude her for a brief spell.

He understood. Marilyn Palmer needed time to prepare for what was to come.

THREE
1956

Some women indulged in sweets to relieve stress. Others cleaned house, went shopping, or drank alcohol. Marilyn would set off for the zoo. It wasn't just the animals she went to see. People strolled down paths in unusually high spirits. The genial atmosphere put her at ease, and the exotic environment offered a reprieve from everyday life.

As she watched an aged lion meticulously clean his paws, sharp spasms all but caused her to double over. She hobbled over to a bench underneath a massive eucalyptus tree, where she popped a couple aspirins and closed her eyes. Marilyn pondered the combative stance she'd taken earlier in the detective's office. Why had she been so belligerent with him when he was only trying to help? Where had her manners run off to? The note was obviously menacing. Believing otherwise might prove to be foolhardy, maybe even dangerous.

Marilyn leaned back and willed her violent stomach and intestinal pains to settle down. She studied the quaking leaves, listened to the cries from the monkey house, and yearned for tranquility. In tranquility's place, what did she have? She had been confronted with a threatening note. She was suffering from what might be a serious stomach ailment, and facing a whole lot of uncertainty.

Stability remained elusive and dramatics reigned supreme, a constant theme since her earliest days.

1929

Grandfather pounded at the door one evening. He was in a huff over the ever-growing crisis after the stock market crash. Mama and Papa sat by the fire, as they often did whenever Papa saw fit to come home at a decent hour. Mama was crocheting and Papa had his face buried in the evening paper.

"Those crackpots on Wall Street have done it now," Grandfather exclaimed, as he entered the room.

Beryl sat on the floor by the hearth, cutting out paper dolls with scissors. She saw Grandfather's nostrils flare wildly. "I saw this coming," he bellowed. Short of breath and with a final sputter, the old man added, "Didn't I, Son?"

Papa set down his paper and motioned for his father to have a seat on the nearby divan.

"I'll make tea," Mama said. Scalding hot Earl Grey was one thing Nicole and James both drew immense comfort from.

"You called it," Papa said. "You sure did."

"Boom euphoria," Grandfather shouted. "They're all credit-poor. I own my land. Quinns don't borrow. Remember that. Never a borrower or a lender be—leave all that to the Jews. I can see we're in for hard times. But we'll weather this storm, my boy. Mark my words."

Papa picked up the paper and read aloud. "In Milwaukee, one gentleman, who took his own life, left a note reading, 'My body should go to science, my soul to Andrew W. Mellon, and sympathy to my creditors.'"

"Good Lord in Heaven!" Grandfather made the sign of The Father, The Son, and The Holy Ghost.

"They're jumping out of tall buildings in New York City, and gassing themselves in Philadelphia," Papa told him.

It was a good thing Mama was out of the room, because she would have put an end to such talk for sure, and Beryl would have missed out on the grisly discussion.

"Thank God we have a Republican in the White House," Grandfather said. "Clear heads prevail. We will survive."

1932

Times got harder. Opal never left the house on Saturday night anymore, but stayed put seven days a week. She told Mama all her friends had left the city because they couldn't get by. She had no one to visit anymore. Reports of escalating desperation circulated. Beryl's cousins told stories of young children roaming the streets, begging right out in the open in the great city of Detroit.

"Our family's lucky," Cousin Ginny said. "We don't have to worry. My daddy can't lose his job because he works for Grandfather."

"You bet," Cousin Mildred chimed in. "We have what Mommy calls *security*. But Daddy's sister in Windsor doesn't have it so good. Daddy had to drive over to Canada to give her money, because she couldn't afford milk or bread."

Beryl came to understand how desperately everyone in the family relied on Grandfather. They were slashing prices at Swifty's in order to keep customers. Ice cream, sodas, and banana splits were luxuries. Papa added sandwiches and soup at discount prices, because Grandfather said discount was the only way to go. Hard times called for desperate measures.

Anxious to be of service, Nicole volunteered at the relief society and began to spend lots of time away, which gave James ample opportunity to swing by and call for Beryl at random intervals.

"Why he draggin' you to and fro?" Opal asked.

Beryl didn't answer. If she had, her resolve might have collapsed, and she would have spilled the beans for sure.

News spread about bread lines and tent camps. Papa worried endlessly, and his ulcers caused him so much grief he was forced to give up whiskey, coffee, and Vernors too. The handsome face of Beryl's father became pinched and he bore a tense grimace much of the time. He would sip warm milk and prescription formula from a brown glass bottle for relief. He spent two days in the hospital. The doctors did not approve when he up and checked himself out. He came home all pasty white, just skin and bones.

Beryl dreaded Grandfather more and more with each passing day. He would drive to a deserted and broken-down warehouse on the outskirts of town. Beryl would stand on the rickety stairwell behind him while he nervously peered back and forth, his liver-spotted hands jiggling the lock open on the squeaky old door. Inside, he demanded Beryl disrobe, in an emotionless voice. As soon as she was naked, and once his pants were down around his ankles and he'd had an eyeful, she was instructed to yank at his crooked wiener. He leaned back in the rickety chair, his eyes shut tight, while Beryl distracted herself from the vile task by staring trance-like at a tattered Eveready Battery poster on the wall behind the old man. The nimble black cat leaped through the number nine, with the word *LIVES* printed beneath. A caption read: *Bounces back for extra life*. Beryl wished she were a cat. She imagined herself being anywhere but that old warehouse.

She always complied with Grandfather. Her mama wouldn't stand in bread lines if she could keep the pantry full by simply satisfying his urges, and Opal wouldn't live on the streets if she could help it. The more sob stories Mama relayed over dinner, and the more Papa's ulcers bled, the more Beryl knew she was doing what must be done. It was her duty to protect her family from certain poverty.

Grandfather showered her with extravagant presents, and whatever he bought for Beryl, he bought a more refined, more expensive version for Mama.

"James," Nicole said, one day after he had produced a costly pair of gloves for her consideration, "in case you haven't noticed, some folks live in rusted-out old car bodies these days. The money you're wasting on baubles ought to be donated to charity. I'm trying to teach Beryl to be charitable. You could be an example of that temperament."

Beryl's mouth hung open as she listened to Mama ream Grandfather.

The old man swayed in place and was forced to steady himself with his walking stick.

Opal witnessed the lecture. Grandfather suddenly turned on the poor girl. "What are you looking at, you monkey-faced wench?" he yelled. He thrust his arthritic finger in her direction, wagging the digit madly.

Frightened out of her wits, the nanny took off, her arms flapping through the air like a whirligig as she made a hasty retreat down the hallway towards the kitchen.

Mama let him have it with both barrels. "Such foul, racially prejudiced language will not be tolerated in my house! I will not have you abusing Opal, she's a member of my family!"

"I'm sorry," he lamented. "But, you tell me, why should my family suffer because of hastily drawn reforms and weakly-administered policies? Greater regulation will not solve these current economic woes, and neither will the mistaken mindset of scarcity. If I'm in the mood to shower my loved ones with gifts, I'll do so with my head held high. I can afford to."

Nicole was not in the least bit impressed with her bloviating father-in-law. "Never mind all that," she said, sternly. "No more gifts. No more dropping by unannounced and disrupting Beryl's schedule. She's getting older. It's not proper for you and my developing daughter to be traipsing off alone."

By the baffled expression on Grandfather's face, Beryl knew he suspected she'd snitched.

But she hadn't!

Papa got an earful when he arrived home from Swifty's. Beryl listened and watched from behind the balustrade.

"That father of yours is an intolerant buffoon," Mama cried. "He can't see the forest for the trees."

Papa removed his fedora. He'd recently fallen off the wagon and looked soused to the gills. "You don't understand. Pop's got the world on his shoulders. You have no idea."

"Regardless, he's oblivious to the suffering *out there*. He's positively disconnected. The very fabric of society is unraveling Patrick, *unraveling*. And your father's buying jewelry, frocks, and music boxes, as if it were still the roaring '20s!"

"He's sentimental," Papa offered. "Humor him."

"I will not!" Mama cried, before storming off.

1934

Grandfather stopped coming for Beryl altogether, and remained distant at family functions. But Papa still kept his managerial position down at Swifty's. Nothing changed. The family still had a home and enough food to eat. Grandfather must have realized that she had not tattled. Mama was a hardheaded woman and that was all there was to it. Surely, the old man understood.

With all the sordid business with her randy grandfather out of the way, she felt more like a kid again. Shirley Bell Cole was performing the role of *Little Orphan Annie* on the radio. The show was produced out of Chicago, not far from Detroit. The close proximity thrilled Beryl and her cousins, and she found it remarkable that Shirley was only a few months older than her and already a famous radio star.

Beryl would get so worked up before each program that her extreme enthusiasm caused her mother great alarm.

"Good grief, Beryl," she'd say, "Annie's fiction. A complete and utter fabrication, and look at you, you're positively fitful!"

Opal didn't share Beryl's enthusiasm for *Little Orphan Annie*, either. The two women were nothing but a pair of spoilsports as far as Beryl was concerned—bona-fide detractors.

One time Mama had the audacity to accuse the entertaining radio program of spewing conservative propaganda, and Papa told her to stuff it. Beryl had to fight back a smile.

The nuns at school were killjoys as well. They put the kibosh on all the harmless antics Beryl and her friends engaged in, their girlish exuberance squelched. It seemed to her that the world was full of an endless stream of strife and turmoil. Beryl longed for distraction and a little harmless fun made sense. Restless and jumpy, she felt held back, like a horse at the gate waiting to run an upcoming race.

She had recently discovered her power, and a miraculous one at that. Beryl deduced how and why she had caused the old man to behave like a letch. She was beautiful, that much was certain. A knockout, and not even a full-fledged woman yet. All the girls said so. Boys gawked at her. *Not only boys.* Yes, grown men stared when Beryl Quinn passed by, and they frightened her. It was one thing to be a young girl and to be admired by a boy in your class, but quite another thing to feel the eyes of a grown man boring holes through your clothing.

✛ ✛ ✛

The Depression wore on. Stress mounted as Patrick did his level best to keep Swifty's profits high enough to placate James.

"You know," Beryl overheard Nicole confide in her friend, Vi Edison. "Patrick's a young man of poor health. He's about to kill himself with the booze. I'm afraid I'll end up widowed, and with that horrible James Quinn lording over me—a bird of prey over road-kill. That man is a vulture."

✛ ✛ ✛

Nicole appeared to be shrinking of late, right along with her husband. Beryl still thought she was the prettiest mother on the block, but she looked awfully tired and worn down.

Grandfather took notice. "I pay you good money," he said, after getting a gander at his emaciated son and daughter-in-law one evening. "Don't you stock the pantry? Should I send my cook over to fatten you two up?"

"Nonsense, James," Mama said. "Opal is a fine cook."

The state of the economy grew more and more dire with each passing day. When Papa's salary dwindled, and the maid and cook were let go, Opal was expected to take on all the additional work. As a result, she and Beryl often dined alone in the kitchen. Beryl would dish gossip about what the kids at school were up to, and Opal regarded their frolics as knee-slapping entertainment. One night, over breaded pork chops, Beryl asked Opal her opinion about her father's health.

"The Mister, he be worried sick," Opal said. "Your daddy's troubles be eatin' at his gut, somethin' fierce. That's why he don't eat. Some folks do that way. Me, if I eat, I feel better."

"Do you ever get lonely for your friends and family?" Beryl asked, suddenly feeling bold.

"I do," Opal said, sopping up gravy with a piece of bread. "I be waiting for this Great Depression to pass. We all is, I reckon."

Beryl nodded. Truer words were never spoken.

1936

Nicole discovered her unconscious husband at the bottom of the front stairway. Patrick Quinn was rushed to the hospital and died a few days later. Beryl would only use the back stairs forevermore.

With Papa gone, Beryl thrashed about all night and cried until her tears dried out. Then her troubled mind switched gears, and she worried about all the hobo youths.

Destitute kids of all ages rode the rails. Bands of them searched for scraps of food and opportunity, and slept in shacks by the tracks made out of tin and old crates. Certain brave girls were hidden here and there, inside those gangs of roving boys. The tribes were made up of ten or twelve and they were vermin-ridden, always hungry, and in constant danger. Those girls dressed as boys to blend in. Beryl counted her lucky stars. How could they stand it? Forced to pose as the opposite sex, in constant danger and at the mercy of any thug that came along? She shuddered to imagine.

Shortly after Patrick passed, James signed the deed to the house on River Road over to Nicole. She had attended business school before she'd married Patrick and was an excellent typist. James put her in charge of the office at the bottle works. Her salary would ensure there would be enough to live on.

James was heartbroken over the sudden death of his only son. His demeanor changed overnight, from a boisterous and robust bear of a man, to a defeated shadow of his former self. Nicole attempted to bolster her bereaved father-in-law's faltering spirits with tea and sympathy each day after he dropped her home.

They would get into drawn-out discussions about politics. Nicole was a Democrat and a huge fan of the popular president.

She considered FDR to be a savior and the hope for the nation. James criticized FDR's policies, The New Deal, and his Civilian Conservation Corps. After the Social Security Act was passed, James claimed welfare to be an evil that would take hold and transform a previously prosperous republic into a Communist state. He never raised his voice at Nicole. His arguments were more of a plea for her to come around and eventually see things his way.

Opal was afraid of James and stayed hidden each evening until he left. "Why's he here?" she'd ask, in whispered tones. "He should be home with his own wife."

"He misses Papa. He's sad. I think he feels guilty for not treating him better."

Opal would shake her head and roll her eyes. "Let him be sad at his own damn house."

Beryl felt torn. She was sorry for Grandfather, and happy that he had Mama to talk to. But it seemed there were two sides to the man. The evil side had caused him to hurt her and her father so deeply. The good side mourned his son and wanted to take care of Beryl and her mother. Beryl shouldered a deep-rooted shame, and she had been shouldering that shame for such a long time. The weight of it colored her perception of the world.

✥ ✥ ✥

Beryl met a madcap girl at school named June Masterson. June had recently moved to Detroit from Chicago with her Aunt Flo. June's mother had committed suicide shortly after her father had run out on them.

Nicole found Beryl's new friend to be flighty. She saw June as a bad influence, but was happy to see her daughter's spirits lift, and so she conceded to let Beryl go to the movies with her every now and then.

June and Beryl were wild about Shirley Temple. *On the Good Ship Lollipop* was one of their favorite songs, and they also enjoyed her in *Poor Little Rich Girl*. June imitated Shirley Temple perfectly. Beryl often asked her clever friend to sing and dance. She called her Junesy Tunesy. June had curly blonde hair, pale skin, and stunning blue eyes. When the two of them strolled down the street, they often heard a chorus of catcalls and whistles.

James lit up whenever June batted her eyelashes. Junesy's over-the-top, flirtatious behavior infuriated Beryl. She knew what her grandfather was capable of, and she didn't want him to lay one beefy paw on her young friend.

June was drawn to James Quinn, much as a daft little moth is drawn to a burning hot flame. The poor kid didn't have a father or a grandfather, and she wanted to know all about his Detroit mansion and country house on Grosse Isle. She liked to go to Swifty's for sodas or sundaes where they were likely to run into him. June was attracted by Grandfather's power and money. And boy—could that girl flirt. It made no difference to June that he was nothing but an aged coot. Beryl soon learned that when someone's been hungry and broke most of their life, they'd do just about anything to avoid either ever again; improving their lot in life became more than a goal, it became a mission.

Opal announced that she would soon leave Nicole's employ. She was headed back down south to join her sister, in a place called Mobile. Beryl sure was in a world of hurt after hearing the terrible news. Mama's coldhearted response to her daughter's anguish was, "It was to be expected, Beryl. Opal had to leave us eventually."

"Offer her more money!" Beryl pleaded. She would've fallen to her hands and knees if it would have done any good at all—if it meant Opal could stay.

"And where would I get more money? We barely get by as it is."

"Grandfather, who else?"

"Your grandfather has plenty of obligations. We're lucky he saw fit to sign this house over after your father passed, and that he offered me gainful employment."

It was all Beryl could do not to scream out at the top of her lungs… *the old man's lucky I haven't told on him for molesting me!*

Opal's last conversation with Beryl began with, "Stop, child."

Tears ran down Beryl's cheeks, and she wiped at them with one of her monogrammed hankies. She sobbed hysterically.

"Don't you see?" Opal added. "I'm happy. I'm goin' home, after all these years. This ain't about you," she admonished. "For once, this ain't about you."

1937

Keeping occupied with Carole Lombard's screwball comedies and Cole Porter tunes helped Beryl forget how lonely life was in the big old house, without Opal to keep her company or to put up with her nonstop chatter. She couldn't get used to the quiet. Her footsteps sounded harsh against the hardwood floors and echoed against the oak paneled walls. Sometimes, she swore she saw Papa out of the corner of her eye, and imagined him watching over her.

Beryl discovered her breasts were too big. Ma told her so (Beryl never called her "Mama" anymore, because June said she sounded like an itty-bitty baby when she did). Ma's exact words were, "You didn't get those ample bosoms from me—you inherited them from Anne's side of the family. Give them a good binding. You don't want them protruding."

"Huh?" Beryl said, dumbfounded. The thing was, she had outgrown her undergarments and sorely needed a modern bra.

"You must keep yourself under wraps," she advised. "Men—not all of them mind you, but some—go positively daffy for big breasts."

Then Ma launched in to her version of what June had already told Beryl. Her friend's juvenile account of man-woman relations had seemed clear-cut.

But Ma's version, believe it or not, frightened her even more. According to Ma, Beryl was already a sinner.

Going by June's descriptions of various sex acts, Beryl knew she had *polished Grandfather's knob*. Of course, neither her poor unsuspecting mother, nor any other soul on earth, except for her grandfather, the instigator, knew Beryl had ever performed such terrible deeds. Had Ma known, she would have dragged her daughter down to church. Beryl would have been forced to tell Father O'Malley what she had done in the confession booth. Or worse yet, she'd have to tell the young priest, the one all the girls had a crush on, dreamy Father Finnigan.

June told Beryl, "It's like this—some women take pleasure in the sex act, as much, if not more, than most men."

Ma told Beryl, "It's like this—most woman merely endure sex. God expects a woman to have intercourse with her husband.

Pleasing one's man is a sacred duty. When the man's engorged penis enters the vagina, it violates, and it hurts."

Ma made it clear that sex was for procreating and married couples only. "Never let any boy or man talk you into intercourse before you are rightfully wed," she warned. "I don't care if he promises to pull out before ejaculation. I don't care if he wears a condom."

Beryl shuddered, then asked what a condom was, and Nicole explained. Then she poked her finger in Beryl's face and said, "You save all that funny business for your honeymoon."

How odd that Ma referred to intercourse as *funny business*, but obviously didn't find any humor in the act. Beryl figured Ma probably didn't miss Papa all that much. Not in the bedroom, anyway.

June's version went something like this: After a-certain-woman-of-a-certain-type had been fully penetrated by the male member, she would forever-after-constantly feel incomplete when an erect penis wasn't inside her ready-willing-and-able-vagina. Certain women instantly became insatiable sex fiends. And certain women could be worse sex fiends than men. June's aunt worked with one such woman. She referred to her as *The Nymphomaniac*.

Ma's and June's extremely dissimilar versions of sexual relations between men and women didn't jive. The image of Grandfather's withered member and how awful it had felt to the touch came to mind, which served to complicate matters even further. Beryl hoped her future sexual experiences would fall into some sort of superior middle ground, somewhere between the two disparate theories, and would hopefully never resemble anything remotely close to her experiences with the old man.

✚ ✚ ✚

Ma came up with a startling idea. She would rent out rooms in the big house. Grandfather was dead set against her plan. But Ma told him that it was her home, and she'd go ahead and proceed. She hired a German woman to clean and cook, and established her in the maid's room. Cranky Heidi settled in.

Their very first boarder was a librarian named Miss Ruth Lansky. Ruth tended to repeat certain phrases. Mama told Beryl to show the librarian to her room. When Beryl asked if she wanted two blankets, Ruth said, "No, one blanket will do. One blanket will do."

When Beryl told her that the bathroom was at the end of the hall, she asked, "Does the lock work?"

"Of course," Beryl said.

"But does it hold? Does it work?"

Out of patience, Beryl took the woman to the bathroom and proved to her that the lock did indeed function properly.

James tried to discourage Nicole from taking in male boarders, but Nicole couldn't say no to the extremely polite Mr. Bolger, who was willing to pay extra for the room on the second floor with southern exposure. He had an advanced case of rheumatism and had served in The Great War. How could she turn such an elderly gentleman away?

The third boarder arrived on their doorstep in October, with a chest full of costumes. The woman had arrived from Milwaukee that very morning, answered an ad, and had been hired on at the local theatre. Her name was Helen Bitters. Helen's mouth resembled a torn pocket and she favored bright shades of the reddest lipstick.

"Good lord in Heaven," Ma muttered under her breath, once the actress was out of earshot. "That creature resembles a carp."

"She's wonderful," Beryl said. "She's got moxie."

"I suppose June taught you that word," Ma said.

"I learned it from a picture show."

✜ ✜ ✜

They took in five boarders in all. Ma insisted that Beryl vacate the third floor and bunk with her, in order to make room for a father-son team from Toledo. *So much for Grandfather's concerns about taking in male boarders.* Walt Turner had come to Detroit as a junior chiropractor. The widower planned on joining practice with an established chiropractor. And his son Bobby would enroll in public school.

"Why did you decide to take in boarders?" Beryl asked one night. They were lying side by side in the bed Ma used to share with Papa.

"Because I'm going to quit working for your grandfather."

"Why?"

"I can't tell you," she whispered. "Trust me, I have my reasons."

Beryl instantly knew why. Her randy grandfather must have tried *funny business* with Ma, and Ma wasn't having any of it. She should have known; the old geezer had wanted more than tea for two. No wonder he'd stopped coming by, and Ma now took the bus home. Beryl wanted to share all the wrong he had done to her, but couldn't bring herself to confess her sins. She had kept the horrible truth hidden deep inside for so long that it almost didn't seem real anymore; *how the old man had touched her and she had touched him.*

Beryl took Ma's hand in hers and gave her a squeeze. "That's okay," she said, sweetly. "You know what's best for us."

1938

June's aunt decided to return to Chicago. June vowed to write faithfully. But the promise of letters did little to lift Beryl's spirits or to make her feel any better about losing a good friend. She had more fun with Junesy than she'd ever had with anyone else. She was already heartsick over losing Papa. And Opal was gone; *she had also promised letters, but hadn't even sent so much as an address.* Beryl would now pine for June, too. Her soul felt heavy with loss.

Christmas was peculiar that year with all those strangers in the house. Beryl didn't see Papa's family anymore.

"Lord only knows what kind of picture your grandfather painted," Ma said. "As if I care. I'm sorry to tell you this, Beryl, but I never did fit in." Her eyes misted over. "How your father conned me into marrying into that clan, I'll never know."

It was odd, sitting at a table with Ruth Lansky on Christmas Day, listening to her repeat mundane facts. "I love winter squash," she told Beryl. "Yes, I do love winter squash."

As if Ruth wasn't irksome enough, Beryl had to put up with pimply-faced Bobby and his crush on her. He nearly drove the girl around the bend, sitting across the table all moony-eyed, as he shoveled enough mashed potatoes to satisfy ten grown men down his big trap. Not to mention Mr. Bolger and his tendency to knock over glasses with his spastic hand movements. At least Helen was entertaining, as she told zany stories about the theatre company. Her animated accounts lent a veneer of sanity to what Beryl considered a holiday meal so surreal, it could have been a Salvador Dali painting.

Ma seemed dazed. Walt sat at the head of the table in Papa's old chair. Oddly enough, his expression was nearly as peculiar as Ma's.

A knock came at the door, and wasn't Beryl surprised to spot her grandparents out on the porch bearing gifts. They were invited in, but only stayed a short spell, refusing to be seated. The look on their faces said it all when they saw the dining room table assembled with that hodgepodge of boarders. It was obvious they pitied Nicole, with that house chock-full of misfits and outsiders. Beryl could have crawled under a rock. When they suggested she go along to visit Aunt Linda, Ma began to shake her head before they could even finish asking, and then delivered a line about Beryl needing to stick around to clean up. What a crock—Heidi always did the dishes.

Although Beryl was angry with Grandfather and always would be, she missed Aunt Linda and her cousins, and longed to see them. She momentarily considered pitching a fit to get her way. It would have worked on Papa, but Ma would never tolerate such blatant rebelliousness.

They left in a huff and Beryl pouted for the remainder of the evening, *for all the good it did her.* Ma and the boarders played parlor games while she curled up on the window seat, and none of them paid her long face one speck of attention.

1939

The newspapers were full of the turmoil in Europe. Beryl had a limited grasp of such things, but understood FDR was doing his level best to steer the country clear of involvement. Hitler was a menace, and yet he had many supporters stateside. Beryl overheard countless heated arguments and grew more puzzled and troubled with each passing day.

Mr. Bolger had fought in the Great War, and that man hated Germans with a passion.

Walt Turner piped up one night at the dinner table. He claimed America should flat-out keep its nose out of Europe's business.

Mr. Bolger grew agitated and launched into a tirade about fascists, and then accused Walt of being both a coward and a pacifist.

Bobby dropped a glistening drumstick. It hit his plate with a smack, and the silverware rattled. Then the boy popped out of his chair and took the old man's side. "Mr. Bolger's got it right, Dad. When I'm old enough, I'm joining up. I for one will do my duty!"

Ma picked up a fork and pinged a crystal glass. "Need I remind the lot of you that this is my house?" she scolded. "I ask that you keep your manners in check at this dinner table."

The men proceeded with their conversation as if they hadn't even heard Nicole. "Son," Walt said in an even voice, "you don't know the first thing about war."

Bobby's eyes brimmed with tears of passion, or fury, or maybe both. He confronted his father. "I know I wouldn't or couldn't stay home, not when other men are marching off to battle. You might be anti-war, but I'm not."

Ma held both hands high in the air. "President Roosevelt isn't about to declare war on Germany," she announced. "This argument is moot."

"You never know," Walt said. "Anything's possible."

Heidi had only just come to the table to replenish the mashed potatoes. Upset by the subject matter, she turned on her heels and headed back towards the kitchen. Ma went after her.

"Dried up old Kraut," Mr. Bolger said, under his breath.

Helen Bitters shook her head. "What a world we live in," she observed.

Bobby dropped down into his seat, retrieved his drumstick, and tore into it with angry teeth. Beryl looked away.

⬧ ⬧ ⬧

That September, Canada declared war on Germany, and several of Nicole's relatives enlisted immediately. Mémère (Beryl always referred to her grandmother by this commonly used French Canadian term of endearment) literally flipped her lid, and came to live with Nicole after her son joined the Canadian army. Mémère had always made her living as a seamstress, but had become so distraught over her son's enlisting that she was unable to stay focused on her work any longer.

Heidi was let go to ensure that Mémère and her dress forms, sewing machines, and scads of belongings could be crammed into the maid's room.

Two hired women took over the cooking and cleaning, but they didn't live in. The cook's name was Minnie, and her food was scrumptious. The housekeeper's name was Madge. She smoked too much and the sallow woman took one lengthy cigarette break after another. How she got any work done remained a mystery. But Ma seemed satisfied enough with her performance.

Since Nicole forbade anyone from smoking in the house, Madge was often firmly planted on the service porch, puffing away. Mémère was an equally voracious smoker. She joined the housekeeper with a cigarette in one hand and a cup of tea in the other. Side by side, they'd commiserate. Since all three of their names started with the letter M, Beryl took to calling Mémère *Number One*, Madge *Number Two*, and Minnie *Number Three*. She eventually shortened their nicknames to simply *One*, *Two*, and *Three*. "Hey, Three," she'd say. "What's for dinner?"

✠ ✠ ✠

At school one day, Beryl came down sick. The nurse instructed one of the younger nuns to accompany her home. By the time she pushed the heavy front door open, her strength had just about given out. She called out for Ma—no answer. She discovered Three in the kitchen, covered in flour and kneading bread dough. It was such a rare occurrence to find Three alone.

"Where is everybody?" Beryl asked.

"Your grandmother and Madge went to fetch—what else—cigarettes. I suppose your mother went with them, because I haven't seen her since they left. What are you doing home?"

"I'm sick. The school nurse thinks I have the mumps."

"Cripes!" Three said. "You do look awful, kid. Get yourself to bed. I'll check on you after I put these loaves in the oven. Luckily, I've had the mumps, but I'm afraid you'll have to stay clear of those who haven't."

"Okay then," Beryl muttered, so weak she thought she might keel over. "I'll go lay down."

A slow ascent up the steep staircase made her feel worse by the second, and her leg muscles ached with the effort. She shifted most of her weight to the handrail. Feverish and dizzy, her head spun, and it hurt to swallow. She crossed the landing, wobbled down the hallway, and braced herself with one hand against the wall. As she opened the bedroom door, in much need of a mattress to flop on, Beryl was instantly confronted by bare skin in motion.

Upon hearing her daughter's involuntary gasp, Nicole's nude body halted midair and hovered momentarily over Walt Sander's nude body. The inconceivable image—all those bare-naked body parts—coupled with Beryl's weakening condition, caused the poor girl to faint dead away.

Walt and Bobby moved out that night, and Beryl returned to her lair. She had suffered complications from the mumps and remained bedridden for nearly a month. Nicole merely pretended her daughter hadn't seen her atop Walt Turner. Beryl put the image right out of her mind, along with all the other images she didn't care to remember. She was quite practiced at denying unpleasant realities by then.

She finally got a letter from June, who loved public school (no more stern nuns for her) and had started dating Horace Cameron, a boy doing his best to reach first base. June wouldn't let him, though. First of all, he wasn't all that good-looking. She mostly went out with him because he bought her malts and paid her way into movies. Her aunt wanted her to get a job, and she was trying, but it wasn't easy when she didn't have any experience.

Beryl remained friendless and isolated. A girl could live in a big house full of people and feel as lonesome as a prisoner in solitary confinement.

FOUR
1956

Doris held out her hand. Reg plucked a message from her palm as he rushed by and gave it a quick read.

"Uh-oh, Toots," he said. "Guess I forgot to call Eve, *again.*"

"She's on the warpath this time," the bossy secretary warned.

"Is that right?" Reg asked, making a beeline for the percolator.

"You'd better call her."

"Maybe later."

"What have you been doing, camping out at your mother's old place?"

"I'm thinking of letting my apartment go. I'm at ease out there."

Doris slapped a file folder down on the desk. "Way out in Montebello?"

"Home sweet home."

"You'd better let Eve know. She has other plans for you."

Reg grimaced.

"Don't give me that look." She whipped out a file. "I told you I was a budinski—Remember?"

"I remember."

"Speaking of nosy, I'm dying to know if you've heard from that *goddess* yet."

"Marilyn Palmer?"

"The knockout. Gosh, if I only had half her good looks, I'd own the world."

"She has nothing over you, sweetheart."

Doris frowned. She wasn't easily cajoled, and she was way too sensible to fall for bogus flattery. "Right," she replied.

"I haven't heard a thing from Marilyn Palmer—but I will."

Up in his office, the detective thought about calling Eve, but didn't. His head hurt. Playing poker with Javier—his dead stepfather Ruben's bachelor brother—and his amigos had proved to be an all-night ordeal. Reg won the last pot and announced he was throwing in the towel for the night, and one of the players by the name of Chuy (a guy known to detest gringos) had threatened to shoot him.

"Go ahead," Reg told him, "Put me out of my misery."

The hothead let out an insane hoot, before saying, "You must return next week so I can win my money back."

To hell with that old pachuco.

Reg looked hard at the big black phone and sighed. Eve had made a fine sometime-companion until a few weeks ago. Trouble was, she thought he would be better company after his mother passed. But he hadn't been. Not even close. Reg wasn't husband material and never would be. Even though he'd warned Eve that marriage was out of the question at least a hundred times, she held on to the mistaken belief that it all came down to his sick mother dying and exiting the picture. A few swallows of coffee later, he mustered up the gumption to grab the receiver and dial.

Eve sounded sleepy when she answered with a throaty, "Hallo."

"Hey, Babe," Reg chirped. "You alive and kicking yet?"

"So you decided to call, did you? Look, I've had it. I accepted a date with Andy Bell. We're over, Reg. Four years is a long time to spend with a guy who refuses to grow up."

He was all at sea, and not just because she'd accepted a date with a cop. He'd always known Eve had a thing for uniforms. Hell, that's why she'd gone for him in the first place. He had worn his share of uniforms—first army issue, and then LAPD. Reg was genuinely baffled by Eve's refusal to give him another chance, since she always had before. Besides, he was the most adult person around.

He was virtually steeped in the realities of the human condition. But at that moment, he just wasn't inclined to try and change her mind.

"Okay," he said, flatly. "That's it, then?"

"It's been a long time coming, as if you didn't know. Have a good life out there in Tortilla Flats."

He heard a click and then Eve was gone.

Andy Bell. He'd treat the poor kid like crap. But, Andy would *marry* her. Eve would get what she was after. She'd quit working in that sleazy cocktail lounge, move into a shit box out in the valley, and squirt out three kids in no time flat. Andy would knock her around and she'd relive her mother's life. End of story.

Reg gave his chin stubble a good rub, swiveled his chair around, and gazed out the grimy window. He did all this just in time to spot a Cadillac pull alongside the curb. The door swung open and one well-turned ankle stepped out. His lousy day was looking up, because he knew who that silky leg was attached to.

Minutes later, Marilyn Palmer handed Reg an envelope. "I found this note under my windshield wiper. Came out of the salon, and there it was, plain as day."

"This morning?"

"Yes, I hurried right over. Check it out, won't you? I'd like to know what you think."

Reg began to read the letter out loud. "I know who you are." He stopped, looked up, and caught Marilyn's eye. He wanted her to consider the gravity of the words. "Follow these instructions, and I won't tell Dr. Palmer what kind of woman he married. Bring ten thousand dollars in unmarked bills to the enclosed address on November seventh. Make sure nobody follows you. Don't tell the cops. Come alone. Wear the red dress you wore to the country club's Valentine's gala."

Reg scrutinized Marilyn Palmer's reaction. "Is the dress remarkable?" He couldn't resist asking.

"I think it's the blackmailer's way of letting me know they're spying on me, don't you?" she replied, cool as a cucumber.

"Sure," he agreed. "Hey, you're sharp as a tack."

She wasn't in the mood for compliments. "What now?"

"You still intend to pay this guy off?"

"How do you know it's a man?"

"I don't."

"Thought you didn't make assumptions."

"Okay, let's assume it could be anyone. Say it's a woman, or a woman and a man, or a group of individuals. Ten thousand clams is nothing to sneeze at. You still want to pay up?"

"Yes, I want this over."

"No guarantees. You pay, they ask for more, and so it goes. That's how these scenarios play out, *sometimes*."

"Could be, but I have no choice. I have a family—a husband and a daughter to protect. Maybe the blackmailer will take the money and run. You never know. It could happen."

"Or, you could tell your husband the truth."

Marilyn flipped open the flap of her small shoulder bag and pulled out a cigarette. Reg got up to search for the ashtray, which must've grown legs and walked away.

"Look, Hartman." She anxiously fingered a matchbook. "I told you before, I won't even consider telling my husband. He's planning on running for Congress, his father's dream. I don't understand why, but there you have it."

Reg wondered why Dr. Palmer would want to become a congressman. Why would anyone? "Doris must have decided to wash the only ashtray I own. Hold on, I'll go find it."

Downstairs, the secretary retrieved the freshly scrubbed ashtray from a cabinet and handed it to Reg.

"Sorry," she said. "I meant to put it back, but got busy. Is the goddess officially hiring you?"

"Looks like," he replied.

"Can't wait to hear the juicy details."

"She's not giving me much to work on."

Doris's coral-lipped mouth made an O shape. "Fascinating."

He rushed upstairs, but Marilyn hadn't waited for his return. She'd already lit up. Her nicotine fit must have gotten the best of her.

"Tell me, have you handled this sort of case before?" she asked.

"You bet."

"How do we proceed from here?"

"Can you get away without causing suspicion?"

The dame appeared composed, but a visible contracting of her neck muscles told Reg just how anxious she truly was.

"I have a friend," she said. "She assists Edith Head. I used to work with her, and I know for a fact she can be trusted to cover for me."

Reg was ignorant about the movie business, but even he knew Edith Head was a big-time costume designer. Maybe Marilyn Palmer had once been an actress; he wouldn't have been surprised.

"Alright then," he said, as he considered the address in the black-mailer's note. "This location is just north of Redlands. I'll drive out there, take a look around, and see what I can find."

Marilyn placed her supple lips around the cigarette filter and took a disturbingly long drag.

Reg thought of his mother's heavy smoking habit and her slow death from emphysema. Damn coffin nails. He didn't understand how people fell for the phony mystique.

"I suppose I'll have to drive in my car, won't I? My husband has a habit of checking the mileage. Redlands, that's where the orange groves are. That's a long way out."

"Sixty miles—give or take."

Marilyn bit her lip. "I normally don't travel any distance to speak of. I meet friends for lunch in Hollywood, that's about it. Gary will wonder how I put so many miles on the speedometer."

"Don't sweat it," Reg said. "I'll come up with a plausible explanation."

She stood and leaned over to smash out her cigarette butt. A touch of cleavage showed through the low-cut V-neck of her slinky dress. No wonder her husband liked to check the odometer. Men must've made passes at her on a regular basis. Women as lovely as Marilyn Palmer could steal a man's breath away, just like Helen of Troy with the face that launched a thousand ships. The male of the species have never been any damn good at resisting beauty. Reg included himself in the mix.

"I'll ring you tomorrow," she said.

Reg nodded. His calculating had already commenced. He would find the guy. He would do his job and put an end to the extortion. Marilyn Palmer would have her domestic harmony restored, unscathed. He would see to it.

FIVE
1956

"I need a damn martini," Gary said, as he jiggled the shaker force-fully. The effort behind his machinations exposed his frustration. He smirked at Marilyn. "What's Freya's problem this time?"

What nerve she had, to sour the mellow mood of her husband's prime relaxation hour with news that her good friend would need her help in a few days. In reality, Freya didn't need her help at all. The story was a cover for when Marilyn would meet the blackmailer.

"Freya's having female troubles," she said, resurrecting a term her mother had often used to put her father off. Gary became even more annoyed when Marilyn used the silly phrase. He was a doctor and well versed in the mechanics of a woman's anatomy. Such mealy-mouthed expressions irritated him.

"Be specific," he advised.

"Goodness," Marilyn said, softly. "How can I, when she won't?"

"Nothing annoys me more than a female practicing subterfuge. Women should learn how to shoot straight. You always do, and I appreciate that."

A pang stabbed her sorry heart with a thousand pointed arrows. What a fraud she was.

"What's for dinner tonight?"

Marilyn latched on to the distraction. "I made your favorite root beer stew." It was one of Lillian's specialties—the Palmer family favored recipes clipped from *Family Circle* and *Good Housekeeping*.

Gary poured them each a drink. "Terrific. I knew something smelled delicious."

The martini went straight to Marilyn's head and soured her sensitive stomach. It bothered her as she fed Lilly peaches for dessert. Her eyes filled with tears as she gingerly reached across the metal highchair tray to wipe her daughter's cherub-like face. The idea that someone horrible might ruin her secure life knocked Marilyn off kilter. *Compose yourself,* she thought. *Pull yourself together.* No more tears, and no more slip-ups.

Armida the live-in nanny materialized. Where on earth had she come from? What a blatant example of Marilyn's lack of control. She must stay focused. What if the sly nanny sensed her trepidation? Armida's mother, Consuela, had been in Lillian's employ practically forever, as had Armida's sisters and brother. The siblings were hardworking and loyal. If Armida got whiff of any dubious behavior on Marilyn's part, she probably wouldn't hesitate to run to her mother and Consuela would surely supply Lillian with every detail.

With Lilly tucked in bed for the night, safe and sound, Marilyn entered the kitchen to find Gary fussing over the stew. He stirred the pot madly. What odd behavior. He wasn't normally attentive to what she had going on the stove, or at least not until it appeared on his plate. She feigned interest in the portion he served up for her (odd as well, as she was always the one to serve him). But her appetite had flown the coop, replaced with stomach pains.

"Not hungry?" he asked.

"Got to stay slim," she said. "You don't want a fat wife, do you?"

"No, but you've never had a weight problem, I venture to guess. A little stew won't make you heavy."

"Don't worry about me," she said. "Don't let your supper grow cold."

⊹ ⊹ ⊹

The secretary always answered the phone at the Western Detective Agency, and Doris told Marilyn that Mr. Hartman would not be available until the following morning.

"He won't?" Marilyn cried.

"No, dear," Doris said. "Don't fret, he'll speak with you tomorrow."

"I need to talk with him," Marilyn said. "I'm a ball of nerves."

"Mrs. Palmer, I don't technically work for Mr. Hartman. I just take his messages." Doris let out a sympathetic sigh. "But, I can assure you, I've seen him in action and Mr. Hartman will do his best to solve your case. You can count on that."

"You don't have any way to get a message to him?"

"Sorry, I don't. He's out of the office until tomorrow morning."

Marilyn's heart pounded with such force she could barely catch her breath.

As she wandered up and down the aisles of the recently opened, ultra-modern grocery store (an enormous place with an overwhelming display of abundance), Marilyn did her best to remember the ingredients for Lillian's oven-fried cornflake chicken recipe. It was another of her husband's favorites.

How she longed for the superior cuisine back home. The tourtière (delectable French Canadian meat pies), roasted maple-glazed leg of lamb, yellow pea soup, and sugar pies. She remembered trips to the butcher made with her mother, and Nicole's frequent requests for fresh rabbit.

Once, Marilyn mentioned her fondness for rabbit to Lillian, and her stern mother-in-law had rudely asked if rabbit was a *down-home* Florida favorite. Marilyn quickly learned to edit what slipped out during moments of recklessness.

The last time she ate dinner at her mother's table, Three had served rabbit fried in the French method. It was crisp as could be, but non-greasy and served alongside scalloped potatoes baked in thick cream and butter. Heavenly.

If only Marilyn had known what a colossal mistake she was about to make. *If only* she hadn't left Michigan to meet June Masterson in Chicago.

✥ ✥ ✥

1939

June had cooked up the scheme. "Jeepers, you ought to threaten to tell anybody and everybody about what James Quinn did to you," she suggested during a visit to Detroit. "Your perverted grandfather better shell out the bucks, or you'll tell on him."

"Stop it, Junesy!" Beryl said. She regretted telling her friend about the molestations. But as Ma often said, it did no good to shut the barn door after the cows were out.

Her friend would simply not let it go. June was certain Beryl could win out if only her evil-doing grandfather was forced to pay a hefty price for what he had done. Keen to Beryl's fear and revulsion, June decided to visit the old man in her place. "I know he'll pay," she insisted. And in the end, when all was said and done, June had it right. James Quinn's only stipulation—his granddaughter must claim the proceeds. Beryl would be forced to take delivery of the money.

Arguments ensued.

"You can face that old coot," June insisted.

"No, I can't," Beryl said, in a small, frightened voice.

"You can."

"No. He scares me."

"Ha. You scare him, silly. If you let the cat out of the bag, he's in big trouble—talk about scary. Come on. Do you want to go to Hollywood or not?"

"How will I ever make Ma understand?"

"You can't! If you tell her about our plans, she'll stop you from leaving, and you know it. We'll get the money from your grandfather and we'll disappear. You can never tell anybody what we're up to. Not a living soul!"

Beryl met her grandfather in an alley behind the Catholic Church, a location she chose for its ironic relevance. Although she feared becoming a nervous wreck while in close proximity to her grandfather, Beryl felt oddly detached. He handed her a bundle. She mechanically accepted the money and coldly turned away.

"Sweet child," he said, in a shaky voice that was unrecognizable to her. "I have no idea what you intend to do with this money, but may God be with you. And may God forgive me."

Although she'd rehearsed a thousand reprimands, she did not give any of them a voice, because she was reduced to his level the moment she accepted his tainted money.

Beryl spent the next few months learning all she could about sewing and patternmaking from Mémère. Junesy had the idea that

if Beryl paid close enough attention, she would have a valuable skill
to fall back on: She could always be a seamstress for the studios. The
more skills gained before they left, the easier it would be to edge out
the competition in Hollywood.

Mémère was excited by her granddaughter's interest in her
chosen profession, and prattled on endlessly. She predicted that
Beryl would have a storefront of her own one day. The ideal locale
would be New York City.

"You are talented," Mémère gushed. "Better than I ever was.
You have a genuine flair for improvisation and design—like the
divine Coco."

Coco Chanel was Mémère's idol. When guilt over her deceptive
plans threatened to dash Beryl's resolve to flee Detroit for brighter
vistas, she dreamed about being a famous actress one day. In her
fantasies, she'd earn gobs of money and buy a lovely house near
the Pacific Ocean for her mother and grandmother. No more cold
winters and arthritis flare-ups for either one of them! And then they
could forgive her for running away.

With nothing more than a satchel in hand, Beryl boarded a passenger
train for Chicago where she would meet up with June, and then the
two girls would travel on to Los Angeles. Neither one of them had
whispered so much as a word to anybody about leaving home. If
they had left a note, it would've invited interference. They'd inform
their families about their whereabouts once they were settled in and
gainfully employed. June had the brains—she had the ideas and
made all the plans—and Beryl followed her best friend's commands.

The girls arrived at Union Station in Los Angeles, at last. The
two of them went bonkers during the taxi ride—oohing and aahing
over the diverse palm trees, how there were short ones, tall ones,
shaggy ones, and smooth ones; so many endless varieties. June
leaned forward and told the driver to take them to the Hollywood
Studio Club. She had in her possession one ancient dog-eared copy
of *Photoplay Magazine*. The article, *Breaking Into The Movies*, had
provided the inspiration, which had captured her imagination and
prompted the trip.

June studied the magazine's map of Hollywood and began to read the address on Lodi Court out loud, but the driver waved his hand in dismissal and told her not to bother. He knew the joint well.

"'Girls staying at the Hollywood Studio Club,'" June read to Beryl, from the pages of the magazine, "'must be seeking employment of one kind or another in the motion picture business. They offer classes in various aspects of the performing arts, two meals a day are provided, along with laundry facilities and'—*get this*—'sewing machines!' Jeepers, the place sounds perfect for us!"

Beryl agreed.

But, not one week later, June practically dragged Beryl kicking and screaming *away from the dorm-like atmosphere of the Studio Club*, to a place she'd heard about from a few of the other girls. She had managed to make heaps of friends in just a few short days.

They were on their way across town, bound for a legendary hotel on Sunset Boulevard, at the east end of the Sunset Strip. A Russian-born silent film and stage actress named Alla Nazimova had purchased a mansion at the height of her career. In an effort to increase diminishing income due to a waning screen presence, she'd had twenty-five Spanish-Moorish villas built on the property, and had named her hotel the Garden of Allah.

Frugal Beryl had been quite happy at the Studio Club, but spendthrift June had other ideas. The cost of living in their own casita was hefty, but June honestly believed she would land many well-paying acting jobs straight away. They resided next to the huge built-in swimming pool Nazimova had designed in the shape of the Black Sea, where the water glowed a supernatural bluish-green after sunset. In their room, they took baths in a black porcelain tub surrounded by Moorish tiles in bright colors.

The girls would make the short walk over to Schwab's Drug Store whenever they got bored. Beryl preferred root beer floats and June ordered chocolate malts. They'd stargaze.

They were sitting at the counter one day, when June leaned close and whispered, "I think that's Myrna Loy. Imagine, Myrna Loy plops down in a chair and eats a sandwich the same as any of us. Isn't that amazing? I wonder who her friend is."

Beryl glanced over—she doubted the woman was Myrna Loy. In fact, she was positive it wasn't, but didn't say so.

June was waiting to be discovered. She posed whenever they ventured out, sure to mind her posture, and to smile, smile, smile. "Look at you," she said to Beryl one day, while they were playing ping-pong on the grounds of the Garden of Allah. "You don't have any makeup on at all, when a marvelous star could waltz on by anytime."

"Oh Junesy," Beryl quipped. "What difference would it make if someone did come by?"

"You're hopeless," June said. "You don't understand anything."

✛ ✛ ✛

June rushed into the casita one day, breathless and excited. "We're going to the Troc! Can you believe it?"

"The Troc?"

"*Beryl, Beryl*...the Trocadero? It just happens to be the snazziest nightclub in town. Robert L. Hamilton—the Broadway star, in case you don't know who he is—invited us. He's got a friend he wants you to meet who was in an actual movie with Betty Grable, of all people! You've got to get dressed up, and I mean dressed up!"

After arriving at the Trocadero that night, Beryl took everything in. She decided it would be fun to be a camera, cigarette, or coat-check girl in such a glamourous setting. She told June this when they went to the restroom to powder their noses.

"You've got to think bigger," June scolded. "You've got to expand your horizons!"

Beryl enjoyed her meal. As they left the club, June invited the fellas to the casita for a drink.

Mark Whitaker, Beryl's date, grew animated when he learned where the girls were staying. "I've always wanted to visit the Garden of Allah," he said.

June rang up the bellboy as soon as she got in the door and asked him to bring around a couple of bottles of champagne and a bucket of ice.

Beryl changed out of her evening dress into comfy slacks and a blouse. She knew June resented her reluctance to invite their dates over, but she wasn't going to let her friend run her life entirely.

Enough was enough. As far as Beryl was concerned, Mark was a good-looking fella, but not her type. He was too eager to please.

Several of June's friends soon filed in, carrying trays of sandwiches and bottles of booze. Another knock-down-drag-out party was breaking out, one that would likely last all night. Beryl knew she wouldn't be missed, so she ducked into her bedroom to finish reading *To Have and to Have Not*. Hemingway was one of countless writers who had chosen to stay in the villas of the Garden of Allah while visiting Hollywood. Writers gravitated towards the villas and the list of luminaries intrigued her to no end: Dorothy Parker and Alan Campbell, Garson Kanin, Robert Benchley, Lillian Hellman and Dashiell Hammett, F. Scott Fitzgerald, William Faulkner, Elmer Rice, Thornton Wilder, Somerset Maugham, Ring Lardner Jr., and P.G. Wodehouse, just to name a few. Beryl loved to read. It was a pastime June never made time for, unless you counted trashy magazines.

The walls of the casitas were extremely thin. Beryl awoke to passionate wailing coming from June's bedroom. She must have decided to go to bed with Bobby Hamilton. Beryl went to the kitchen for a drink of water and spotted Bobby curled up on the sofa, snoring away. Oh drat—June must have gone to bed with *Mark Whitaker*!

Beryl retrieved a glass of water and tiptoed to her room. She was sorry she'd allowed June to talk her out of leaving the Studio Club, where men were not allowed in the rooms and were required to wait downstairs in the lobby whenever they came a-calling. Why did June have to be impetuous? What if her friend got pregnant? Then what would they do?

✥ ✥ ✥

One day Beryl found herself all alone and bored. She impulsively called a taxi and told the driver to take her to the Griffith Observatory. The building was a lovely art deco marvel with a domed top. The site offered an amazing view. Although Beryl had always been afraid of heights, she stood on a deck and stared out at the City of Angels spread before her.

An older couple soon joined her. "Evolution schmevolution," the wife remarked.

"To each his own," the husband said.

"Do you believe in evolution?" The wife suddenly addressed Beryl, as if she'd been a part of the conversation all along.

They must have come from the new exhibit, and the wife obviously didn't agree with its subject matter. "Not really," Beryl said, honestly. There were so many things she wasn't sure about.

"Why don't they just toss the Old Testament right over this cliff?" the well-coifed older woman cried. She turned to Beryl and extended her hand. "I'm Ruth Adler, and this is my husband, Melvin. He's retired now. He used to be a doctor at Sinai Home for the Incurables, a sanitarium."

Beryl shook the woman's hand. "I'm Beryl Quinn," she said. She quickly turned to address the doctor. "A sanitarium?" she asked. She was captivated by the concept of being incurable.

"A sanitarium and a hospital," Dr. Adler replied.

"Glad to meet you, Beryl Quinn," Ruth said. "What brings you up here today?"

"I wanted to see what all the fuss was about," she answered. "I have to say, the observatory is incredible."

"We think so, too, except for the promotion of evolution."

"Ruth," Dr. Adler said, "you sound radical."

"They call it science, when it's basically theory. It's nonsense. God created the heavens and Earth."

Dr. Adler smiled at Beryl. "She won't stop," he said. "I can't make her."

"Are you all alone here?" Ruth asked.

"Yes," Beryl admitted, sensing the older woman's displeasure at the news.

"A beautiful young girl such as yourself should not be out and about without a chaperone. What happened to good sense?"

"Ruth!" Dr. Adler grabbed his wife by the arm.

"It's true," Ruth said. "I insist you stay with us for the rest of your stay. Have you seen the riff-raff lurking about?"

Beryl smiled. She hadn't seen anyone she would consider riff-raff. This Ruth Adler was certainly opinionated.

"And," the older woman said, "you'll lunch with us."

Beryl dined in a deli with the couple, where Ruth insisted she try the matzo ball soup. She couldn't believe Beryl had never tasted matzo.

When they pulled over to drop Beryl off, Ruth shook her head in disgust. "I've heard of this place," she said, as she carefully scrutinized the Garden of Allah sign. "My nephew works in pictures. I'm not ignorant about what goes on with these Hollywood types. It's not a place for a young girl."

"I'm careful," Beryl told her. "Don't worry." She thanked them for buying her lunch and said goodbye.

When she told June about the encounter, her friend suggested Beryl had holes in her head for eating lunch with old people.

"But he was a retired doctor," Beryl told her. "They were so nice."

June crinkled her nose in disbelief. "I was frolicking in the same swimming pool with Gillian Chase, and there you were, eating in a deli with two old Jews you don't even know! Honestly, Beryl, you're hopelessly boring."

"I am not boring," Beryl snapped. "You should have seen the observatory: It was remarkable. And the Adlers were intelligent and interesting. Jeez, you're so narrow-minded."

"It's obvious we're interested in different kinds of stars," Junesy declared.

Mark Whitaker invited June to join him for the weekend up the coast, in Malibu Colony.

"I'm not going unless you come," June told Beryl.

Beryl was reluctant to commit. "Who's going along?"

"Mark and his sister. Emily's as sweet as can be—I met her yesterday. Come on, Beryl, neither one of us has ever seen the ocean!"

"Need I remind you, I've swum in three of the Great Lakes?"

"That's not the same. Not by a long shot."

Beryl decided not to protest any longer. It did seem ridiculous—they'd been in Southern California for two whole weeks and she hadn't once laid eyes on the Pacific. "You talked me into it. I'll tag along. Why not?"

Gilbert Dann, the silent film star, had built the cottage they were staying in for his wife back in the early '20s. After his car had veered off the Pacific Coast Highway and he'd been decapitated, his wife moved into town and decided to rent the cottage out for extra income.

The cottage sported a weathered deck facing the water. It was April, and too chilly for Mark and his snotty sister. It was warm in the sun, though. Beryl left the deck, flopped on the beach and stayed put all day long.

June marched over. "We're off to the local watering hole," she announced.

Why had they come to Malibu if all they were going to do was tie one on? Beryl shook her head. "I'm loving it here."

"Fine—be antisocial." June darted away, spewing sand with her bare feet.

Beryl brushed herself off. She was determined to finish Marjorie Kinnan Rawling's *The Yearling*. And finish it she did, just as the sun began its retreat and the light grew too dim for her to make out the words on the page any longer. She folded her chair and hurried over the dune towards the cottage.

When they returned, June and Mark had two fellas and a gal in tow, but the bratty sister was nowhere to be seen.

"What happened to Emily?" Beryl asked June, once they were in the kitchen unpacking groceries.

"You bored her to tears. She's visiting friends."

"I bored her to tears? I didn't know it was my job to keep that brat amused!"

"Don't get all bent outta shape. Mark got rid of her, didn't he? We're going to have ourselves a bash. Will you fix us that great chicken soup of yours? I think I brought all the necessary ingredients."

"Sure." Soup sounded good. Beryl had skipped lunch and was starving.

One of the fellas they'd met up with was an actor named Chet Rove, and Beryl found him charming. He brought out his guitar and played a few cowboy tunes after dinner. His goal was to follow in the footsteps of his idol, Gene Autry. Chet did have a nice voice. Maybe he would be a big star one day. Just about everyone they ran into intended to make their name in Hollywood. Beryl was beginning to feel as if anything was possible.

Not a few days later, Mark alienated June when he demanded she marry him. Beryl heard them arguing through the thin walls.

"I can't get married!" June cried.

"You must marry me," he said. "I love you!"

"Say, you're nice and all, but *I don't love you*. Not by a long shot. I'm too young to even consider marriage."

"But you slept with me!"

"Mark, be realistic. We were just having some laughs."

He had no answer.

Beryl sighed. Mark was a nice fella and she felt sorry about his broken heart.

Chet Rove rang Beryl a few weeks after they'd first met, to ask if she'd like to go for a drive. He was off to take a meeting at a movie location in the valley. He thought she might get a kick out of the mock Western town and oodles of costumed extras roaming around.

June was out and about, so Beryl didn't have to invite her along. She was glad. Her friend exhibited unpredictable behavior and clearly lacked common sense. After she dumped Mark, she had taken up with a shady character by the name of Ronny Wiley. Out by the pool one day, an awkward girl with crooked teeth suggested Ronny Wiley was affiliated with the mob.

"The mob?" Beryl bristled at the news. "In *Los Angeles*?"

"Especially in Los Angeles," was the awkward girl's deadpan response. "What are you, *stupid*?"

Beryl thought: *Maybe I am stupid. June is running amuck, with a mobster of all people. I am her roommate. At this rate, it's certain I'll earn a terrible reputation by association.*

"We have a drive ahead of us," Chet told her, once they'd set out on the highway. "Sure hope you don't mind."

"I don't mind the ride," Beryl said. "In fact, I'd love to learn to drive myself."

"You don't know how?"

"Nope," she said, feeling like a kid.

"Not a lick?"

"That's a funny way to put it."

"Remind me to teach you," he said. "It won't take any time at all. You're sharp, you won't have any problem."

Beryl hoped so.

"About that friend of yours, June. Has she gone on any auditions yet?"

"No auditions that I know of. She's too busy living the high life." Beryl felt bad. She shouldn't speak poorly about her friend. But when was that girl going to get on the stick and try to land work?

"I gave her a couple of contact numbers," Chet said. "Maybe she's not all that serious about acting after all. I sensed a little apprehension on her part."

"I've known June for a long time. Believe me, she's always wanted to be an actress."

Chet cocked his head thoughtfully. "Many a slip between the cup and the lip," he offered.

Beryl had given it some thought; what the heck held Junesy back, anyway? Why did she run around with every Tom, Dick, and Harry, instead of taking acting lessons or trying out for parts? Was she fearful? She had never thought of her friend as insecure. June was vivacious and outgoing, always posing and smiling and acting comical. Beryl felt like a wet blanket in comparison.

"I'm sure she's only doing her best to get the lay of the land," she told Chet.

"Maybe. What about you? You're stunning, if you don't mind my saying. You wouldn't have any problem getting work."

"I think I'd prefer the costume department. I love to sew. To be honest, I don't know the first thing about being an actress."

"Acting's easy—we're not talking Shakespeare. Ham it up like there's no tomorrow. That's all I do."

"But you've got talent! You sing and play the guitar so well."

"Take it from me, getting paid good money to say lines some writer spent hours and hours writing is akin to larceny. You should try. You'll never know, otherwise."

While Chet took a meeting, Beryl wandered around the set. She marveled at the Western costumes and at how much work must have gone into designing and sewing them. She had barely sat down on a bench outside the phony front of a general store when she discovered the bench was so poorly put together that the wooden frame quaked under her weight. She sprang up, not wanting to topple the flimsy thing. The town was nothing but an illusion of a town.

Beryl made her way over to a corral and watched the horses, suddenly aware of how odd she must appear in her long knit dress cinched with a patent leather belt and wide-lapel jacket, navigating the uneven dusty dirt roads in open-toed platform pumps. She leaned against the fence rail and admired a palomino.

A cowboy seemed to materialize out of thin air. "You go in for horses?" he asked.

"I think I could, given the chance."

"That one's Flo," he said, pointing at the horse. "She's a beauty, ain't she?"

"Sure is."

"I know a pretty filly when I see one." He thrust out his hand. "Boots Parker."

"Beryl Quinn."

"Glad to make your acquaintance. I haven't seen you around before. How about we walk over to the mess house and grab a cup of coffee?"

She tried not to grin when he tipped his cowboy hat. "I'd better not disappear," Beryl told Boots. "I'm waiting for someone."

"Who might that lucky someone be?"

"Chet Rove."

"Chet Rove, the guitar-playing cowboy?" Boots Parker took two steps back. "Shucks," he cried. "I'm broke right in two."

Beryl wished Junesy could have been there to hear him speak. Boots was charming, with his curly hair, bowed legs, and likable crooked smile. June would have shamelessly flirted with Boots.

"Don't be silly," Beryl said. "Chet thought I should see a movie set."

"First time?" Boots kicked at the dust.

Beryl scowled; her shoes were dusty enough as it was.

"Sorry!" he cried.

"That's all right," she said. "This is my first time on a set of any kind. I suppose I should have worn more practical shoes. You see, I hope to get a job in a costume department. I'm a seamstress."

"You, in the cotton-picking costume department? Why, that's cock-eyed."

Beryl smiled. "Where are you from, Boots?" she asked. His accent was so pronounced.

"I was born in Oklahoma but raised north of here, in Bakersfield. Where you from?"

"Detroit, Michigan. I guess I sound different, too."

"Detroit, Michigan, where they build cars?"

She heard Chet call her name and Beryl turned her head.

"Uh-oh," Boots said. "My luck's plum wore out!"

"I see you've found the horses," Chet said, in his good-natured manner.

"I did," Beryl replied.

Chet offered Beryl his arm. "Come with me." He then tipped his hat at Boots. "Thanks for keeping her amused," he said, coldly.

Boots lifted his chin in acknowledgement and turned away.

"That cowboy sure is colorful," she remarked.

"He tries too hard," Chet said, under his breath. "He's too much of a caricature for my taste. I don't buy into that hick routine."

It was the first time she'd heard Chet say anything negative about anyone, and Beryl was a little shocked to hear him put Boots down. "Where are we going now?" she asked, doing her best to follow along. Next time she would wear flats.

"You'll see."

If somebody had told Beryl she would meet face to face with Joyce Baxter that morning, she would have thought they had a screw loose. Joyce was a big star who'd gotten her start in movies with Mary Pickford and Lillian Gish. Her face had filled out and she'd aged some, but she was one hundred percent recognizable. Beryl was thrilled to meet her, and nearly dumbstruck.

When Chet ran off to handle a little business, Beryl sat with the famous actress.

"I came from Chicago," Joyce said, after Beryl mentioned she was from Detroit.

"My roommate's from Chicago," Beryl told her.

"Midwestern girls do fine out here in Hollywood," the movie star stated, "if they keep their heads." Beryl bit her tongue. It wouldn't do to badmouth June to a complete stranger. "There are wolves, and then there are plain old dogs," Joyce added. "If you get my drift."

"You bet," Beryl replied. "I'm staying at the Garden of Allah. I know exactly what you mean."

"That den of iniquity?"

"It was my friend's idea." Beryl's face grew warm. My, but the hotel had a bad reputation.

"All sorts of shenanigans go on over there. I've heard rumors…"

"But, but…" Beryl stammered, "there are some lovely people. Quite well known. Writers…"

"Writers!" Joyce interrupted. "They're the worst! You be careful. A beauty like you. I was never beautiful, but I was attractive and I was innocent. I can tell you're still innocent. Hey, are you and Chet an item?"

"No, we only just met."

"He's a good kid."

"He's sweet, but I'm not looking to get involved."

"Heavens to Betsy, girl," Joyce said, "that might not stop you. I only knew my second husband for two weeks before we headed for Santa Barbara one Friday. We tied the knot that Sunday and were back in town by Monday, for the *Rescue Rachel* shoot. He was the producer, and I played the villainess. The public didn't buy me in that role—not my fault, mind you. They were used to seeing me play the blameless victim; the frightened little lamb. I was determined to break the mold, and I went on to many varied roles, thank God."

"You didn't play a victim in *Time for Honey*," Beryl said. "I love that movie."

"Yes, that's right…and thank you. I have a special place in my heart for that picture. My first truly well-rounded role, Miss Penelope Purdy, the wayward woman with a heart of gold."

They sat for quite a spell that afternoon, while Chet was doing whatever it was he was doing, and Beryl learned that Joyce was now married to her fourth husband. He owned restaurants. "I'll never marry another man in the movie business if it doesn't work out with Edward," she said.

It seemed the movie star was unruffled at the prospect of parting with yet another husband, as if she were simply making another costume change. How strange these Hollywood folk were.

One night, during a roaring party in one of the most remote casitas at the Garden of Allah, Beryl was introduced to a model turned
costume designer. She was working at MGM and her name was
Freya Simard. Shortly after they met, the two of them launched
into a lengthy conversation about costume designers. Beryl gushed
on and on about Walter Plunkett, but Freya preferred Adrian and
praised his work on *The Philadelphia Story.* Katharine Hepburn had
never looked as lovely.

Beryl unfortunately had trouble hearing what Freya had to
say over the din in the room, which was building to a crescendo.
Besides, she was preoccupied, too busy trying to spot June in the
crowd. They had arrived arm in arm, but her friend was nowhere
to be seen.

Beryl would not lay eyes on June again for three long days.

Once she ventured out and let it be known her friend was missing,
Beryl was urged not to report June's disappearance by several Allah
residents. The general consensus seemed to be that June was a wild
child and Beryl shouldn't overreact. June would surface eventually.

A tall woman with cropped black hair showed up at the door of
the casita one morning.

"My name's Toni Goodman," she proclaimed, as she took a drag
from an extra-long, ruby-encrusted cigarette holder. After she'd
sent a cloud of smoke into the room, she continued speaking. "I
hear your friend is missing. June is it?"

"Yes," Beryl said. "June Masterson. I'm worried sick."

"Look, give it more time," the mysterious woman said. "I heard
through the grapevine that your pal disappeared with Kay Rennick.
Everyone knows Kay's a possessive lesbian with a penchant for
young blondes."

"But June isn't...*of that persuasion,*" Beryl said earnestly. She had
only just learned what a lesbian was.

Toni Goodman threw her head back and let out a throaty laugh,
her charcoal-lined eyes shimmering. "How fantastically naïve!" she
said. "Here's my advice, don't call the cops. I wouldn't tarnish your
little friend's reputation with the infamously disreputable LAPD if I
were you. Don't open that can of worms. She'll show up, you'll see."

Later on that day, a rumor began to circulate. People said the reclusive Nazimova, the owner of the Garden of Allah, had been the one to send Toni Goodman to Beryl's door.

With no further reports of June's whereabouts or welfare, Beryl stayed close to home and waited for news, a nervous wreck all the while. Sure enough, her uneasiness had been valid. As soon as her friend pounded on the door and Beryl opened it wide, she saw straight away—Junesy had returned all battered and black and blue.

"We'd better scram!" June cried through swollen lips. "Some crazy broad's obsessed with me. Kept me prisoner in a shack out on Mount Washington!" Marilyn watched June tear around the place like a chicken with its head cut off. June grabbed Beryl by the arm. "I only escaped because she didn't tie me up tight enough before she left for work this morning. She was hungover from drinking tequila all night long, sick as a poisoned dog. I stole a wad of cash, caught a cab, and hightailed it outta that dump. Start packing, kid. We're heading for San Francisco! I know a woman who can get us a job on Treasure Island."

Typical June. She just assumed Beryl would comply.

Beryl wasn't as willing to go along with her friend as she had been in the past. She was only beginning to acclimate to Hollywood. And besides, since they'd set foot on California soil, they'd been spending money like drunken sailors. A trip to San Francisco would cost a mint. But her attitude changed instantly once June clued her into but a fraction of what had happened while she had been imprisoned in Kay Rennick's remote hideaway. Under duress, and horrified by what she'd heard, Beryl agreed to accompany her friend north. Junesy insisted Kay would be in fast pursuit. She claimed Kay would never leave her be if she stayed in Hollywood.

Beryl was losing out, throwing away a job offer to work in the costume department with Freya. And Chet had been so sweet— he'd even given her that driving lesson. There was a producer too, what was his name? He said she was gorgeous and hinted about arranging an audition. She hoped her allure wouldn't dim while she was away.

Nevertheless, it was plain to see she had no choice but to take pity on her injured friend. They had to skedaddle. She would find out what the heck June had been thinking when she'd left the party with that strange woman, and what Treasure Island was, once things settled down a bit and they were aboard the train and safe.

June slept like a dead woman for most of the trip. Beryl enjoyed the peace and quiet. She needed time to think over all that had transpired in but a few short weeks.

All manner of depravity took place in and around the private casitas of the Garden of Allah. She'd heard rumors of drunken rows, numerous sexual couplings between members of the same gender, nude swimming—even prostitution.

Beryl had witnessed outrageous hijinks with her own two eyes. By mistake, she had once walked in on a group of partygoers sharing what she later learned was a marijuana cigarette.

And once, she'd heard a bang against the side of her casita at three in the morning. An inebriated guest, a very tall man in a rumpled suit, had crashed a bicycle straight into the stucco wall of the casita. June had heard the commotion, too, and she'd pushed Beryl aside, scampered out the door wearing nothing but a flimsy nightgown, and helped the tipsy klutz untangle himself from the bougainvillea. She'd promptly accepted his offer to accompany him to a nearby early-morning-gathering a few doors down. They'd stumbled across the lawn, arm in arm, leaving the bicycle abandoned in the bushes.

Beryl got caught up in the hijinks once or twice herself. Why, she had nearly lost her virginity to a fast-talking, wavy-haired dreamboat. In the midst of the throes of passion, she had rediscovered her nearly abandoned resolve to never risk an unexpected visit from the stork, and she'd ended the encounter. She'd broken loose from his clutches just in the nick of time. Thwarted, the dreamboat had called her a cock-tease and had threatened to spread the news. Maybe cock-tease was a fitting description. She blamed her irresistible allure.

At least the men and women carrying on in the Garden of Allah were consenting adults. In Detroit, grandfathers saw fit to seek relations with their own granddaughters. Beryl decided most human beings were absolute slaves to their sexual desires. Better they exercise those impulses and urges than attempt to keep such inclinations under wraps, which was what she imagined James Quinn had attempted to do. And what good had that accomplished, in the long run? Bottling up his passions had led the old man down the road to abject perversion. Sex, it seemed, was a thorny affair. Why her mother had seen fit to tutor her in such matters by using the term *funny business* puzzled her. Or maybe *funny business* was an apt description after all. A hilarious comedy was taking place all around her and Beryl ought to surrender and participate in the farce.

SIX
1956

Reg parked his Buick a couple of miles away from the cabin. Dressed like a fisherman and carrying a pole to complete the disguise, he made his way down to what was nothing more than a creek, flanked on both sides by heaps of rocks and boulders. He had expected a great deal more water from what he'd seen on the map. His intention was to follow the rocky riverbed towards the address supplied by the blackmailer. The high elevation made him dizzy. The rough terrain tripped him up every now and then. He wasn't exactly mountain man material. Reg had come from the plains of Kansas, and had grown up running the streets of Montelbello and East L.A., rough and ready towns on the outskirts of Los Angeles. Windy mountain roads and significant heights were foreign to him. Evergreens, camping, fishing, and hunting were all unfamiliar territory.

Down in the Los Angeles basin, there wasn't much display when it came to foliage during the autumn months. Color simply leaked out of the leaves, which took their time drying up, and merely turned brown and brittle before falling to the ground. Up the mountain it was cloudy, and trees glowed in vibrant shades of yellow, orange, and red. The scenery was pleasing, if not the trek. He'd had the good sense to listen to the outfitter at the sporting goods shop, and had begrudgingly purchased sturdy hiking boots. Without the boots, it would have been impossible to gain the amount of headway he was making.

Reg discovered the remote and rustic cabin. It was built on a river-rock foundation, nestled among tall pines and cedars. The windows and doors were shuttered and secured with heavy padlocks. All he heard was the wind in the treetops high above him. Not an unpleasant sound. Next to the front door was posted the same address he had jotted at the top of the map tucked inside his shirt pocket, alongside a small metal sign, which read: *Jackson's Vacation Rentals, Nightly, Weekly, Monthly*. Reg pulled out a small notepad and scribbled down the phone number of the rental outfit.

He followed the road back to his car and never ran into a soul. All that sneaking around and the purchases at the sporting goods store really hadn't been necessary after all. He could've driven straight to the door of the cabin and nobody would have been the wiser.

Down the mountain, he pulled up to a country store, where he dropped a coin into the outside pay phone. A cheery voice rang out with, "Jackson's!"

"Hi," Reg said. "I'd like to rent the cabin at sixty-two Northstar, for the night of November seventh."

"Okey-dokey, can you hold for a sec?"

"Sure," he said. His stomach rumbled. Once the call finished, he'd go inside and inquire about the nearest place to grab a bite.

"I'm sorry," the girl said, "it's rented out for the seventh. You can have it the night before, or the following night, though."

Reg let out a frustrated sigh. "But I need *that date*. You see, it's my wife's birthday and I wanted to surprise her."

"We have others!" the girl offered. "In fact, it's been a little slow and I can rent you a much nicer cabin with a fireplace. I'll even give you the same price."

He lowered his voice and tried to reason with her. "But I want that one, you see. For sentimental reasons."

"Darn it all. I feel awful about this," the girl said pleasantly.

Growing a tad over-confident, Reg overstepped the boundaries by asking a risky question. "Could you give me the number of the person that reserved the cabin? I think I could persuade them to change their minds."

"I couldn't," she said. "It wouldn't do. I've got to consider privacy issues and all."

"Where's your office, sweetheart?"

She rattled off an address in downtown Redlands. Reg wondered how late she'd be open. When he asked about a nearby place to eat, she told him about a sandwich shop right next-door, one where they served "yummy" grinders. He climbed back in his car and made a made a mad dash down the highway to the office.

The girl's name-tag read Carrie, so Reg said, "Hi Carrie, I called earlier about the cabin on Northstar."

"Well hello there," she replied. "You know, there's more to do in Big Bear. Jackson's rents up there, too. It's not purely the attraction of the lake, you see. There are shops, restaurants—more fun stuff. You really ought to take your wife *farther up the mountain.*"

Evidently, Carrie's hackles hadn't been raised when Reg had stupidly asked if she'd give him the number of the person who had rented the cabin. She wasn't the distrustful type. He couldn't get over his luck—the rental roster lay right there on the counter.

"You say the sandwiches next door are good?"

She grinned. "Better than good. My boyfriend works there. Do you like salami? Because I'm telling you, they serve the best salami I've ever had."

"Who doesn't?"

"I have an idea. Wait right here and I'll run over and get you one."

"That's a generous offer," Reg said. "I am starving, but I couldn't let you go to all that trouble."

"I don't mind," she replied, already on her way out from behind the counter. "Mind the shop for a second, won't you?"

He told her he was a big fan of mustard before she took off like a rocket. Reg kept one watchful eye on the door while he copied down the name and number from the roster in short order.

When she got back, he made up some lame excuse about an appointment he had to get to. He said he'd give her a call the next day to make arrangements for a cabin up in Big Bear, and then he got out of there.

As he drove home and devoured the sandwich, Reg believed his job could be far too easy—so easy he ought to feel bad about taking his client's money. Carrie hadn't lied. He'd never eaten better salami, and the sweet kid wouldn't let him give her a dime, either. She'd said the sandwich was on the house because she felt so bad about him not getting the cabin he wanted.

✛ ✛ ✛

By the time Reg arrived back to the office, Doris had gone to lunch. Her new assistant, snotty Martha, hadn't bothered to make any fresh coffee. The damn percolator sat dry as a bone. One of the encyclopedia salesmen told Reg everybody in the building wanted to see the girl fired. "She's lazy as the day is long," he had complained.

"Can you do me a favor, Toots?" Reg asked Doris when she finally popped her head through his office door.

"You betcha," she said, eager to get his request out of the way. He knew she wanted to know how things had gone for him out in Redlands.

"Would you arrange for the guys to move my stuff over to my mother's place? I'm gonna give up the apartment."

"Sure," she said. "When?"

"I don't have to be out till the end of the month. Most of my clothes are over in Montelbello already. Will they pack the kitchen stuff? There's not much."

"That's what we do around here. But, forget all that—it's as good as done. What happened out in Redlands?"

"I hiked to the address in my new boots." He kicked up his foot so Doris could get a look at one of them. "Pity," he shook his head, "doubt I'll ever need these again. Turned out to be a rustic cabin rented by one J.T. Wodehouse. I managed to get my paws on the telephone number and address. Got to run out to San Pedro now to check it out."

"You sure do have to travel in this line of work. I don't get around much. For instance, I haven't been to Redlands or Montebello. And I've never laid eyes on San Pedro either, but I hear it can be a rough town."

"What you're saying is you have opinions about all those places, whether or not you've been there or not."

Doris laughed out loud. "Mister," she said, regaining composure, "if opinions were dinero, I'd be loaded."

"Don't fret about me. I come from a tough town, and I've patrolled some unsafe streets in my day."

"I suppose so. Look," she said, "this may or may not be relevant, but I read a story once, written by an Englishman by the name of P.G. Wodehouse. It was called *The Juice of an Orange*. He lived in Hollywood for a spell, back in the '30s. He was hired by the studios to write scripts, and once bragged in an interview with *The Times* about how all he did was float around in the pool in the hills and loaf about on the studio's fat dime. There was a big to-do over his flippant comments, and MGM fired him. Who knows if any of this is relevant to your case, but I thought I'd throw his name out there, because, J.T. Wodehouse, P.G. Wodehouse, that had to mean *something*."

Reg wrote the author's name down. "You never know, Toots," he said. "Thanks for the tip. Now, why don't you go down and fire that snotty Martha, that useless hunk of woman flesh? Seems she's afraid of the percolator." The sweet clerk in Redlands had been so much more helpful and upbeat in contrast to the sour-faced assistant downstairs.

"Jeez Louise, what's with you guys, trying to get that girl canned?" Doris puzzled. "Martha's a war widow with a son to raise, and God knows she needs this job."

Reg waved her away. "Go read her the riot act, then. If she doesn't shape up, ship her out."

⊹ ⊹ ⊹

As he crept up Ocean View Terrace, Reg spotted a house with the address J.T. Wodehouse had supplied to Jackson's Rentals. It was one of those typical Southern California Spanish-influenced structures, with a prominent arched plate glass window perfectly situated for viewing Catalina Island on a clear day. He parked across the street and switched off his engine. As luck would have it, not ten minutes later, an attractive blonde emerged from the side entrance and climbed into a banged-up Ford. He trailed her all the way to Torrance and followed her into a Tiki bar parking lot.

He hung back a few minutes before going inside to see what the blonde was up to. Reg had no trouble spotting her. She was sitting in a cushy booth with a lively group, a fancy cherry-red drink on the table in front of her, the rim of the glass holding a pineapple wedge that sported a pink paper umbrella. Judging by the animated behavior of her pals, they were about half in the bag. The detective took a seat at the end of the bar, where he could keep an eye on her, and asked the bartender for a beer.

It wasn't too long before the blonde was on her feet and dancing with some pimply-faced sailor. Reg wasn't much of a dancer, but when she finished with the sailor, he left the comfort of the bar to tap her on the shoulder. And when he did, she told him she thought he'd never ask. The theme to *Picnic* came up next, which suited him fine. He had enjoyed the movie. The film was set in Kansas, for one thing. Thankfully, the slower song didn't require him to make any tricky moves on the dance floor.

"What's your name, handsome?" she asked.

"Stephen Hartman." He often used the alias Stephen.

"I'm June. June Gordon."

June started with J. *A start.* "Stephen's really my middle name, if you want to know the truth. My first name is awful, so I go by Stephen."

She pulled back slightly to get a good look at him. "Horrible names—that's a sore subject with me. You see, my middle name's *Tilda*. I got saddled with my great aunt's name. Can you believe it? How awful is *Tilda*?"

"June's a nice name, that's what counts."

"I guess," she said, relaxed enough to rest her pretty head on his shoulder.

So, she had taken the bait. Her first two initials *were* J.T. He had to admit, Miss J.T. *Wodehouse* was certainly well put together. "You from around here?" he asked, doing his best to keep the conversation going.

"Sort of. I moved to San Pedro a while ago, from up north."

"Up north, as in Alaska?"

"No silly, San Francisco."

"Ah, the city by the bay."

"One and the same. With its hills and ocean views, San Pedro makes me feel as if I'm still up there."

"I see the similarities."

"And you?" June Gordon asked. "Where do you hail from?"

"Kansas."

"As in the Land of Oz?"

"One and the same."

The blonde pulled away again, threw him a dazzling smile, and suggested they sit down. "These shoes are killing me," she said, limping back to the table.

They joined the others in the noisy booth and he learned how easily she made friends. The blonde had only just met the gang that night when she waltzed into the joint. The booth was noisy, full of guys and gals out to tie one on and mix with members of the opposite sex. He couldn't hear himself think. Regrettably, he didn't dig up any more information. But, he scored at the end of the evening when June handed over her phone number, which she'd scribbled on the back of a matchbook. She invited him to call her *any old time*.

Once the Buick fired up, he decided to stay in his apartment for the night, too beat to make the drive out to Montelbello. Maybe he wouldn't be able to move out there after all. He often worked late; sometimes a case would send him all over hell and gone. He really should unload his mother's house. But the place had meant so much to her and his stepfather Ruben. Ah, it wasn't necessary to get all bothered over the situation. He didn't have to decide what to do right then and there. The detective pulled out onto Hawthorne Boulevard and made his way towards the apartment, doing his best not to shut his weary eyes.

Reg was irritated to have his meal interrupted when a knock came at the door. He was astounded to find his old girlfriend Wendy standing on the stoop with a black eye and a suitcase in hand. He smelled trouble. "Don't give me that look," she said. "I only need to stay tonight. I'm taking a bus home to North Dakota tomorrow. I'm sure glad to find you still here. Please, Reg? I don't have anywhere else to go." He carried the bag inside and offered her a plate of hash.

They sat down and ate together. They each drank two beers before she relaxed enough to tell her story.

"I started going out with this guy. I should've known better—he's a repo man. What did I expect, huh? A lousy repo man. Anyway, we got along, and he insisted I move in with him. What a mistake! I swore I'd never shack up with anyone. But, I admit, it's my fault. I took the easy way out because I was having trouble making the rent. I took him up on his offer to move into his place. I lost my job at the co-op and I was nervous about finding another. You know how it goes. He felt as if I should kiss his feet because he was supporting me. He didn't initiate sex—he demanded it. He's a certified rat bastard."

"Sounds like a hell of a guy," Reg said. He brought the plates over to the sink and began to rinse them.

"A real prince. He took to knocking me around right after I moved in. I think he gets more pleasure out of beating me than he does out of screwing me. I've been working for a couple of weeks. I earned enough to buy a ticket home, and I just left him."

She threw their empty bottles in the trash and wiped the table clean. "You were the best boyfriend I ever had," she said. "You broke my damn heart—you know that?"

Reg had heard this routine before. He sighed and reached for the dishtowel. "I was on the level with you," he said. His practiced response followed. "I made it clear that I was only in it for laughs and company."

"Yeah, yeah, yeah, that's what you said. Don't you think most ordinary couples start out that way, though, both the men and the women—overcome with infatuation instead of good sense? Overcome with the newness of the thing, and the lightness. But then you get involved. If you're human, you do. And you want more. It's inevitable. Most of us want more, especially us women. We can't help ourselves. You, Reg, you're afraid of all that."

He knew what she meant. Beginnings were always breezy. Yeah, it was all fun and games in the beginning. There was a long pause, because he wanted to respond, but was no longer of the mind to defend his actions.

Wendy broke the silence. "How's your mother? She's such a nice lady."

He had forgotten Wendy was one of the few girlfriends he'd ever seen fit to bring home to meet his mother. "She's gone. Ruben is, too."

"Ah, I'm sorry to hear that."

"She was bad at the end. It's a terrible thing when you find your-self willing someone you love to die, when you look forward to them checking out."

They drank more beer. And at one point, Reg felt compelled to delicately touch his old girlfriend's cheek, just below her seriously bruised eye. Wendy was a handsome girl, a sturdy girl, with big brown eyes and chestnut hair. "I could make sure that rat bastard gets his, if you want me to."

"Nah, what's the point? What's done is done. I'm going home and I'm through with him anyways. I'm sick of this town. Nothing feels real here."

"These bruises look awfully real," he said, lightly running his finger alongside the purple stain.

Wendy had hold of his hand and she gave him a squeeze. "I believe there's too damn many people with too damn many points of view packed in too tightly together around here. It's easy to get lost in the chaos. At least I did. You knew me when I was young and naïve. Now I'm jaded—more of a realist. In the end, I'm a fish out of water. All the temptations that lured me out here in the first place don't mean squat anymore."

"It's only been four years since we parted," Reg said. "Have things been going that badly for you?"

"You don't know the half of it."

"I'm sorry," he said, feeling down.

"It's not your fault," she told him, sadly.

Maybe it was his fault. Maybe he'd set a series of events in motion when he recklessly threw the poor kid to the wayside. His self-centeredness was monumental. Men and women and the nature of their push-pull relationships confounded him. He didn't want his women to need him—that was the truth of the thing. He needed them, he used them, but he didn't want them to expect too much. Wendy had a point. The reason a man needs a woman differs greatly from the reason a woman needs a man. A woman needs a man to watch out for her, to protect her, and Reg had never been set to provide that level of reliability.

It was all coming back to him. Wendy didn't belong with a cop. He'd been with the force when they were together. She needed a Joe-lunch-bucket-type, somebody who would leave home and return the same time every evening during the week. Somebody who would spend weekends at home fussing over what she wanted him to fuss over. She had herself figured out. As he recalled, Wendy was a fairly simple girl with fairly simple needs.

When she kissed his neck, he pulled away. "You don't want to do that," he said.

"But I do," she told him. "I'm leaving forever. Come on, Reg. How can you act so cold? Be with me, for old time's sake?"

Reg touched Wendy's warmth where her dress had ridden up. The silkiness of a woman's thigh always had the same effect. It reminded him of other soft spots, hidden spots, and sent his wandering hands looking for more.

Despite her bruises, Wendy seemed hungry for contact. She slipped her dress over her shoulders and unclasped her bra. Reg pushed her underpants down and put his kisser to the place where she wanted it to be. His fingers worked over Wendy's supple ass while she came to climax. Then it was his turn. He made the sofa into a bed, and undressed. "You are one desirable man," she said, as she took him into her waiting arms.

The next morning he drove her to the train station. Who was the rat bastard now? He wanted to give her a few bucks but didn't want her to think he was paying for sex. "Do you need any cash for the trip?" he asked.

"No thanks. I've got enough. When I get to Fargo, I'll clerk at my uncle's shoe repair shop. I'll be fine. It'll be nice to be back home."

He kissed her cheek. She gave him a squeeze, picked up her beat-up suitcase, and climbed aboard the bus. It was probably for the best. She'd be happier up there in North Dakota. Wendy was an angel that didn't belong in the City of Angels.

SEVEN
1956

Over the phone, detective Hartman insisted Marilyn come into his office that very afternoon. He sounded uncharacteristically anxious at the start of their conversation and grew audibly more so as time went on. If she expected him to get anywhere, she had better trust him, because he'd been out and about, investigating, and believed the blackmailer to be a blonde woman by the name of June Tilda Gordon.

So, Junesy must be responsible for the notes! It could not be a coincidence that the blackmailer was a blonde who just happened to be named June and who also shared the peculiar middle name Tilda.

Marilyn left her daughter with Armida before hightailing it across town. As the pain in her stomach grew worse it became obvious she must have ulcers, just like Papa. If only she could just bleed to death like he had, right then and there—what a convenient way to dodge her predicament.

1940

June woke up on the train several hours after they tore out of Hollywood in a mad dash for San Francisco. She gingerly touched her injured left eye. "Beryl, you're the best friend in the whole entire world," she declared through bruised lips. "Thanks for saving my life."

What was a girl to do—turn her back on her best friend? Beryl couldn't bring herself to do it.

Even boy-crazy June wasn't interested in any of the servicemen's advances while they took lunch in the dining car. She behaved demurely and discouraged interested males with severe glances. Maybe the incident with Kay Rennick had taught Junesy a thing or two about discretion.

They disembarked into a throng of humanity at the station, jostled into line, and waited for a taxi, which June directed to the apartment of a woman she had met during one of her many escapades.

The woman's name was Lydia Lark, and she invited the girls to stay with her. She had an extra bedroom and said she was lonely, anyway. Lydia's manner of speaking, upswept platinum hair, and full hourglass shape brought Mae West to mind.

"Kid, I'm sure glad you listened to me about coming up to see us. You won't be sorry," Lydia told June, followed with a quick wink and a smile. "The San Francisco Exposition reopens on Treasure Island in three weeks, and runs for four months. You two will earn yourselves a pile of dough working in the Gayway. That FDR sure does know how to throw a party. The New Deal built the Magic City, you know."

"I hear it's out of this world," June said.

"I'll say. Just you wait," Lydia assured her.

Beryl removed her hat and tried to fluff her matted hair. "Oh, I see—it's a fair," she said. She remembered all the stories about The World's Fair in Chicago in 1933. Her grandparents had attended several times, and they'd discussed the centennial celebration of Grandmother Anne's hometown with much enthusiasm. They heard Judy Garland sing. They saw a zeppelin fly.

"Not any old fair! It's bigger than life and too marvelous for words! They're vamping the island up right now. It's gonna be even better than it was last year, if that's feasible." Lydia motioned for them to sit then strolled across the room to a teacart, which served as a portable bar, and generously filled three crystal glasses with straight scotch.

Beryl wasn't much for hard liquor, but was so relieved to be safe and off the train that she gulped the burning liquid straight down, which caused June to follow suit and cringe afterwards.

"You've got quite a figure," Lydia told Beryl, appraising her openly. "That'll pay off."

"What am I anyways—chopped liver?" Junesy wondered.

"You, little woman," Lydia said. "Have I got plans for you!"

⊹ ⊹ ⊹

Beryl woke up that morning with a sour stomach. The whiskey had burned her sensitive gut. She munched on a piece of dry toast and hoped the bread might soak up the smoldering substance that had caused such discomfort.

Earlier, while June was still asleep, Beryl had unfastened the lining of her suitcase and hid the majority of the money inside. She had tucked and sewed it all neatly in place with a needle and thread, and kept only a few bills to cover the cost of living. June probably wouldn't steal from her, but then she wasn't all that predictable, either. And Beryl didn't know Lydia from Adam. It was a good thing they would soon be working. At the rate they were spending, it wouldn't take long to drain their stash of money that had been earned in the most abominable manner imaginable. Beryl knew she shouldn't dwell on how she'd come into possession of the cash to begin with, but couldn't help it. Her own grandfather!

She fantasized about returning to Hollywood and working alongside professional seamstresses for notable costume designers. She ought to give up on Hollywood altogether, since that pipe dream now seemed highly improbable. June had put the brakes on all Beryl's splendid plans with her unbridled recklessness.

Lydia did her best to cover up the bruises on June's face with gobs of make-up. "Look Hon, I'm gonna give you girls the grand tour. We'll paint this town red!"

San Francisco was a marvel. The busy streets were very steep and the hills impossibly vertical. Lydia explained the precipitous conditions were precisely why the cable cars were originally invented. Imagine horses and carriages able to scale such inclines!

The cable cars moved at a good clip, up to ten miles per hour. At every stop, men, women, and even children hustled to scramble off and on, in a frenzy of activity. The process rather frightened Beryl. Lydia shared an account of a man losing his foot, which only added to Beryl's anxiety about hopping off whenever they approached an upcoming stop.

That first day, they visited Fisherman's Wharf and dined on stacks of cracked crab and cups of clam chowder piled high with oyster crackers, while they sat near a window with a bird's eye view of Alcatraz. The warm soup went down nicely and eased Beryl's stomach.

"You know, Al Capone was on The Rock, until they moved him down south," Lydia said, then she licked some butter sauce off her fingers. "He hated the warden."

"You sure know a lot about the city," Beryl told her.

"I ought to," Lydia replied. "Been living in the North Beach Quarter since I was fourteen. My folks came all the way out here from Brooklyn. I'm crazy about California. Los Angeles and San Francisco beat out New York City hands down, no contest."

June wanted to know more about the Golden Gate Exposition, but Beryl couldn't focus on their discussion. Alcatraz intrigued her. Capone had been incarcerated on that island—imagine that. She knew a little something about Al Capone. She'd grown up on stories about the St. Valentine's Day Massacre. Capone and Bugs Moran had operated out of Chicago. The Purple Gang had operated out of Detroit. They'd preyed on rumrunners and hijacked loads of liquor. Some fought to the death along the waterfront of the Detroit River and Lake Eerie over bootleg shipments.

The foreboding prison loomed across the water. Beryl tried to imagine life encased within those dank walls, isolated, and behind bars. How often did the prisoners venture outside? When they did go out, what did they think of when they saw the vibrant city across the water? Did those criminals regret what they had done? Did they regret the decisions that landed them in such bleak surroundings? Would they change their evil ways, if and when they got out?

"Hey!" Lydia cried. "You still with us, kiddo?"

Beryl smiled and stopped picturing life on Alcatraz. "Sure," she said.

"Let's go home and take a nap," Lydia suggested. "Tonight we're going up to the Top of the Mark, on Nob Hill. We'll need our beauty sleep."

✛ ✛ ✛

"Try this on for size," Lydia said. The lobby of the Mark Hopkins Hotel was full of servicemen having their picture snapped while standing proudly beside their sweethearts.

"Looky there, how do you like that?" June said, nodding in the direction of one good-looking sailor who had his arm draped over the shoulder of a redhead with handlebar hips. "I want one of my own! I'm a goner for those sailor outfits."

"You love what that feller's packing inside that outfit," Lydia said, leading the way to the elevator.

Beryl blushed. She should've gotten used to dirty jokes after spending time at the Garden of Allah, but she hadn't.

Once seated at a window-side table, Lydia ordered a bottle of champagne, and the girls enjoyed an unfettered view of the city at night.

"Isn't it marvelous?" June asked, as she elbowed Beryl. "Aren't you glad you left Hollywood now?"

As if she'd had a choice. Beryl nodded. "It's a wonderful city, that's for sure," she said.

"The Paris of the West," Lydia declared.

Beryl had heard her own Papa call Detroit the *Paris of the Midwest.*

A confident, but very short-statured gentleman strolled over. "Why hello, Sweet Lydia," he said. "I see you're keeping excellent company tonight."

"Don't you know it?" Lydia replied. "Girls, meet Mr. Billy Rose. He's bringing his fantastic Aquacade here from New York." She turned back to Billy. "I've heard through the grapevine that the act promises to be better than ever," she told him, in a confidential manner.

"I think so. Hey, we're interviewing," he said. "What about you two lovely bookends? *Do you swim?*"

Junesy cocked her head, batted her eyelashes Mr. Rose's way, and held out her dimpled hand. Although the bruising was fairly well hidden, Beryl noticed that the make-up could not mask the swelling surrounding her eye.

"My name's June Masterson, and I sure do wish I could swim," June gushed, unabashedly.

"And you?" he asked, addressing Beryl.

Beryl was too nervous and shy to offer her hand, so she simply shook her head. "I can keep myself afloat, but that's the extent of my swimming abilities," she admitted.

Billy Rose's gaze remained focused on Beryl, even as he asked Lydia another question. "Promise me you won't let these two go to waste, will you, Sweet Lydia?"

"You can bet I won't," she assured him.

"Wonderful," he said, and then he finally turned his eyes away from Beryl and looked at Lydia. "I'll see you in the Gayway." He sauntered across the room to another table.

"He's called Bantam Barnum, for obvious reasons," Lydia told Beryl and June. "But don't forget, Billy's a good person to know—a real connection. He used to be married to Fanny Brice, *the* Fanny Brice. And he's the reason Sally Rand is famous. Don't you two ever forget it."

"I sure won't," June said.

"Diminutive in height but long in reach, if you get my drift." Lydia picked up her glass and downed her champagne. "Hey girl," she said, addressing Beryl, "you need to warm up a bit and learn a thing or two about turning on the charm." Lydia's harsh tone was not lost on Beryl.

After they finished the champagne, they made their way to Chinatown. It was so festive, Beryl could barely take it all in. Brightly lit neon signs promoting everything from art goods to jewelry affronted her senses. But mostly, it seemed, the signs shone in fantastic colors and existed primarily to draw attention to something called *chop suey*. Letters and symbols blinked on and off, directing people to window displays of upside down ducks, silky garments, and tea-sets covered in dragons, abundant bazaars, and rows of shops filled with exotic merchandise from the far away Orient. Beryl's head buzzed with excitement. She longed to purchase treasures, but dared not spend a penny, except to pick up the dinner tab. Lydia had been awfully kind and had given them a place to stay, so Beryl insisted on picking up the check.

Lydia ordered without consulting a menu. While Beryl drank hot tea, Lydia and June gulped beer from small glasses, one glass after the other after the other.

"You know, chop suey was invented in America," Lydia informed them, as they helped themselves to heaping servings from various steaming plates of exotic delicacies. "Order it in China, and they won't even know what it is."

Beryl didn't care what it was called—the food was scrumptious.

Two adorable children wearing funny little bowl-shaped hats peered through a curtain from a back room. They merely stared in silence while the women ate, laughed, and gossiped. Beryl decided to give a slight wave, which caused the poor things to grow bashful and duck for cover. Intrigued by the Chinese people and the sights and sounds of their ways, she vowed to return to Chinatown alone to explore and absorb the foreign impressions on her own, without distraction.

They were to be ready by ten the following morning. "My pal, Woody Malkin, is coming to take us sightseeing. He's special to me, so be nice—*real* nice," Lydia announced, before tapping Beryl on the forearm to indicate that she was referring to her.

Woody Malkin showed on time, as promised. He was a tall, youngish man with a glowing face, a prominent nose, and slightly showy ears. There he stood in all his proud glory, sizing up the world from two of the most expressive, long-lashed, deep-brown eyes Beryl had ever seen. She tried her best not to stare. Lydia was head over heels for the guy, that much was clear.

Woody drove a ruby-colored four-door Hudson touring sedan. As a result of being raised in the motor city and immersed in the world of the automobile from an early age, Beryl loved cars. She resisted the urge to run her hand over the shimmering finish, but once in the backseat, sank into the upholstery and sighed with longing. She would learn how to drive, one day. She thought of Chet, but immediately did her best to put him out of her mind.

"Not too shabby," June said.

"All's I know is," Woody said, "if I was getting the grand tour of this town, I'd be out of sorts if anybody left out Golden Gate Park, so that's where I'm taking you girls."

"Fine, then drive!" Lydia commanded.

And drive he did. They spotted herds of buffalo, bridle paths with horsemen and women dressed to the nines in full-on equestrian gear, sheep grazing in pastures and golfers chipping away at little white balls. When they stopped briefly to admire a waterfall, Lydia instructed Woody to drive right on by the botanical gardens, since she had allergies.

Lydia waited in the car while everyone else got out to get a closer look at Seal Rocks. "Those seals reek," she said, as she sipped deftly from a flask. "Listen, you kids get a quick gander at those squawking creatures, and then let's go find lunch. I'm starving."

As the three of them admired the bright blue day, they were startled by a scream from just down the path. A quick glance told them a gull had unleashed a lashing of dense droppings on the head of an unsuspecting woman. She launched into a scandalous tirade fit to shame a seasoned longshoreman.

June joined suit. "Oh shit, is Lydia the smart one, or what?"

They took off for the car, and the three of them were cutting up fitfully. It took them a few moments to compose themselves and explain to Lydia what they'd witnessed.

"See?" Lydia told them. "There you have it—Mother Nature. That broad's brutal!"

Lunch at The Cliff House was lovely.

"This joint has burned down and been rebuilt so many times it makes my head spin," Lydia said.

"You should see the Victorian version," Woody told her. "There's a picture hanging around here somewhere. It's really something."

"Forget all that," Lydia said. "I need a drink."

They had a nice view of the water and enjoyed a leisurely lunch. Woody was from New Jersey, and he ran several concessions on the Gayway. By the sound of things, one of his concessions had something to do with modeling. Woody was humble and sat quietly while Lydia bragged him up. "This guy can charm bees," she said, winding down after a spell of singing his praises that had visibly energized her.

Woody blushed. He did have excellent coloring. Beryl pretended to be interested in a brochure she picked up about the Sutro Baths, which were adjacent to The Cliff House. She could see Lydia was desperately in love.

"Sutro's is a barrel of fun," Woody told Beryl.

"What is it, exactly?" June asked, leaning over Beryl's shoulder to get a gander at the brochure.

"It's a swimming complex," Beryl said, turning the picture so Junesy could get a better view.

"It's a good place to catch polio," Lydia snapped.

What a killjoy Lydia could be. Beryl thought she understood why. With her tight girdle, Lydia wouldn't want to go swimming with her beau. She wouldn't want to climb on rocks to see the seals, or do anything that required much physical exertion. How she could bear to be so bound up all day long? Beryl couldn't imagine.

They left The Cliff House and headed to Lydia's place. Shortly after they arrived, Lydia went to her room to slip into something comfortable, and June ran across the street to buy ice. Woody sat down at the piano and began to noodle around. Beryl went into the kitchen to feed the neglected cat, Sylvie. Outside the window she witnessed a wondrous site. After sundown the city transformed. Detroit, and even Hollywood, always seemed to crawl to a halt and practically shut down, *save for a few nightspots*, as the day darkened. But San Francisco jumped to life. Beryl sensed a lively energy building in the air, and she enjoyed the surge.

June rushed in and dumped the ice, said something about changing out of her street clothes, and disappeared. Lydia emerged; she now looked far more comfortable, if not a tad more ample. Woody asked her if she'd like him to play anything special.

"I don't know," she said. "Maybe I do, and maybe I don't." Then she poured a few drinks and passed them around. Before long, Beryl had curled up in her favorite chair with the cat. Junesy emerged in short pants, looking as fresh as a peach. She sat on the floor beside her friend and scratched the kitty's neck.

"I'll choose the tune," Woody announced. "And you'll sing for us, Sweet Lydia."

"Is that right?" Lydia asked. But Beryl could tell the lady was more than willing to do whatever pleased Woody.

He launched into a bluesy tune. Beryl hoped against hope that Lydia wouldn't ruin the lovely music Woody was making on that piano—that her voice wasn't shrill.

Lydia took a sip of her drink, set it down, and walked closer to Woody. She leaned against the piano and began to sing. "You said it was me, but it wasn't me, it was my shoulder you were lookin' for. You said it was me, but it wasn't me, it was my sympathy you were lookin' for…"

And oh, but the woman's voice was smooth as silk, a hint of raspiness highlighting the sorrowful lyrics. The two of them took it slow. That's how Beryl thought the song should be sung, nice and slow.

Lydia's voice rang out like a bell and filled the room with tender melody that sent shivers down Beryl's spine. How dare she imagine Woody a fool? No wonder he was sweet for the singer, and no wonder everyone called her Sweet Lydia. Good lord up in heaven, what a voice!

June reached for Beryl's hand and gave it a quick squeeze as if to say: *See how wonderful she is?* Beryl gazed down at her friend and smiled.

The next morning Beryl hopped out of bed, slipped on a sundress and cropped sweater, rinsed out the soiled glasses and ashtrays, and then hurried down to the corner market to pick up eggs and bacon. She practically ran back up to the apartment to fix breakfast. By the time the coffee had begun to percolate, Woody wandered out of Lydia's bedroom and into the kitchen. He yawned and made noise about eating the asshole out of a bear, he was that hungry.

Beryl knew certain so-called respectable citizens would frown upon her and June sleeping under the same roof as an unmarried man and woman. She thought about the church's view on such relations and remembered how she'd found her mother and Walt fornicating. It seemed to her that Woody and Lydia weren't hurting a soul. Who cared if they wanted to lie down together? She certainly wasn't about to judge them. Beryl didn't hold her mother's human-ness against her anymore. In fact, Beryl thought she might set about losing her own virginity soon.

Woody sat down at the tiny table in the kitchen, dwarfing it even further, and lit up a cigarette. "Want one, kiddo?" he asked.

For some unknown reason, Beryl said yes. Although she pre-tended to know what she was doing, mostly the cigarette burnt away in the ashtray while she fried up the bacon and beat the eggs to scramble. She felt Woody's eyes on her and tried to appear con-fident in the kitchen.

Beryl could remember Mémère's voice telling her the recipe for fluffy scrambled eggs: *You must melt the butter but you mustn't brown it, and you shouldn't over-stir or over-cook, or you'll make the eggs tough.*

Woody considerately volunteered to make the toast while she set off to rouse the girls out of bed.

After breakfast, Woody and Lydia withdrew to Lydia's bedroom. Their voices were slightly audible, but Beryl couldn't make out what they were saying.

"Woody's married, you know," June whispered in her ear, while they did up the dishes.

"*He is?*" Beryl's heart skipped a beat; she didn't want to think less of either one of them.

"He lives in a house in Oakland with his wife. I hear she's a gimp, and they have a little son."

"How horrible," Beryl said.

"Lydia's heartsick most of the time. She's only happy when he can get away. It's all very tragic."

Beryl didn't think Woody should two-time on his wife just because she was a cripple. She wondered what had happened to the poor thing to make her that way, but didn't dare ask. The flippant manner her friend used to talk about Woody's wife bothered her. It wasn't kind to refer to the woman as a gimp.

"Married men make the best lovers," June added, breathlessly.

"Who says so?" Beryl asked. June could be so annoying—so crass and forward. And the way she always forced Beryl to dry the dishes, because damp dishtowels *felt icky*, also grated on Beryl's nerves.

"Everybody knows that, silly."

"Oh brother," Beryl huffed. "You don't know half of what you think you do."

"So happens, I've been with married men before."

Shaking her head, Beryl disbelieved her friend's confession. She set the dishes in the small cabinet near the window. Lydia's dishes were mismatched, but delicate and covered in red flowers—roses mostly. Beryl couldn't wait until she had a place full of nice things to call her own.

Junesy began to do the jitterbug, right there on the linoleum. Her yellow curls bounced as she shouted, "I'm bursting with energy, that coffee's got me revved up!"

"No kidding," Beryl said. "Why don't you make yourself useful and go pick up your clothes off the floor then?"

"Wet blanket," June said. She tried to grab hold of Beryl, but Beryl resisted. "Come on you glum girl—dance!" June insisted. "Be happy!"

Beryl would be happy when she felt like being happy, not because Junesy told her to.

✚ ✚ ✚

The ferry ride to Treasure Island cost ten cents. "I'll be glad when I start working and you don't have to shell out your dough on my account all the time," June told Beryl. "It gets old."

Beryl didn't hand cash over to June willy-nilly anymore, and not because she was a tightwad. On the first leg of their journey she'd given June a stack of her own spending money, and June had seen fit to purchase whatever caught her eye: hats, magazines, gum, gloves, candy bars—you name it, she had to have it. Junesy was very proud, Beryl soon discovered. When her friend was forced to ask for money, her spending stayed under control.

They were on their way to meet Lydia. For business reasons, Lydia had gone over to the island earlier in the day. Junesy's face had finally healed up nicely, and they were both gussied up in their finest outfits, anxious to meet anybody and everybody capable of gainfully employing them. Lydia was a personnel administrator, recruiting girls for various positions. With such a lovely singing voice, Beryl wondered why Lydia wasn't making her living as a songstress.

Lucky for them, June had befriended Lydia. June always made friends easily. People gravitated towards her carefree and sunny personality. The girl didn't have a shy bone in her body. She grinned and spoke freely with any old stranger she happened to meet. Beryl couldn't smile for no good reason, and she just didn't excel at small talk.

As the ferry approached Treasure Island, all Beryl could think about was how much Ma and Mémère would have loved San Francisco. And the looming Golden Gate Exposition, which was sometimes known as the Magic City, did not disappoint. Beryl wished she could dial home and tell them all about it. Maybe when she got a job, she would call. Ma would be icy at first, without a doubt. But Beryl would explain. She would explain running away had been June's idea and she had naively gone along. Ma would forgive her—wouldn't she?

They were greeted by a sign reading: *Purchase Your Tickets Here.* Lydia got them past the guard with no problem, as the ticket booths weren't open yet. She took each of the girls by the arm. "We don't have time to get a good look around right now," she said. "We'll save all that 'til tomorrow. I've got a ton of work ahead of me, and you two have interviews."

As they walked along, Lydia pointed to an enormous statue. "There's Pacifica, ain't she something?" she said. Lydia then turned and gestured towards a beautiful white glowing tower. "And that," she told them, "is the Tower of the Sun."

Beryl remembered Lydia had pointed out the spire from atop a steep hill near her apartment the day before. The flat topography of the island stood in stark contrast to the hilliness of the city across the bay.

"Let's sit for a spell," Lydia suggested. "I need to ask you girls a few questions." They lined up on a nearby bench, and Lydia continued speaking. "How modest are you?"

June giggled.

"I'm serious. Do you think you could take your clothes off if you were compensated royally for doing it?"

Beryl's mouth fell open.

"I could!" June said, anxiously. "I'm sure I could."

"I'm not saying you have to go nude. There are plenty of jobs here, if you're not interested. But, if you girls want the big bucks, you'll have to disrobe."

Beryl sat there like a bump on a log—speechless. Lydia smiled and patted her on the hand. "For you, I'm thinking modeling. All you have to do is stand there and look like a living statue. You don't have to talk—you merely pose while customers snap photos. No big deal. No performing. All you'd have to do is be your beautiful self."

Lydia turned and nodded in June's direction. "Sweetie, I'm thinking you'd be perfect for Sally Rand's Nude Ranch. You'll romp around with groups of other girls, wearing cowboy hats, bandanas, boots, a G-string, and nothing else, participating in outdoor sports, pitching horseshoes, that kind of thing. It's a fun, campy environment. I think you'd fit right in."

"*The* Sally Rand?"

"Yes, *the* Sally Rand!"

"Count me in," June said. "But I have to tell you, I have no experience. I've never done anything like this before."

Lydia brushed back a lock of hair that had fallen loose from her hairpin. "They'll train you, kid."

June gave Beryl a slight shove. "What do you think?"

"I, I, well…" Beryl stammered. She didn't know who Sally Rand was, and she didn't think she could take her clothes off and pose in front of ogling men.

"I'll bring you over there and have Woody show you around," Lydia offered. "You can get a feel for what's it's all about. If you don't want to pose—if you're not comfortable—I can set you up somewhere else. There's plenty of jobs to be had. It would be a waste if you said no, though. They need stunning beauties like you to draw the men in."

Beryl's eyes grew wide. "*Woody?*"

"Yes, *Woody*," Lydia said. "It's one of many concessions he operates. And he told me personally—he thinks you'd be perfect."

The thought of parading around naked in front of Woody made Beryl blush.

When she'd heard he had something to do with models the first day she had met him, nude modeling in a carnival atmosphere wasn't what had popped into her head. What kind of place was this Gayway?

As soon as they took a seat on the ferry and headed back to the city, June began to chatter nonstop. "Sally Rand doesn't perform with us. She's the big name, she draws in the crowds. Well, her name, that is, and us being naked and all. You know, one girl told me, when there's over forty of us parading around in our birthday suits at any given time, it's not so bad really. She said you get used to it. Her name's Cora, and she worked here last year. Said she earned more money than anyone in her family ever had. We walked over to the Maxwell House doughnut house and she warned me, 'Coffee only, no fattening food, nobody's interested in watching jiggly women shoot basketball.'" June chuckled.

A man two seats over outwardly stared at June. She simply chattered on without a care in the world as to whether anyone might be listening in. Beryl shot him a dirty look and he turned away. "For crying out loud," she told June, under her breath, "can't we talk about this at Lydia's place?"

Junesy's animated face fell. "Spoilsport," she snapped. Her feelings were hurt. Beryl would have to make it up to her.

"Let's stop at that little Italian place and pick up dinner to go," Beryl suggested. They were limping along the sidewalk, as both of them had sore feet from walking all day in open-toed heels.

"I guess we'll have to order salad," June said, in a gloomy tone.

"I'm ordering spaghetti," Beryl said. "All this walking, I'm starving, and we can afford a proper dinner. We'll soon be working girls."

Junesy beamed. "That's right. A girl can be too skinny—can't she? Nobody wants to watch a bag of bones shoot basketball!"

They broke out in laughter.

Beryl confided in June over heaping plates of food, in Lydia's cozy kitchen. "The Model Studio is pretty tame, as far as that goes," she said. "From what I understand, most exhibits on the Gayway are more than a little tacky and naughty. One's called Virgins in Cellophane. Imagine? And then there's Adam and Eve in the Garden of Eden."

"You don't say," June said. "That's a hoot."

"Anyhow, all I'd be doing is standing nude in front of silken draperies—sometimes alone, sometimes with one of the other girls—posing like I was a Roman goddess. Woody said I should think of it as doing my part to inspire a famous artist, like I should pretend to be Mona Lisa."

"He did, *did he*?" June said. "That's probably a good way for you to look at it. I think you'll be inspiring a moment with Madame Palm and her five sisters. But who cares? What's the difference? That's what I say. Men like to look at women, the nakeder, the better."

"Oh, June, that's not even a real word."

"If they had a big old sign that read 'The Nakeder, the Better,' they'd be wheeling barrels of money down the Gayway."

"Sweetie, they already are."

"Yoo-hoo!" June let out. Then she settled down. "Did Woody convince you to take the job," she asked, "or will you be flinging hash or dressing prim and proper and old-timey over at Cavalcade of a Nation?"

"I told him I would think on it."

"Don't be all hard to get," June warned. "He might hire somebody else and you'll miss out on all the greenies."

Madame Palm and her five sisters? Greenies? Beryl learned as she went along, and she now knew Sally Rand was a famous burlesque queen. As usual, June always seemed to be a hop, skip, and a jump ahead of her.

✛ ✛ ✛

Lydia came home looking like something the cat dragged in. The girls were already in their pajamas.

"Lucky girl," June told Lydia. "We kept a plate of spaghetti and a side of garlic bread warming in the oven."

"Yeah?" Lydia said. "I'll take a glass of Scotch whiskey. The jury's out on whether or not I got the strength to eat." She kicked off her shoes, her swollen flesh imprinted with strap indents.

It was almost eleven o'clock.

"You want me to fill the roasting pan with hot water so you can soak those dogs?" June asked, pointing to Lydia's swollen feet.

"Sweet offer, kid. But let me get outta this monkey suit and I'll be right back." She disappeared into her room.

Beryl had been reading the evening paper, and now she folded it and placed it on the side table. How strange, San Francisco was preparing to reopen an exposition that only a year earlier was meant to be a celebration of the *unity* of the Pacific Rim. But in light of the ongoing conflict between Japan and China (and absolute brutal behavior on Japan's part), the ongoing festivities were a bit of a sham to her way of thinking. All the mingling of architectural styles and cultural themes, the millions of dollars spent, the apparent rejection of reality — what a farce! If the world was a melting pot, that pot was boiling over on the stove. Beryl knew America would eventually get burnt. Humankind had gone stark raving mad and there was no avoiding involvement. It seemed as if Roosevelt was only putting off the inevitable.

"Why do you read those nasty rags when you can't do a thing to change any of it?" June asked. "Look at you, all down in the dumps now."

"You know, I feel it's my duty to keep up with current events," Beryl admitted, feeling sapped.

Lydia emerged from her room in a colorful kimono, of all things. The irony wasn't lost on Beryl.

"I am ready for that drink," Lydia said. "We're so far behind, I can't believe it. Why didn't they call me in earlier? I'm expected to do months' worth of work in a few short weeks."

"Gosh, Lydia," June said. "Wish I could help."

"I'll tell you what," she said. "Bring out that *I-talian* food. I'm getting as fat as a pig, but I'm not the one who has to parade around without my clothes on."

✠ ✠ ✠

Treasure Island at night was a spectacle, showcasing acres of educational exhibits, pavilions, reflecting pools, massive flower gardens, murals and fine art displays, freaks and flesh, high-wire artists, food stands, and more. The likes of Benny Goodman and even crooner Bing Crosby performed in person — for free. It was virtually impossible to take it all in.

Beryl would sit and let cotton candy melt on her tongue as she watched people rush by. Men in overcoats, women with scarves tied under their chins, children near hysterics, their eyes wild with excitement, teens dashing here and there, and old people desperate for a place to rest their tired bones, all seemed unable to sort out the kinetic activity. The need for diversion was palatable (servicemen teemed, the stark reality of the ominous threat of war on parade), and every single soul seemed to be frantic to have a good time, as they tried to escape the inevitable *what-will-be-will-be*.

People were out to seek a means of escape, a temporary diversion at best. Beryl was sure of it.

✚ ✚ ✚

Whenever men visited the modeling studio—and most visitors were male—they would only have a small allotment of time in which to snap a few hasty photographs, as they were paraded through, all very rush-rush. A few returned several times in a day. Beryl's eyes would gloss over; she would pretend to be a statue just as she had done as a child while being molested. The first few days were uncomfortable. But once she adjusted to the routine, she would simply clock-in and clock-out.

June enjoyed frolicking at the nude ranch with other like-minded girls. Lydia knew her stuff and had matched up her new roommates' personalities to their work.

Others Beryl modeled with tended to be discreet and shared her temperament. Although they weren't ecstatic to be doing what they were doing, they were resigned. It was all about the money. The cash they brought home provided incentive and a rationale.

Beryl and the others were encouraged to change their appearance whenever they went out and about. It would not be advantageous to be recognized as one of the *girlies* by an obsessed fan. Beryl always swept her hair into a ponytail and slipped on a beret whenever venturing out. She wore dark clothes and big sunglasses to hide her eyes.

"You look as if you're perpetually in mourning," June told Beryl. Junesy didn't make any attempt to hide her identity. Sometimes she didn't even remove her bandana. But, Beryl maintained, what June did was another story. Sure June was undressed all day, but she didn't perform in an intimate setting like Beryl did.

"I don't care to be recognized," Beryl told Junesy. The men who took photographs were an entirely different breed than the fellas (and curious ladies) who viewed the girls through glass windows at the nude ranch. The men that came into the modeling studio were extremely intense and focused, visually inclined, and more perfidious. They slunk in the shadows in their well-pressed gabardine slacks, and skulked under creased fedoras. Their determined cameras threatened to steal her very soul. They took Beryl's image and they took that image home.

June shook her head, and added, "Aw, you're too mistrustful."

"Maybe," Beryl said. But she wasn't taking any chances.

✧ ✧ ✧

Woody had a night off so he took them to Chinatown for chop suey and fried rice. As Beryl laughed hysterically at one of Lydia's amusing stories, an unassuming bald man crept up to her side. "I know who you are," he said, softly. "You're one of those nude models from the Gayway."

Woody sprang from his chair. "Move along pal," he warned.

The man didn't budge. He focused on Beryl. "You're the most beautiful model by far," he insisted. "I come to see you and only you."

"You heard me," Woody said sternly, as he took one step closer.

The man ignored Woody and didn't take his eyes off Beryl. "I'm doing a study," he told her.

Woody shoved him, and the stranger seemed genuinely shocked. "Hey, it's a free country, mister."

"I'm gonna take you outside and kick the living shit outta you if you don't beat it," Woody growled.

Lydia stood up and addressed the man civilly. "Come on, now, we're not looking for trouble. Do yourself a favor and listen up, won't you?"

The bald man smoothed the sleeves of his coat. "Goodbye, beauty," he told Beryl. "I'll see you soon."

The stranger left the restaurant and Woody turned to Beryl. "What a creep," he said. "That does it, we're gonna move you."

Lydia placed her hand lightly on Woody's tense arm. "Where to?"

"I'll think of something," he told Lydia. He turned back to Beryl. "Don't worry," he said, "I know how to handle guys like him. I'm gonna deep-six that schmuck. I'm gonna put a bulletin out on him. He won't get into our fair again, not if I have anything to say about it."

✢ ✢ ✢

One afternoon, June whispered, "Lydia's locked in her room. She's down in the dumps. Woody's wife landed in the hospital again. She can't even walk anymore. Her mother moved in with them because she's too sick to look after their little son. No wonder Woody's been so jumpy lately. It's all so sad."

"Is it polio?" Beryl asked.

June sighed. "Guess not—some mystery disease."

"I have an aunt who's very ill."

"I remember."

Beryl hadn't thought of Francis in a while. "If I was out here on the up-and-up, I could've visited her in that sanitarium in San Diego."

June ignored the up-and-up remark. "I never get sick," she bragged.

"But surely you've had the measles?"

"Nope."

"The mumps?"

"Nope."

"Influenza? Pneumonia?"

"Nope and nope. Healthy as a horse."

"How lucky for you!" Beryl feared illness.

"The women in our family tend to be hale and hearty. We don't die until we grow really old, and then we simply seize up and keel over. With the possible exception of my crazy mother, and she killed herself, so I won't count her." Junesy could be so flippant about her mother's suicide. She suddenly switched subjects, as June often did. She dropped her voice back to a whisper. "Woody's never gonna leave his wife, not with her in such bad shape, and Lydia knows it. I'm telling you, she's had a rough go of it."

"I need bath salts," Beryl said. "Let's go to the drugstore."

The girls set out. It was sunny but chilly and Beryl thought of a quote attributed to Mark Twain, something about how he spent the coldest winter he'd ever known during summertime in San Francisco.

"I'm fresh out of red nail polish," June said, as she examined her pretty but unpainted nails. "Maybe I'll get some. It's nice having my own dough to spend. This is the first time in my life I've ever had any of my own."

"Hang on to most of it, don't blow it all," Beryl warned.

"Yeah, I know—you want me to save half of what I earn. But that's hard to do."

"We don't know what's going to happen after the Gayway closes at the end of September. It's better to be prepared."

"You sound like Lydia. She's so blue right now, says she might leave San Francisco in October and head for New York. That's where she was living with her husband."

Beryl stopped walking and took hold of June's arm. "Lydia has a husband?"

"Did have. They're divorced. I forgot, *you don't know*. Don't tell her I told you, but she had a little girl, and that little girl drowned in the bathtub. All Lydia did was leave briefly to answer the phone. Her husband was a bandleader, and he was on the road, and she didn't want to miss his call. She was excited to hear his voice and they talked for a spell. By the time she returned to the bathroom, the child was under water and wouldn't come to. Lydia's little girl drowned in a few inches of bath water at only three years old. The husband never forgave Lydia, and she won't forgive herself, either."

Beryl stopped dead in her tracks again and leaned against a tiled wall. The sidewalk reeked of urine. "That's horrible," she said. "I feel so bad for her."

"She was a popular singer," June told her. "They called her Sweet Lydia, and she sang for her husband in his band. But she gave her career up to stay home with the baby." The urine odor burnt Beryl's nostrils so she took June firmly by the arm once more and yanked her forward. "Lousy things happen, but we have to keep on keeping on. What else can we do?"

Beryl began to formulate a plan as they made their way down the sidewalk. "I'll roast a chicken for dinner," she said. "A nice meal might make Lydia feel better."

"Good idea. She'll snap out of her doldrums," June said. "She always does."

Woody was inspired to create a new attraction as he sat in Lydia's kitchen and watched Beryl make breakfast. That's when he realized men might get a charge out of scantily clad women performing everyday tasks.

He dressed Beryl and the other girls in nothing but frilly aprons and high heels. They decorated cakes, ironed shirts, mopped the floor, and all the while men gawked through the glass. The new exhibit was called, *What's Cooking Good Looking?* and was an instant success. Beryl preferred working on the kitchen set, as opposed to modeling. She lost herself in the tasks she performed and time went by quicker.

Every night Treasure Island glowed like a make-believe fairyland. Illuminated seventy-foot lanterns, translucent glass pillars radiating bright colors, fluorescent tubes of black light, ultraviolet floods, and underwater lamps produced the effect. All this artificial moonlight created a magical city of light. Beryl tried her best to commit the scene to memory as she strolled by the reflecting pools lit with colorful Siamese umbrella lanterns along the spectacular Court of Reflections. She stopped to take in the tranquil beauty. Talk of the war heating up had put her on edge of late. She must remember this peaceful night, and all the splendor and serenity.

Beryl tore herself away. She had to meet June soon. They would grab a quick cup of coffee before hurrying to catch the ferry. It was chilly, and she longed to feel the warm cup in her cold hands more than she wanted the brew itself.

He caught her off guard. It happened so fast. It seemed impossible for anything to happen so fast. He grabbed her and dragged her into the bushes between buildings. One strong hand held her mouth shut, the other held her torso tight. She cried out and tried to wiggle out of his grasp but could not break free. Beryl had heard time and again a girl should always fight back, and fight she did. She kicked him in the shin. She used her elbows as weapons. It was no use. He punched her head without mercy. Instead of blackness, she saw red. Veiled in the color of blood, her will to live waned. He would do her in, she just knew it.

He pulled away when he finished with her, but didn't leave right after the rape. She did not open her eyes. He crouched nearby. Like a dog after a fight, his panting eased, his breathing regulated. This was when he spoke to her. She would never forget the sound of his voice, nor his choice of words. "That ought to show you," the brute finally said. "You had it coming. You asked for it." And then he fled.

When Beryl didn't show at their usual meeting place, June made a stink. A search began. Luckily, a night watchman spotted and followed a trail of blood droplets, which led to the bushes where Beryl lay unconscious and completely hidden from view. She had injured the assailant.

Beryl's jaw had been fractured, and she lost her upper front teeth and molars on her left side. Her battered head was bandaged up like a mummy. Her left arm was broken above and below the elbow, and wrapped in a long bulky cast.

The attack was kept secret. It would be bad for business if word got out about a maniac rapist on the loose in the Magic City.

When Beryl came to, she was under the influence of the morphine they had given her for pain. Woody wanted to know if she thought the attacker had been the bald man from the restaurant. Unable to speak, she could barely scribble on a piece of paper. She wrote in squiggly, almost unreadable script: *Not him, too big, deeper voice.* No, it hadn't been the man from the Chinese restaurant.

Woody paced the room. Junesy sat in a corner and wept for her battered friend. Lydia fussed with the blankets and made small talk.

They kept Beryl in a private room with a twenty-four-hour guard outside the door. As she floated in and out of consciousness, she remembered the day she had visited the Griffith Observatory. She wished she could be with the Adlers. She wished she could be nursed back to health at the Sinai Home for the Incurables.

Beryl's friends brought her home from the hospital to an apartment full of flower arrangements. They did their best to create an air of festivity. But drinking a liquid potion through a straw while they all feasted on June's fried chicken dampened her spirits. Beryl hated the idea of wearing dentures for the rest of her life.

Stuck in bed, horrible thoughts took over. Beryl fought self-doubt, a familiar demon from the past. Malicious echoes of blame affronted her—*you asked for it, you had it coming, you made me do this.* But Beryl battled the familiar damnation. She was practiced at squelching unwelcome reproach by then.

If she didn't take up for herself, who would?

Junesy tried her best to cheer Beryl up by donning silly costumes and singing and dancing like a wild woman. Lydia did not want the cat shedding in the house all day but June snuck Sylvie into the bed whenever possible. Sylvie would lie by Beryl's side and purr. Beryl felt sorry for the poor neglected creature. She didn't understand why Lydia had gotten Sylvie to begin with if she was going to lock her out of the apartment most of the time. Beryl loved animals. She felt they should have a fair shake. If you took on a pet, you took on a considerable responsibility. Ma hadn't been much for animals, and she would never allow Beryl to keep one. Not even a goldfish. Sylvie offered company and solace as Beryl convalesced. As her body recuperated, her wounded spirit cowered and slipped silently into hibernation.

EIGHT
1956

Reg was pissed about being forced to park clear down the street because the parking lot was jam-packed whenever Caravan Moving and Storage held a meeting. What did movers conference about anyway? He couldn't imagine.

"What's the matter?" Doris asked. "You look as if your dog up and died."

"I don't own a dog," Reg said.

"You miss Eve. I just knew you would."

He smirked. "No, I don't!" he snapped. "She saved me the trouble of dumping her." He was in no mood to discuss Eve with the bossy secretary. And he fought the urge to complain about the overcrowded parking lot. After all, his rent was dirt-cheap, and the moving company had a right to hold a powwow whenever they saw fit. "Never mind me. I'm out of sorts with Marilyn Palmer. She called earlier and I had to set her straight. She's on her way over."

Snotty Martha came strutting out of the meeting room. "They want more doughnuts," she cried.

"Okay," Doris told her, as she reached into the desk drawer for petty cash. "Here." She handed the girl a couple of bills. "Run around the corner and buy more."

"You expect me to do it?" Martha said, as if Doris had asked her to skin a coon.

"Yes—you!"

"Well, you're just sitting here, *can't you go?*"

"Go get the damn doughnuts like you were told!" Reg erupted.

The girl snatched the money and flew out the door.

Reg shook his head at Doris. "Why do you put up with that treatment?"

"I know. I *know.* I'm a guppy. But you should see her little kid, he's such a sweetie pie."

"She's useless as tits on a bull. Get rid of her."

"Let me do my job!" Doris bellowed. "I was running things before you turned up. I'll handle this little problem in my own way."

"I'm sure you will, no reason to think otherwise," Reg conceded. "Listen, can you hold off on moving my stuff out of the apartment? I'm not so sure it's a good idea to set up clear out in Montebello, after all. I work late all the time, and the drive's too damn far after a long day."

"Glad to hear you've had second thoughts," Doris said. "I can see why you wouldn't want to leave the area, since most of your cases are in and around L.A. It's about time you came to your senses. I'll go ahead and erase you off the board. I had your move scheduled for next week."

Reg wasn't sure why, but he had a habit of attaching himself to hardheaded women. His mother had been the most domineering woman in the world. Most of his girlfriends had been stubborn, including Eve. And now here he was, all tangled up with Doris in a roundabout way. The secretary would run his life if she could get away with it.

The coffee urn had been moved to the meeting room, so Reg reluctantly headed upstairs empty-handed.

The detective hadn't noticed the size of the rock on Marilyn Palmer's ring finger before. It was a dandy—at least two carats, maybe three.

"Before you lay into me," Marilyn said, "you should know—I can't sleep a wink, I'm smoking like a fiend, and I'm scared out of my mind."

"Get one thing straight," he said. "We're both after the same thing. I'm on your side, but you've got to work with me. Who is June Gordon to you?"

"I met her way back in grade school. Back when her name was June Masterson. And I suppose you should know—we ran away from home together, bound for Hollywood. She made a habit of getting into trouble and involving me in her mischief. We ended up in San Francisco due to some hot water she'd gotten herself into. And, not long before they bombed Pearl Harbor, we were in Honolulu." She looked into Reg's eyes. "Did you serve in the war?"

"The army, but I didn't see the Pacific."

"I'm glad you made it home in one piece."

She looked sincere, and he believed her. "Thanks," he said. "I'm one of the lucky ones."

"Anyway, we lost touch. I returned to the mainland and never saw June Masterson again."

"That hot water you mentioned, I suppose it's the kind of hot water your husband might find scalding?"

"After I returned to Hollywood, I changed my name legally to Marilyn Walsh and started with a clean slate. Gary doesn't even know that much. Everything he thinks he knows about me is a complete fabrication. How would you feel if your wife had deceived you? Lied about who she was? He thinks I'm an orphan from Florida. And I'm not."

"This is good news."

"Good news?"

Reg sure could have used a cup of hot coffee. "I've come to the conclusion we're dealing with a lightweight. I'll expose June Gordon but *good*. You won't have to give her one red dime. Aside from what you pay me, you'll come out smelling like a rose."

"You think?"

"Absolutely positively. Now go back to Pasadena. And keep in touch. I might need to talk to you." Since he couldn't call her at home, she'd been instructed to call the office and his house periodically.

Marilyn Palmer stood up. "I don't know what to say. It almost seems too good to be true. But nothing bad will happen to June, will it? I mean, we were quite good friends at one time."

"Don't get all wishy-washy," he advised. "The woman's out to blackmail you—remember?"

✚ ✚ ✚

Before he dialed June Gordon's number, alias J.T. Wodehouse, Reg grabbed a bottle of beer, opened it, and plopped down in his favorite chair. The blackmailing blonde answered on the first ring.

"Hello there," he said. "We danced together, you remember?"

"Stephen, isn't it?"

"None other. How are you tonight?"

"I'm blue, if you want to know the truth."

"Ah, that's too bad."

"I get this way. So low I could give Billie Holiday a run for her money."

"Do you sing?"

"I'm not singing tonight. I hate it when it's cloudy. I moved down here looking for the sun and where is it? Can you tell me that?"

"We do get dreary weather, now and then."

"My dumb luck."

"I thought we could go out for a drink? But it sounds like you're too low for company."

"Haven't you heard?" June asked. "Misery loves company."

"I'll tell you what, I'll bring food. Do you like pastrami?"

"*You'll come anyway?* That's swell, Stephen."

She supplied Reg with her address—how could she know he already had it?

"Look for me within the hour," he said.

✚ ✚ ✚

"Hey, you!" June Gordon trilled, as she swung the heavy oak door open. All made up and dressed to the nines, she wore a full-skirted crimson cocktail dress. "I'm reborn!" she said. "I'm not letting you go to waste, you wonderful man. We're going out!" In one deft move, she nabbed the bag of sandwiches from Reg's hand and tossed them onto a nearby table.

Once they were in the car, June asked him what he did for a living.

"I sell tires," Reg said. "I hope to own my own store soon." He had no idea where the fib came from.

"A salesman," she said. "I wouldn't have pegged you for a salesman."

"What did you peg me for?" he asked.

She winked. "I'm not sure exactly."

June instructed Reg drive her to a joint in Long Beach named the Pago Pago, yet another tropical-themed bar. She proceeded to order a difficult-to-pronounce rum drink. Reg asked for a beer and a dinner menu.

"Aren't you hungry?" he inquired.

"I rarely eat," she said, cheerfully. "How do you think I keep my girlish figure?"

June's drink disappeared in no time flat. The blonde didn't act drunk, but she was obviously high as a kite. Maybe it was from cocaine, but he guessed it was more than likely diet pills that had her cranked up like a manic wind-up doll. No wonder she'd gone from being despondent over the phone to euphoric by the time he'd arrived.

"Here," he said, "try a rumaki. They're terrific." They weren't. Nothing on the appetizer plate tasted good, but the girl ought to eat.

"Okay, okay," she said. "Jeepers, why are you trying to fatten me up? You're not one of *those* are you?" she asked, before biting into a sample.

Reg had no idea what she meant. He intended to let her get all sauced up and then pump her for information. Chances were she wouldn't even remember a thing come morning.

"See?" he said. "Not bad."

"I need another drink," June cried. "You don't understand, I'm buried! I'm in way over my head!"

Pay dirt. He would bide his time and ply her with enough food to hopefully keep the sugary booze concoctions from making her sick. He hoped her tongue would wag recklessly.

✠ ✠ ✠

Reg dropped June Gordon off at home at one in the morning. She'd knocked 'em back like they were going out of style, but he hadn't learned a goddamned thing. He tried to pump her for more information, to no avail. Drunk as a skunk, the blonde instantly passed out once they were in the car and on the move. He had to carry her into the house. Reg arranged her limp body on the sofa, removed her shoes, and covered her with a blanket.

"You see," she mumbled, as her eyes fluttered, "I got a plan."

"I'm sure you do."

"Going back to Hawaii. Gonna live in paradise—wanna come with?"

"Hawaii?" Reg asked, arranging the pillow behind her head for better support.

"Makin' it happen, wait and see. Comin' into money, goin' back to Honolulu." She let out a grunt followed by a long moan, before conking out.

Reg retrieved the bag with the pastrami sandwiches and went to the kitchen. He opened the fridge on the search for milk, only to find emptiness. There wasn't a speck of food or drink, and the interior was clean as a whistle. Maybe June had been serious—maybe she didn't bother with food. No wonder she'd been so light to carry. He poured a glass of tap water and parked his butt at the dinette, where he wolfed down both sandwiches. They hit the spot.

Before taking off, he adjusted the pillow under June's head again. She was dead to the world.

He phoned the next morning. "How sweet are you?" the sleepy-sounding blonde said. "I must have tied one on, 'cause I don't remember a thing. Did you tuck me in?"

"I did," he told her. "Right after we ate the sandwiches, remember?" He aimed to knock her off her game.

"I ate a sandwich? Jeepers, then why am I so famished? Hey, did we...?"

He cut her off at the pass. "Don't worry, we didn't. You conked out, and gentlemen that I am, I went on home."

"Shucks, what a guy."

Reg promised to call her later on and hung up. He should remember what kind of girl he was dealing with because, like a chump, he found the blackmailing blonde incredibly attractive.

Anxious to get cracking, Reg stormed through the door. "Hey, Toots," he asked Doris, "you heard from Marilyn Palmer today?"

"In fact, she's up in your office waiting."

"She is?"

He suddenly realized that all was right with the world. There stood the coffee urn, returned to its rightful position.

"You go on up," Doris said. "I'll bring you a cuppa. The goddess has been waiting a while."

Reg took the stairs two at a time.

Marilyn Palmer's head was bowed, her pretty nose in a book.

"Hope I haven't kept you waiting too long," Reg said.

She closed her book and set it on the edge of the battered desk. He read the title as he passed by. *From Here to Eternity.*

"Listen," she said. "Gary's behaving strangely. I think he's suspicious. I try to act nonchalant, but I must be sending out a desperate signal. He's jittery."

"Jittery?"

"He's touchy. And I know I haven't been myself."

"Maybe he's picking up on your mood?"

"Could very well be."

"I need to know why would June be obsessed with Hawaii?"

Marilyn's eyes darted over the cover of the novel, and Reg recalled *From Here to Eternity* was set in Pearl Harbor.

"June's obsessed with Hawaii?"

"Don't pussy foot around. 'Fess up."

She sighed. "I told you we were there. I left in '41, before the bombings."

"Whatever happened to June?"

"Can't say. We parted ways before I ever left the island."

"Ironic. I barge in here, asking about Hawaii, and find you reading that particular book?"

The beauty shrugged her slender shoulders and shook her head, as if she couldn't quite believe the coincidence either. "It is a bestseller," she said.

A muffled knock came at the door. "Come in," Reg called.

"'Fraid I can't," Doris cried. "My hands are full!"

Marilyn jumped up before Reg had a chance to open the door.

"Two coffees," Doris announced, as she strode over and set the cups down on the desk. She spotted the copy of *From Here to Eternity.* "Have you seen the movie?" she asked.

"No," Marilyn replied. "I don't get out to the theatre much anymore. But I used to be a real movie buff at one time."

"How's the book? I've been meaning to read it."

"Good, this is my second go round."

"My, my, it must be good if you're reading it all over again! Well, that comes as no surprise. The movie was sensational. That Burt Lancaster, what an actor. And Deborah Kerr—she's tops."

Reg had a mind to clear his throat to send a signal, but it wasn't necessary because Doris did an about-face. "Got to run," she called. "Had to let Martha go, got a million things to do. See ya in the funny papers!"

"Would you consider June dangerous?" Reg asked Marilyn, once they were alone.

"Dangerous?" she repeated, sounding skeptical. "What are you getting at?"

"I need to know what I'm up against."

"No! For Pete's sake, no! She can be underhanded and devious. And she isn't virtuous by any means, but she's not dangerous."

"That's good to know," Reg said, and he meant it.

"Why, what's your plan?"

"I'm gonna frame her."

Her perfectly shaped eyebrows shot up. "*You are?*"

"You better believe it. She'll rue the day she cooked up this hare-brained scheme."

"Like I said, the June I knew wasn't dangerous." She leaned forward, and he caught a whiff of her intoxicating scent from across the desk. "But stay alert," she added. "Who knows what she's capable of. After all, I haven't had anything to do with her in years."

✛ ✛ ✛

Reg called in a dependable gal, one he relied on quite frequently. Her name was Danni Lopez Weaver and he asked her to tail the blonde for the day. He didn't want June Gordon to catch him following her around, and Danni knew how to make herself invisible. Meanwhile, he headed to Montebello to see if Javier knew of anyone who might be interested in renting his parents' house.

Javier was out in the garden, the old bachelor's favorite place on Earth. He had always enjoyed fiddle-farting around. And now that he was retired, fiddle-farting was how he passed the time when he wasn't getting hammered with his pals.

As a child, Reg had hung out in the garden and watched him work. Javier used to snatch fat green worms off his tomato plants and drop them in a dented bucket. Reg had an aversion to earthiness. Mucking around in dirt or battling bugs and worms and blight only made him cringe.

"I know this one guy who might be interested," Javier said, as he leaned his shovel against the makeshift shed he'd built from nothing but accumulated junk.

"I'm looking for a long-term tenant," Reg told the old bachelor, taking care to watch where he stepped, reluctant to soil his leather shoes. "Someone who will take care of the place."

"Sure, Reggie," Javier said. "I know you want someone reliable. It's disappointing that you're not moving in. I wished you would."

"I know, but Montebello's out of the way. The kind of hours I keep, it would mean more driving than ever, and I need my sleep or I'm no good."

Javier pulled off his straw hat, wiped his brow, placed it back on his sweaty head, and nodded. "I'm well aware," he said. "I remember when you were working that case last year, up in...*where was that*, Camarillo?"

"Ojai," Reg replied.

"Man, you put on a lot of mileage."

"Don't I know it. And lately I find myself worn thin somehow. Losing both folks was hard. I expected Ma to go, she was sick for so long. But Ruben I wasn't prepared for. I just can't bring myself to sell their house."

"I know, son. I didn't expect them to go so soon. We all thought my brother was the healthy type. He wasn't fat, and he didn't drink. At least he died in his sleep, that's something to be grateful for. Not like your mother, all that suffering. I think he missed her too much and just couldn't go on without her."

Reg realized he wasn't the only lonely guy. "Ruben was a decent man," he told Javier.

"And he took real good care of you and your mother."

"That he did."

"Better than your real father."

"No contest. We left my old man, a shiftless bastard if there ever was one, and headed west, looking for a better life. Maybe the old man's still in Kansas, or he could be dead for all I know."

"Your mother didn't want you around him anymore, said he was violent."

"I'm a detective, and I won't bother looking for him. Why should I?"

"No reason to," Javier said. "He doesn't deserve a son like you."

"We got away from him and she led a better life."

"She sure loved California."

"Yep."

Before Reg took off, the old bachelor told him not to worry, as he would locate a suitable tenant.

✚ ✚ ✚

Reg considered his mile-high stack of neglected mail. He didn't have a chance to open even one envelope before Danni knocked at the door. He offered her a beer. Although Danni had been raised in an affluent family (her mother was the Mexican starlet Isabelle Lopez, and her father was Ace Weaver, a prominent real estate tycoon with an insatiable passion for the ponies), she grew up at the track and was a little rough around the edges, to say the least. Her life was all about the horses, or *bangtails*, as she often referred to them. Danni was what some in racing circles called a *wise guy*, a knowledgeable handicapper; she specialized in accumulator bets and exotic wagers. Reg benefitted from her inside knowledge every now and then when he forked over a few bills for her to bet on his behalf. But gambling typically went against his grain. Money was too hard to come by to risk losing on a regular basis.

Reg watched Danni empty half a bottle in one long gulp.

"What I saw," she said, as she sat back and read her notes. "Well, Miss Gordon left the house around ten, hopped in her Ford, and proceeded to drive to Pasadena. She stopped in to Hill Avenue Public Library. Inside, she went straight for the W section and removed a book and sat down to read for a spell. I didn't see her remove anything from the book. She seemed too nervous to concentrate. She didn't bother to put the book back, just left it on the table, hurried outside, hopped in her car, and made a beeline to a pay phone down the street. After placing a call, she drove straight to Huntington Memorial Hospital and parked. Not five minutes later, this tall blonde doctor came walking out of Emergency and climbed in her car…"

"Hold on," Reg asked. "How do you know he was a doctor?"

"White jacket, stethoscope around the neck. Oh, he was a doctor, no doubt."

"Damn," Reg said. *"Marilyn's husband*? What's June Gordon doing, playing two ends against the middle?"

"Seems like. I could see the doctor was ticked off. He was waving his hands around and he raised his voice. I couldn't hear what he was saying, though. I didn't want to get too close and blow my cover."

Reg went to the kitchen for two more beers. They sipped quietly while he collected his thoughts.

"What do you know?" he finally said. "That blonde's way more diabolical than I gave her credit for."

"She could be a double-crosser, she could be scamming both the wife and the doctor."

"I didn't see this coming," Reg told her.

⚕ ⚕ ⚕

"Hey, Stephen," the blonde blackmailer said, "hope you like fried chicken and mashed potatoes. I've been working all day long slaving over a hot stove, just to impress you."

Reg mixed two whiskey drinks. "Fried chicken sounds fine." And it did—he was hungry.

"My aunt's recipe," she said, proudly.

June Gordon was pretty; he had to give her that. Not beautiful like Marilyn Palmer, but attractive all the same, with those sparkly, icy blue, half-moon-shaped-eyes, and her sexy moves. If he didn't know what she was up to, he could really go for her. She hadn't come off as devious, and he'd always been a fairly good judge of character—obviously he'd been deluded.

He walked into the living room and took a good look out the arched picture window. The multi-colored sunset over the Pacific was spectacular. Hawaii was out there, way out there. He wondered what had happened back in '41. Marilyn doled out snippets of information, stingy with the facts. Reg knew she was withholding crucial information. He would put the pieces together come hell or high water.

"I didn't make dessert," June said, when she joined him at the window, glass in hand. The sun had receded quickly and was now a slight sliver of orange, almost spent for the day. "I didn't take you for the type that went in for sweets."

"I like pie," Reg replied.

"I see," June said. "What kind of pie?"

"Apple, rhubarb, any pie—except banana. Bananas give me hives."

"Well, I'll keep that in mind."

They ate dinner (the chicken was delicious and the potatoes creamy) and then Reg suggested they go dancing at the Coconut Grove. Since the date was on Marilyn's dime, Reg, masquerading as Stephen, decided to check the place out. He'd always meant to visit the legendary nightclub. And while they were out, Danni would bug June's house.

NINE
1956

Lillian called to invite Marilyn to lunch, something she'd never done before. Marilyn frantically changed outfits three times and finally chose an unbecoming Chanel suit. She regretted the purchase; Mémère's influence had gotten the best of her. The day she rushed home from Saks and tried the suit on for the second time, she saw how the two-piece garment would better suit a flatter-chested woman. She appeared top-heavy, boxy, and shapeless. But since she was off to have lunch with her mother-in-law in one of her stuffy haunts, the Chanel seemed the perfect choice.

When Marilyn pulled out of her driveway and into the cul-de-sac, she spotted a mysterious blue car parked across the street. The very same car had been parked up the way the day before, and she wondered if it meant anything. On her way to meet Lillian at Flynn's Fish-n-Steak, Marilyn thought she spotted the blue car in her rearview mirror, but when she turned around she realized it was a different vehicle altogether. Her mind must be playing tricks; she had jumped to an absurd conclusion. So what if a strange car showed up two days in a row? Her normally reclusive neighbors must have company — that's all.

"I've gone and ordered a gimlet," Lillian exclaimed when Marilyn showed, her manner far more jovial than expected. "I love that suit!"

"Thanks," Marilyn said, as she placed a hand over her belly of fire. She should have asked for glass of milk, but ordered a pink lady instead. She didn't want Lillian feeling like a lush. "I love your suit, too," she added.

Lillian was dressed head to toe in a brilliant green that caused her skin to appear sickly. Her mother-in-law was big on matchy-matchy hats, gloves, pumps, and handbags. Someone influential had once convinced her that the monochromatic approach made a woman appear slimmer.

"I picked it up at Bullock's Wilshire, on sale for thirty-percent off. I do like a bargain." Lillian ran her hand across her lap to smooth her skirt. "They serve a fine steak sandwich here," she added. "But if you're in the mood for something light, I suggest the turtle soup."

"I am rather hungry," Marilyn said, as she lit a much-needed cig-arette. "I'll try the sandwich."

Her mother-in-law smiled broadly. "Lovely. Neither one of us will go hungry, now will we?"

Pleasantries were exchanged, the gimlet was drained hastily, and another disappeared at a startling clip. Lillian didn't usually imbibe so freely. Something must be terribly wrong. Maybe Gary sent his mother to talk to her! Maybe they knew about the blackmail and Detective Hartman! Marilyn's pulse quickened. A feverish dizzi-ness almost overtook her, but she calmed down enough to make her way to the ladies' room to swallow a few aspirin. This wasn't the time to fall apart, not at lunch with Lillian. She refreshed her lipstick and hurried back to the table.

Her mother-in-law devoured her sandwich with gusto and Marilyn followed suit. Food sometimes squelched the burn in her gut, but other times only added to her discomfort. Lately, painful muscle spasms had become the norm, and her urine appeared darker than it ever had before. Marilyn's digestive woes and strange symp-toms were getting the best of her. She practically lived on Phillips' Milk of Magnesia. The cobalt blue bottles were tucked away all over the house. They might be found under a stack of towels in the linen closet, behind the roasting pan in the pantry, inside an empty coffee can out in the laundry room, or right out in plain sight amongst the toiletries in the bathroom cabinet.

Gary had little sympathy for her various maladies—monthly cramps, headaches, and especially her most common complaints of late—stomach upset, cottonmouth, and flaky skin. When she asked him if he thought she should see a doctor, her husband behaved as if she were a pathetic hypochondriac. He clearly doubted anything could be seriously wrong.

Oh my, why hadn't she slipped one of those little blue bottles in her purse before leaving the house? A good swig of medicine might have eased the pain. Marilyn bit into her sandwich and chewed and chewed. The steak had the consistency of shoe leather, but Lillian ate most of hers.

The waiter cleared away their plates. Lillian folded her arms. "I'll come right out with this," she said. "There's no sense in beating around the bush. The sooner we deal with this problem, the sooner it will all be over and done with."

Marilyn's heart sank clear down to her feet. Her mother-in-law knew something! How could she have waited so long to broach the subject—what kind of woman was she?

"My friend, Peggy Littleton, spied Gary—*my son, your husband*—coming out of the Arches Motel, right in the middle of the afternoon. Seems she was across the street having her oil changed when she saw Gary skulking out of a room from that grungy dive. Any doubt about his identity was squelched, because she knew his car, and she saw him climb in and drive past. Peggy saw his face as clear as day." Lillian's eyes widened like saucers. "And get this," she added. "Not a minute later, a rumpled blonde emerged from that very same room, got into a beat up Ford, and drove away. Imagine how I felt when I heard all this!"

It was all too much. Marilyn couldn't take anymore. "Gary," she squeaked, "two-timing with a rumpled blonde?"

"You look terrible. Keep your head and listen to me, girl. I hired a private investigator. He's been tailing Gary, and Gary's met with that little tart three times since. We know who she is. Her name's June Gordon, and she lives in San Pedro. I sent her a letter stating that I'll gladly pay her off if she promises to go away. Evidently, she moved here from San Francisco a few months ago. I made it all very clear—she gets the money but only if she disappears. My detective will handle the transaction. I don't know how Gary got involved with that little tart. Rest assured, if his father finds out, there will be hell to pay."

Marilyn moaned due to a sudden and intense wave of wooziness. "I'm afraid I don't feel very good," she said. Then she passed out cold, fell off the chair to the floor, and caused quite a scene in the usually dignified dining room of Flynn's Fish-n-Steak.

⛨ ⛨ ⛨

She pleaded and pleaded until the nurse broke down and brought her a phone. Marilyn called Western Detective Agency. Hartman wasn't in.

"Please, Doris," she told the reliable secretary, "deliver this message to the detective as soon as possible. I'm in the hospital. Tell him that my husband, Gary Palmer, was seen leaving a motel room with June. And tell him my mother-in-law hired a private investigator to follow my husband, and that's how I learned this. And tell him that my mother-in-law has offered June money to go away."

Doris gasped. "Good Lord in Heaven!" she cried. "What hospital are you in? What happened to you, you poor thing?"

"Bleeding ulcers. I'm in Huntington Memorial. Don't send Detective Hartman here. Just have him call me, room 509. *Got that?*"

"Yes," Doris said. "I'll pray for you."

"Thank you," Marilyn said. As if God up in Heaven would lift a finger to help a sinner like her. She thought of her mother and her undying faith in the Holy Trinity, which only caused her to feel worse.

No more than three minutes later, Gary strolled in as if he owned the place. He held on to his clipboard as if his life depended on it and tried his best to look official and in control. She fought the urge to spit in his face. All along, she had suffered, worried sick about the lies she had told him. And he had no more respect for their union than to step out with June, *of all people*! For all she knew, Dr. Gary Palmer did this kind of thing all the time. He might have several mistresses on the side.

"Look at you," Gary said. "What a sight."

Marilyn didn't respond. It was important to keep her anger under control. She'd wait to speak with Hartman.

Gary scribbled away on her chart.

Another doctor entered the room. "Hello, Mrs. Palmer," he said. He was an older, rather sympathetic man. But then, Marilyn reminded herself, men were all pigs. They couldn't control their urges. Why had she let her guard down and trusted Gary? Because he was well respected? It didn't matter where they came from, or who they were, the pigs were all the same. She closed her eyes.

"Hey—open up!" Gary said. "This is Dr. Brown, he's come to help you—look alive!"

"Take it easy," Dr. Brown admonished his colleague. Gary bristled at the comment. Marilyn did her best to stifle a grin. It did her heart good to see the older doctor stand up to her despicable husband. Maybe he was an okay guy after all.

Dr. Brown patted her hand gently. "We'll get you back in tip-top shape," he said. "No more aspirin."

"No aspirin?" she cried. *No aspirin*? But aspirin helped.

"You're anemic. We've administered several iron shots. And I'm sending you home with a bland diet. Follow it." Dr. Brown took her chart from Gary and made a few notes.

Gary approached Marilyn's bedside. "You scared my poor mother half to death," he said.

Dr. Brown frowned and turned to his colleague. "That's immaterial."

Marilyn wished she could tell the doctor about her father's health issues. But she didn't dare call attention to the lies she had told Gary about her past. "Do I have ulcers?" she asked.

"Yes," the doctor replied.

"She complains every now and then," Gary said. "But you'd never guess."

"I'm sure she didn't want to burden you," the doctor said. "I see that all the time."

The door swung open, and in came Lillian. "Child," she said, as she rushed to Marilyn's bedside. Suddenly, they were best friends, *les confidants*. "How are you?"

"Better," Marilyn said. "I'm tired. Sleepy." Against her better judgment, she had allowed the nurse to inject her with something for the pain. Her eyelids grew heavy. Marilyn wished they'd all exit the room, in case the detective called.

"Is sleepiness to be expected?" Lillian asked.

"Yes," Dr. Brown said. "We should leave her alone so she can get some much-needed rest."

Gary took Lillian by the arm as if he was truly concerned. "Come along now, Mother," he murmured.

Lillian broke away from her son and reached towards Marilyn. "I'm sorry!" she wailed, as Gary yanked her back.

Marilyn supposed her mother-in-law felt responsible for her condition. "Now, now, Lillian," she said. "You go on home, I'll be fine."

They left the room. Marilyn closed her eyes. Gary hadn't offered any reassurance whatsoever. He hadn't attempted to hold her hand, nor had he communicated a smidge of concern. Never mind, her unfaithful husband's flagrant neglect was nothing new. Besides, she had been in worse shape before and knew she would find the strength to see this crisis through.

Someone touched her arm, and Doris's compassionate face came into focus. "Sorry to wake you, kiddo. Mr. Hartman sent me," she whispered. "If need be, you can say we serve on a women's committee together, or some equally believable fib. How are you feeling?"

"I've felt better."

"Mr. Hartman blew his top when I gave him the news. I have a message for you. But tell me, are you up to this?"

"I think so," Marilyn said. "Don't mind if I keep my eyes closed, though. I'm listening, it's just that I'm awfully woozy."

Doris leaned close. "Detective Hartman is worried about you," she whispered. "He'll proceed with the case unless you tell me he should do otherwise. He wants you to concentrate on getting well and you're to call him if you need anything at all. He feels terrible. All this strain, it's done a number on you, my goodness."

Marilyn took Doris's hand in hers. For some reason, she trusted the woman. "Listen," she said, "you tell him to stay the course, won't you?"

"You bet," Doris said. "Look, I'm gonna scoot. We shouldn't cause undue suspicion."

"Undue suspicion?" Marilyn asked. She cracked a crooked smile. "Under the circumstances, I find that expression amusing."

Doris said her goodbyes and slipped out the door. Marilyn let her mind wander back to her recuperation after the attack in the Magic City, recalling the day Woody unexpectedly showed up at the apartment.

1940

June and Lydia had just left Lydia's apartment to go to work, when Woody let himself in and handed Beryl a check. It was written out to Beryl Quinn, for ten thousand dollars.

"What's this for?" she asked.

He spoke softly. "It's a payoff. The powers that be are willing to do whatever it takes to make sure you don't come forward. Look kid, you've got that money coming. If I'd had a say, it would've been for more. You could have been killed. Keep this to yourself. Don't tell anyone—not June, not Lydia. This payoff is a secret you must keep to the grave."

Beryl folded the check, slipped it into her billfold, and sighed.

Woody sat down. "Your teeth look good," he said.

"You think? Just got fitted yesterday. I think they're better than my real teeth. Whiter and straighter—that's for sure. But dentures do take some getting used to."

"I bet."

She headed for the kitchen. "Hot coffee?" she called over her shoulder.

"No thanks," Woody said. "Today's my kid's birthday—I'd better run."

Beryl stopped in her tracks and turned around. "Sounds like fun."

"I missed it last year, won't do that twice."

"You had better not."

"For the record, I feel rotten about what happened, Beryl. I know money can't erase the nightmare. But it's something."

"Thanks, what else can I say? I think I'm still in shock."

"If I hadn't concocted that stupid set-up, you wouldn't be here. Maybe the kitchen setting was too familiar. Maybe it triggered that nutcase to hurt you."

"You don't know that. We can't know what motivates other people."

"June said it's a bizarre psychological reaction, all tied up with the Oedipus complex. Who the hell knows, she might be right."

"Don't go letting June's attempts at psychoanalyzing the criminal mind influence you. She gets all her information from the movies."

Beryl poured a cup of coffee after Woody left. Then she took a seat at the window and studied the activity on the street below. Money, it seemed, came to her in the most peculiar ways.

Junesy was afraid to return to Hollywood. Beryl advised her to go to the police and report Kay Rennick, but she had refused. The exposition would close on the twenty-ninth, in a few short days. Maybe she ought to leave San Francisco on the fly without June in tow. News of the blitz and all the German attacks on London and other cities fueled her growing anxiety. She couldn't help but wonder how things were back home, in Detroit.

How could she ever explain to Ma why she'd chosen to make a living by parading around naked—or the rape, or the lost teeth and broken bones? There was no way to put it all in words. She wouldn't even try. It was best her mother didn't know who her daughter had become.

✛ ✛ ✛

Treasure Island closed, and Lydia suddenly left town, bound for New York. She left the two girls in the apartment for the remainder of the lease, until the end of October. Lydia had no problem leaving Sylvie the cat behind. "You girls keep her," she told Beryl.

Junesy was busy cooking up another of her outlandish schemes. "We're going to Hawaii," she announced.

Beryl blew a smoke ring and watched it float across the room. "Count me out. I'm going back to Hollywood, and that's that. We can't drag Sylvie to Hawaii."

"I'll never forget Bing Crosby in *Waikiki Wedding*," June reminisced, as she flipped through one of her magazines. "They'll even pay our way over there. You've got to come along. We'll give the cat to the old lady across the hall. She always fed her when we were all off working, anyway."

Beryl decided to humor June. She wasn't about to give the cat away. Sylvie was still young, barely out of kitten-hood, and she needed a stable home. "Who's gonna pay our way over there?" she asked.

"My two new friends will—Samantha Torres and Alberta Carter."

"I'll bite. Who are you talking about?"

"Two ladies I met on the Gayway. They're looking for girls. You know, they've moved The Pacific Fleet to Pearl Harbor. The place is crawling with bored servicemen who have nothing but time and money on their hands."

"And?"

"And Alberta says they're starving for female company in Honolulu."

"And?"

"We'll be entertaining them."

"Not me. Can you hear yourself?"

"Ah, come on. What happened here was a fluke. One freak found you. The chances of anything like that ever happening again are slim to none."

"You bet it won't happen again! Because I'm not going to Hawaii to entertain servicemen."

"And why not? Where's your sense of adventure?"

✣ ✣ ✣

The ride across the Pacific to the islands took five long days. Beryl was ill throughout the entire voyage, and still felt queasy when she spotted Oahu for the first time.

"Paradise," Junesy cooed, at the sight of Diamond Head. Set against waters so blue they seemed to belong to a strange new world.

A chill ran down Beryl's spine. Maybe she should've stayed behind. Maybe joining June in what might be another harebrained scheme would prove to be another monumental mistake. There was something eerie about the unnatural vibrancy of the vista before her, and a foreboding sensation intensified as the ship approached the dock. Beryl dismissed her troubled mood, writing it off to lack of sleep and an extended bout with seasickness.

✣ ✣ ✣

They traveled in a big black car up to a house high in the hills above Honolulu. By the time they got there, Beryl felt so poorly she went straight to bed.

She didn't know how many hours she'd been asleep when she opened her eyes to a looming Alberta and Samantha. "We'll have you back on your feet in no time flat," Alberta said.

"This is gonna hurt me more than it'll hurt you," Samantha snarled, as she plunged a needle in Beryl's vein.

Beryl grimaced and realized her dentures weren't in. She sprang forward and began to thrash about.

"Keep still," Alberta scolded. She shoved Beryl back onto the bed.

Beryl didn't struggle for long. A woozy sensation she knew very well suddenly overcame her. The sensory memories of morphine rushed back with a vengeance, forcing her to close her eyes.

The two women kept Beryl prisoner in a dark room for several days. Repeatedly injecting her with morphine, they referred to themselves as *angels of mercy*, only out to make things easier.

"What do you want with me?" Beryl asked. "What's going on here? Where's June, anyway?"

"We told you," Alberta said. "We're only looking after you, honey. Don't you worry about June. She's just fine—she's swell."

"No, something's off here. What are you up to?" Beryl asked.

Samantha attempted to get her to swallow broth from a big spoon but Beryl pushed her away.

"Look, we're doing you a favor," Alberta snapped, "June told us about the rape. We're here to help you forget."

"I want to see June!" Beryl cried.

"Goddammit, enough already!" Alberta said. "I told you, June's fine."

Beryl tried to focus on the big woman's horsey face but couldn't. Junesy was all she could think about. She wanted to see her in the worst way. "How do I know June's okay?" she asked. "Why can't you bring her to me?"

Alberta loomed over Beryl. "I'm about to explain, so listen up," she said.

Beryl was so sick of lying on that smelly mattress listening to that woman's lies.

Alberta's face contorted. "You think June Masterson is your friend. But that girl wasn't straight with you from the get-go. She didn't tell you why we were bringing you over to Hawaii, did she?"

"She said we'd be entertainers."

Samantha smirked. "In a way she didn't lie, then—did she? What did you think, that you would pose nude like you did in the Gayway?"

"No, I did not! I'll never do *that* again." Beryl was so high she wasn't exactly lucid, but she could still protest.

"Here's the scoop, honey," Alberta said. "June knew all about Hotel Street and our plans for you two. Prostitution's all the go over here. We bring girls from the mainland and the madams pay us. Your friend knew what the score was, and we assumed you did, too. After we got here to the house, June told us you weren't in the know, and we were pissed to say the least. We aren't in the business of having to persuade girls into the sporting life."

"Why are you drugging me then?"

"For obvious reasons. You'll find it much easier to turn tricks under the influence."

"No, I won't! I'm no whore!"

"You aren't?"

Beryl buried her face in the pillow.

"What will you do if she don't get with the program?" Samantha asked Alberta.

"The fix is in," Alberta replied. "As you know, Beryl's already been fingerprinted. Money talks and I greased a few palms. As far as the cops are concerned, Beryl Quinn was operating in San Francisco prior to coming to Honolulu. Yep, the vice squad has our beautiful friend here registered as a sporting girl, and she's got a license now. *She's in the system.* All we have to do is get her lovely ass down to Hotel Street and check her in. They'll take it from there.

"You know the rules of the law, Samantha: Beryl won't be able to visit Waikiki Beach, patronize any bars or better-class cafes, or own property or an automobile. No steady boyfriends. No riding in the front seat of a taxicab or with a man in the back seat. She can't telephone the mainland or attend dances. She can't marry service personnel or wire money to the mainland."

Beryl had placed all her money in a safe deposit box before she left San Francisco. She'd only brought enough to live on—enough for what she thought would be a short trip. How would she get off the island now? "I won't do it," she cried. "I won't go along with your plan."

Alberta leaned closer and whispered in her ear. "You got all that? You listening? You don't have a choice in the matter. I'm sure that mending jaw of yours would be *mighty* susceptible to injury. I bet it would hurt like hell if you took another blow. Wouldn't it, sweetheart? Look on the bright side—sporting girls on Hotel Street rake in the big bucks. Some service a hundred horny boys a day. That, sweetheart, is more money than you'd ever earn posing nude. Which, need I remind you, is what put you in the spotlight in the first place and got you beaten and raped. You may as well take that silken pussy of yours to the cathouse and get paid for it. Do your patriotic duty and see to those servicemen's needs."

How on earth could Junesy have agreed to be a prostitute? Why would she go along with such a plan? It didn't make sense, what Alberta said. No sense at all.

The following day, Beryl was ushered through a back alley and into her new line of work. The so-called hotels were nothing more than seedy houses of prostitution. Preposterous, how they were supervised by local government with military bureaucrats' blessings. She had been hand-delivered to one of the numerous brothels in town, which were much appreciated by commanding officers. They believed the brothels provided a crucial relief valve. Men could satisfy their sexual desires and relentless compulsions without involving the female population of Honolulu at large—those respectable young wives and daughters who were innocents forced to live in a town crawling with roving, sex-starved man flesh in uniform.

The men readily forked over three dollars for three minutes. The prostitute was allowed to keep two dollars, but was expected to pay her room and board, as well as any and all medical costs, including VD tests. Beryl soon learned the morphine she craved wasn't free, either.

Lines formed along the sidewalks each morning and did not let up until the brothels closed up shop.

Beryl entered into a living hell on Earth. She lived for morphine and morphine alone. The disconnect her preferred drug afforded kept her sheltered from reality. She gladly paid for every shot with eager, trembling hands.

The crone responsible for taking the money and wielding the needle recommended Beryl smoke opium instead. She insisted opium wasn't as harmful. But Beryl did not listen. She'd been given morphine in the hospital. To her way of thinking, morphine was preferable because she had stopped taking it once before. Who knew what would happen if she tried the opium? This was flawed logic, to be sure, but it was all that was left to her at the time.

Beryl gave June's name to many a maid, prostitute, and even a madam or two, and finally discovered her friend was working in a brothel on the island of Maui. Beryl sent word several times, but never heard back. She was positive Junesy did not know what they were in for when they voluntarily climbed into the black car and were driven into the hills by Alberta and Samantha—those two horrible, horrible women. June must be in terrible trouble, too.

Loretta Cahill, Beryl's new friend, was a good woman who hailed from Bean Station, Tennessee. At nearly six-feet tall, Loretta stood out from the other whores. In a loud voice, with a thick country-fried accent, she asserted, "These daddy long legs of mine drive the men wild!"

One afternoon when nobody else was around, Loretta leaned down and whispered in Beryl's ear. "You got to wean yourself off that dope, girl," she said. "These madams love junkies, because you junkies don't care about nothin'. Now, that's good for the establishment, but bad for you."

After a concerted effort, Loretta managed to convince Beryl to get out for the day. She arranged for a driver to take them out of town, to a remote beach, where they set up a picnic lunch and sunned themselves.

"I'm saving up my money," Beryl said. "I need to stop whoring."

"You can't stay on the island if you stop humpin' like a bunny," the tall woman from Tennessee warned.

"I couldn't care less. I don't want to stay here."

"You don't like Hawaii?" Loretta asked, running her hand through a short, curly mop of hair. She had tiny crow's feet at the corners of her big brown eyes.

Beryl wondered how old her new friend was, but she knew better than to ask a woman her age. She could have told her about how she'd come to be in the brothel against her own will, but decided against it. "No," she said, quietly. "I hate this place."

"I love it here!" Loretta said. "I'm socking my greenbacks away so I can buy me one of those houses outside of town. A few of the sporting girls are breaking rules these days. Why not me? I intend to get out of this racket. I'm no spring chicken. I'm over thirty years old."

Women in trouble dreamed of having their own home, just as their stable counterparts did. "How'd you get into whoring?" Beryl asked, not knowing how else to put it.

"It's a long story. It started back when I was very, very young. Let's put it to you this way—nobody starts out thinking they're gonna sell their damn body to get by. You fall into it." She laughed, adding, "No pun intended," and began to peel an orange.

"I got caught in a trap myself," Beryl said. "This is not what I want to be doing, either. As soon as I get out of here, things will change."

A formation of military planes flew overhead. They watched them soar in unison across the sky and disappear.

"I fear for the world," Loretta said, as the droning of the engines subsided. "My daddy fought in the Great War and he came home a broken man. I fear for our boys. I know it sounds funny, but I think about what might happen to them while they're busy pokin' me. All these men want is a little touch before they head off to put themselves in harm's way. I don't care how hard Roosevelt tries to keep us out of this thing, too many of those boys will end up dead and gone, that's for certain."

Beryl lived from one fix to another, and while high, she didn't worry. For the first time in a very long time, she wasn't a nervous wreck. In a way, her drugged-out state seemed to be a blessing. She hadn't missed Ma, or Detroit, or even regretted blackmailing Grandfather once. The rape felt like a bad, far-away dream she could barely remember. Nor had she given June's welfare much thought. She was protected and removed from her feelings. Sweet morphine provided shelter from any and all anxiety.

⚜ ⚜ ⚜

"Get yerself prettified," Loretta said. "We're goin' to a party tonight."

"I don't feel like getting dressed up," Beryl whined.

"You know I won't take no for an answer. Get your ass outta bed and put on your face—you'll feel better."

Beryl had to borrow an eyebrow pencil because various belongings kept disappearing. She was so stoned she wasn't cognizant most of the time, and thus fell prey to devious whores and maids, with their thieving ways. Loretta was determined to try and get her friend off the morphine, but Beryl had no desire to straighten.

"Your hair's getting way too long and unruly," Loretta said, as she did her best to pin Beryl's auburn mop up off her neck. "This week we'll march you down to get it done. Enough of this loafing about, lazy bones."

"I always wanted a big sister," Beryl said. "Will you be my big sister?"

Loretta was standing behind Beryl and smiled at their reflection in the mirror. "Aw, that's sweet. I don't have a *little* sister. I think I will take you up on that offer."

Later, as they were driving to the party in a borrowed car, Loretta said, "We could have it worse. There's a rusted-out old truck outside of town being used as a portable whorehouse."

"That's disgusting, but then, our brothel's no picnic."

"Still, can you imagine?"

Maybe Loretta felt above the girls turning tricks in an abandoned truck, but Beryl didn't. What difference did it make where she copulated for money? "Where are we going, anyway?" she asked, anxious to change the subject.

"One of the sporting girls owns a house. It's illegal, but she bought one anyway. She's throwing a Valentine's Day party."

"Is it Valentine's Day?"

"You better get off that dope if you don't even know what day it is," Loretta scolded. Her face softened. "Look, since you're my little sister now, I got something to share with you. I'm pregnant, and I refuse to visit Dr. Doom."

The legendary Dr. Doom was an Englishman who operated out of the back of a Chinese laundry. He performed abortions, and not always successfully. Many bloody tales of the so-called doctor's sloppy—even deadly—practices circulated the rooms and streets of the hotel district.

Loretta had Beryl's full attention. "What will you do?"

"I'll go home. Next week. To Bean Station. I'll have my baby in the good old US of A."

"What are you going to tell everybody when you get back there?"

"That I married a soldier serving in the Pacific and he died of pneumonia. I have enough money to make a run at building a life for the two of us in Tennessee."

"But I thought you loved it here in Hawaii."

"It's not only about me and what I want now, sweetie. There's gonna be two of us."

Beryl was jealous of the baby who would take her friend away. So much for the big sister routine—she would sure miss Loretta.

Loretta left Hawaii and, more than ever, Beryl was dominated by dependence and craving. Any and all desire to leave the confines of the brothel dissipated. The madam grew concerned and urged Beryl to get out for a little sun and air, but Beryl waved her away and refused to join the other girls. Polly, a sweet hapa komoa, felt sorry for Beryl, so she did her shopping for a fee and happily delivered stacks of magazines and books. Beryl read to escape her desperate predicament whenever she wasn't working.

The endless parade of men who traipsed in and out of the curtained workspace behaved themselves, for the most part. They were generally tense, quite often drunk, and some so very young and inexperienced they shot off like a geyser at the sight of Beryl's breasts, or at first touch.

Beryl avoided their pleading eyes and ignored the yearning, humanity, and dread. The men's emotions were palatable. Some were lonely and many were afraid to die. But she had no tolerance for their neediness. She had nothing to give. Her job was to service them sexually, not empathize with their doubts and concerns. Whenever they spoke, other than to grunt or profess, *"I'm coming, I'm coming!"* or variations on that tired old theme, she would tune them out. The sex talk meant nothing to her. But if Beryl let it, she knew their imminent mortality might break her heart.

One buck-toothed sergeant kept telling her she was as beautiful as Hedy Lamar. He'd just seen the racy movie, *Ecstasy*, and couldn't believe his good luck at coupling with such a fine-looking whore as Beryl. "You remind me of her," he repeated, for the third time. She told him to shut the hell up and finish his business.

As the sergeant manhandled her, Beryl thought of her days in Hollywood. How much better off she would have been if only she hadn't left Hollywood in the first place. She didn't want the *what-ifs* crowding her thoughts, so many *what-ifs*. More morphine, please. Memories and regrets were useless to her now.

There was one repeat customer, a local businessman. He would pay for an hour of her time every few weeks. Once, he had asked if she would take him in the mouth. But Beryl did not give fellatio. Although the other girls preferred giving *head* for all sorts of reasons, such maneuvers might hurt Beryl's jaw and loosen her false teeth. "I can't," she cried, pulling at his fleshy arms and encouraging him to mount her instead.

"Sure you can, honey," he pleaded, as he gave the back of her head a quick push south. "I'll make it worth your while."

"I already told you, I can't," she said, coldly. "My jaw's been broken and it's still healing."

The regular ran his fingertip along her jawbone. "I'm sorry," he said. "Forget I asked." He slipped her three one-hundred dollar bills when he left. And she never saw him again.

Mostly they came and went. The blurred faces, torsos, arms, and legs of the three-minute men constantly moving in sequence over Beryl's prone body, a virtual string of inexhaustible longing, desire, and release—always undulating, breathing, moaning, grunting, coming, and going, inside and away.

✠ ✠ ✠

Beryl woke up with a madam in her room, which had never happened before.

"You're leaving," the madam said. She was a stern-faced woman with straw-colored hair and beady, raisin-like eyes. "You're no good to me anymore. You're too strung out."

Stunned and confused, Beryl could barely focus. "But what will happen to me? Where am I to go?" she asked.

"Back to the mainland."

"Home?"

"If San Francisco is home, then yes, you're going home. First, you must be tested. Follow Dua. She will take you where you need to go."

Passengers on the boat witnessed Beryl's agony and assumed the unfortunate girl suffered from an extreme case of seasickness, but as her withdrawal symptoms grew more intense and alarming, a concerned woman went for help. Beryl was carried to the infirmary, where her condition was immediately identified—her track marks were a dead giveaway—and subsequently brought under control. Upon landing, the tormented drug addict was transferred from the shipyard to the hospital by ambulance.

A sweet nurse named Ronda suggested Beryl check into a highly regarded sanitarium outside the city after her imminent discharge from the hospital. Ronda had previously worked at the sanitarium and sang its praises. "There's a wonderful doctor who runs Monte Bahia," she told Beryl. "Dr. Henrick Brenton. He'll do his best to see to it that you never get hooked on morphine, or anything else, ever again. If you can afford it, *and somehow I have the feeling you can*, you deserve to take yourself there. I only left because I got married last year. Otherwise, I'd still be working there."

Beryl agreed to go. Maybe Dr. Henrick Brenton would be as kind as Dr. Adler, the man she'd met at the Griffith Observatory. She thought she might be heading for a place very much like Sinai Home for the Incurables, a good place to be.

Calls ensued and arrangements were made for Dr. Brenton to receive Beryl as a patient. Ronda had previously planned to visit her mother, who lived close to the Monte Bahia, and they made plans for Beryl to ride along. Ronda truly believed Brenton could help Beryl get to the root of what had caused her to embrace such a nasty habit.

Ronda liked to talk. Her passion for nursing and helping others made up the lion's share of her discourse. Uproarious anecdotes regarding dating, her recent wedding, and her spiffy husband made Beryl laugh. Ronda's animated repartee made the trip pass by almost too quickly. Beryl enjoyed chatting with a female who had a brain in her head for a change, with a member of her gender not interested in getting by on her looks or sexuality. She longed to become a woman of accomplishment. Her intention was to follow a path as bright and as purposeful as Ronda's.

Dr. Brenton met Ronda's car in the driveway, walking stick in hand. They embraced, and Ronda hurriedly introduced Beryl. "Isn't she divine?" the nurse exclaimed.

The doctor took Beryl's hand in his. "Utterly divine! Welcome, Miss. My aim is to restore your health as quickly as possible."

Monte Bahia Sanitarium, which had begun life as a mansion on a hill, provided an unsurpassed view of San Francisco Bay, with extensive grounds, heaps of fresh air, and plenty of peace and quiet. Beryl was quite content with her room and the lovely view of the apple orchard outside her window.

What a change from the smelly brothel in Honolulu, where she had been constantly affronted with odors as varied as disinfectant, semen, nail polish, stinky feet, and the scent of foreign midnight snacks of undeterminable origin. She had never grown accustomed to the lack of privacy, living amongst hacking, farting, giggling, crying, singing, squawking women of varied ages and shapes. She'd seen, smelled, and heard enough unpleasantries to last a lifetime.

The events of the last year seemed impossible. Beryl glanced over her shoulder and couldn't believe her eyes when she saw Treasure Island, off in the distance!

✥ ✥ ✥

Beryl called Woody Malkin's office from Monte Bahia but she did not tell him about her life of hell in Hawaii, nor did she say a word about being in recovery for a drug habit.

"Lydia's through with me," he told her. "I couldn't very well leave my wife, so she moved on. I hear she's doing fine out east."

"I'm sorry to hear that. I know how much she cared for you."

"I was over the moon for that woman, I truly was. But I shouldn't have started up with her in the first place. It wasn't fair to her."

Beryl fumbled for a cigarette, feeling shaky.

"How was Hawaii?" he asked. "How's June?"

"I'm afraid I lost touch with her." Beryl had taken the time to send a note back with Dua, the woman who had seen her to the boat, but who knew if Junesy would ever read it? Maybe she wasn't even in Hawaii anymore.

Woody sighed. It was the sort of sigh that told Beryl he had tired of life and all its difficulties. "That's too bad, I hate to hear that. You two were a pair of bookends."

"I sent a letter to her last known address. We'll see if she responds."

"It looks like things are heating up in the Pacific," Woody said. "I hope she'll be okay."

"Me too," Beryl replied, and she was serious. It had become second nature to fret and worry about Junesy Tunesy.

She almost asked about his wife's health and the welfare of his son, but decided against it. Unexpectedly, Beryl couldn't wait to hang up. Woody's despondent attitude made her feel sad, and she couldn't bear any more grief.

✚ ✚ ✚

Dr. Brenton learned about the sordid history with her grandfather, and he decided to call in a psychotherapist, one Dr. Irwin Kerr.

Beryl met with Dr. Kerr for intense therapy every Thursday afternoon.

"Tell me," Dr. Brenton said, the day after Beryl's first meeting with his colleague. "How did it go with Dr. Kerr?"

"I told him about my sixth birthday, when Grandfather gave me Blossom. He wanted to know how having my own pony made me feel."

Dr. Brenton simply nodded and scratched one of his bushy eyebrows with great fervor. One unruly and one tamed brow created a lopsided appearance.

Beryl continued. "I told him that we didn't have facilities to keep a pony on our property, and about how Grandfather sent Blossom to his stable. I told him Grandfather came to get me one day, so I might ride Blossom. I told him about what happened in the car on the way home."

"I'm sure we're on the right track," he said. "What did you have for breakfast?" Dr. Brenton was preoccupied with her dietary habits.

"I tried the goat milk," Beryl offered, "but..."

"No buts!" he advised. "No rash judgments—you must give your palette time to adjust."

"Sure," she said, eager to please him. "I know. I did enjoy the honey, though. It was the best I've ever had."

"We will reconstitute your constitution one cell at a time," he said, in his booming voice. "My next step is to convince you to give up those nasty cigarettes."

"Is smoking bad?"

"I've had two patients with tongue cancer, and both of them were pipe smokers. Coincidence? I hardly think so. Listen to your body, Miss Quinn! Your body will always provide the correct answer."

When he said this, she thought about how her body had told her it wanted the morphine—no, how her body had *demanded* morphine. Would the same thing happen with goat milk?

Most patients in the sanitarium were moneyed people. When Dr. Brenton came to know Beryl's story of having no parents and no husband, he refused to charge for her stay at Monte Bahia.

"I will not take your money, Miss Quinn," he told her. "I feel it is my duty to help you without draining you financially."

She protested, but he wouldn't discuss the matter further.

Mrs. Diane Graver Strand had been admitted when the voices in her head told her to drive her car over a cliff. She shared this information with Beryl over tea one day. They had been admiring a little yellow bird when Mrs. Strand said, "We, *me and my voices*, had it all planned out...I was told to drive out to Point Reyes, but it got so foggy I crashed into an elk. Killed the poor thing, mangled the car, and cracked my skull. But do you think that shut *them* up? Oh no, the voices are constantly urging me to try again!"

A striking young man named Wesley Murray had dropped out of Stanford. He sought help to curb his homosexual leanings. "You see," he told Beryl, as they hiked a trail down to where the goats roamed free, "I cannot bear to be queer. Some are able. I'm not. I want to marry and have children. How old are you, Miss Quinn?"

"Nineteen," she said. "Call me Beryl."

"I'm twenty, Beryl. Maybe you and I shall marry one day."

"Really, Wesley!" she cried. "You can't be serious."

"Why not? You're stunning. I'm incredibly handsome. We'd make beautiful children."

"I'm not the sort of girl you ought to marry," she said. "Besides, I'm going to be very honest with you. I doubt you have one thing to say about being homosexual. If you are—you are. Fighting your inclination will only make matters worse."

Wesley stopped in his tracks and picked up a fallen palm frond. He waved it through the air. "Don't tell my father that," he said. "He's sure I'm *curable*. Besides, my dear girl, even Oscar Wilde married."

"I'm afraid I don't know much about Oscar Wilde," Beryl admitted, "but I know a little something about sexuality, and I believe that suppressing urges only causes perversion. Nobody's curable."

"Well," Wesley proposed, "many consider homosexuality the ultimate perversion. I think I'm a bisexual anyway; it's not that I'm *not* attracted to women. Take you, for instance. I'm very attracted to you."

Beryl ignored his comment and went on to make her point. She decided she had learned to be sensible, maybe even wise. "Two consenting adults should be able to carry on, as long as it's in private and they aren't hurting anyone. Should you marry me, you would only hurt me in the end. Because eventually you'd be compelled to go off with a man, and my heart would be broken. Don't you see?"

"I do believe you are interfering with my therapy. If that's not discouraging enough, now you're dashing my plans to make you my wife. You're the prettiest girl I've ever met. I want you!"

Bisexual was a new term Beryl would have to study up on.

✛ ✛ ✛

Twin sisters, Emily and Amy Stitch, were recuperating from a severe bout with malaria and syphilis, respectively. Emily had contracted malaria while on a safari in Africa with her third husband, George, and Amy had contracted syphilis from a lover in Europe. They returned home to California for treatment and had decided to recuperate at Monte Bahia.

"George killed a zebra," Emily said, as she read from one of her adventurous husband's lengthy letters. "Doesn't seem all that brave, now does it?"

"I don't understand hunting at all," Amy said, sadly.

"You wouldn't," Emily told her. "You wouldn't hurt a fly. But George—he thinks he's the great white hunter."

"He may never come home."

"I hope not. Better he mounts the heads of animals on the wall—rather than me!"

Amy shook her head. "Spare Miss Quinn, won't you, sister?"

"Have I offended you Beryl?" Emily asked.

"No," Beryl answered.

"I shouldn't have married old George," she admitted. "I wasn't over Peter. I long for Peter still, and he's gone and married that Boehm girl."

"Old George will tire of Africa one day," Amy said. "You'll see."

The sisters were quite entertaining.

Dr. Brenton played records before and after dinner on weekday evenings, but most weekends, a string quartet would arrive and set up in the parlor. He believed music and dance served to lift the spirit. He also insisted patients spend considerable time outside in nature. They participated in various activities, such as gardening, hiking, feeding the animals, and bird-watching.

✚ ✚ ✚

Dr. Kerr forced Beryl to go over each and every detail of her grandfather's interactions with her. And, to her dismay, he believed she romanticized her relationship with her papa. "Surely," he said, "you realize how remote he was."

"I do not!"

"Your father spent little time with you. It was as if Patrick allowed James to fill his shoes. And James knew his son wouldn't interfere. It was your mother who stepped in and put an end to your grandfather's visits."

"Papa had too much on his mind," she insisted. "You don't understand the pressure he was under."

"He was a weak man, a lush," he insisted.

Beryl cried to hear him rake Papa over the coals and went through tissue after tissue. "Why are you doing this to me?" she whined. "Why do you insist on degrading my memories of Papa?"

"Because every man you meet, and every relationship you have, will hinge on your examination of your earliest experiences with your father and grandfather. I want you to explore the past, and only then will you come to view the two of them in a realistic light. I want you to examine your life, year by year, week by week, and day by day."

The prospect of probing every detail of past events did not sit well.

Wesley and Beryl were sitting in the orchard on a sunny day, sharing a picnic lunch the cook had prepared. Wesley saw a different psychiatrist than Beryl did. His doctor's name was Rupert Hawking.

"What's Dr. Hawking like?" Beryl asked.

"He's a decent chap," Wesley replied, "a student of Carl Jung. He's trying to encourage my spiritual side. He believes I'm too worldly; he thinks I need to cultivate a belief in a higher order."

"Do you agree?"

"I suppose, but I've come to the conclusion that I'm too young to care about some omnipresent being. I'm too caught up in the fleshly side of things. What about you?"

"I was raised Catholic. I'm an admitted sinner, but I'm not ready to confront my wicked ways."

"Catholic? I've never been close to a Catholic. Shouldn't you go to confession and get all those sins off your chest?"

"I should. But I won't."

Wesley's brow furrowed. "Girl—what horrible things have you done? That expression on your face is vexing."

"I won't tell you! And those days when I used to go sit in a booth with a priest on the other side of the screen and confess my sins are long over. Could you ever do that?"

"This fool's confessions," Wesley cried, "would make a priest's ears bleed!" He broke out into hysterical laughter. Beryl watched him roll around in the grass until he calmed down. Wesley sobered up and added, "I won't ever tell Dr. Hawking the truth. I worry he'll tell Daddy. I love my father and I don't want him to think poorly of me."

"Your therapy might never succeed, then."

Wesley carefully brushed some breadcrumbs off his pant leg. "I think you may be onto something," he said. "Hey, maybe my father should pay you instead of Dr. Hawking and Dr. Brenton. I haven't been able to stop visualizing myself with men. For instance, the delivery boy—the one that brings the staples to the cook daily—I can't get him out of my mind. I want to ravish the poor kid. I could never tell Dr. Hawking. I *won't* tell him. Like you with the priest, it seems too bloody horrible to admit. The truth hurts sometimes, doesn't it?"

Beryl nodded. The truth frightened her, too. She should ask Dr. Brenton to switch psychiatrists. But suddenly, there on the blanket under a tree with Wesley, it hit her—she had to stick with her Dr. Kerr. No matter how daunting the task of delving into her disgusting past proved to be.

TEN
1956

Danni met Reg in front of his apartment. They pulled up to the curb simultaneously.

"Get this!" Reg said, once they were inside. "Marilyn Palmer is in the hospital with ulcers. She suffered an attack. Seems her mother-in-law's friend saw her son, the doctor—Marilyn's husband, Gary Palmer—coming out of a no-tell-motel with a *blonde*. And, get this—the old lady hired a P.I. to follow her own son. And, get this—the blonde is none other than June Gordon."

"You don't say?" Danni exclaimed, her dark eyes dancing.

"We've got a whole lot of shadowing going on; a whole lot of backstabbing and deception. I'm trying to piece this mess together."

"Who's the gumshoe?" she asked.

"No clue. Have you worked for anyone in Pasadena?"

"Russell Unger. Tommy Hope. You must remember Tommy Hope?"

"I do my best to forget all those guys," Reg told her.

"You shouldn't let all that ancient history get to you anymore. Let it go. Crooked sons of bitches. I'm glad you're out of there."

Reg's demeanor changed. His departure from the department would always be a sore spot.

"No telling who old Mrs. Palmer hired," Danni said. "I'll put my feelers out. And, now that I've bugged the joint, we'll learn more about Little-Miss-Double-Crosser." She stood up. "I'm off to the track. Gonna put my cabbage on an unbackable sleeper, we'll see how it all pans out. Wish me luck."

Reg momentarily considered handing over a few bucks. Maybe he'd make a little money grabbing hold of Danni's shirttail, but she darted out the door before he had time to reach for his wallet.

✛ ✛ ✛

Doris asked Reg if they could speak alone. "Marilyn called," she said, once they were up in his office and the door was closed. "She thinks her husband's poisoning her."

"Poisoning her?" Reg couldn't believe what the secretary had just told him.

Doris was wringing her hands and he didn't know her to be a handwringer. "When Marilyn returned from the hospital this morning, the nanny told her how she'd seen Dr. Palmer pouring something in one of her bottles of Milk of Magnesia. She'd witnessed him doing so on more than one occasion. Marilyn's collected several bottles and she's on her way over here."

"Find a lab where I can get them tested, could you, please?" Reg asked. "I'll compensate you for your time."

Doris nodded eagerly. "Do you think it might be true?" she wanted to know. "Do you think he put something in the medicine and that's what sent her to the hospital?"

"Who can say at this point?" Reg told her. "But, as you know, the good doctor's having an affair with June Gordon, so let's not rule anything out."

What had first seemed like a relatively clear-cut case of an amateur blackmailer trying to take advantage of an old friend had taken more twists and turns than Reg could have ever imagined. June Gordon had sent those notes to Marilyn Palmer. And, she was having an affair with the doctor on top of the bargain. As if that all wasn't bizarre enough, the doctor's mother knew about their trysts and was trying to pay June off so she'd go away forever. Hell, maybe June Gordon knew his identity. Maybe she had played him like a cheap fiddle, right along with everyone else.

Marilyn opened a satchel, removed seven blue glass bottles, and placed them on Reg's desk. "I like to keep them hidden," she told him. "Gary wasn't sympathetic when it came to my belly aches."

"How absurd," Reg said. "You're telling me that your husband, *the guy who took the Hippocratic oath*, gets pissed when your stomach hurts?"

Marilyn sighed. "He's short on patience. He's an intolerant man."

"Let me get this straight, the nanny saw him tinkering with your stash of Milk of Magnesia?"

"She saw him adding something, more than once. She wasn't sure if she should make anything of it—until I was hospitalized. He is a doctor, after all. The day I landed in the hospital, she saw me take a big swig out of the bottle I keep in the laundry room, right before I left the house. And, thankfully, she came to me when I got home and told me."

"We'll rush the tests," Reg said.

"I'm getting the hang of being sneaky," Marilyn told him. "I bought new bottles and replaced the ones I removed, so Gary won't get suspicious. I think he might want me out of the way for good, don't you?"

Reg dodged her question. "How are you holding up?" he asked. He genuinely felt sorry for the woman.

"I'm angry. I've been terrified and worried my past might catch up with me—that Gary will find out what a liar I am."

"I guess I don't have to tell you not to drink any more Milk of Magnesia."

She pulled a brown bottle from her purse and showed it to Reg. "I have prescription medicine now. But, what if he *is* trying to poison me? What if he tries to put something in here?"

"Keep that hidden in a safe place."

"What if Gary realizes I'm on to him?"

"What color is your medicine?"

"White."

"Good. Here's what you do. Pour that prescription medicine into a different container and hide it in a safe place. Then fill that prescription bottle with Milk of Magnesia. Pour out each dose as if you were taking it, and then save it. If he tampers with the bottle, we'll find out."

"How long before we see the test results?"

"I don't know yet."

Marilyn sighed.

"The alternative," Reg said, "would be to go to the police and tell them everything. Maybe you ought to."

"I'm sure there's a reasonable explanation. Maybe Gary's trying to help me by adding something beneficial. It's possible. I wouldn't want to accuse him of anything without proof. How would it look if I falsely accused the father of my child of trying to poison me, a doctor at that?"

Reg tried to appreciate her point of view. It couldn't be an easy pill to swallow. It had to be difficult for a woman to believe her husband could be capable of something so horrific. "Be watchful, just in case," he warned.

✚ ✚ ✚

Doris made several phone calls. It turned out her cousin was a grad student at the lab at USC and was willing to analyze the samples. Reg decided to run them over without delay. It was imperative to expedite matters.

"What do you think?" Doris asked. "Is the doctor poisoning his wife?"

"Could be, Toots," Reg said, reluctantly. "I almost feel responsible. If he is guilty, I'll regret not calling in the cops."

"Never a dull moment since you moved leased that upstairs office," the bossy secretary declared.

"Ended up with a lively case this time."

"You know what? I like that Marilyn Palmer. Let's hope there's a reasonable explanation, and the doctor isn't a murdering bastard. I mean, adultery's one thing, but poisoning your spouse is quite another."

June answered the door in a huff. "Stephen? What are you doing here in the middle of the day?"

"Sorry," Reg said, hanging his head. "Should I have called first?"

"I'm always happy to see you, but it's just...I'm on my way out."

Danni's wiretap had served a purpose. Reg knew June was on her way to meet Dr. Palmer. He just had to see her, though. He wanted to search her face for a clue as to why she was so diabolical. Something in him had a hard time accepting her dark side, and something in him wanted to believe June was a better person than she obviously was.

"That's what I get for being so spontaneous," he said.

"We could make a date for later," she suggested, her rosy-cheeked face as appealing as ever.

"Okay," he said, trying not to appear anxious. "I'll call you later." He made his way out to the car, taking his time. Danni was parked down the street, poised to follow June.

Later that day, he met Danni for dinner at Clifton's on Broadway. Since neither one of them had found the time to stop for lunch, Reg figured they might as well chow down and kill two birds with one stone.

"I love this place," Danni said. "Been coming since I was a kid. They used to feed people for free during the depression, you know."

"I've heard," Reg replied.

Danni didn't have the best table manners. She used her fork as if it were a shovel. Her parents were so exacting and classy; he couldn't understand how or why she'd turned out so coarse. Reg began to discuss the case, as a means of distraction. He considered waiting to tell Danni about the suspected poisoning 'til after dinner, but he went ahead and spilled his guts over cheesy macaroni and salty meatloaf.

"News flash," he said. "Marilyn's maid saw Dr. Palmer pouring something into her Milk of Magnesia. She brought in several samples and I dropped them off at a lab earlier."

Danni reached for her milk and took a good long drink. Reg detected the wheels spinning in her quick mind and was somewhat disappointed when she went on drinking without comment. He cleared his throat. "I suppose there's a slight chance he could have been adding something beneficial," he said.

"Why do that?" Danni asked. "Why not simply offer her the medicine, if he wanted to help her? No, this guy's up to no good."

"I suspect you might be right, but I don't want you to be right. I keep saying this, but if he's hell-bent on poisoning Mrs. Palmer, he could accomplish it in many ways."

"When will the test results come in?"

"Tomorrow. Sometime tomorrow."

"You should know, the two lovebirds met on the Santa Monica Pier this afternoon. It was too crowded and too noisy to hear what they were talking about. The doctor was all over the blonde, like stink on shit."

"So, he didn't call it off?"

"If reaching down the front of her blouse in broad daylight means he dumped her, yeah, he dumped her."

Reg cringed. His pulse quickened at the thought of the doctor's hands all over June. "He must really be taken with the girl."

"Who knows what angle he's playing? By the way, I had a little confrontational meeting with the senior Mrs. Palmer's detective; he was tailing them, too."

"You didn't tell him you were working for Marilyn Palmer, did you?"

Danni frowned. "You know me better than that. I told him I worked for Dr. Palmer." She chuckled. "And I told him to scram and he listened. He took off, anyway."

"What if he tells Mrs. Palmer that Dr. Palmer has a private detective working for him?"

Danni smirked. "Doesn't matter, this goat-fuck is lousy with treachery and bound to blow up sooner or later. That doctor's a real letch."

"If he is poisoning his wife, that's the understatement of understatements." Reg knew he shouldn't, but he was eyeing the dessert table. "You going for dessert?" he asked.

"I'm not leaving till I dig into that Jell-O salad," Danni answered. "No way."

"In that case, I'll try some of that butterscotch pie," Reg said.

✛ ✛ ✛

As Reg fumbled with the key in the lock, his phone began to ring. He almost tripped on the threadbare rug rushing across the room.

"Detective Hartman?" Marilyn Palmer said.

"Yes," he answered, somewhat breathlessly.

"I know it's kind of late. I'm calling from a phone booth. I think Gary may have fooled around with my medicine bottle tonight. It was sitting in the medicine chest in a different spot than where I left it."

"Are you sure?"

"I could swear I set it on the second shelf up. Later on I found it on the first shelf. But…maybe I'm wrong. I have to admit I am a bundle of nerves."

Reg fell into his chair. "Relax, if you can," he said. "Hopefully, we'll get an answer tomorrow. In the meantime, keep up the ruse and pretend to take that medicine."

"I will."

"What excuse did you use to get out of the house?"

"The nanny asked me to run out and get baby aspirin for Lilly. We're pretending she's sick."

"Go on home. Don't give him cause for suspicion."

Reg felt stuffed. He shouldn't have gone for the pie. The phone rang again. It was Javier. By the sound of things, he'd gotten into the tequila.

"My cousin Lupe might rent the house," Javier said. "She's got three kids and a decent job in El Monte. She cooks at the high school cafeteria. Her oldest son contributes to the household. I'm sure they will make the rent on time every month, if she decides she likes it."

"Okay," Reg replied. He had too much on his mind to pay attention to what was going on in Montebello.

The old bachelor's voice sounded thick with the liquor. "What do ya wanna do with your mother's things? And the furniture?"

"I just don't have the time to deal with any of this, Javier. Go through and take what you want and get rid of the rest. I'll pay you."

"Man, you don't got to pay me," he said. "But there's some good stuff over there. Number one, the wheelbarrow's only five years old.

And then there's the lawnmower, it's still in working order. And the radio—don't you want that nice radio?"

"Nah, you keep it. I've got a radio. All I want are Mom's most personal items. Her jewelry, what's left is of it. And her brush and mirror set. You deal with the rest."

"Wait, don't you want the photos?"

"Yeah, of course. Pack up the photos."

"Don't worry, Reggie. I'll save the good stuff for you. How's the case goin'?"

"This one's a dandy. I'm knee deep in intrigue."

"You come across all kinds in your line of work."

"I do, all kinds."

They said their goodbyes and hung up. The phone rang again, almost instantly. June Gordon was on the horn.

"It's crazy windy here," she said, "trees are hitting the side of the house and a pack of cats are screaming and crying outside. I'm unhinged. There's no moon and it's darker than hell. I thought I'd call so you could do your best to help me relax. Your voice calms me."

"First of all, there's no such thing as a pack of cats. Dogs travel in packs. What you're more than likely hearing is a clowder of feral cats."

"A clowder? Huh? I guess you learn something new every day. Anyway, they're loud, and now the neighbor's dogs are in the mix and barking their fool heads off."

"Funny. It's not windy here."

"Hey, that reminds me—I keep meaning to ask—where do you live, anyway?"

He needed to remember that he was *Stephen* and not Reg. "Off Santa Monica Boulevard," he lied.

"Do you have a house?"

"Nope. I live in a dump, a real rat trap. I rent a tiny apartment." *That much was true.*

"I rent this place," she said. "The landlord's anxious to sell it, he wants to retire in Arizona. I could buy it for a song, but I'm going back to Hawaii."

"You're intent, aren't you? What's so special about Hawaii?"

"Only everything. The weather, the water, the sky, the people. Have you been?"

"Nope. I did enough traveling to suit me during the war."

"Where were you?"

"All over—Morocco, Italy, France, England."

"You got around."

"Yep."

"What are you up to right now?"

"Thinking about getting a little shut-eye."

"But it's only eight-thirty," she told him. "How do you do that, go to sleep so darn early? I sure wish I could."

"I close my eyes," he said.

"Very funny. I can close my eyes, but I'm not about to meet the sandman. Especially with those cats going ape-shit outside."

"Put on music—music helps."

"I need company," she said. "I hate to be alone."

Reg knew he shouldn't feel sorry for June, but he did. There was something vulnerable and appealing about her. It was a mystery what any particular woman might have going for her—what might draw a fella in. For him, it was always more than good looks. It was *something intangible*. If he had met June under different circumstances (if she hadn't turned to blackmailing her childhood friend), he would have already been involved with her, no doubt about it.

"You still there?"

"I'm here," he answered. He reminded himself to pull away, to detach himself from this two-faced wench. "I ate too much. I had pie right after dinner. I know better than to overeat. And I'm sitting here on my couch like a lump on a log while my body tries its best to break this grub down."

"What kind of pie?"

"Butterscotch."

"Icky," she said. "A foul substance. I like chocolate."

"I happen to love butterscotch. But for some reason, it didn't agree with me tonight."

"Hey, those cats stopped with the racket. Maybe they moved on."

"Glad to hear it. Maybe you can catch a little sleep."

"You trying to get rid of me?"

"Absolutely not." *Yes—yes I am.*

"I should buy myself a television."

"I don't own one, either."

"No?"

The Los Angeles Basin was experiencing a cold snap. Reg shivered in the dark. It was time to fold out the bed and get under the covers. He asked June to hang on while he threw the cushions on the floor with abandon, unfolded the bed, slipped out of his clothes, and covered up.

"I'm back," he told her.

"What were you doing?"

"Trying my best to get warm. It's freezing in here."

"I lit a fire in the fireplace for the first time. I went out in the backyard and broke all the dead branches from the neighbor's tree. I hope they don't mind. The branches were hanging over the fence. I found lots of dry twigs and leaves on the ground for kindling. I scratched my arms badly, but the fire's well worth all that. If you were here, we could cuddle."

He wouldn't have minded getting warm with June Gordon about then, but hated himself for thinking it. He really ought to get off the damn phone. She was probably waiting for him to tell her he'd be right over.

"Did you open the flue?" he asked, redirecting the conversation.

Needless to say, June wasn't pleased. "Of course I opened the flue," she snapped. "What do you think I am, a simpleton?"

"No, but it happens. People forget. It sounds like you're the rugged type when you want to be."

"I do what I need to do when I need to do it," she said, emphatically. "I can be resourceful when properly motivated."

"Sounds like."

"A girl's got to be enterprising."

"Damn," he said, "I'm so cold my teeth are chattering."

"Turn on the heater, why don't you?"

"It's on the fritz."

"Poor baby."

Nobody had ever called him *baby* before. Reg could have told her about how he stayed out at his mother's much of the time, about how the heater worked fine out there, but he didn't feel like going into the whole story. Besides, he shouldn't reveal anything remotely pertinent to his true identity. It was nuts to get involved with his client's nemesis. He knew better.

"I'm never in contact with my landlady," he told her. "I drop the checks in the box and I never think to tell her the heater doesn't work, or how the bathroom faucet drips. I guess I should."

"You're likely to catch your death, or maybe even pneumonia."

"I don't think you catch pneumonia from being cold."

"It's unhealthy, in any event."

"I could use at least two more blankets," he said. "I think I'll do what my mother used to do in the old days. I'll heat a pan on the stove, wrap it in a towel, and bring it under the covers. I'll say good-bye now."

"Get warm. Goodbye, Stephen."

His feet felt like chunks of ice as Reg hurried over to his tiny closet and began to root through a duffle bag for a pair of pajamas he almost never wore. He slipped them on, along with his heaviest pair of socks. At the stove, he cranked up the flame and heated the heavy cast iron skillet. He then wrapped the heavy skillet in a bath towel and maneuvered it clumsily under the covers, doing his best to warm up the mattress and blankets without burning his hands. Wrapped in his winter coat, he climbed in, pulled the covers up over his head, and closed his eyes. If only he could fall asleep while he still felt warm.

ELEVEN
1956

Armida cornered Marilyn in the laundry room. "We need to talk," she said, in the most serious manner. "I've come up with a plan. I'll do all the cooking from now on. Tell the doctor we made a new arrangement. I'm going to watch his every move. If he comes into the kitchen, if he tries anything—anything at all—I'll be here to prevent him. Don't you worry."

"I'm having the Milk of Magnesia tested," Marilyn confided. It felt good to know the nanny was on her side. "Hopefully, we'll have an answer tomorrow." She studied Armida's concerned face. Marilyn had always imagined the diminutive woman to be an intruder infiltrating her home—someone from Lillian's enemy camp. How wrongheaded!

"No need to wait 'til tomorrow for the answer," Armida said. "It's common sense. Why else would he fool around with your medicine behind your back if he wasn't adding something to make you sicker?"

"I know, I know, it does seem kind of fishy. But I'm giving him the benefit of the doubt. For the time being, anyway."

"All this must be a hard pill to swallow, *no pun intended*. Meantime, I'm not letting him near the food, the coffee, nothing. And don't you brush your teeth with your toothpaste. Use the baby's."

"Right, he wouldn't poison Lilly," Marilyn said, her resolve to be brave suddenly evaporating. "I don't know how I can sleep in the same bed. The thought of lying next to him makes my skin crawl."

"We'll make up a story: Lilly needs you, because she had a bad dream. You'll sleep with her tonight."

� ✚ ✚ ✚

Gary arrived home shortly after six, and he appeared to be in an uncharacteristically good mood. He hurried over to the bar and offered to make Marilyn a cocktail.

"No," she said. "I'm not supposed to have alcohol, remember?"

"One little drink won't hurt," he argued, a familiar edge creeping into his voice.

What kind of doctor would go against the hospital's recommendation? One who didn't give a hoot about his wife's welfare—that's what kind. She tried to appear calm. "No, I'd rather not," she said.

"Well, I'm having one. It's been a long day."

According to Gary, every day was too long. Marilyn wondered what he'd been up to on that particular day. Maybe he'd met up with June for a quickie earlier at *their* motel. "Armida's cooking tonight. Since I'm not myself, she's taking over the kitchen duties."

He frowned. "I hope she's not making beans. You know how I hate beans."

"She's not making beans," she assured him. Marilyn was irritated to think that Doc believed beans were all Armida knew how to cook. "I gave her my recipe for cabbage rolls. You love cabbage rolls."

"Not if they're spicy."

"I gave her my recipe," Marilyn repeated.

After dinner, Gary switched on the TV. From the kitchen Marilyn heard, "Ladies and gentlemen: the story you are about to hear is true. Only the names have been changed to protect the innocent." *Dragnet*—how ironic. Marilyn felt as if she were living in a *Dragnet* episode lately. She went outside and rolled up the hose. Then she put a load of towels in the washer.

Armida was seeing to Lilly's bath. Marilyn headed towards the hallway to help, but Gary patted the couch cushion next to him. "Come over here," he told her.

"Not now, Doc," she replied. "Enjoy your show. Lilly's in the tub and I need to check on her."

Dragnet was Doc's favorite program, and he especially hated to miss the beginning. Maybe he'd gotten the idea to poison her from the program in the first place. Or maybe he wasn't poisoning her after all.

Her thoughts seesawed back and forth. The ghastly situation seemed too far-fetched.

In the bathroom, Lilly splashed in the bubbles. Armida perched on a little stool next to her, doing her best to discourage the child from being too unruly in the slippery tub.

"Do you mind if I smoke in here?" Marilyn asked. "I'm edgy."

"Do what you must."

"Mama, Mama!" Lilly cried. Marilyn reached down to scoop up a handful of bubbles and fashioned a beard on her chin. The beard sent the child into fits of laughter.

"How's your tummy?" Armida asked Marilyn.

"Not too bad, thanks." Marilyn wiped her bubble beard away with a hand towel. She had eaten oatmeal for dinner, because she had made up her mind to adhere to a strict diet in order to heal her gut. But still, her tummy ached. She lit her cigarette and took a long drag.

"You haven't taken any Milk of Magnesia?" Armida said. "*No wonder you're better.*"

Marilyn put a finger to her lips as if to say shush, and gave a pointed look at the closed door. What if Gary decided to listen in during the commercial break?

"Dolly!" Lilly cried, fretfully.

Armida jumped up. "Oh dear, I forgot her Kewpie doll! I'll be right back." She took off for the bedroom.

The little girl tried to stand up but lost her footing. Marilyn immediately dropped her cigarette and grabbed hold of her daughter's tiny arm before she had a chance to slip and fall. Gently, she lowered Lilly back down in to the warm bubbly water. "Oopsy daisy," she said, taking in the soapy smell of the bathwater, relieved to see her daughter was fine. Marilyn worried that Lilly might already be too close to Armida. Nannies came and went.

Marilyn had become far too attached to her nanny and it had broken her heart when Opal had departed so abruptly. Sometimes Marilyn wondered if losing someone so close, so unexpectedly, had contributed to her troubles.

Lilly blinked a few times and settled back down, as if nothing had happened.

Armida returned, carrying the plastic doll with the big black eyes. She handed it to Lilly.

"She tried to stand up but almost fell and cracked her head open," Marilyn said, as she snatched her discarded cigarette off the tile floor. "Brought to mind an incident that happened to an old friend. She was giving her daughter a bath when the phone rang. She went to answer it and got involved in the conversation. When she returned to the bathroom, her daughter was underwater. The child drowned." Marilyn shivered.

"How horrible!" Armida reached her hand out protectively towards Lilly. "You put such thoughts right out of your mind," she told Marilyn. Lowering her voice, she added, "Don't worry—I would never leave the baby alone, especially for the telephone. The telephone can always wait."

Marilyn ran what was left of the cigarette under the faucet and tossed the soggy thing in the trashcan. She wanted to defend Lydia and say she hadn't left the child to take just any old phone call—her absentee husband had been on the other end of the line—but Marilyn realized what a paltry excuse that was. She had an entirely different perspective now that she was a mother with a child of her own.

The guilt must be an insufferable burden. Marilyn wondered how Lydia was getting along in New York City, and hoped the trag-ic-but-gifted songstress had found peace.

It hit Marilyn how tired she was. "I think I'll change into my paja-mas," she said, watching Armida pull Lilly out of the tub. Then she wandered out of the bathroom. Once she had changed, she sat on the divan deep in thought, remembering her time in the city by the bay with great fondness. She could practically see, taste and feel the bright lights, chop suey, hustle-bustle, and her youthful glee, before the attack had changed everything.

1941

Just outside San Francisco, Marilyn used to sit in the gardens of Monte Bahia and look out across that incredible skyline, wondering if she'd ever return to the city.

"Don't you get bored, being locked up in this place?" Wesley asked her once.

"No, never."

"Never *ever*?"

"I may one day, but not yet."

"Good grief, I'm going positively bonkers, and they've forbidden me from venturing into the city. If I'm serious about changing my ways, I must *auger in*. Those are the words of Dr. Hawking. If I don't *auger in*, Daddy's sure to pull the plug, and I don't know what will happen to me if he does. I doubt he wants a queer for an heir. I'm forever seeking his approval. And I do enjoy being a rich man's son. I'd better straighten up."

"I stopped resisting altogether," Beryl told him, hoping to make a valid point. "I suppose you could say I'm finally auguring in, getting on with my therapy."

"Honestly, I feel as if I'm trying to drag a dead elephant up an endless flight of stairs," he said.

"Well then, just pretend to drag that dead elephant, why don't you? Do what the doctors say and pretty soon you can pretend you no longer find members of the same sex attractive. They'll pronounce you cured, you can go back to school, graduate, and live your life."

"You make it sound so easy."

"I had a long visit with a homosexual actor at the Garden of Allah once," she said. Wesley *lived* for her stories about Hollywood. "He was married, even had a wife and kiddies in Connecticut. But he carried on with several actors. You see, such affairs are kept hidden in Hollywood."

"Like Cary Grant and Randolph Scott?"

"Yes, or so I've heard."

"Pray tell, what's this actor's name?"

"I won't say—he doesn't want this to get out. My point is, he told me he wished he'd never married, that he'd never had children at all. Maybe you should keep his story in mind. Stay single, make bachelorhood a lifelong circumstance."

"No! I'm still planning to marry you, Beryl. We'll have those beautiful children, and we'll understand each other. I'll have boyfriends. You'll have boyfriends. Why, we might even share."

"I'm afraid that's far too twisted for this girl!"

"Please, say you'll marry me. Daddy would be pleased as punch if I brought a girl like you home."

"You're loopy." She ruffled her fingers through Wesley's thick curly hair, and then tore off down the hill with him in fast pursuit.

✥ ✥ ✥

Dr. Brenton saw to rebuilding her physiology, and Dr. Kerr saw to rebuilding her psyche. Dr. Brenton finally persuaded Beryl to pour goat's milk over her oats every morning. Loads of honey helped mask the pungent flavor and the thick amber syrup had come from his very own bees. According to the bee-keeping doctor, such a farm-healthy diet would help cure what ailed her.

The solemn Dr. Kerr insisted Beryl tell him about the day her mother found her father at the bottom of the stairs. "Where were you?"

Beryl struggled to remember.

"You must have been in the house, somewhere?" he insisted.

"Naturally. It happened early in the morning."

"Were you in your room? Eating breakfast?"

"I can't remember exactly."

"Did your mother cry out?"

"It seems I heard about her finding him *after the fact*, but I can't say where I was when she did find him. What difference does it make?"

"Think. Can you see him?"

"I always imagined what he looked like, if that's what you mean."

"Tell me what you see."

Beryl closed her eyes; she wanted to get it right. "One hand's stretched out, stuck between the spindles of the banister. He's flat on his back. I can even see the patterned carpet with the trailing red roses under his head. His neck is all crooked, his eyes are wide open, and they're impossibly blue."

"Does he see you?"

"No, of course not. This is me *imagining* what he looked like."

"Beryl, you saw him before anyone else did, didn't you?"

"No. I didn't *see* him at all. You aren't listening."

"Think girl. *You did see him.* What do you do next?"

"I don't *do* anything."

"What do you do?"

"I'm in bed." Beryl opened her eyes. "Ma screams. I don't move."

"You saw him first and went back to your room."

"Why do you say that? Ma found him. If I had, I would have been the one screaming." She shook her head. "Don't be ridiculous, doctor."

Beryl and Mrs. Strand were strolling through the rose garden when Mrs. Strand lost her footing and tripped. She grabbed hold of Beryl's hand. "I do believe I'm awfully dizzy today," she said.

"I've got you," Beryl told her, doing her best to keep the old lady steady.

"If I had my way, I'd still be in bed. I'd be working on my cross-word puzzles and eating cake."

Beryl smiled.

"My voices tell me the answers, which makes it nice because I don't have to think."

Did Mrs. Strand believe her creepy voices knew the answers to questions she didn't? Beryl felt as if she were a member of a club she no longer wished to belong to. She had better get herself cured, and quickly. It was high time she began to live a responsible life among healthy people.

"They won't send me home," Mrs. Strand said. "My husband won't let me leave until they tell him I'm better. The thing is, if they think I'll stop hearing the voices, then they're the crazy ones. We stayed in an ancient castle in England five years ago and that's when it all started. I believe a demon lives inside me, plain and simple. His name is Fire, and he's not leaving until I die. I claimed the voices told me to drive off the cliff at Point Reyes, but it's the angels telling me to do it. And soon enough, I'll figure out another way to kill Fire—mark my words, I will." She looked Beryl square in the eye. "Am I scaring you, child? I don't mean to."

"Don't worry," Beryl said. "I don't scare easily." The old woman was obviously off her rocker. She sure hoped the doctor could help the poor thing.

✛ ✛ ✛

"It's high time you call your mother," Dr. Kerr announced at their next meeting.

Beryl had been staring out the window, watching the Stitch sisters play a peculiar slow-motion game of croquet. "No way," she said.

"You owe it to her to let her know you're alive and well."

"Dr. Kerr, promise me you won't call my mother."

"How could I call her? I don't even know her name." The resolve in his eyes upset Beryl. She didn't believe him.

That night she grew more panicked as several fretful hours passed. Dr. Kerr had all the pieces necessary to track down her mother if he decided to do so—or her grandfather, for that matter. He might contact them soon. In fact, he could have done it already. She had better leave, and it had better be now. But what if her imagination was just overactive? No, he could very well expose her. She was not ready to speak to her mother. Not yet. Maybe never!

Beryl bolted out of her chair, tiptoed to Wesley's room, and shook him awake. She whispered in his year, telling him she needed to sneak out of the sanitarium right away.

Once Wes sprang to life, he told her to put together only what she absolutely needed. It had to fit into the picnic basket. "We'll take one of our picnics tomorrow. There'll be a car at the bottom of the hill waiting for us. I'll arrange everything."

"So, you're coming with me?" she asked.

"You bet. I'd better get out of here, too, or I'll go squirrelly."

The following morning, they asked the cook to pack up a basket, which Beryl carried up to her room and emptied. She proceeded to fill it to the brim with the most important of her belongings. She had to tear the lining of her poor old suitcase apart one last time, to get at her hidden bankbook and extra cash. Regretfully, she left most of her clothes and her favorite boots behind. It couldn't be helped.

But Wesley had somehow managed to hide an entire set of luggage in the orchard during the night. He wasn't about to part with one stitch of his exquisite clothing. They had quite a time lugging the suitcases down the hill, along with the picnic basket full of what few belongings Beryl had carefully chosen.

The driver showed promptly at twelve-thirty, and the delivery boy happened to pass by in his rickety truck. Wesley flagged him down and gave him five bucks to keep his mouth shut about his seeing them on the road. The boy promised he would, and waved and winked at Beryl as he drove away.

"That boy has a terrible crush on you—I bet he thinks I'm the luckiest man in the world," Wesley said to Beryl, once the bags were loaded and they were speeding away. "Step on it, won't you?" he then told the driver. "We're in a hurry to get to the city."

They rented a room in a fleabag hotel as husband and wife. Wesley signed them in as Mr. and Mrs. Wesley Wilde.

"Father will search for me at every hotel in Union Square," he said, "but here I am, staying in a hovel off Market. If he has me tailed, they'll be looking for me at the train station, but we're picking up my car from a friend of mine. He'll never suspect we're on our way to Hollywood, of all places. How marvelous! Hey, you never mentioned the Garden of Allah to the shrink— did you?"

"We never got any further than my childhood in Detroit. Luckily, Dr. Kerr's a firm believer that the first five years of life define us," she said. "If you ask me, he was far too interested in my toddlerhood."

Beryl took Wesley to Chinatown after their nap and introduced him to chop suey. He bought a jade ring, two sets of Chinese pajamas with embroidered lions on the back—red for her and blue for him—and a set of ivory chopsticks.

Afterwards, they caught a taxi and rode over to Wesley's friend's house. The friend's name was Henry and he was every bit as sweet as Wesley. They planned on leaving for Los Angeles first thing in the morning, so they only visited a short while. Henry handed over the keys to Wesley's Jaguar (he hated to let the convertible go), and assured Wesley he'd be down to L.A. soon enough for a visit.

"Quick question," Beryl asked, once they were speeding back to the fleabag hotel. "Do you think you can teach me how to drive?"

"You can't drive? Well, that beats all. I barely know how myself."

"Wesley," she said. "Don't scare me."

"I'm not trying to scare you," he said. "Everyone agrees I'm the worst driver around."

The following morning, he did manage to find his way out of the city without incident, but all the swerving and subsequent honking terrified Beryl. Wesley hadn't been kidding; his incompetence behind the wheel was positively monumental. Consequently, Beryl practically taught herself to drive with very little help from him, in order to save their skins.

She felt like a practiced pro by the time they passed Salinas on the main highway. Wesley snoozed while she flew along, invigorated by her newfound self-taught skill.

"You know what I think I'll do?" she said, when he finally woke up. "I'll change my name. I don't want to be Beryl Quinn anymore."

"Excellent idea," he exclaimed, with his own special brand of infectious enthusiasm. "Let's choose your new name right now. What is it you don't like about Beryl?"

"It's not that I don't like my name," she said, with her hands firmly on the steering wheel. "But, I'm starting over, and I want to be someone else."

"I get it, I do!" Wesley concentrated hard before finally calling out, "*How about Marilyn*? You've still got the *r*, the *y*, and the *l*, just like you do in Beryl. It's lovely, the name Marilyn, don't you think?"

She said it three times. "Marilyn, Marilyn, Marilyn. I *do* like it!"

"Excellent. We're halfway there, unless you want a middle name."

"Do you think I need one?"

"Probably, it's the thing to do. How about we stick 'Ann' or something equally as mundane in the middle?"

"Sure," she said. "Marilyn Ann, *what*?"

"I know," he said. "I had a teacher in school, his name was Walsh. I always thought Walsh was such an elegant name."

"Fine then, I'll have my name legally changed to Marilyn Ann Walsh. Thanks, Wesley!"

"I'll stay *me*, thank you very much. My Mama chose Wesley and Daddy's proud of Murray, which is apropos since it means sailor, and he's a sailor and I'm a sailor."

"Wesley Murray is a fine name, no need to tamper with it."

✥ ✥ ✥

They checked in at the Garden of Allah. "The first thing we have to do after we get settled," Marilyn told Wesley, "is run on over to Schwab's for milkshakes."

"*Milkshakes?*" Wesley whined. "I'd prefer a stiff drink."

"Oh, you can get drunk later," she said. "I want a damn milkshake."

"Sour puss," he quipped. Wesley had begun to unpack. He tossed his socks in an open drawer and hung his suits in a neat row in the cedar-lined closet.

"It's what June and I used to do." Realizing what few belongings were left to her, Beryl complained, "Gosh, I don't have any decent clothes to speak of."

"We'll go shopping, don't worry. I'll buy you a new wardrobe. Don't fret. I've got a bank account my mother established for me years ago, long before she up and died. Daddy doesn't even know about it."

"How rich are you?"

"*Stinky, smelly rich.* Now do you want to marry me?" He arched his eyebrows fetchingly. "Become Mrs. Murray forever and ever?"

"Oh, Wesley."

Over the next few days they kept very busy. They hired a lawyer to change her name from Beryl Quinn to Marilyn Walsh. They shopped. They saw the sights. Wesley insisted they visit the Brown Derby.

Beryl was near the pool, searching for Wesley, when she ran into Freya Simard. It hadn't been that long since she'd given up the opportunity to work with the kind costume designer at MGM. To Beryl, though, it felt like a lifetime.

"Beryl!" Freya called.

"Hey, Freya, how are you?"

"You're back. I missed you."

"I didn't want to leave, but June got herself into hot water and we took off together."

"And so I heard."

"Sorry. I wanted to return sooner, but you know how it goes."

"You still looking for a job, Beryl?"

"I sure am, but I go by Marilyn now."

Freya shrugged. It wasn't unusual for people to change their names in Hollywood, and she didn't seem to think much of it. She handed over her card. "All right, Marilyn. Give me a call next week, we could use you."

"Wonderful! Thanks, Freya, I will."

Freya gave her a quick wave. "I look forward to hearing from you."

From here on in she would definitely be Marilyn Walsh. Beryl Quinn was dead.

She gazed at the card Freya handed her. MGM—three glorious letters. She was dying to tell Wesley but he was nowhere to be found. She returned to their villa and slipped Freya's card into her wallet for safekeeping. Would she even remember how to sew a straight stitch? She hadn't touched a machine in ages. Wesley showed up a few minutes later (he had run out to pick up a bottle of vodka), and he was beyond thrilled to hear that she had bumped into Freya, with the prospect of her possibly working with such an illustrious costume production department.

"The thing is," Beryl told him, "I haven't touched a machine or traced a pattern in such a long time. What if I've forgotten how?"

"We'll fix you up, kiddo," he said, setting down the bottle of vodka. "I'll put the Bloody Marys off till later."

They hopped in the car, and Wes took Marilyn shopping. Wesley was an excellent shopper, a seasoned pro. They visited the garment district and picked up a new machine, several bolts of fabric, and all the miscellaneous materials she needed to practice.

At Wesley's suggestion, Marilyn set about sewing an elegant evening gown. When first seated before the shiny new machine, she found the method for threading the bobbin mechanism so different, and the very act of sewing seemed a bit foreign. She hadn't handled patterns and fabric in such a long time. This strange machine was supposedly new and improved, but the learning curve intimidated her. When Mémère had sat her down in front of her Singer for the first time, her hands had been shaking even worse than they were now. The first thing she had ever made was a frilly yellow apron for Ma. The sense of achievement had sent a surge of triumph through to her very core. For the first time since the molestations, her younger self had felt fulfilled. She had accomplished something. She might have a talent.

Why had she let Junesy fill her head with dreams of some glamourous pie-in-the-sky Hollywood life? Worse than that, why had she followed her impetuous friend to San Francisco? If she had stayed behind in Hollywood, she wouldn't have been raped, wouldn't have sailed to Honolulu, and wouldn't have been tarnished. She would be so much farther along in her craft.

Enough! Wesley believed in her, didn't he? He expected her to produce something lovely. It was time to hunker down and prove herself. It was time to honor Mémère's legacy.

When he caught sight of the finished gown, Wesley exclaimed, "You're the cleverest girl I've ever met!"

✠ ✠ ✠

Wes became instantly popular with the Allah residents, which was no big surprise to Marilyn. They were invited to all the best parties. One night, they drove up Nepeta Road to attend a formal dinner party given by a producer Wes had recently befriended. As they passed a for-sale sign, Wesley instructed Marilyn to slow down. He studied the house for a minute and then asked what she thought of it.

"It's adorable," she said. "A real doll house. It looks like an English cottage."

"I'll buy it for you."

Marilyn threw back her head and laughed. "Sure you will."

The party was tame compared to the bashes they soon became accustomed to. But Marilyn had come down with a headache, so they left early. On the way home, Wesley pulled up to the curb of the same house he'd stopped to admire on his way up the hill.

"I love the view from up here," he said. "Look at all those twinkling lights, below."

✛ ✛ ✛

Marilyn bravely drove the Jaguar to the studio to visit the wardrobe department for a scheduled meeting with Freya Simard. Metro Goldwyn Mayer was a prolific factory where hundreds of people produced thousands of costumes. There were senior and junior designers, cutter-fitters, tailors, beaders, embroiderers, and seamstresses galore. Marilyn was immediately hired on as a seamstress. She had brought along the dress she'd constructed, in order to show Freya what she was capable of.

"You designed this?" Freya asked, as she inspected the hem of the evening gown.

"I sure did."

"Most excellent. If you work hard, you'll move up the ladder quickly."

To celebrate her new job, Wesley took Marilyn to dinner at the little Mexican place they'd recently discovered.

"I have news, too," he announced over guacamole. "I'm trying out for a part!"

Wesley had acted in theatre back in college and had impulsively decided to give film acting a try. Marilyn held up her margarita to propose a toast.

"To our new endeavors," she said, as their glasses touched.

"I'll be playing a rich boy," he said, with a smirk. "I know it's a stretch, but you've gotta start somewhere!"

✛ ✛ ✛

They moved into the English cottage on Nepeta Road during a torrential downpour. It rained so hard and so long, the swimming pool nearly overflowed. Marilyn insisted Wesley take the master bedroom. She would take the bedroom closest to the main bathroom.

The shipment of furniture from Wesley's house up north had been delayed. For three nights in a row, they ate Chinese takeout straight from containers. They slept on pillows and piles of blankets placed on the floor in front of the raging fire they'd built in the stone fireplace in the vaulted living room.

Wes's furniture, when it arrived, proved to be oversized for such a small space. The ceilings in his room were too low for his ridiculously tall four-poster bed, and he was forced to send most pieces to storage.

A decorator was hired to expedite matters. His name was Jean Paul and he was determined to paint Marilyn's bedroom walls yellow.

"I would rather you didn't," she told him.

Jean Paul shrunk back. "I am the professional—you must trust me!" he exclaimed.

"But they're my walls, and I would rather sleep in a pink room."

"*Pink?*" the decorator cried, aghast.

"A dusty pink."

"Very well," he said. "But yellow will be our complimentary color."

Over her dead body.

Wesley had little time to supervise the project, or to rein in Jean Paul's expenditures. He had gotten his wish and had landed the role of Charles Cunningham, the spoiled son of a greedy industrialist, in a film with the working title, *Save Me, Won't You?*

"I was born to play this part," he told Marilyn. "I tell you, I'm not even acting. All I'm doing is memorizing lines."

"I went ahead and let Jean Paul order the draperies for the living room," she said. "I hope you like them."

"At this point, I couldn't care less about any of that." He handed her his script. "Help me rehearse, won't you?"

They sat at the kitchen table and she fed him lines until neither of them could keep their eyes open.

⊹ ⊹ ⊹

Wesley flew off to begin filming in New York. Marilyn oversaw the decorating project in his place, but Jean Paul disagreed with her every decision.

After a heated argument over the placement of an armoire, Marilyn confronted the decorator on another sore point. "As far as I'm concerned, you forego that loud fabric or I leave the upholstering of the sofa until Wesley returns." Jean Paul insisted on using a garish, bright green, leafy print she absolutely despised and that Wesley had never okayed.

"What would you have me use?" he asked, his exasperation evident.

"Something that doesn't conflict with the feeling we're trying to evoke; something elegant and fitting our vision."

"Why you people hire me when you think you know it all, is a complete mystery," Jean Paul said.

Marilyn placed her hands firmly on her slender hips and stood her ground. "It seems to me, if we are to live here, shouldn't our sensibilities come into play? Shouldn't our taste be paramount?" She stared him down.

Jean Paul threw his hands up in the air. "Fine," he said, "I'll bring swatches by tomorrow. I have bigger fish to fry, missy. I've got an appointment to meet with Barbara Stanwyck at her country house next week. We've got to wrap things up here."

"Leave the sofa be, then," Marilyn said. "I'll buy a new one and put this one in storage with the rest of the furniture."

"Tell me what you have in mind," the decorator suggested. "I'll find something marvelous."

But she was finished with him. "No thank you, I'll handle it myself." She couldn't be rid of Jean Paul soon enough.

✢ ✢ ✢

They kept Marilyn busy at the studio, but still, she was lonely without Wesley and filled the time in with work. The smallest bedroom had been transformed into a sewing room against Jean Paul's wishes, because he thought they needed a den. Marilyn bought a drafting table and set about learning to sketch. She hovered around the sketch artists at the studio whenever possible, studying their work. Some were patient and answered all her questions. Others, protective of their creative process, simply brushed her off.

Freya did not do her own sketches. Eventually, Marilyn gained enough skill and dredged up the courage to ask if Freya might give her work a quick look-see.

"You draw?" Freya asked.

"I'm learning." Marilyn hoped she hadn't made a mistake, and that she had the chops to impress her boss.

"You *do* draw, and *well*," Freya said, as she flipped through a stack of renderings. "You have a fantastic style, too!"

Freya approached Marilyn a few days later and asked if she would be her assistant. Marilyn said yes.

The work was grueling. Most nights she crawled into bed in her street clothes, and she would barely have time to shower and change before she headed back to the studio. Freya claimed trial by fire would pay off. She said Marilyn had to pay her apprenticeship dues.

✛ ✛ ✛

Wes wrote beautiful letters. Sitting around the set was tedious and mind numbing, he explained. But he absolutely loved, loved, loved the work. Compared to studies at Stanford, acting was undemanding. But he missed her. He wondered if he was experiencing true love. Because his heart hurt, now that he was so far away from her. Yes he was sure of it—this must be true love. They should commence a physical relationship at once, he wrote. He was pining away. What other explanation could there be? He had fallen in love with a woman and, how amusing, he had met her in a sanitarium. When he returned home, he said they would share a bed. He would grow up once and for all, graduate from his adolescent fantasies and move right on up into the man's world his father wanted him to discover. She read Wesley's letters with eyes full of tears. He was absolutely insane and totally delusional.

Marilyn believed they could love each other with all their hearts, but they would never know bliss in each other's arms.

No telling how many men Marilyn had copulated with. She knew a girl back in the brothel who did her best to keep count, but it had never occurred to Marilyn to do such a thing. She wanted to forget each encounter as soon as it ended. But, despite the constant parade of sexual activity, she had never experienced any sensation even remotely resembling what she understood to be an orgasm. She must not encourage Wesley. It was futile to expect he could ever fulfill her needs. Maybe she'd been ruined for life by the rape and Hotel Street. Maybe she was unable to experience sexual satisfaction. And it was difficult to imagine Wesley could ever repress seductive homosexual urges.

Marilyn wrote Wesley often. She did her best to convey affection and support, but she discouraged a romantic relationship.

Her letters were also full of stimulating gossip from the various wardrobe workrooms, including reports about the high demand for sought-after and newsworthy costume designers, and how tired and worn down she felt. Had he heard about the U.S. freezing German and Italian assets? She told him she wished he was closer, because she feared the power-driven fury currently sweeping the four corners of the Earth. How long could their nation remain sheltered from the oncoming storm? *Do hurry home,* she wrote. *It's lovely here in our stylish little house. There are loads of lemons growing on the tree out back. Their flesh is tinged orange, and they're almost sweet.*

There were times when it seemed scandalous to find herself working in a mammoth dream factory—one responsible for churning out fantasy. Was she helping to produce subject matter that kept people entertained and perpetually deceived into believing they lived in a different world from the real one? Didn't people understand they were under threat of imminent peril? Did they believe borders mattered? Didn't they watch, listen, and read about the global calamity? No, most buried their heads in the sand. They flocked to the movie theatres instead, to bask in the artificial glow cast by the silver screen.

⊹ ⊹ ⊹

Golda Kaminski was one of Freya's most gifted cutter-fitters. Older than most and headstrong, she had a thick accent and was one of Freya's favorites.

"I can't find Golda," Marilyn announced, after searching for her in all the usual places. "She's been working on that cape, and the beads came in. I wanted to see if the beads match the fabric perfectly. I fear they may be the wrong hue."

"Golda had to leave," Freya told Marilyn. "She's taking the day off."

"I thought you said she hadn't taken a day off in years?" Marilyn interjected.

"Come into my office." Freya led the way in a brusque manner. Once inside, she reached into a cabinet, pulled out a bottle and a couple of glasses, then poured two shots of vodka. Marilyn wasn't a vodka drinker. No matter. Freya took a gulp, so she took a gulp.

Such behavior at work was out of character for Freya. "Is Golda okay?" Marilyn asked.

"The Nazis have ordered the Jews to wear yellow stars so they can be identified. Many in our industry have family members over there."

"Good God," Marilyn said.

Freya downed what was left of the vodka. "Stalin is wicked. Hitler is evil. And that lunatic Mussolini…"

"I couldn't agree more," Marilyn replied. "It's as if everyone lives in a bubble of disbelief. And this mass delusion blinds people to the threat."

Freya leaned forward. "Believe me—it's human to be fearful about speaking out and drawing attention to oneself, or to appear paranoid or obsessed with such matters, because it can put others off."

"I know what you mean. It has happened to me. The girls called me a wet blanket, and one guy said I reminded him of Chicken Little."

Freya shook her head. "On a lighter note, I'm having a get-together tonight. Would you like to come?"

⊹ ⊹ ⊹

Wesley returned. Marilyn was driving him home when he told her he'd been tagged to play a small role in a big production. "At least it's scheduled to be shot here, in town," he said. "I'm happy to be home."

"I'm happy to have you home. It was lonesome and boring around here without you." She pulled in the driveway and slammed the brake pedal with too much force. Marilyn felt skittish. The prospect of Wesley seeing the fruits of Jean Paul's labor for the first time had her on edge. "Don't be afraid to tell me what you think of the place."

Inside, Wesley first ran his hand along the length of the drapery fabric. "Nice, subtle," he said. Then he stopped at the sofa. "This looks out of place. I think we'll put it in storage and buy another."

"That's what I thought you'd say," Marilyn said, "I was going to put it in storage but I decided to wait for you. Jean Paul wanted to reupholster it in the ugliest pea-green fabric, and we had a tiff. I said no."

"Good girl. *Why pea-green?*"

"You've got me, it was jungle-inspired. He's full of strange ideas. But he did a fantastic job in *your room*."

"Let's eat before the tour," he said. "I'm famished. And then I'll take a gander at what you call *my room*. I need a nap."

She prepared sandwiches and a pot of tea. "How does it feel to be a movie star?"

"It hasn't sunk in. You know, I told Daddy what I'm up to. Called him and came clean."

Marilyn studied her friend's face for distress, but he seemed relatively calm. "What was his reaction?"

"He laughed. I told him I signed a contract with Paramount, and he said he wished I'd have let his lawyers look at it first. Of course, I reminded him that I had studied law. Overall, the conversation went well. I think. He's coming to visit. You and I are going to get hitched before he gets here."

"Wesley," she said. "Not that again."

"You'll see," he said. "We'll be good together."

✚ ✚ ✚

As Marilyn spent a good deal of time with Wesley, she came to trust him more than she had ever trusted anyone besides her father. She came to understand that Wesley's feminine side was highly developed, and that his insight into the mind of a woman tended to be spot-on. His warmth and compassion did not negate his masculinity in her eyes. There were lots of manly aspects to his character. He encouraged her to speak about her grandfather's molestations, the rape, and the time she spent on her back in the filthy brothel. Wesley said the way he dealt with his homosexual urges was to face them head on. The more she talked about her sordid past, the easier it was to accept what had happened as horrible, but over. She was doing her best to forget and move on.

Wes found Marilyn sexually attractive, and he wasn't shy about letting her know how he felt. But, unlike what she'd experienced in the past, his displays of affection felt clean, sinless—almost virginal. She knew he would never intentionally hurt her. Marilyn had desires, and her desires were mixed in with feelings of shame and guilt. If she was to overcome all that shame and guilt and her fear of men, who better with than trustworthy Wesley?

Marilyn soon succumbed to Wesley's long lingering kisses. His sweet lips and whispered endearments melted Marilyn's resolve that they remain just friends. She finally agreed to risk heart and soul. How did she square herself with this rationale? She realized they were both cured. Wes loved her. It was that simple.

"But," she confided, "There's much you need to know, before you go through with this marriage."

Beryl shared every detail with Wesley about Grandfather's molestations, about her involvement in June's blackmail scheme, about running away from home and abandoning Ma and Mémère, about posing naked in The Gayway, about the rape, about Alberta and the morphine and the brothel, and she didn't leave out the *three-minute men.*

Wesley cradled Marilyn in his arms and insisted the past did not matter.

"I won't divulge past sins to you," he told her. "What's done is done. We're starting a new life together."

"No, you're right about that. I don't want to know anything, not unless there's something you absolutely must confess.

"Darling, we're starting over. It's just you and me from here on in, and now that we have each other, the past will fade away. Our separate histories will become a distant memory."

⊕ ⊕ ⊕

They wed in a tiny chapel, with Freya and Henry in attendance, and immediately rushed off to honeymoon. They only had three days, as Wesley was expected on the set right away.

Marilyn drove—she always drove. Wesley directed her to the marina south of Santa Monica. He took her by the hand and led her to a gleaming sailboat.

"See the name?" he said, proudly.

The name on the hull, painted in blue letters, read: *The Moon and Sixpence.*

"Do you know Maugham?" Wesley asked.

"Yes!" Marilyn said. She had read the novel he'd taken the title from. Somerset Maugham was one of her favorite authors. "I have to say, that's a most excellent name for a boat."

"It's all about art and beauty, in the end."

Marilyn placed her hand over her heart. "Please tell me you know how to operate this thing."

Wesley wrapped his arms around her. "This *thing*? It's not an automobile! No, no, no. Always refer to a vessel in female terms, *she or her*. And yes, I am the son of a sailor, experienced and reliable and at your service." He took a quick bow. "Have you ever been on a boat?"

"Besides the one that brought me to Hawaii, and the one that brought me back? Well, small motorboats. I did grow up on the Detroit River and spent time on Lake Eerie and Lake Michigan. But I've never been in a sailboat on the sea."

"You have much to learn."

"I have to warn you, I get seasick on open water."

"Landlubber!" Wesley cried.

He helped her aboard and immediately led her down into the cabin, where he promptly familiarized his new wife with the bed, which he called a berth.

A patient and adept lover, Wesley was greatly experienced, and the first ever to make Marilyn's body sing. "See?" he told her. "I'm dynamite in the sack."

"I'll say you are, Captain," she said. "If I had only known. We've wasted so much time!"

"Ah, is that my new name?"

"You bet it is, my sweet *Captain*." She threw her arms around his long neck, and felt they ought to never leave that safe and cozy berth, with the row of little round windows offering up a view of marina and sky. "Let's do that *all over again*," she suggested.

✚ ✚ ✚

Just after his father arrived from back east, Wes rang Marilyn. "Try to get home early," he whispered. "Daddy's here! He's just dying to meet you."

Marilyn couldn't ask for any more time off. Things were hopping in the workroom, and she'd already taken three days for their honeymoon. But she finished up right on time, something she rarely did, and hurriedly clocked out.

Harris Murray was just as charming as his son. He was beaming. It was obvious that the man was immensely relieved to find Wesley in the arms of a woman. He instantly took to Marilyn, and once they were all comfortably seated and deep in conversation, he asked about her parents.

"Dad," Wesley said, "Marilyn's father has passed and she's alienated from her mother. Hopefully that alienation will be rectified in short order, but she doesn't discuss her family. You understand?"

"Well, give me a smidgen of information," Mr. Murray responded. "Any brothers or sisters?"

"No," Marilyn replied. Wesley thought she should get in touch with her mother? This was news. "I'm an only child."

"Where were you born?"

"Detroit, Michigan."

"I see. And what nationality are you, dear?"

"My father's family is Irish, my mother's is French Canadian."

"You have a strain of Irish, from your mother's side," Mr. Murray reminded his son. "And it just occurred to me, you lost your mother and Marilyn lost her father. You have that in common."

"That's right," Wesley said.

"Your mother," Mr. Murray said, "loved weddings with a vengeance. She would've made a big to-do."

"True, it would have shattered her dreams if we didn't go all out," Wesley placed his hand over his heart. "But, mother's no longer with us, bless her soul. And I was anxious to begin our life together." He then took Marilyn's hand in his, and smiled.

"I can see why you were so inclined," Mr. Murray told his son. "Marilyn's a beautiful girl. You wouldn't want some other chap to come along and sweep her off her feet, right out from under you."

Marilyn laughed. "Mr. Murray, that's what your Wesley did. He swept me right off my feet."

They hadn't told him that they'd met at the sanitarium. Why open that can of worms? Dr. Brenton had told Mr. Murray that

Wesley had left with a girl named Beryl Quinn. There was no reason for him to deduce that Marilyn was that girl.

"I hear you work at MGM?"

"Yes, I do. I'm an assistant to a costume designer. I hope to be a designer myself someday."

"But surely, when the children come, you'll give all that up."

"I suppose so," she said. "We haven't talked about it."

Wesley got up and poured more coffee. "We are going to have the most gorgeous children, Daddy. That is something we have discussed." He winked at Marilyn.

"I look forward to grandchildren. Looks like your brother's wife isn't able. Bit of a tragedy, I'm afraid."

"Poor Earl, poor Rachel," Wesley said. "Perhaps they'll adopt?"

"I haven't heard them mention adoption. They keep trying and she keeps miscarrying. It's all very discouraging."

Wesley turned to Marilyn. "I can't wait for you to meet them. Rachel's very sweet and my brother's a cut-up. You wouldn't expect a lawyer to be such a comic."

"Your brother's not in good spirits these days," Mr. Murray said. "Neither of them is."

"Gosh Daddy, you paint a bleak picture."

"It's late," he said, standing up. "My driver will be here shortly. I'm off for the night. See you kids tomorrow?"

"I told you, you're welcome to stay here." Wesley reminded him.

"No, you newlyweds don't need an old geezer like me hanging around."

"I wish you would," Marilyn insisted.

"My secretary reserved a suite at the Hotel Knickerbocker, so don't you worry about me."

They walked him out to his car and made a date to meet at Musso and Frank's for lunch the next day.

"I hate to think about him going to that hotel room, all alone," Marilyn said.

"He won't spend the night alone. Mark my words, his secretary's probably waiting for him. If she's not, they'll speak on the telephone."

"You think he's fooling around with her?"

"I know he is, and why shouldn't he? My mother's been dead and buried three years now. When she was alive, he was true blue. They were madly in love and he took the loss hard. A little hanky-panky keeps the blues away."

"I like your father."

"Daddy is nice, isn't he? But, trouble is, he plainly doesn't approve of queers. That's the long and the short of it. And now that he doesn't have to worry about me anymore, we'll get along splendidly."

Marilyn pushed him playfully. "If I didn't know better, I'd think you married me so that your father won't leave you out of his will!"

"Simply a side benefit," he said. "Plus, we'll give him grandbabies, and I get to be married to the most beautiful girl in Hollywood, and my best friend, to boot. Even Henry, who's the biggest homosexual this side of the Mississippi, said he'd marry you if I didn't."

His father wanted to see the orange groves, so Wesley told the driver to head east. Mr. Murray spoke as they rode along. "When I was a boy, growing up in Boston, my mother brought home a crate of oranges. I fell in love with the beautiful label, and the artful depiction of rows and rows of trees, the groves set against the foothills with the snow-capped mountains in the distance. And, I thought to myself, California must indeed be the land of sunshine. Been crazy about oranges ever since. I was so excited for Wesley to go to Stanford. I thought being out west would suit his independent spirit."

The driver parked on a knoll, near a fruit stand. Mr. Murray bought a bag of oranges. "Why, this view of the grove and the mountains beyond very much resembles the artwork on the crate that had captured my imagination as a boy," he declared. "The only difference between this scene and the one on the crate is today there's no snow on the mountains."

"We should go to the mountains tomorrow," Wesley suggested. "We could spend the night in a cabin. We could go fishing!"

"Afraid I have to get back," Mr. Murray said. "But I will take you up on that offer. I'll return in a few months' time, and we'll make that trip. Maybe we'll go skiing."

✛ ✛ ✛

The attack on Pearl Harbor put everyone in a daze. The citizens of Los Angeles, and almost every soul living on the west coast, felt uneasy and very much like sitting ducks. Wesley finally wrapped up the film shoot. Now, he spent most of his time in front of the radio or with his head in the paper.

Germany declared war on the United States. "That's it," Wesley told Marilyn, "I'd better enlist. I will not serve in the infantry. I aim to be a Navy man."

"The son of a sailor," Marilyn said, doing her best to hide her panic.

Wesley hurried off to call his father. He enlisted the next day.

✛ ✛ ✛

Mr. Murray wrote Marilyn frequently, and his most recent letter read:

Dear Girl,

News from our fine boy arrived today, and it sounds as though he's mucking through. I know you miss him as much as I do. His brother tried to enlist but was denied due to a ruptured eardrum. I fear the guilt is eating away at him. Here in Boston, it's winter as usual and I slipped on the ice and twisted my ankle, so I'm hobbling about like the geezer that I am. I've been working long hours (spending much time searching for growth opportunities, capitalist that I am), and when I get home, I sit by the roaring fire. Currently I am reading Black Lamb and Gray Falcon *by Rebecca West, learning more about Nazism and Yugoslavia. Hope all is well out in the land of oranges and lemons.*

Your loving father-in-law, Harris Murray

She hadn't received a new letter from Wesley, so she reread his last one for the umpteenth time:

My Flower,

They're doing their best to whip me into shape. After toting a nine-pound rifle in the drill field all day, I'm so beat I fall into bed, and so tired my bones melt into the lousy mattress (referred to as a fartbag around here). My eyes close instantly and even the surrounding snoring and smelly feet can't keep me awake. Besides, sleep brings dreams of you and that's what I'm after at the end of a grueling day of soldiering. I taped your latest photograph next to my bunk and caused a small riot. The fellas think you should be on the cover of Yank *magazine. I told them to mind their own beeswax. I'm keeping you to myself.*

Daddy's been writing often. He's trying his best to keep me updated on what's going on with my brother Earl and the whole sordid not-being-able-to-have-a-child business. When I get back, we'd better get cracking on making him a grandbaby (censored by me). I had a dream that we were back at Monte Bahia and, get this, we were running the place! Isn't that a hoot? The food here is horrible. The coffee's pure sludge, and I'm getting skinnier and skinnier. This Adam's apple of mine appears to grow larger every day.

Well, I know you'd prefer a longer letter, but I'm bushed, so I'll stop now. If I try to keep writing, I'll bore you to tears. Know that my goal is to return to you as soon as this thing is over.

Your Captain, Wesley.

As soon as she finished the letter, Marilyn grabbed the dictionary and looked up Adam's apple. The medical term was 'prominentia laryngea' (prominence of the larynx). She was simply wild about Wesley's Adam's apple—his whole body, really, every square inch of flesh and bone. At night she would do her best to memorize the length of him. She thought about his dream—that the two of them were running Monte Bahia. It seemed a good sign to her—an encouraging omen. They were reduced to only being connected through letters once again, and she had so much to miss this time around. He just had to come home to her.

TWELVE
1956

"Hurry, take this call, it's the lab!" Doris urged Reg. She stood enrapt as she listened to his one-sided conversation, hopping from one foot to the other and nervously biting at the side of her thumb. "Fill me in," she demanded, as soon as Reg set the receiver down it its cradle.

"Just regular old Milk of Magnesia."

She cocked her head the way a confused dog might. "Hogwash!" she shouted.

"I agree."

The secretary calmed down. "I mean...sure, it would be great if Dr. Palmer was innocent. Definitely preferable. But something's fishy in Denmark."

"I'm with you, Toots," Reg admitted. "Got an ace up my sleeve, though. Hey, has Marilyn Palmer called yet?"

"She did. She's calling back at eleven." Doris put her hands on her hips. "Don't leave me hanging, what ace are you referring to?"

"You see, we set Gary Palmer up. Marilyn exchanged her new medicine for Milk of Magnesia, and she removes and saves her regular doses. If the doctor's tampered with it, we'll find out. I doubt he could resist the temptation, if he is guilty. I'm sure he changed out those other bottles from the house for clean ones after Marilyn landed in the hospital, and that's why the test came out negative. She's bringing me the sample this afternoon."

"Tricky," Doris said. "You know your stuff, guess that's why they call you detective."

✚ ✚ ✚

Reg met Marilyn Palmer at a place in Alhambra with a neon chef's toque, called *The Hat*. Pastrami sandwiches were their specialty, and Reg had never come across a pastrami sandwich he didn't like.

She took a seat in his car, reached in her purse, and handed him the medicine bottle.

"I'm a little surprised the test came out negative," he told her. "No trace of poison." He couldn't read Marilyn's face. She remained passive. "But, bear in mind, your husband may have switched the tainted bottles for clean ones. Maybe he picked up on Armida's suspicions. We're not dealing with a dummy."

"I'm tired," Marilyn Palmer said. "Bone tired."

"I'll put a rush on this," he offered, showing her the bottle he held in his hand.

"You know," she said, quietly, "our anniversary's coming up, and Gary's making noise about taking me to Mexico. Would he propose such a trip if he were plotting to kill me? You've had experience with these kinds of situations, detective. What's your opinion? Do you think he's innocent?"

"Sorry, I really don't have any way of knowing. But, if I was you, I wouldn't leave the country with the doctor."

"I'll take your advice. I'll use these ulcers for an excuse to stay close to home. I really need this to be over. I can't wait to see June and give her a piece of my mind."

Marilyn was distraught. Reg regretted mistaking panic-stricken for passive.

"You want to go ahead and pretend we're paying June off?" he asked.

"No, we *will* pay her off. I don't want her blabbing details about my past. Don't you see? I hired you to look after my interests, and it's in my best interest to keep my good name. Please make it clear, if I give her this money, she can never contact me again." She reached for the car door. "Ever," she added.

Reg nodded. He had to admit, Marilyn Palmer was one tough cookie. Not many women could play this little cat-and-mouse game. His stomach growled. The detective remembered he had met up with Marilyn for a dual purpose—he needed food and he needed it now. "I'm starving," he told her. "Care for a sandwich?"

"I have to watch what I eat," Marilyn replied. "But I am hungry. I'll take milk, and maybe some French fries. A few potatoes shouldn't hurt."

"Wait here," Reg said. He took off to get the food.

When he returned, Marilyn's head lay against the seat and her eyes were closed. Her dewy eyelids were fetching, to say the least.

"How are you feeling?" he asked, once seated. "Healing up?"

The beauty straightened herself. "Not too bad—today, anyway. Thanks for asking. I'm not spry though, not by a long shot. But, I think the medicine the doctor prescribed is helping. I went to the library and did a little reading. If there was a lethal substance in those bottles, there's no telling how much I've ingested. The doctors just assumed my ulcers were out of control." She looked at him with pained eyes. "Why would they assume otherwise?"

"Here," the detective said, handing her the French fries and milk container. "Enjoy. At least we know this food's safe."

"Armida's watching Gary like a hawk. I think she sleeps with one eye open. She's convinced he's guilty."

"Good for her. It's good to know someone's got your back."

"I suppose so. But still, I feel confused. I don't know which end is up anymore."

They ate in silence. Reg resisted the urge to brag about how good the pastrami was. He doubted that he'd be able to stick to such a bland diet, even if he had to.

✛ ✛ ✛

Good old Stephen headed over to San Pedro to see June. How or why she found the time to work him in, Reg couldn't figure out. Why did she keep on seeing him if she was so crazy about the doctor? If June Gordon knew his true identity, she sure was skilled at pretending otherwise. What was the bit about going back to Hawaii, anyway? Was the doctor in on it? Were they plotting together? Poison the wife and head off to paradise once she's out of the way? Maybe

Palmer was on board. But what about his political aspirations, or were they merely his *father's* political aspirations? These questions and others raced through Reg's mind.

June wanted to see a movie. They met outside her house. "Come with me," she said, "we'll take my car. If we don't hurry, we'll miss the beginning, and I hate missing the beginning. Don't you?"

She weaved her way in and out of traffic, and Reg was forced to ask her to take it easy.

"Sorry," she said. "I'll slow it down. How's the tire business?"

He'd almost forgotten he'd told her he was a tire salesman. He'd better stay on his game and pay closer attention to his fibs. "Kind of slow."

"You never asked me what I do."

"You told me that night I took you home," he lied.

"I did?"

"You sure did."

"What'd I say?"

"You said you were between jobs."

"That's the long and the short of it," she said. "I gave up my profession and haven't replaced it with another one, *yet*. Still investigating my options. Yessiree Bob, investigating my options." She was really cranked up.

Reg swallowed hard when he saw the marquee. June had chosen to see *The Man Who Knew Too Much*, and he followed her up to the ticket counter. How diabolical was this blonde?

June could barely sit still during the movie, which was filled with plenty of intrigue and double-crossers. But Reg didn't catch anything that applied to him.

"What'd ya think?" she asked, as they left the theatre.

"I'm a Hitchcock fan, and this film didn't disappoint."

"I'm a Hitchcock fan, too—always been attracted to the darker side of things. I don't sugarcoat life. Never owned a pair of rose-colored glasses. Did I tell you my old man ran off when I was a kid and my mother jumped off the Ambassador Bridge?"

Reg was always amazed when people confessed traumatic events in such matter-of-fact terms. June's mother had thrown herself off a damn bridge to her death. Reg studied June's crystal-blue eyes for some kind of clue. The kid had to be in pain. Everyone had their way of dealing with a rotten childhood. Hers was to simply pretend there was nothing wrong and to just push those bad feelings down even deeper. Yeah, he could see the pain all right. It's what made her shine so bright.

"What a lousy break," was all he could say.

"Being raised by an aunt who resented the job made growing up tougher than it had to be. I used to have this well-to-do friend who lived in a big fancy house. Her father died, but her mother was wonderful. I was envious. She had this idea that she had it rough, but that silly girl didn't have the vaguest notion of how awful life could be. You know what I mean? You ever have a friend like that? Somebody who had it made, but didn't think they did?"

June asked questions, but Reg could see she wasn't really looking for answers. "This friend of mine was beautiful," she rambled on. "I'm not using the word loosely, either. I mean *beautiful*. It almost hurt to look at her. Being around her made me feel like a comical little elf. Guys only went for me because I was easygoing. She was aloof and cold as ice, and boy that drives you menfolk over the deep end."

Reg knew very well June meant Marilyn. Marilyn must've done June wrong somehow. What had happened between them? Reg intended to find out. "For the record," he told her, "nobody's gonna take you for a comical little elf. Where's this friend now?"

"Say, *thanks*. But you're only saying that because you've never laid eyes on her. She's living the good life. She has everything I want. But not to worry, I'm working on changing all that. What about you, Stephen? What do you want, besides your own tire store?"

He puzzled over how to answer.

"Never mind," she said. "I'm getting too personal—too heavy. Let's go to my place and make mad, passionate love."

Had he heard her right? "Jesus, June."

"Don't you want to nail me? Why else would you come around?"

June took delight in shocking Reg. Was this girl really a tramp or was she putting on some kind of an act? Was she only testing him, trying to determine if he was just another guy out for easy sex? And that suicidal mother of hers—how dare she just leave her young daughter alone in the world. His mother had always looked out for him. She hadn't been a perfect mother, but she had done her best.

"Look, I just lost my girl," he said. "I like you, but I don't want to rush in to anything."

June unlocked the passenger door and opened it. "You aren't light in your loafers, are you, Stephen?"

"Nobody has ever accused me of being queer before."

"Oh, just get in the car," she snapped.

She picked up where she'd left off. "I'm seeing a married man right now. You probably think that's despicable, don't you? But he was supposed to be my husband. We were in love. When I told him I couldn't have children, he dumped me. He was out to please his wealthy parents and they wanted him to produce an heir. Anyway, after he threw me to the wayside, I ran off to San Francisco.

"And guess what I up and did? I ran straight into the arms of a married man. What a fool! I knew he was impossible to get. His wife was very sick. I was younger and a lot more innocent. I had met him back when he was seeing a friend of mine—a talented, dynamic woman—and he wouldn't leave his sick wife for her, so I knew he wouldn't leave his sick wife for me, either. But he was handsome as all get out, and fun. And I hate to be alone. I'm one of those girls who mistakes sex for love. But he eventually called it off and there I was, all alone, all over again."

She had a death grip on the steering wheel. "After all that, I got myself married to the first sap who came along," she continued. "He was a lazy, shiftless, mean bastard. I stood on the Golden Gate Bridge one windy day. I had planned to jump off. I thought, well the fruit doesn't fall far from the tree—it falls from the bridge. Ah, but I couldn't bring myself to do it. Instead, I went home. I left my ratfink husband a few months later and returned to L.A."

June stopped talking. Reg rolled down the window and gulped cool air in an attempt to clear his head.

"Hey," she said, "let's stop and have ourselves a nip or two."

Reg hoped she wasn't hadn't finished talking. There was more to June's story, he was ready to listen, so he nodded in agreement. No time at all passed before she pulled in front of a bar called The Whistle. He ordered two scotches with a splash of water, on the rocks. And his hunch proved right. June was in the mood to talk.

"I had lost touch with the most beautiful girl I had ever known. But I ran into a mutual acquaintance, and that's how I learned my

friend was working in the costume department at MGM, and that
she lived in a cozy little cottage off the Sunset Strip, thank you very
much. That's my friend! Throw her up in the air and she'll land on
her perfectly-arched feet. She was going by a different name. Me
and my big mouth, I told my boyfriend all about her and how we'd
parted ways. I went on and on about how beautiful she was, prettier
than most movie stars. And what did I discover when I returned
from San Francisco? That my fella, the man *I* was supposed to marry,
had sought out that beautiful friend and he'd gone and married her.
The dirty son of a bitch had married her!"

"That's insane," Reg said, and he meant it. "Does your friend
know all this?"

"Nah, she doesn't know anything."

"And you're still seeing him?"

"Try to understand," she paused to take a sip of her drink. "I
had to confront him—didn't I? And oh boy, did we start up again,
with a vengeance. And guess what? He *hates* Marilyn. Claims she's
no good in bed, that I'm livelier and more playful. But he doesn't
want to leave his child, his little girl. Here I am again—in the same
position I was in with the fella up in San Francisco. I've tried to
break up with Gary Palmer, but he says he's going to leave her. He
says he can't live without me. I don't know if that's true, or if he's
just looking to keep me on the line. We meet in this dive motel three
times a week. He's a goddamned sex maniac, that's what he is." She
suddenly stopped talking and touched Reg's knee. "But hey, I'm
talking your ear off, here."

June was really spilling the beans now, using Marilyn's name,
and Gary's, too. Was she throwing caution to the wind because
she was high? Was she just riled up? Those pills probably had her
cranked. He wondered if she'd taken some more when she'd visited
the restroom.

"If you're so far gone for this married guy," Reg asked, "why
proposition me?"

"I guess I'm a sex maniac, too."

Reg shook his head in disbelief.

"You must think I'm mad as a hatter," she said. "There's more to
the story, but you wouldn't believe it if I told you."

"Give it a whirl," he said. "You've gone this far."

"I like you, Stephen. I like you a lot. What if I told you I could buy you a tire store? We could move to Hawaii. Start a new life. Could you go for that kind of set-up?" The light was dim over the dingy booth, but Reg thought he saw June bat her eyelashes.

"What kind of a timeframe are you talking about?" he asked.

"Not far down the road. Not far at all. It's my turn for happiness."

"I'm at a loss for words," he said. And he truly was.

"You think about it. I'm coming into money, and I could go for a decent fella like you."

Reg took a healthy gulp of whiskey, eager to rinse the nasty taste out of his mouth.

✛ ✛ ✛

On the way home, Reg saw flashing lights in his rearview mirror. He was pulled over, not a block from his apartment by a cop he used to work with. And Andy Bell just happened to be Eve's new boyfriend.

"What do ya know?" Andy exclaimed, after Reg rolled down his car window.

"Why'd you pull me over?" Reg asked the jerk.

"You were weaving?"

Weaving, my ass, Reg thought.

"You tired?" Andy asked.

"Yeah," Reg said, anxious to be on his way. "I've had a long day."

Andy looked inside the car, as if he expected to see something interesting. "You hear from Eve lately?"

"Nope, can't say that I have. Not since she broke it off and told me she was dating you."

Andy forced back a grin. "That's good, because I like her. And I wouldn't want to think she was the type to step out on me."

"You don't have to worry about Eve." Reg wondered just why Andy was skunking around. He was sure the jerk knew his car and had pulled him over intentionally.

"I'm gonna let you go. You smell like whiskey, and you were weaving all over the road, but since you're so close to home, I'll ignore all that. You are going home, aren't you?"

Reg fought the urge to get obstinate. He nodded. "Thanks. Yeah, of course I'm headed straight home."

Andy performed a quick drumbeat against the roof of the car. "Eve went out with the girls the other night. Did she ever do that when you were with her?"

So that's why he'd pulled him over. The cop was insecure. "At least once, twice a week," Reg told him. "I didn't mind. Like I said, you don't have to worry about Eve."

"If you say so."

"Look, she's your girl now. She's your problem. What you two got going on is your business."

"What are you trying to insinuate?" Andy asked, his voice growing irate. "You think I have something to worry about?"

Eve was driving her new boyfriend wild—that much was obvious. Reg should've shut the hell up, but didn't. "I told you, you don't have to worry about Eve. If you're unhappy, have it out with her. The last person you want involved is me."

"You think so?" Clearly, Andy wasn't pleased. "And why's that?"

"Because the last thing a woman wants to hear is that her ex, *the one she dumped because he was a horrible boyfriend*, might be talking about her, or offering advice to her new lover. Think about it."

Andy saw the sense in what Reg had proposed. "You're probably right. Well, that's all then. You get on home now."

How fucking generous! Andy would let *him* leave? Reg should hop out of the car and kick the ever-loving shit out of the jealous chump, but he didn't. He mumbled something civil and got the hell out of there instead. Most cops were assholes. He always had trouble remembering why he'd ever wanted to be one.

⚕ ⚕ ⚕

"Eve called," Doris said. Reg winced. "She's mad because her new boyfriend said the two of you had a talk about her."

"I don't need this." Reg leaned against the counter for support. "Andy pulled me over last night for no stinking reason—wanted to know if Eve used to go out with her girlfriends when we were dating. I told him he didn't have anything to worry about. Look, I didn't want a ticket. I didn't want any trouble. I could have gotten into it with him, but I behaved myself."

"Eve's upset."

"Here's the deal," Reg said. "She broke up with me. I don't have to talk to her anymore. If she calls here again, tell her I said so."

Doris opened her mouth as if to say something, but closed it quickly. She turned away. "I'll tell her," she called over her shoulder. "I'll tell her to call you at home if she wants to talk, because I'm not interested in being a go-between."

"No, tell her I don't want to talk with her. Simple. That's it. I'm begging off. I'm out of the loop. We're through, and there's nothing more to discuss."

"Fine, I'll tell her to bug off in no uncertain terms."

"Good." He walked over to the coffee urn.

"Can we get back to business?" Doris asked, after she'd returned to her desk. "There's a message from a man who wants you to follow his daughter around because he thinks she's fooling around with his brother—her *uncle*. Isn't that *sick*?"

"How old is his daughter?"

"Seventeen. The brother's thirty-two."

"Great."

"He wants you to get started right away. He says if you can't do it, he'll get somebody else."

"You know what?" Reg told her. "Call him and tell him I wish I could help him out, but my hands are full right now. The last thing I need to do is to follow some wayward girl around and find out she's meeting her uncle. I might find out he's taking advantage of her, and I might tear him a new asshole for being such a degenerate. And, like I said, I don't need trouble."

"I think it's smart of you to pass on this one. Seamy business—*incest*. I jot this all down, you know. Some fine day I'll do something with all these notes. I'll write a doozy of a book."

Her ambition was news to him. "I believe you might, at that," he replied.

"I won a short story contest once. I've read all of Agatha Christie's mysteries. Except for a couple of the more boring ones, and I believe I could write a decent crime yarn."

"Glad to do my part," Reg said, as he poured the dregs of the coffee into his cup.

The landlady had tacked a note to the door. The heater was fixed, and the tap wouldn't drip anymore. Inside, the room was sweltering. Reg checked the thermostat. The repairman had set it at seventy-eight. No wonder it was so damn hot. He changed the setting to sixty degrees and opened a window to cool the place down. Things were all cockamamie. June Gordon was a blackmailer fooling around with Marilyn Palmer's husband, but Reg continued to be intrigued and bewitched by her. And Andy, the jealous cop, sought romantic advice from him about his ex. What a mess.

His perpetually needy stomach growled, so he fixed a ham sandwich. The apartment was not only stifling; it was a damn dreary place. He looked out the picture window beyond the row of tall palm trees to the Hollywood sign in the distance. The sun was about to set. There was a curving snake of bright headlights—a seemingly endless line of commuters. The bread was dry and difficult to chew. He tossed his sandwich off the fire escape. It landed on a small patch of lawn. A needy critter would hopefully enjoy the meal. Wildlife somehow managed to flourish in the city—raccoons, possums, squirrels, and even coyotes.

Reg closed the window and made a mad dash outside. He had to get away. He couldn't bear the stifling room any longer, or the loneliness closing in.

Not anxious to get in traffic with everyone else, he walked down the street to Napoli, his favorite Italian restaurant. The grumpy waiter sat him by the front window and promptly set a bottle of Chianti on the table. "We have a special tonight," he said. "Veal Marsala. Also, the soup comes highly recommended. It's the chef's mother's recipe, two squashes."

Reg felt bad because he wasn't going to order either of the waiter's suggestions. He knew what he liked and he was sticking with it. "Bring a bowl of the minestrone," he said. "And an order of linguini with clam sauce. I'll drink this red with the soup, and I'll have white with the entrée."

The waiter frowned. "The usual," he said.

"What can I say?" Reg told him. "I'm a creature of habit. Nobody else's linguini with clam sauce measures up. Believe me, I've tried it all over town. I always order it when I come here because I can't stand how they prepare it anywhere else."

"I hate to hear that you eat Italian elsewhere," the waiter said, shaking his head as he walked away.

A busboy dropped off a basket of hot bread and the Chianti. Reg eagerly dug into the bread and filled a glass. He leaned back to enjoy the continental atmosphere and flickering candlelight.

A ruckus outside the window caught his attention. Two guys were going at it heatedly. That's how it was sometimes. You could be having a good time, relaxing, but steps away a tussle could be in play. You might be in a nice hotel making love to a beautiful woman, but in the next room, atrocities may be under way. Maybe even homicide. That's how it went. Reg knew how things were and such things bothered him. The two men outside almost came to blows, but the slighter guy backed down. Good move. The bigger guy would've rubbed the pavement with him.

The waiter brought out a bowl of steaming soup. "What's goin' on out there?" he asked.

"It's breaking up."

"Bad for business."

"Don't worry. It's over."

"Last week we had trouble. A drunken bum accosted a customer as they were leaving. I'm afraid this neighborhood's going down the toilet. But the boss can't move. He's got a lease, not to mention the investment in that kitchen, and these fancy new red booths."

Reg shook pepper into his soup. "Blame Stubby's down on the corner," he said. "Taverns draw lowlifes."

"Yes, *Stubby's.*"

Reg took his time with the minestrone and went easy with the bread. He didn't want to fill up, because the linguini was coming.

Reg stopped eating the soup, leaving half of it untouched. He placed the bowl at the edge of the table. When the waiter saw Reg hadn't finished, he frowned again. "What was wrong with it?"

"Nothing. Don't want to get too full."

"Big guy like you—what's the problem?"

"I eat too much, that's all," Reg admitted. "Got to slow down or I'll get porky."

More agitated than ever, the waiter brusquely scooped the bowl into his big hands and took off. A couple entered the restaurant, followed by a trio of businessmen. It was the kind of place that got packed fast. Reg sat in the smoky air, surrounded by nonstop chatter and laughter, clinking silverware, and the music they piped into the room to create ambiance. He recognized the voice of Caruso as he'd grown up with Ruben's favorite operas playing on the phonograph.

The familiar arias and clouds of tobacco smoke reminded him of home, and brought on a melancholy mood. The detective's appetite vanished. The waiter exchanged the bottle of Chianti for a bottle of white, which he'd already opened and placed in a bucket of ice at the side of the table. "Your dish will be right out," he said.

Reg wondered if the sting of losing his mother and stepfather would've been lessened if he'd had siblings to commiserate with. It couldn't be more personal, when death takes the very person who brought you into the world—when you've been robbed of an integral part of your own damn self. Reg filled his glass with the chilled white wine and took a swallow, pushing the sorry lump down his throat, for he knew he was nothing more than a motherless child in need of love.

THIRTEEN
1956

It was customary for Armida to take Lilly to visit her grandmother every Wednesday. Not long after she kissed her little daughter goodbye, Marilyn hurriedly dialed the Western Detective Agency.

"Did you get the test results?" she asked Hartman.

"I just did. I was about to call you. I'm afraid they found arsenic and strychnine."

Marilyn stared out the sliding glass door, past the wispy willow tree to the pond. "Strychnine *and* arsenic?" was all she could think to say.

"Stay put. Wait for me. I'll be right over."

She hung up the phone.

"Who was that?"

She nearly jumped out of her skin. Gary was in the room, standing behind her. "You scared me half to death!"

He smiled. "Half to death? You look fine to me."

"I didn't hear you come in. What are you doing home?"

"Who was that?"

"Nobody."

"Nobody?"

"Nobody important. The tailor, he's taking in that suit for me."

"The tailor? *Is that right?*"

He must have overheard her conversation with Hartman. Marilyn did her best to appear at ease. "Would you care for lunch, Doc?"

"No, I'm not hungry."

"What are you doing home so early in the day?"

"Came to see you. How about a cold one?"

"Sure." The last thing she wanted was a drink, but she was trying to appease him. "Armida took Lilly over to your mother's."

"I ran into them outside," Gary said.

Something about the odd expression on his face spooked her. Marilyn watched as Gary poured the gin. There was no way in hell she would ingest one drop. "Did you see Lilly's little dress?" she asked.

"I didn't notice."

"I finished it this morning. My, but she looks sweet in yellow."

He took his martini shaker in hand. "Lilly is a doll come to life. Dress her in a potato sack and she'd look sweet."

"Why would I dress her in a potato sack?"

"Sometimes you can be so damn literal, it astounds me."

"I'll be right back," Marilyn said. She turned away and made a beeline for the front door.

"Where are you off to?" he asked, as he raised his glass to his lips. "Your drink's ready."

"I need to check the mail, before I forget."

"Are you expecting something special?" he asked, and then he drained the martini in one long gulp.

Marilyn stepped into her Keds. She must not appear frantic. "Oh, you know. Just bills."

Gary set his glass down and reached for hers. "If you don't want this martini, I do. What's so all-fired important? The damn bills can wait."

"I haven't checked the mail in days. I really should…"

He raised his voice. "All I want to do is to share a drink with my wife. Is that too much to ask?"

"Gosh, Gary, relax. I'll be right back."

Once outside, she sprinted down the driveway and up the cul-de-sac. She hid in the bushes to wait for Hartman. From her vantage point, she watched the house. A couple minutes passed before her husband ventured outside and stood by his car. Marilyn watched him cover his eyes to block out the sun as he searched for her in vain. The leaves underfoot crackled beneath her feet. There was a red hibiscus flower not six inches from her face. Gary stood, a sentinel in the middle of the driveway, sipping that confounded martini. What would the neighbors think? Her husband. What a joke—what a cruel joke. She remembered her captain, and a tear came to her eye.

1942

Living alone didn't suit Marilyn, but Wesley's letters kept her sane. She was forced to learn how to handle rationing books, tokens, and the like. Everyone had to make adjustments during wartime. Her car bore a sticker that prominently displayed the letter *A*, which meant she was allowed to buy only four gallons of gasoline a week. After she saw a poster reading, *You ride alone, you ride with Hitler*, she followed the advice of the government and began to drive Freya to and from work. The Jaguar only sat two people, or she would have carpooled with more passengers. She did her best to get with the program, to do without. She even bought the wartime edition of *American Woman's Cookbook*. She studied her handy point chart for processed foods. She consumed far less sugar and reluctantly gave up cigarettes.

On February twenty-third, a Japanese submarine fired on an oil production refinery in Santa Barbara, causing grave alarm and concern along the entire west coast. Two days later, the Battle of Los Angeles ensued. Air raid sirens sounded off as twenty-five silvery plane-like objects made their way slowly from Santa Monica to Long Beach. Fourteen-hundred shells were fired, but no aircraft whatsoever was shot down. Speculation circulated as to whether the silvery objects were indeed airplanes, or weather balloons, or mysterious flying objects from another world. Sometimes Marilyn wished she could take a sleeping pill. But she didn't dare. She was through with drugs. She would drink chamomile tea to make herself sleepy. It was too easy to lie in bed fretting about flying objects and gunfire and bombs and such. Sometimes she was so scared she cried herself to sleep.

Marilyn was so pleased when Freya, her mother, Kika, and their little dog Patch moved in. There was a housing shortage; people poured into the city. Mother and daughter lost their apartment when the lease was up because the landlord threatened to raise the rent by fifty percent. Marilyn offered them two rooms. She now had company at the breakfast table; they read the headlines and analyzed the ongoing drama playing out worldwide. Their companionship did her good.

Wesley wrote from New Orleans:

My Flower,

One of the fellas here in New Orleans is Italian, and he brought me out to the country to his parents' place, where we ate like kings. I tried deep-fried squid, which they call calamari. If you get a chance, try some. I highly recommend it. We tossed the baseball around with his little brother out on the lawn for a bit. What a fine way to spend the afternoon. We ship out the day after tomorrow. After the war's over, I'll bring you down here. The jazz is one reason, the architecture quite another, plus the people are awfully fine. I'd get all poetic on you and stuff but, to tell you the truth, the reality of where I might be going and the inevitability of combat is weighing heavy on me. I wish we could have spent more time together. I wish we'd made a baby before I had to leave. I wish a lot. My wishes get me through. Go find an Italian restaurant and order calamari. I'm anxious to see if you like it as much as I did. And if possible, get your hands on some New Orleans style jazz recordings. You won't be sorry.

All my love,
Your Captain, Wesley

Marilyn stashed all of Wesley's letters in a hatbox under the bed. She read them when she woke up and before she went to sleep. She stashed his father's in her nightstand. She wrote to both of them almost every night, keeping two letters in progress simultaneously. Her correspondence tended to run many pages long and she mailed two a week to Wesley, and one a week to his father.

⊹ ⊹ ⊹

Out of necessity, times were changing. For one thing, women held down jobs that had traditionally been held by men. It seemed odd when Marilyn tried on a pair of shoes and was fitted by a saleslady. Women now worked as bank tellers, aircraft workers, and ship builders. Marilyn was shocked to be greeted by a female mechanic at Tracy's automotive, and to learn that she was the sole proprietor and in charge of the whole shebang.

The wardrobe workroom had undergone many changes, as well. The atmosphere was generally more reserved. The hive behaved like bees enveloped in smoke. Spirits had been dampened and tempered by the war. Those on the home front were encouraged to support the troops, and this was accomplished in many ways.

Freya and Marilyn volunteered to help out at the Hollywood Canteen over on Cahuenga Boulevard. "Bette Davis and John Garfield are responsible for starting the Hollywood Canteen, did you know that?" Freya asked.

Marilyn had been trying to maneuver the Jaguar into a tight spot on a side street. "Of course, everyone knows that," she replied.

"I didn't, not till today. The servicemen must get a kick out of seeing all the famous actors and actresses." That night they had been instructed to tend the soft bar, as they did not offer alcohol at the Hollywood Canteen. Marilyn found herself serving soldiers once again. The irony wasn't lost on her, but she was pleased to dole out sodas and coffee, instead of sex.

"Beryl, is that you!" a soldier cried out.

Momentarily scared out of her wits that someone might have recognized her from the brothel, she was immensely relieved to see Chet Rove. "Chet? *Look at you.* I'm Marilyn now, Marilyn Murray! I got married."

"You did? So did I. But I didn't change my name." He offered one of those kind smiles she remembered fondly. His hair was shorter, but he looked much the same.

"You look good, Chet. I see you're in the Army. My husband's a Navy man."

"Ah, he's a bluejacket."

Marilyn had never heard the term before.

"You're prettier than ever," he said, blushing slightly. She had always been drawn to his reverent demeanor.

"You don't look half-bad yourself."

"Meet me tomorrow?"

"I don't think so."

"Hey, I told you. I'm married, too. A little chitchat's in order, for old time's sake."

"I'll tell you what," she said. "You come over for dinner. My roommates and I will make you a home-cooked meal."

✠ ✠ ✠

Chet arrived on time. He brought his guitar and entertained after dinner. Freya and Kika were rather solemn women. Unlike Junesy and Lydia, they never danced around the house in their stocking feet, they didn't play the piano, and they certainly never sang at the top of their lungs. They crocheted, and Freya furiously worked crossword puzzles. Kika spent loads of time alone in her room. The poor woman had experienced many horrors back in the old country and preferred to be alone with her dark thoughts, or so Freya said.

But that night, Chet had them going. They tapped their feet, hummed, and even laughed out loud.

Chet had to leave early. Marilyn walked him out. "Hey, lovely girl," he said. "Will you write to me? My wife isn't much for letters, and I get awful lonesome."

Marilyn hardly knew how to respond; she was married and found it unfitting to write to another man. She didn't want to hurt Chet, but she had to say no. "I'm sorry your wife is so selfish," she said. "I can't write you, Chet. Try to understand, it wouldn't be fair to Wesley." She regretted inviting the singing cowboy to dinner. She should have known better than to encourage him.

"I hear you," Chet said. "Don't mind me. I'm a homesick fella. I should never have asked you to write. Forgive me?"

"There's nothing to forgive." She decided to offer advice. "Write that wife of yours and tell her what you told me. Tell her you need those letters."

They said their goodbyes, and Marilyn went back inside.

"He's a nice boy," Kika said, as she collected soiled coffee cups and saucers.

Freya threw her two cents in. "Chet's a talented fella. I hope he comes home in one piece to resume his acting career."

Kika paused. "Why do you say that?" she asked.

"Sorry, Mama. But that's how it is, why beat around the bush? He's a soldier, isn't he? You of all people should know what that means."

"Don't be so gloomy," Kika said. "You should find yourself such a nice boy and marry him."

Freya rolled her eyes. Kika had no idea that her daughter was a lesbian and didn't know about Freya's lover, Gladys. Freya visited Gladys all day every Sunday, and would go out to meet her one night during the week. "I'm thirty-six years old," Freya reminded her mother. "I don't think I'll marry now."

The old woman sulked as she carried a tray of cups to the kitchen.

"I'll help," Freya called after her, before turning to let out a snicker and whispering in Marilyn's ear. "Too bad I can't knock Gladys up, so Mama might have a grandbaby to spoil. That would make our relationship worthwhile in her eyes."

Freya and Kika were more troubled than usual when thousands of Japanese were given only forty-eight hours to evacuate their homes, and were housed in barracks before eventually being interned in camps.

"And they call this a free country," Kika said. "We came here to escape this sort of treatment. Two-thirds of those Japanese displaced were born in America, and half of them are children!"

Frustrated, Freya threw her bony hands up in the air. "Hysteria, plain and simple," she said.

Marilyn thought the military must know something that the two of them didn't—surely they must.

Freya began to pace. "The United States was the first country to practice eugenics when they began compulsory sterilization. I fear the direction certain policies are taking."

"What on earth are you talking about?" Marilyn asked. She often felt uninformed and ignorant in the company of her intelligent, knowledgeable friend.

"You don't know *eugenics*?" Freya asked. "To use a German term, *life unworthy of life*. Hitler and his ilk intend to rid the world of the feeble-minded, the insane, the weak, and all homosexuals. And they aren't targeting only those groups. Hitler's now embracing racial hygiene as the so-called final solution for dealing with Jews."

"*Life unworthy of life*," Marilyn repeated.

Kika began to wring her hands. "These monsters, they do all these horrible things in the name of the people. They always claim to act in the best interests of the people."

"The Nazi's are fiends. Have you never heard of Dachau? The rest of the world knows what they are up to, but won't act." Freya said.

Marilyn had never seen Freya so fired up. "But we're in the war now. My husband could die. Many have and will." She thought Freya was far too hard on the U.S. government.

"It's always hard to confront the truth," Freya pointed out. "It's extremely difficult to fathom what atrocities human beings are capable of."

"Spare me, not all that again. *Are you trying to torture me?*" Marilyn couldn't bear to hear of such horror. "Besides, you bring up what the Japanese are capable of, but then you get mad when we round them up and put them in internment camps. Nothing makes sense anymore."

"You have to understand," Freya insisted, "they are Americans! They have assimilated. We all had a reason for leaving our countries to come here. Doesn't anybody think of that? It's not easy, leaving your homeland. You do it for a reason. I feel for those poor people, they have been ripped apart from everything they've worked for. It's a crime."

Kika put her arms around Marilyn. "Stop! This poor girl. Her husband is in harm's way. We should not speak of such things."

"It's time you grew up, Marilyn," Freya snapped.

"We are guests in her house!" Kika cried.

Freya threw her head back and shrieked. "So I'm not free to speak my mind?"

"Of course you are," Marilyn assured her.

Kika began to cry.

"Please, don't do that," Freya said. "I'm sorry, I get so angry." She went to comfort her mother. But Kika became inconsolable and hurried off to her room.

Freya did not go after her mother. She stood in front of the fireplace and continued speaking to Marilyn. "Mama says if women ruled the world, it would be a very different place."

"Maybe," Marilyn said. "Probably."

✚ ✚ ✚

Marilyn took up crochet, but her stitches were irregular and crooked. She tried crossword puzzles, but they bored her silly. She pulled out her sewing machine, which had been relegated to the garage after the sewing room had been turned into Kika's bedroom. Marilyn set up camp in the utility room, where she first sewed a set of frilly floral curtains to brighten up the kitchen. Then she made Kika a few house dresses. Sewing kept Marilyn occupied as letters from Wesley were sporadic, and her insecurities often got the best of her. After all, he was in such close proximity to so many young, virile men. What if Wes decided he didn't love her anymore?

Mr. Murray's letters were always welcome.

Dear Girl,

I'm afraid I had a scare. Thought I had a heart attack last week, but the doctors claim the severe pain I experienced was only angina. I am now on a rather bland salt-free diet, which I hate with a vengeance. I have taken up walking but feel odd indeed as I amble down the street heading nowhere

*in particular. It is not in my nature to amble. I am too old
and out of shape to row as I used to, and so I walk.*

*Yes, letters from Wesley are precious and I wait, as I know
you do, for each and every one. I have become quite religious.
I go to church and pray to God that my son will be spared.
How egocentric of me. But I'm afraid I cannot stop myself
from being so obviously selfish in front of my maker.*

*I'll keep this letter short. (Like father, like son?) I feel tired
tonight and intend to read until I cannot keep my eyes open
anymore.*

> *Your loving father-in-law, Harris Murray*

Marilyn did not attend church anymore. She did not pray, either.
How could she worship a God who was asleep at the wheel? Why
did He let the world go stark raving mad? No, she wasn't about to
pray for Wesley. She hoped the Almighty would find the time to
listen to Mr. Murray, though.

Although she had often criticized others for escaping unpleas-
antness at the picture show or in dance halls, she found music
and movies lifted her spirits immensely. She often went to the
theatre alone.

She just had to go see *For Me and My Gal*, starring Judy Garland
and newcomer Gene Kelly. Mr. Kelly danced remarkably well and
she adored Gile Steele, the costume designer who was responsible
for dressing Mr. Kelly so wonderfully.

Woman of the Year was another MGM picture. Marilyn thought
there was no actress more clever, funny, and classy than Katharine
Hepburn. Spencer Tracy was a marvel. What a team!

One night, Marilyn ventured out to see *Cat People*. The movie
poster intrigued her. It depicted a beautiful woman with a panther
lurking in the background. The caption read: *She was marked with the
curse of those who slink and court and kill by night!*

Marilyn normally didn't go in for spooky pictures, and after
viewing *Cat People*, she remembered why. By the time she arrived
home, her nerves were a jangled mess. She brewed a cup of Kika's

special blend herbal tea to calm them. Freya and Kika's bedroom doors were shut. Marilyn did her best to keep quiet as she carried the cup to her room in stocking feet. The herbal tea did the trick. Her restless mind quieted and she soon fell asleep.

"It's a dream, only a dream," a voice said. Marilyn felt a cool hand against her cheek. She heard the lamp switch click, opened her eyes, and Kika came into focus.

"A nightmare," Kika explained.

Marilyn sat up. She remembered—the cat woman had been after her. And she had turned into a cat, too. Her waking mind felt jumbled and confused. She began to weep.

"Ah," Kika said, sitting on the edge of the bed. Patch, her little Lhasa Apso, followed suit, and then dove under the covers. "What's the matter?"

"I went to see a movie. It was about this woman who came from Serbia, and she happened to be a fashion designer. Anyway, she comes from people who transform into cats, and she fears that when her husband ignites her passions, she'll turn into a cat and kill him. I know it sounds silly, but it must have gotten to me."

"We never know what will haunt us."

"Kika," Marilyn said, "I was raped. Do you think that's what's bothering me?" Marilyn didn't bring up the three-minute men. She could never tell Kika she had once been a whore.

Kika's cloudy grey eyes fluttered and closed. "I too was raped, by three soldiers," she whispered.

"Dear Kika," Marilyn said. "I'm sorry."

"This is how I came to carry Freya."

"Dear Kika," Marilyn repeated. "Does Freya know?"

"Yes," she said, before her mouth became a thin line of resignation. "She knows."

The ficus tree outside Marilyn's bedroom window made an attractive haven for noisy songbirds and she would often wake to a cacophony of peeps, twitters, and squawks. She would feel guilty lying in that sunlit room, warm and safe in her bed, while Wesley was out there in the big world, stuck on that damp ship, living among all those foul-smelling males, navigating foreign waters, and in constant peril.

One such morning, after Marilyn had woken to the songbirds and sat in the cheery breakfast nook with her solemn roommates, tapping against a soft-boiled egg with a butter knife, she wished she could share breakfast with her lively captain instead. When Patch begged for toast scraps, she tossed him bits of crust and longed for the day she would be with Wesley once again.

Freya was reading the morning paper. "The Americans attacked from the air for the first time over Europe," she called out. "Here's a picture of them gunning after German planes."

Kika looked at the photo and let out a sigh. "Talk of war, so early in the morning," she said.

"We shouldn't bury our heads in the sand," Freya warned. "We shouldn't enjoy our comforts and ignore reality."

"And why shouldn't we?" Kika asked, indignantly. "Women do not start these wars. Women do not fight these wars. We are always the victims."

"That old argument! Well, mother, I'm no victim."

Kika shook her head. "How can you say that?" she muttered.

Marilyn missed the way cigarettes had once calmed her nerves. She had to make do with a sip of coffee, and not good coffee, either. Due to rationing, they'd been forced to cut it with chicory and add condensed milk to make it go farther.

Kika pointed towards the icebox. "Care for some jam?" she asked.

Both girls shook their heads no.

"It is not the best, but it is sweet," Kika said, absentmindedly.

"I wish I could run over to Bullock's and buy this suit," Freya said, as she held up the paper to display an appealing full-page ad.

"I can make you one exactly like it," Marilyn told her.

"I can't see spending money on fabric," Freya said. "Besides, where would I wear something so tailored? I don't go anywhere fancy and I dress practically for work."

"Dear girl, try to understand," Kika told Marilyn. "We strive to put away every extra penny, and Freya has never been one for finery. Ironic, isn't it, considering her occupation?"

Marilyn could afford to buy all the fabric she wanted, but she kept her fat bank account to herself and lived frugally. "Clip it out and give it to me," she said, feeling generous. "We'll see what kind of bargain I can find. It's always nice to have a suit hanging in the closet. You never know when you might need one."

"Thank you, but no," Freya said. "It's too extravagant. I need a suit like I need a hole in my head."

✛ ✛ ✛

The tone of Wesley's letters altered. Marilyn noticed detachment creeping into his text. He didn't write about babies. Nor did he mention how he looked forward to taking a spin in his beloved Jaguar, or to going sailing. He wrote about practical things, describing a Moroccan marketplace in detail—the strange spices, a meal of gamey lamb, or how the sweet syrupy tea tasted. He described the desert. Camels were horrid creatures, he wrote. They smelled worse than death.

His tone upset her. She obsessed over his welfare and often stayed up late, sick with worry. She decided to write to her father-in-law and seek his opinion.

Dear Mr. Murray,

Have you noticed a difference in Wesley's letters? I fear he's feeling somewhat downhearted. I suppose I should understand that this is to be expected. But I can't help but feel concerned. It's not that he's pessimistic exactly; he's always very clinical and detached. Maybe that's how one deals with living on a ship and fighting a war. I wouldn't know the first thing about how he must feel. I have stopped reading the papers. I find that my powerlessness only causes me great anxiety and I want to write letters that convey a warm, optimistic tone. I surely don't want to come across as a self-centered wife, insecure and fretful. I don't want to do that. I am anxious to hear your opinion on the matter. Are his letters to you merely an account of the mundane—do they read like a travel guide?

Your concerned daughter-in-law, Marilyn

She pored over the letter Mr. Murray sent in return, looking for clues, and trying to determine if he knew something she didn't. It was maddening, trying to understand what her husband might be going through.

Dear Girl,

Yes, I suppose I have detected objectivity, and an impersonal air in the communications I've received from the boy, of late. But, bear in mind, he is under a great deal of stress and not likely to share all his insecurities and fears with us. And why would he? He may not be able to fully express his misgivings. I served in The Great War. And I would go for months and months without writing home. I simply couldn't think of anything to say. Perhaps we should consider ourselves fortunate that Wes writes us at all?

I had to purchase new clothes, and I am down three belt sizes. It seems my efforts to become healthier are paying off. Winter is here in force. Without my fleshly padding, I am considerably colder than ever. I sit by the fire and pen these letters, dreaming of sunny California and those magnificent orange groves. I will never forget the scent of those white blossoms.

Do your best to keep busy. I'm glad you have Freya and her mother to keep you company, I hate to think of you all alone out there. I encourage you to read. I have just finished A Tale of Two Cities; *I had read the volume many years ago and got far more out of it the second go-round. Do you ever read Dickens? I don't believe I've ever asked you. Or are you more the Austen type? When Wes was in school, he discovered* Lady Chatterley's Lover. *Although certain people consider the novel smut, I do not. People can be such hypocrites! I don't suggest reading it (if it is even possible to get your hands on a copy) with Wes so far away. It would surely stir your emotions and, without an outlet,*

I'm afraid that would prove to be rather frustrating! Please
don't consider this old man too bold. I do ramble on.

Your loving father-in-law, Harris Murray

✚ ✚ ✚

Everyone felt sorry and shocked about the Sullivan brothers and
the mother who tragically lost five sons in one dreadful disaster.
It was customary for a mother to hang a blue star in the window
while her child served. All five of Mrs. Sullivan's sons were aboard
the Juneau when a Japanese torpedo hit the ship. Five blue stars
turned to gold in one window belonging to one mother, and the
country wept in unison.

It was heartbreaking enough, those blue stars in windows here
and there, but the gold stars were a horrifying sight to behold.

"Imagine," Freya said, "those poor fellas whose job it is to deliver
the news to the parents and the wives."

Marilyn shivered.

"Why must you continue to speak of such things?" Kika asked.
"This business of pretending is futile."

"It's not that I'm pretending," Marilyn said. "I'm trying to stay
sane! Can't you imagine what it's like? To love someone the way I
love Wesley, and to wait and wait and wait? Not knowing? Fearing
the worst? Can't you?"

"Of course I can," Freya answered. "I feel for you. I think you
know that. But I'm not good at pretense. I never have been and I
never shall be. I don't see the point in delusion. When we deny reality, we don't do ourselves any favors."

Kika was busy making dough. She had placed the breadboard on
the kitchen table and was going to town, punching and kneading,
kneading and punching. The yeasty aroma permeated the kitchen.

"Oh, hell," Marilyn said. She was thinking about how hypocrit-
ical Freya was. She hid her homosexuality from her mother—so
much for not being a fan of pretense!

"War is hell, everyone knows that," Freya snapped.

"Waiting is worse than fighting, I think," Marilyn said, forcefully.

"Waiting is purgatory, fighting is hell," Kika added.

Marilyn hadn't thought about purgatory in quite some time. The idea of waiting for final judgment sent shivers down her spine.

"Don't forget," Kika said, her accent weighing heavy on the g, "purgatory is temporary."

"It's all temporary," Freya declared.

"No, death is permanent," her mother pointed out.

Fleetingly, Marilyn longed for the sweet release of morphine, which shocked her.

Sensing Marilyn's distress, Freya stepped over to the cupboard and pulled out a bottle of vodka. She poured three glasses, and the women sipped their drinks slowly. Soon, the oven did its job and filled the air with a mouth-watering scent. The timer sounded and Kika removed the bread. She carefully loosened the warm golden loaves from the pans and brushed the fragrant crust with melted butter.

Marilyn drained her glass. She drank alcohol but did not over-indulge, and came to realize she didn't have the personality of an addict after all. She had been forced into addiction. Morphine, Marilyn had learned, was a highly addictive substance.

"We are fortunate," Kika reminded the girls. "I have known true hunger, which is another hellish state."

✥ ✥ ✥

Working at the Hollywood Cantina provided respite from the dreariness of life outside work. Marilyn couldn't spend all her time in the movie theatre, or reading Wesley's letters over and over again. She enjoyed serving sandwiches and beverages, listening to the swing music that was so popular, and watching enlisted men hobnobbing with starlets. She was encouraged to dance, but never did. It didn't seem proper to trip the light fantastic when her husband was off fighting a war.

Unlike some other celebrities Marilyn often saw at work or about town, Gary Cooper was immediately identifiable when he approached her at the Cantina. Those eyes, those penetrating blue eyes locked on to hers, and she saw that he was every bit as dashing in person as he had been on the big screen wearing that foreign legion uniform in the last film she'd seen him in, *Beau Geste*.

"Hello beautiful, what's your name?" he asked.

"Marilyn."

"When do you get off? We could grab a bite."

"I couldn't do that," she said, showing him her wedding ring. "You see, I'm married."

He flashed a cavalier smile. "I'm married too, never stopped me."

"My husband's off to war," she said, feeling indignant. "I could never go to dinner with another man."

His expression changed, his gaze softened. "Good girl," he said. "Your fella's lucky. You're a beaut."

Marilyn had become accustomed to flattery, almost immune. The movie star's behavior put her off but she never told anyone about Gary Cooper's invitation. People thought highly of him; let them have their illusions.

✥ ✥ ✥

They decided to throw a Christmas party. Marilyn and Freya chose a small tree. Since the Jaguar only had two seats, they had to pay extra to have it delivered, despite its diminutive size. They set the fragrant little tree on a table in front of the bay window in the living room and decorated it with tinsel, angel hair, and ornaments bought from Woolworths. Kika produced the beloved angel that had belonged to her mother. Freya climbed up on a chair and wired it firmly in place at the top of the tree.

They set up a makeshift bar in the utility room.

Kika offered to cook, but Marilyn urged her to relax and enjoy the festivities. She hired a catering company to perform the task.

The house was bursting at the seams by ten o'clock. Suddenly, Freya grabbed Marilyn by the arm and led her down the hallway. "Listen," she whispered. "I want you to check out the woman in the kitchen, the one with Audrey. It's none other than Kay Rennick. *Remember her?*"

"Of course I do," Marilyn said. "She's the one that kidnapped June. Look, I don't want any trouble."

"She's with Audrey. They're a couple. I wouldn't worry."

"I never understood why June went off with her in the first place."

"Your friend used to swing both ways," Freya told her.

Marilyn frowned.

"You know how that goes," Freya continued. "Any port in a storm."

"You're wrong." Marilyn snapped, then smoothed her skirt and headed back to the party.

Freya followed her. "Have you ever heard from June?" she asked.

"Not a word," Marilyn said. Freya did not know about Hawaii, and Marilyn intended to keep it that way. Freya knew the two friends had lost track of one another somewhere along the line, but she wasn't the nosy type, and didn't ask many questions.

Freya took hold of Marilyn's arm again. "Look there. That dapper gent is Travis Banton!" They shrank back into the hallway. "You know, *Edith Head's mentor*? He works at Fox now. I need to calm down."

"Relax," said Marilyn. "Breathe." Marilyn had often heard Freya sing Travis Banton's praises because she admired his stunning designs.

"My idol is standing right here, in *our* house." Freya sounded breathless. "I hear he likes to drink. Go offer him liquor."

Marilyn strolled over, introduced herself, and told Travis she worked in the wardrobe department at MGM. She said she admired him greatly, and then got down to the business of asking if he'd prefer a glass of champagne or a cocktail.

"Good Lord," he gushed, "your face is perfectly symmetrical. *And that swan neck.* Turn around."

Marilyn reluctantly did as she was told.

"Why are you behind the scenes? You ought to be on the big screen!"

"I'm shy," she told him. People were gathering. Several nodded in agreement.

"Forget all that. Can you act?"

"I've never tried."

He shook his head. "And that figure. *What a waste.*"

"I agree with you Travis!" a woman Marilyn didn't recognize cried out. "Every time I see her around, I can't help but wonder why she's not an actress."

Freya intervened. "Marilyn's a gifted designer in her own right," she said. "And she does all my sketches, too."

"Is that so?" Travis replied. He took Marilyn by the arm and turned his back on Freya. Marilyn felt horrible. "I'll take that drink now. Lead the way," he declared.

Travis offered to get her a screen test, but Marilyn told him she wasn't interested. No way would she ever step foot in front of a camera. Those days when she foresaw a career as a Hollywood actress seemed ludicrous. Besides, that's all she needed, for some-body to recognize her from the brothel, or to identify her as a former morphine addict. No, she would stay out of sight in the costume department, where she belonged.

✛ ✛ ✛

Wesley Murray, the proud son of a sailor, died not sixteen miles offshore, in the Sicilian invasion. The destroyer he was on board was struck from above by a German dive-bomber. Mercifully, he'd suffered a fatal blow upon impact. Wesley's lifeless body had been hurled into the ocean waters, several onlookers reported.

Marilyn learned of her sweet husband's death and immediately took to her bed. When Mr. Murray telephoned from back east, Freya explained that Marilyn would not stop wailing long enough to muster up the strength to come to the phone. Harris called a local facility and had a qualified nurse sent straight away to tend to his mourning daughter-in-law's needs and welfare. Her name was Sandra Larson. The nurse fed Marilyn tranquilizers and Kika's rich and nutritious beef broth.

Sandra would sit in the kitchen with Kika, Patch atop her bony lap, while Marilyn slept. The women drank tea. Sandra watched the older woman putter and listened to her stories about life in Latvia during the First World War. Her own grandparents had come from Sweden, but she admitted that she hadn't given the First World War all that much thought. Sandra found it interesting to hear about how it used to be back in the old country, and about how the Latvians dealt with the Russian Bolsheviks and the advancing German army.

Marilyn stayed in bed all day long, with her teeth shamelessly on display in a jar on the nightstand. She kept a pillow over her head to block out unwanted light. Every last ounce of her strength had been squelched, she was sure of it. There was nothing left for her now. She was twenty-two years old and all used up. How could she ever return to Ma and Mémère? How would she face either one of them? She'd gone off in search of a pipe dream, only to fall prey to depravity and prostitution, her good name a faint memory. Beryl Quinn was dead and gone. And now, Marilyn's only hope for happiness, her one true love, was but another lost remembrance. She felt the memory of Wesley slip away. What did his laugh sound like? How had his fingers felt upon her skin? His lips upon her lips? If only they had made a baby. Marilyn mourned not only for the loss of her young husband, but also for the loss of a child never conceived. How different things would be if she had a child to care for in his absence—a living, breathing reminder of Wes, her captain.

Mr. Murray came out for a visit in March. He reserved a room at the Hotel Knickerbocker, as he had enjoyed his previous stay. Marilyn wondered if his secretary had accompanied him. His first night in town, Kika went all out and prepared a lovely meal of pickled mushrooms, borsch, breaded pork chops, and sauerkraut. For dessert, she made a raspberry torte.

"Such wonderful food—I'm likely to put back on every last pound I lost," Harris told Kika. She took it upon herself to cut him another slice of torte and pour another cup of coffee.

"I've never met anyone from Latvia before," Harris told her.

"My country is small. We live in the shadow of Russia to the east, with the Baltic Sea to the west."

"As a young man, I traveled extensively. I have been to Sweden."

"We are quite different than the Swedes, in culture and in language."

"Do you miss home?"

"Yes and no. And so it goes."

Harris nodded. "And so it goes," he repeated. His voice cracked and Kika's eyes filled with tears. The old woman spent much of her time deep in thought, reliving the past, and now Marilyn would, too.

They made a gloomy trio. Freya's reluctance to be around their despondent souls was apparent. She couldn't wait to bolt. When Gladys came to pick her up, she tossed out a polite goodbye, and hurried out the door.

"You must come with us tomorrow," Harris told Kika. "We're driving out to Redlands, where the orange groves meet the foothills of the mountains."

Kika rarely left the house. "No, Mr. Murray," she replied. "Thank you, but no. I am happy here. The riding in the car, it makes me sick to my stomach."

"But have you seen the orange groves?"

"Bring me back the fruit," she said. "I'll make juice and little cakes."

✛ ✛ ✛

Marilyn drove the Jaguar. The top was lowered and the sun was intense and, even though she wore sunglasses, her eyes remained in a permanent squint.

"I have something to tell you, Mr. Murray," she said.

"Call me Dad, won't you?"

Marilyn complied. "Well, Dad, Wesley put a ton of money in a bank account with my name on it. His mother left it to him, and I know you didn't know about it."

Harris threw back his head and laughed. "Coconspirators, those two. Don't worry. I knew."

"You did?"

"That money was hers, to manage as she saw fit. I just didn't understand why she didn't leave any to our other son, Earl, but maybe she figured he didn't need it as much as Wesley did. I think she thought Wes was going to have a harder time of it. Mother and son were extremely close."

"I know that much. Wes told me."

"She felt I was too hard on the boy. And maybe I was."

"He adored you."

"And I adored him. But I won't paint a rosy picture; I was an ambitious man and an absentee father. My wife, bless her soul, was overprotective of Wesley. She practically suffocated the boy. He wasn't close to his brother, either, which complicated matters. Maybe it's because Earl was six years older than him, or maybe it was something else. Who knows? When I wasn't busy working, I took the boys sailing. That was our bond."

"I hope you don't mind that I sold Wesley's sailboat," Marilyn interjected. "It broke my heart to do it, but I had to. I don't know the first thing about boats, and I know you already have one."

"I understood."

"Sorry, I didn't mean to interrupt."

"All I was saying was I sure wish I had a do-over. But we don't get do-overs in this life."

"Wouldn't that be something?" Marilyn said. Given the chance, she would choose to do so many things differently.

✛ ✛ ✛

Marilyn found Redlands beautiful. The mountains loomed so close, it seemed as if she could reach right out and touch them. They were covered in snow that had fallen during a storm a couple of days before, even though the weather had since turned warm, as it usually did in Southern California.

They stopped by to visit a friend of Mr. Murray's who lived in a lovely Victorian, smack dab in the middle of an orange grove on Citrus Avenue—how appropriate. Carl and Jeanette Sanders had left Boston before the war, after Carl inherited the house and its extensive groves from an uncle.

Carl put his arm around Mr. Murray. "You ought to sell out and come west," he advised.

"Business is going like gangbusters with this war on and I can't leave my interests," Harris replied. "But I tell you, it's tempting. I left thirty-degree weather and icy conditions behind."

Jeanette took Marilyn by the arm and walked her through the kitchen, out to the massive back porch. "Sit right down," she said. "Funny how riding in a car for any amount of time can take it out of a person."

Marilyn took a seat on the wicker chair offered. Beyond the porch was a flower garden surrounded by a white picket fence, with a statue of a child amongst the blooms. Beyond that, row after row of orange trees with dark shiny leaves stretched on and on.

"I noticed your accent, Jeanette. Because you don't sound remotely Bostonian."

Jeanette smiled sweetly. "I'll say not. I'm from Georgia. Went from peaches to apples, and now to oranges."

"I'm originally from Detroit," Marilyn told her.

"How long have you been out here?"

"Not long, a few years."

Jeanette's eyes lit up. "I hear you work at MGM. That must be exciting as all get out!"

"I mostly sketch and sew. Believe me, it's not as marvelous as it sounds."

"But Lordy mercy, you're surrounded by beautiful costumes and *movie stars.*"

"Yes…well."

"Name names. Who have you met?"

People who weren't surrounded by celebrities just didn't understand. No member of the workroom team should—or would—ever fawn over actors or actresses. Everyone was expected to keep their distance and act respectful and dignified.

"It's not as if I'm friendly with any of them," Marilyn said.

Jeanette poured two glasses of lemonade. "Don't split hairs, darlin'."

Marilyn couldn't help but giggle. "Okay," she said. "Names? Let's see… Greer Garson, Irene Dunne, Norma Shearer, and how about Clark Gable, Shirley Temple, Micky Rooney, and my personal favorite, Judy Garland. How's that?"

"*Do go on,*" the lady of the house insisted.

"I volunteer at the Hollywood Canteen, so I've seen Bette Davis, Frank Sinatra, George Raft, and Lana Turner. I've learned that celebrities are people, imperfect and flawed to be sure."

"I saw Ingrid Bergman once," Jeanette confided. "She was as pretty in person as she is on the screen—so European. Who's the most beautiful actress you've ever seen?"

"I'm going to say Lana Turner. She's the same age as me, a couple of months older. And she's fresh-looking."

"Ah, come on," Jeanette said. "*Lana Turner?* I can't stand that tramp. You're *ten* times prettier than her—why, you could be a *star.* I used to be quite a looker in my day, too. But I up and lost my looks. They flew the coop in my forties when I wasn't payin' any attention."

Marilyn thought about Kika, and how she had said the exact same thing, but in her own way. Kika told Marilyn how one day she felt attractive, but not the next. When she looked in the mirror, it seemed her reflection had changed virtually overnight, as if a magical spark inside her had gone up in smoke. "Poof," she had said, eerily. "You see, it is in the eyes. The light goes out."

Jeanette sighed. "There are worse things," she noted, philosophically. "Once your looks go, you can make better friends with women. The competitive factor dissipates. And you don't have to worry about impressing men—you can finally take a breath and relax." When Jeanette said relax, it sounded like *ree-la-xx*.

Marilyn nodded. She thought it might be nice to ree-la-xx…

On the way home, Mr. Murray fell asleep. He slept all the way from San Bernardino to Santa Monica. Upon waking, he cleared his throat and complained about being such a self-centered buffoon.

"Nonsense," Marilyn said, "it's been a long day. Do you want to come over, or should I drop you off?"

"Drop me off, but come inside, won't you? I want you to meet someone."

And that someone Harris was anxious for Marilyn to meet was his secretary, Clara Tucker. Their suite was huge, and Clara was anxiously waiting. She looked to be a good deal younger than Mr. Murray, a vivacious redhead with a buxom build and remarkable topaz eyes.

"I've heard a lot about you, Marilyn," she said. "Please accept my condolences about Wes."

They sat down. Clara uncorked a bottle of wine and they got to know each other.

"The first time I met Wesley, he was fourteen years old," Clara shared. "He told me that I had nice breasts and I nearly choked on an olive!"

"He was a bold lad," Harris declared.

"He was up front about everything," Clara said. "And I mean *everything*!"

"He really was," Marilyn told her. "I've never met anyone quite like Wesley. And I don't expect I ever will."

"He was so sweet," Clara said, wistfully. "Sage for one so young, and so insightful."

Marilyn smiled. "He was wise, wasn't he?"

Harris stood up. "I will never get over losing him."

Marilyn stood up too. "Me neither, Mr….I mean, Harris," she said.

"Music!" Clara cried. "I'm phoning down to the desk for a phonograph. Wesley adored music!"

"I have a better idea," Harris said. "Let's go out. Call for a car! We'll go dancing."

Marilyn didn't protest. She knew that Wesley would want her to go out with his father and Clara.

FOURTEEN
1956

Reg had just turned onto the cul-de-sac when Marilyn materialized from the manicured shrubbery that ran along a high fence line. Stunned by the distraught expression on her face, he swerved to the side of the road. She scrambled over to the passenger side of the car, opened the door, and stuck her head in.

"What the hell were you doing, hiding in the bushes?" he asked.

"Gary knows I know!" she cried, her voice unrecognizably shrill. "He heard me on the phone with you. He's in the house. I thought you'd never get here."

Two police cruisers whizzed by and pulled into the Palmer driveway. "Did you call them?" she asked.

"Nope," he replied. "I wanted to meet with you first. So, if I didn't call, and you didn't call, who did?"

"I can't imagine."

"We'd better go see," Reg said. Marilyn hopped in and he drove straight ahead and parked near the mailbox.

A cop positioned in front of the door queried Marilyn as they approached the stoop. "Who're you?" He had a strange accent, one Reg couldn't peg.

"Marilyn Palmer. I live here."

"Stay put. Don't move a muscle, and I *mean* don't move a muscle," the cop said, before ducking inside.

Reg scowled. "Why are cops so curt?"

A few minutes passed, and a different officer opened the door and peered out. "Mrs. Gary Palmer?"

"Yes," Marilyn said.

"Got any I.D.?"

"Inside. My purse is sitting on the bench in the entry hall."

"Hold on," he said.

The second cop reappeared. "We got a call. A woman claimed that a Dr. Palmer was trying to poison his wife."

Marilyn looked at Reg. "A woman called?" she asked. "Well," she added, "you need to know I have no idea who that woman might be, but I am aware of the poisoning."

"*Is that so?*" the cop asked.

Marilyn pointed towards Reg. "This is Reg Hartman, a detective I hired. I suspected that my husband was tampering with my medicine. Who called you?"

"I can't answer that," the cop told her. "Look, you two go back to the car and wait there. Don't even think about leaving. Officer Heinz will be watching you."

Reg nodded and led the way to his car. "I'm guessing June Gordon turned Dr. Palmer in," he said, once they were seated.

"I wonder why she'd do that?" Marilyn asked.

"Who can say? At this point, it's anybody's guess."

"This beats all. My husband—my very own husband. You know, I've never been one for mysteries. Maybe if I'd read more of them, I would have caught on. I knew Gary was hard on me, and he wasn't the most affectionate husband, but I foolishly believed he cared for me in his own way."

Reg studied her face. It appeared she wasn't wearing any makeup whatsoever, and yet even with her auburn hair pulled back in a ponytail, the woman was still radiant. Hard to say what had gone through the doctor's mind, but if Reg had a wife as beautiful as Marilyn, he couldn't imagine cheating on her. It was time to fill his client in on a few key details.

"I have to tell you, June was seeing Gary before you ever met him. Seems she told him all about you, about how beautiful you were, and about how the two of you had come out west from Detroit."

Marilyn wouldn't have looked more wounded if Reg had hauled off and slapped her across the face. "They were together, before I ever met him?" she asked. "He knew who I was all along? How do you know all this?"

"I went undercover. June believes my name is Stephen, and she confided in me. I've got something else to tell you, so brace yourself."

When Marilyn's pretty brow furrowed, he felt like a bad guy for delivering more terrible news. Reg knew he'd better come right out with it. He took in a deep breath then let it out. "Gary broke it off with June because she couldn't have children," he said. "As you know, he was determined to have kids. And afterwards, June returned to San Francisco."

"She did?"

"While she was in Frisco, June started an affair with a guy she used to know. Some guy with a sick wife and a kid."

Marilyn put her hand to her chin and paused to think for a moment. "*Woody*?" she asked.

"You know the guy? Well, seems they saw each other for a time, but he wasn't about to leave his wife. They broke up, and June married and divorced some bum, and that's how she ended up with the name Gordon. Eventually, she returned south. When she learned Dr. Palmer had married you, she went nuts."

"Junesy's been awfully busy."

"No kidding. She cornered Gary, to have it out, and somehow he convinced her to start seeing him again."

Reg paused to give Marilyn time to absorb what he'd just told her. "I'm sorry to be the one to tell you all this," he added after a moment.

Understandably, Marilyn was overcome. Before his distressed client had a chance to respond, another car drove up. The plain-clothes detectives had arrived on the scene.

Marilyn didn't seem to notice. "Gary was June's lover, before we ever met?" she muttered.

Reg realized what a tough pill it was to swallow. "That's what she claims."

"I believe her," Marilyn said. "Do you?"

"Yeah, I believe it's all true."

"Gary knew I was lying about being an orphan all along?" Marilyn's nose was leaking, but she didn't seem to notice, or maybe she just didn't care. "He knew who I was? He knew my name was Beryl Quinn?"

Reg fished around in the glove compartment for unused napkins, located a couple, and handed them to her. "I'm afraid so," he said.

June's jalopy careened up the cul-de-sac. She slammed on the brakes, barely missing one of the parked cruisers. The car door flew open and she tore straight for the door.

"Junesy!" Marilyn cried. She dropped the napkins and took off after her.

Reg should have stayed behind, but didn't have the good sense.

June screamed at the cop who stood guard at the door. "Let me see him!"

"Look, lady," the irate cop told the hysterical blonde. "Give it up. You aren't going in there."

"Junesy!" Marilyn cried once more.

June turned and gaped at Marilyn. It was as if she'd seen a ghost.

"Mrs. Palmer," the cop said, "I told you to wait in the car."

Marilyn ignored the cop and faced June. "You're the one who called, aren't you?"

June ignored the question. Wearing a confused expression, she turned to Reg and cried "*Stephen*? What are you doing here?"

"His name's not Stephen," Marilyn snapped. "This is Detective Hartman."

June rushed at Reg and hit him in the chest with both hands. It hurt—for a tiny woman she was strong as hell.

"Hold on!" the cop yelled. "Simmer down, missy!"

Reg pulled June away from the scene and into a stand of young birch trees at the side of the property. "Listen to me," he whispered. "Get ahold of yourself. You don't want them to know you tried to blackmail Marilyn, do you?"

Marilyn joined them. "I won't protect you," she warned June.

June glared at her old friend. "Have it your way. When Gary told me what he was up to, I called the cops. I might be a lot of things, but I'm not willing to be an accomplice to murder. Gary wanted you out of the way so he could marry me and keep Lilly. He had a duffel bag containing the bottles of tainted Milk of Magnesia. I thought they might be hard evidence, so I threw them in the trunk of my car."

"And just when did Gary tell you that?" Reg asked.

"Just today." She then turned to Marilyn. "I had no idea, I swear, Beryl."

Marilyn scowled. "How dare you call me Beryl?"

The hurt registered on June's face. "Have it your way, *Marilyn*," she said.

Moments later, a couple of plainclothes detectives emerged. They told the three of them to get down to the station for questioning, straight away.

Reg turned to June after the cops rushed back inside. "We're off to see the wizard," he said. "Park your car across the street, grab those bottles, and ride over with us."

June did as she was told, no argument.

On the way over to the station, Reg turned to Marilyn. "You have a decision to make," he told her. "Will you turn her in?"

June had curled up in the fetal position in the backseat. "I don't care if she turns me in," she wailed. "I'm sick with it. I've brought nothing but trouble Beryl's way — nothing but trouble."

"Oh shut up!" Marilyn said. "I can't hear myself think with you bellyaching back there. And stop calling me Beryl."

"It was such a shock!" June said. "To discover you two were married. You don't know what I've been through!"

Marilyn turned around. "You tried to blackmail me!"

"I needed money! I wanted to get the hell out of here and go back to Hawaii."

"Hawaii!" Marilyn exclaimed. "Don't tell me you actually *want* to go back to that island? Do you know what Alberta did to me? Why would you set me up like that?"

Reg wondered what had happened in June's so-called paradise.

"Do you think it was a picnic for me?" June cried.

Marilyn's face grew red. "You know what? I don't give a damn what it was like for you."

"Okay, all right," Reg said. "Listen, it's not a long drive to the station. We have some tough decisions to make before we get there. What's our story?"

Doris waited patiently for Reg to return. "I wasn't going to leave until you got here," she told the detective. "So I kept myself busy. I finished all my paperwork, cleaned the coffee station top to bottom, swept the floor, and did some filing. I'm telling you, I'm beat. I thought you'd never get here."

It was long past closing time and nobody was around, so there wasn't the usual need to go upstairs to his office to carry on a private conversation. Reg took a seat behind the counter, and the secretary poured them each a stiff jigger of Jim Beam.

"Lay it on me," she said. "All the juicy details. Don't be sketchy."

Reg belted back his drink and let the warmth sink in. "I got over there to find Marilyn waiting for me, *in the bushes mind you*, hiding from Dr. Palmer. Seems he had snuck in the house and listened in on her end of our telephone conversation, that's how he discovered that she knew about the poison."

"Hell's bells," Doris said, her color high.

"The cops showed up and they wouldn't let us in the house. They told us to wait in the car. Naturally, we did. We were out there when June showed up. Man, she was fit to be tied."

"The blackmailing blonde?"

"Yep, turns out she was the one who called the cops. You see, the doctor confessed. He told June he was trying to slowly poison his wife so they could be together."

Doris hung on to the detective's every word.

"Now, bear in mind, June had told him that ulcers killed Marilyn's father. So he must have put two and two together. His wife had a history of stomach problems. He studied her symptoms for a while and figured he could blame Marilyn's death on bleeding ulcers. That's why he was poisoning her slowly, bit by bit."

"What a slime-ball," Doris declared.

"Those two started going hats and bats, right outside the house, with *the cops inside*, so I did my best to defuse the situation. I felt sorry for June. I knew if Marilyn turned her in for the blackmail, she'd be in for it."

"You felt sorry for June Gordon? Jumping Jehoshaphat, if that don't beat all!" Doris reached over and refilled Reg's glass, but she hadn't touched hers.

Reg nodded. "June Gordon is one complicated broad. I guess all you women are. I don't know. Anyway, Marilyn didn't bring up the blackmail to the cops. When we heard what Dr. Palmer had done inside the house, the three of us went blank. We were all in shock. Just dumbfounded, absolutely dumbfounded. I still can't believe it."

Doris placed her hand against her cheek. "Well, tell me, just what did that nutcase doctor do?"

Reg took another quick drink. "After he overheard Marilyn talking to me on the phone, he went over to the bar and whipped up a batch of martinis. He tried to get her to join him, but she made up a story about checking the mail and hightailed it outta there. So, the doctor proceeded to drink the entire batch of martinis on his own."

"What a lush."

"Well, the lush up and died. Those martinis were poisoned."

"He committed suicide?"

"That he did. I guess he figured it was just a matter of time before his house of cards crumbled. So he just checked out to avoid disgrace, certain scandal, and a trip to the big house."

"What a strange man. Most people would figure a guy like Dr. Palmer had it made in the shade. I mean, he had it *all*. Came from a good family with plenty of money, had a successful career and a beautiful wife, but he put it all on the line. Very strange behavior."

"It is mystifying."

"Mark my words, you be careful. That June Gordon is trouble with a capital *T*."

"Hey, don't forget, June was the one who discovered the empty Milk of Magnesia bottles in the motel room where they had their trysts. And she did turn them in. So, thanks to her, we have concrete evidence."

"I wouldn't trust that blonde farther than I could throw her," Doris said. "The doctor's dead. Who needs more evidence? He's gone."

"Wait a minute, *June's sorry*. She really is."

"What about Marilyn?"

"She's in the hospital. They put her into detoxification immediately. Now that they know what's in her system, they can give her antidotes. Dangerous business, being poisoned over God only knows how many days or months. She's lucky to be alive."

"What they say is bloody right, about truth being stranger than fiction," Doris said, when she finally reached for the whiskey.

✥ ✥ ✥

Javier had cleaned the little house thoroughly. Every stick of furniture was gone, and he had repainted the place. The walls were stark white and devoid of personality, and the floors were scrubbed. A dozen or so boxes were piled on the front porch.

"The fridge wasn't working properly," the old bachelor told Reg. "Wouldn't keep the milk cold. I replaced it with a used one. You owe me twenty-four bucks."

"I owe you more than a few lousy bucks," Reg said. "You've done a lot of work here. Plus there's the cost of the paint."

"Ah, my brother-in-law gave me the paint. If you look close, you'll see that the white in the bedrooms is cooler, and the white out here in the living areas is warmer."

Reg figured white was white. "It's clean," he said. "It's so much better."

Javier led the way. "Come see the bathroom."

Reg stuck his head through the door for a look-see. The chipped tub had been replaced with a tiled walk-in shower, and where the old pedestal sink had once stood was a vanity cabinet fitted with a built-in sink bowl. The tiny bathroom had been transformed from shabby to presentable.

"Holy smokes, Javier," Reg declared. "I owe you big time."

"Nobody takes baths these days," the old bachelor said. "It's all about the shower."

They loaded the boxes into Reg's car. "Come on," he told Javier, "I'll buy you lunch."

They drove over to Javier's cousin's place, Casa Flores, where they met up with several of his amigos. Rounds of tequila shots, slices of lime, and tomato juice chasers were ordered all around. Javier's cousin's wife brought out platter after platter of tacos and chimichangas. Reg enjoyed authentic Mexican food.

"The cold hard fact," one of Javier's louder friends shouted, "is this entire area's turning into a shit hole, nothing but a shit hole. I'm moving to Riverside—it's nice out there."

"Nah," another friend told him. "You gotta go farther out, man. I prefer the desert. Indio. Land is cheap out there."

The old bachelor's eyebrows twitched. "You can't leave Montebello," he said. "This is our home."

"Times are changing," the cousin's wife replied. "Montebello's getting too congested."

Reg listened as they hashed it out. If possible, he would live in San Diego. San Diego was a nice town. Hell, he liked where June Gordon lived, out in San Pedro. He took it easy and relaxed under the influence of the tequila, daydreaming about the various interconnected towns that made up the fabric of Southern California.

When Danni Lopez showed unexpectedly, Reg asked for two more beers and they took a seat in the back, in a private booth.

"What a turn of events," Danni said. "Who would have thunk the doctor would do himself in?"

"Not me," Reg answered.

"Son of a bitch, how could he willingly drink poison? I'm somewhat of a gore hound, and I can tell you, he basically suffocated."

"What about Marilyn? She's got that shit in her tissues. Can't help but wonder what the long-term effects might be."

Danni gulped the beer greedily. She set the bottle down. "I hope she's in the clear. By the way, I managed to debug June Gordon's place."

"Good, thanks. Well, I can say this much for June—at least she drew the line at murder."

"I was shocked to hear Marilyn didn't turn her in."

"If not for June, Marilyn might not be here."

"I suppose," Danni conceded.

"As it goes, Marilyn figures the doctor did them both wrong. Hey, how'd you know I was here?" Reg suddenly thought to ask.

"I dropped by your Mom's place. People were moving in, and they said you'd come over here with Javier."

"Aha."

"I thought maybe I could help you load up, but they said you only took a few boxes."

"Just some of Mom's stuff, and my yearbooks and trophies from school. There's not all that much I'm interested in."

"Good policy," she said. "I figure the least amount of crap I accumulate, the least amount of crap I have to worry about. I travel light. In this line of business, you see what money and possessions can do to people. Plus, my mother's the most materialistic woman I ever met. She's one sick puppy. I vowed I was never gonna place so much importance on *things*."

Reg had met Danni's mother. Danni didn't resemble her in any way, shape, or form. "You're the polar opposite of your mother," he assured her.

Danni pulled her head back and smirked. "You can say that again. Hey," she added, "on a side note—did you know June Gordon's waiting tables at a place called Pago Pago?"

Reg cracked a smile. "She sure goes in for those tropical-themed joints."

"So, onto the new. What's this other case Doris called me about?"

"Another worried wife. She thinks her husband's planning on setting fire to their mattress factory, which has been running in the red, so he might cash in on the insurance loot. She doesn't want to turn him in if she's mistaken, but she doesn't want him to go through with it, either."

"Should I tail him?"

"Yep. Here's his name and address." Reg reached into his pocket and pulled out a piece of paper, then handed it to Danni.

"What the hell am I supposed to do if he turns out to be a fire bug?"

"Break out the marshmallows?" Reg offered. He saw Danni's alarmed expression. "Sorry about that, just a lame joke. This is a hard one. I've been wondering how we find out what's on this fella's mind? It's not likely he's running around telling anybody about his plans, except the wife, *the woman he mistakenly thinks he can trust.*"

"I'll get on it. He'll probably go shopping for whatever it is you shop for when you're about to burn down a mattress factory. Then we'll have proof."

"You're on the right track."

"Okay," Danni said, standing up. "I guess I'd better quit swilling brewskis. Sounds as if I have my work cut out for me."

Danni took off and Reg walked over and nudged the half-tanked Javier. "Come on, pal," he said. "I'll take you home."

"I'm staying put," the old bachelor said. There was a stubborn edge to his voice, as if he thought Reg might try to talk him into leaving, which would have been sensible. "You go on ahead."

"Suit yourself," Reg told him. He wasn't up for persuading anyone to do anything they didn't want to do.

He drove by the old place for one last look. The family had settled in already. Two little kids were playing tag in the side yard. When he looked out his car window, old memories had their way with him. Soon, the woman sent one of the kids over.

"Mama wants to know if you'd like to come in for a cup of coffee, Mr. Hartman."

"No thanks," he answered. To the kid, he probably looked like some creepy old white landlord. With that image in mind, he vamoosed.

Reg drove clear out to Pago Pago in Long Beach, as there was an outside chance June might be working. Maybe Doris was right—maybe he should have his fool head examined.

June was at work, busy filling numerous pairs of salt and pepper shakers, but she hadn't seen him yet. Reg took a seat at the bar and ordered a beer. That's when she spotted him, but didn't budge. She topped off each shaker carefully, robotically.

The once-pleasant buzz from the tequila had left him and he hoped to stave off an inevitable headache by drinking a bit more. If June didn't acknowledge him soon, he'd get the hell out of there and find some dinner. He was a knucklehead to think he'd ever be able to make amends with her. Reg wasn't sure he understood why it mattered what June Gordon thought about him, why he worried about her, or why he was drawn to a woman with so many faults, one who was capable of such twisted deeds.

A supervisor came out from the back room and asked June if she wouldn't mind working late because one of the other waitresses had called in sick.

"Why not?" she said. "I don't have anything else to do." She looked at Reg. "And God knows I need the money."

The supervisor nodded and returned to the back room.

Reg got up and walked over to her. "For the record," he said, "I wish we'd met under different circumstances."

The way she paused before she answered and the stricken look on her face caused Reg to regret the surprise visit. Same old thing—he didn't know how to leave well enough alone. He'd never known when to give up, or when to back down. He had a habit of going after hopeless causes. That's why he had left the force. He just never learned how to let sleeping dogs lie.

He took in the pseudo-tropical décor. June wanted to return to Hawaii in the worst way, but she'd been forced to settle for *such a pathetic substitute*. He returned to the bar, drained the dregs of the beer, and dropped a bill down for the bartender.

Reg was almost out to his car when June emerged from Pago Pago.

"Hartman," she called, "I'd ask how you know where I work, but then, you are a detective. Why come here? I can't figure you out."

"I just wanted to see you," he said. "Kind of stupid, I guess."

"I think so."

"Yeah, well…"

"Thanks for talking Marilyn out of turning me in." June took a step backward and signaled her retreat into the tropical oasis. "I'd be in big trouble if it wasn't for you."

"I didn't talk her out of it. I discouraged her. I think your decision to call the police held a lot of weight."

"Anyway, thanks. I'd better get back. We're running a special on Pupu platters tonight. It's a sure bet it'll be busy. Goodbye, Hartman." She turned around and made a speedy beeline for the door. They sure did dress the waitresses in snazzy outfits. She looked cute as she ducked inside, with blonde curls bobbing.

Reg unlocked his car door, climbed in, and the dreaded headache kicked in with a vengeance. What business did he have, pounding shots of tequila in the middle of the day? He really shouldn't start up unless he intended to drink all night.

Exhausted, Reg unlocked the door to his apartment, intent on more than a little shut-eye. Needless to say, the sight of Eve's cop boyfriend at his kitchen table, in uniform, eating his Fig Newtons, more than rattled him.

"Make yourself right at home," Reg said. "Don't mind me."

"I let myself in. Eve still had a key. Did you know that? I set it over there on the coffee table."

Reg circled Andy Bell. He debated whether or not he should listen to what the asshole had to say, or if he should maybe smack him around some. "What do you want?"

"Are you fucking my woman?"

"Is that what this is all about? Why involve me in your business? If I wanted Eve, I would've treated her better, and she would have stuck around."

"Why didn't you want her anymore? You find out she was cheating?"

"No—get that through your thick skull. She wanted to get married, and I didn't. Now clear out of here."

"I'd marry her," the cop said. "But she thinks I'm too jealous."

"No shit?"

"I don't know how you gave her up. She's like cocaine to me. I'm crazy about her. I can't get enough."

"Take your story somewhere else," Reg said. His head was pounding. He went to the fridge for a little hair of the dog that bit him, grabbed a beer, popped it open, and emptied most of the contents in a few hungry gulps. His life was getting crazier and crazier.

"Hey, where's your hospitality?"

The cop had a screw loose somewhere. Reg gave him the evil eye. "Look, you crazy son of a bitch, hit the road." Reg walked over to the door, opened it, and made a sweeping motion with his hand to indicate he wanted him out, and *now*.

Andy didn't budge. His eyes were closed.

Reg slammed the door. He stood at the window and finished his beer to give Andy time to get it together. Outside, the Foursquare church across the way was filling up. He watched a terrier chase a tomcat down the sidewalk and a Mexican push his tamale cart across the street. Eventually, Reg's gaze drifted up toward the hills. He noticed that someone had blacked out the "Holly" on the Hollywood sign—it simply read, *wood*.

Andy raised his head and cleared his throat. "I'm losing it," he said, looking at Reg. "If a woman has the ability to make a man this loopy, he ought to give her up."

"You're using your bean now."

"You advising me to leave Eve?"

"Hell no, I'm not telling you to do anything. You made a statement and I agreed with you—nothing more, nothing less."

"The thing is, I'm not ready to give her up."

"Why don't you go home? Talk to *her*."

"How do you *do it*?"

"Do what?"

"How do you keep your head? How do you stay so detached? Eve says you're coldhearted. How do you *not* care? I lose my head and then I can't get my bearings. I always fall for them. I fall hard, and usually make a fool out of myself. Eve stays out too late and I imagine she's with you or some other cop. Guys like you have it made in the shade. Coldhearted bastards like you get all the women. They dig that hard-to-get shit."

"I'm not hard to get," Reg told him. "I'm hard to keep."

Andy nodded. "I see how it is. I do."

"My patience is wearing thin," Reg warned.

"Are you honest with your women?"

"From the get-go. I tell 'em I'm in it for the company, and for a few laughs."

"Who the hell isn't?" Andy cried, with a pinched face.

"Some guys want the whole ball of wax—marriage, kids, the mortgage, and all that jazz. Some guys go for that life."

"I'm guess I'm one of those guys, I want all that," the cop admitted.

"Eve does too—what's the problem then?"

"She claims I'm pathologically jealous, and out to control her."

"I can see why she'd get barmy." Reg dropped his empty bottle in the trash and fetched another. Andy didn't dare ask to be included.

"I vow to behave myself but I act stupid, like coming here tonight."

"It *was* stupid to come here. It was stupider to let yourself in."

"I know."

Reg sat across from him and gave him the evil eye once again. "I might have responded violently. You don't know me. You think because you're wearing that uniform, you're safe? It doesn't work that way."

"I got a gun," Andy said.

Reg slammed his hand on the table. "So what? So do I! So do half the clowns in this town, you fucking idiot."

"You have a gun? Is it legal?"

"That's it," Reg said. "I've been more than cordial, considering the circumstances. This conversation's over."

"I hate being a cop. I'm not cut out for this line of work. Eve's against my quitting the force."

"Eve likes a man in uniform."

"She told me she made an exception for you."

"Did she now?"

"My father owns a window-washing outfit in Fresno. I want to go back to work there. One day he might turn the whole shebang over to me. That's a future. You think Eve sees it that way? No."

"Look, pal. I can't help you."

"You quit, though. She stayed with you."

"Lay down the law. Tell her you don't want to be a cop anymore, and tell her she can take it or leave it."

"She'll leave it."

"Did you ever once stop to think that there might be something wrong with a broad so fixated on men in uniform? Did ya?"

Reg regretted the question as soon as he asked it. Why inflame the situation? Eve liked to play games in the bedroom. Andy was obviously a jealous guy and he might realize his handcuffs weren't the only handcuffs that had marked up Eve's brass bedposts. He might fly off the handle. He had broken in. He was a wild card.

Maybe Reg missed his ex sometimes, especially late at night when he found himself alone. They had some good times, but he wasn't the man for her. He attracted troubled broads and then he went for them. Take June—wasn't he intrigued?

Reg's question had stunned Andy. Andy gave no response, he just sat there, looking defeated. "Never mind," Reg said. He was now officially hungry. He got up, went to the fridge, and took an inventory. There was an apple, two eggs, a nearly empty milk bottle, and all the damn beer was gone. "I'm starving half to death," he said. "I'm out of here, got a hankering for Italian."

Andy stood up. "I need to get going, anyway," he muttered.

Reg ushered his uninvited guest out the door, following him outside and then locking the door behind him. He thought he might order something different for a change. Maybe he'd try the scaloppini on for size. He headed down the sidewalk for Napoli, drawn towards their glowing neon sign.

"Hey!" the cop called after the detective. "Thanks, man, for helping me out."

Reg shrugged. He hadn't done anything at all. He turned around and answered Andy. "If you ever pull a stunt like that again, if I ever find you in my apartment, I'm liable to shoot you." The detective did an about-face and made his way towards dinner.

FIFTEEN
1956

It had always irritated Gary to no end when Marilyn had the audacity to sneeze or yawn in his presence. He claimed her face morphed hideously whenever she yawned, and she resembled an alley cat in heat. And she sneezed so loud, he thought his eardrums would burst.

He found hair curlers, bathrobes, and slippers unsightly. Marilyn was expected to rise long before Doc, to guarantee her hypersensitive husband wouldn't view her when she was *less than presentable*. He should never be forced to witness her brushing, gargling, plucking, moisturizing, scrubbing, or God forbid—tinkling. He should never, ever see his wife tousled and undressed. Did she want to spoil his morning?

Now, whenever her deceased husband's endless lists sprang to mind, Marilyn was able to access his demands from a more detached point of view. She finally realized just how absurd Doc's expectations had been. The toothpaste tube should only be squeezed from the end, no bread other than white allowed in the house, the garden hose must be rolled into a precise circle after every use, she was expected to wear heels whenever they went out together, each newspaper must be refolded and placed on the coffee table until the next edition arrived and only then could the old copy be trashed, she was expected to change the bed sheets every Monday and Friday without fail, and hand towels were unhygienic—he even hired a sanitary worker from the hospital to install commercial paper towel dispensers next to every sink in all three bathrooms and in the kitchen.

Marilyn didn't dare serve the same dish for dinner twice in a month's time—Doc had kept track. His lists had been endless, varied, and bothersome. She didn't have to cater to his every whim any longer and felt as if she were on an extended vacation.

No, life with Gary Palmer had never been breezy. He didn't even wait until after the honeymoon to bark orders—often conflicting orders. She never knew what might be on his outlandish agenda from one day to the next. Doc seemed to be at odds with himself, unaware of his own volatile mood swings. Marilyn wondered if his bizarre behavior ever had a detrimental effect on his performance at the hospital.

Their first morning together, he rolled over to face her, and said, "Quite frankly, Marilyn, your breath smells dreadful. Go brush your damn teeth." Then he turned away. But he hadn't brushed *his* teeth yet and his mouth didn't smell like roses, either. "From here on in, don't you dare speak to me until your mouth is minty-fresh," he added.

Gary broke her heart when he insisted she quit her job at MGM and wouldn't take no for an answer.

Jobless and stuck at home every day, Marilyn was forced to deal with Doc's newfound and most irksome habit. He took to presenting a detailed agenda, which he taped to the fridge door every morning before leaving for the hospital. As if she couldn't function in the world without a rigid set of dictates where he listed exactly what she should accomplish over the course of any given day. As soon as he was out the door, Marilyn would tear his agenda into tiny pieces and toss it in the compost bin with the eggshells and coffee grounds.

Doc didn't like her friends, either. Marilyn never told her new husband that she owned the Nepeta house. He'd assumed the quaint cottage belonged to Kika and Freya. She didn't tell him about her marriage to Wesley, or the bank accounts she held in the surname of Murray. She knew she'd be out on the street if he ever discovered her past, and so kept her assets under cover.

"Why do you insist on hanging around with those old maids, those foreigners?" Doc asked, referring to Kika and Freya.

"Don't call them that," she replied, crossly.

"You're a Palmer now," he reminded her. "There's no need to pal around with the likes of *them*."

Marilyn lost her temper. "They mean a lot to me! Freya got me into the costume department. Don't speak poorly of them—I won't have it."

Whenever they socialized with other doctors and their stuck-up wives, he urged Marilyn not to mention how she used to work at MGM, as if he were ashamed of her profession.

He claimed she wasn't cheerful enough. "Smile once in a while, why don't you? I sure do wish you had a sunnier disposition to go with that beautiful puss of yours," he'd say.

Smile? When he constantly scolded her about every piddly irritant that didn't amount to a hill of beans—what did she have to smile about, anyway?

Marilyn sometimes questioned why she almost always readily complied and why she hadn't rebelled more often. The man couldn't have been more difficult to please. Still, she had tried to win his love, striving against the odds to earn his respect and admiration, one impossible day at a time. If only she could have pleased him, if only she could have become the woman he wanted her to be, then she could have atoned for past sins. What a foolish girl. She honestly believed that if Gary Palmer had been able to truly love her, she would have been liberated.

Her dedication to Doc made no sense. Deep inside, she knew it didn't. But she remembered what she had learned at Monte Bahia, that feelings aren't right or wrong, they just *are*.

Doc had been ecstatic when Marilyn delivered the news that she might be pregnant. His parents were thrilled when the pregnancy was verified by one of his colleagues. They all hoped for a boy. Doc's sour attitude toward his new wife altered considerably when he learned she was expecting. He began to treat her as if she were starring on *Queen for a Day*. Lillian sent Armida over to be a live-in housekeeper, but once the baby was born, she would be the nanny. For the time being, she was to run the house and take care of Marilyn.

"This preferential treatment is unnecessary," Marilyn complained. "I'm not sick. I can still cook and clean."

"No," Gary insisted, "you take it easy. Don't lift a finger around here."

Their home became a tolerable for a change, if not a downright agreeable place to be. Doc began to show affection, which Marilyn craved in the worst way, but he shunned sexual relations. "Let's not," he said. "Let's wait. I don't want your hormones fluctuating wildly. Something could go horribly wrong."

Well, Marilyn thought, *he's the doctor*. But she missed making love nonetheless.

She found herself nearly bored to tears with so little to do. To keep herself occupied, she sewed baby clothes and accumulated colorful stacks of neatly folded crawlers, rompers, gowns, T-shirts, bibs, spit-up-shields, crib sheets, blankets, and quilts.

Gary's father had his heart set on a boy to carry on the Palmer name, and he turned a cold shoulder to Lilly. But Gary and Lillian had fallen instantly in love with the child.

"Don't sweat it, Dad," Doc announced. "We'll have a boy next time around."

"That's right," Lillian said, as she reached out to touch Lilly's tiny perfect pink toes. "This one will look after her brother when he comes."

Old man Palmer's lack of interest in her daughter didn't offend Marilyn in the least. He reminded her of her own grandfather, and she prayed he never would warm up to Lilly.

Gary's unrelenting focus on the household transformed into a powerful compulsion once his daughter arrived; his increasing need to control every detail mushroomed, and his rigorous and exacting expectations seemed impossible to satisfy.

Once freed from Gary's control, Marilyn realized how downtrodden and disenchanted she had been in her marriage. The machinations necessary to keep such a bully satisfied had exhausted her.

Kika was instrumental in her recovery, instructing Marilyn to drink apple cider vinegar upon waking and before going to bed. In the old country, vinegar was considered a natural antidote to poison.

Not only was Marilyn's body on the mend from the poisoning—her mind was as well. As the toxic effects of Doc's abuse began to wane, her strength returned.

� ✷ ✷

Lillian led Marilyn into her husband's study and promptly strolled over to a tall oak file cabinet. Her mother-in-law pulled out a leather-bound folder, which she presented to Marilyn with aplomb.

"What's this?" Marilyn asked, eyeing the folder cynically.

"Mr. Palmer put it together. You have it coming."

"Okay, again, *what is it?*"

"Stocks, bonds, whatnot, for you and Lilly."

"I see," she said, taken aback. "Well, tell him thank you."

"He's having a hard time," Lillian confided. "As you can imagine, he's devastated. We all are."

Marilyn put her hand on her mother-in-law's shoulder. "I know, and I'm sorry," she said, doing her best to bolster Lillian's spirits.

"I suppose neither one of us can fathom how we've ended up in this position. After all, I'm his mother, and you're his wife, the two people in the world who should have known Gary best. It's hard to come to grips with just who we wanted him to be, and who he really was."

Marilyn related to Lillian like never before. Why had they both buried their heads in the sand? The first night she met Gary, he had ditched his date to come over to her table. Why hadn't she taken heed of that particular red flag?

"It's inconceivable. My son tried to *murder* you, his wife." Lillian's lip quivered as she placed her hands on her hips in a noticeable effort to regain her composure. "In all honesty, I have to admit, Gary could be so odd, *so vexing*. When he was five, he was caught spying on the nanny while she took a shower. I often thought he was over-sexed."

He certainly hadn't behaved that way towards *her*. Marilyn had practically begged Gary to make love to her. She had never been able to determine just why he'd married her in the first place. And she'd been brainless enough to beg and plead for his love and atten-tion. Vexing—what an apropos term.

"I have an announcement to make," Lillian said, changing the subject abruptly. "We're selling out. Mr. Palmer wants to move to Palm Springs. He's *retiring*. His heart's broken right in two. The poor man can't concentrate on his work any longer. I barely recognize my husband." She stopped long enough to clear her throat, and then added, "I'll drive into town twice a month to visit with Lilly."

A few tears escaped and ran down Lillian's cheeks. She pulled a tissue from her sweater sleeve and dabbed at her face absentmindedly. Marilyn reached over and touched her. "I certainly don't expect you to drive clear out to the desert," Lillian said. Marilyn's mother-in-law had aged immeasurably in a short period of time. It seemed her face had gone slack virtually overnight.

It momentarily appeared as if Lillian might throw up, but she quickly recovered. "The detective I hired supplied me with a written report," she blurted out. *"Gary had more than one girlfriend. Besides June Gordon, there were a couple of nurses. My son sure liked nurses. I probably shouldn't share this sordid information with you. Gary made good use of that motel room he rented. Oh, he got his money's worth, all right. There was also a red-headed switch-board operator, and a patient he took up with."*

Why was Lillian telling her all this? Marilyn supposed she had to unload her burden onto someone, and who the heck else would she tell? "Busy guy," Marilyn mumbled. She could have launched into a tirade, *no wonder he hadn't been interested in me, he was worn out!* But she didn't sound off. "I guess he lived two lives," she simply said.

Lillian stared off into space, the way people do when fixated on the past. She began to manically rub her forearms as if fending off a chill. "I should have seen it coming. I suppose it's genetic. My father was a philanderer of the highest order," she confided. "I remember my mother following him around. She used to bring me along to go spy on him. We watched him enter hotels with his chippies. Sometimes he just carried on in the backseat of cars. She'd cry and call him a *cheating, no-good bastard,* and worse." Lillian's arms went slack and she let out a ragged sigh. "But Mother never left Father. She didn't want to give up her lifestyle, or the San Marino house.

Marilyn bit her lip. It seemed imperative to offer support. "That must've been awful for you." *You think you know people, but you never really do,* she thought. *They reveal themselves in layers as they unravel like a peeled onion.*

"Never mind all that. I worry about you," Lillian said. "You've been through so much."

"Don't worry about me. I'm tough. You should know something—I won't ever tell Lilly about what happened. I hope you and Mr. Palmer agree with me. It would scar her to discover the circumstances of her father's death." Marilyn felt relieved all at once. She'd been dreading this very conversation.

"I agree," Lillian said. She placed her hand on Marilyn's shoulder. "And I should tell you, it means everything to me that you find it in your heart to let me see her at all."

The door opened, and Marilyn's taciturn father-in-law entered the study. "I see you've given her the paperwork," he said. He plucked a pen off the blotter on his desk and set it back in the holder where it belonged.

"I did," Lillian replied, her back ramrod straight. Her previously pained face suddenly took on a phony expression of cheerfulness.

"All right then," Mr. Palmer answered, without looking at either of them.

"Thank you, sir," Marilyn replied, pointing at the folder. "I'll put all this into a trust for Lilly."

He nodded. "Very well, I'm off to the lodge. Goodbye all." He turned and left.

Once the door clicked shut behind her husband, Lillian crumpled and collapsed into the nearest chair. Marilyn held the old man's detachment responsible in part—or maybe entirely—for Gary's madness. Why did the mother receive most of either criticism or praise whenever a child turned out to be a bad seed or an exemplary citizen? It seemed to her, anyway, the father's involvement in any given child's upbringing was just as consequential and crucial. Marilyn was certain her father had imparted a sympathetic outlook that her mother hadn't possessed. Especially precious memories were those of time spent alone with her wonderful blue-eyed Papa.

1936

Patrick had a hard time convincing Nicole to allow him to take Beryl with him on his trip up to Northern Ontario. He had business to tend to and looked forward to his daughter's company. Nicole protested mightily, but he put his foot down. His stubborn wife relinquished control and let him take the girl.

Father and daughter crossed the Ambassador Bridge into Canada. With a few miles behind them, Patrick's somber demeanor brightened. He began to hum a little tune.

"Hey, Papa, what kind of business do you have up in Red Cedar Lake?" Beryl asked, as the lines around his mouth softened. He'd been tense of late and she was pleased to see him loosen up.

"I'm off to inspect a hunting camp, thinking of buying it from a friend. If things go right, I might expand the facilities. Beef things up."

"We'll own a hunting camp?"

"Hopefully, if it all comes together."

Beryl had been to Canada, but only as far as Windsor. As they drove north, she settled in and watched the scenery fly by. It was late September and the leaves were changing color. They stopped at a small roadside cafe for lunch. Beryl ordered a double stack of pancakes, which she covered in plenty of butter and maple syrup but couldn't finish. It was impossible to eat so much at one sitting. Papa drank several cups of coffee, and Beryl noticed how the young waitress fawned all over him. If her handsome father had picked up on the waitress's interest, he didn't show it.

"I used to go north every July," he said. "The summer camp was located right outside of North Bay, on Lake Nipissing."

"I wish I'd gotten to go to camp with my cousins. But Ma always said no."

"I tried to talk sense to that woman, convince her to let you go, but she can be pig-headed when her mind is made up."

Ma had feared that some sex-crazed counselor would molest Beryl, but she had no way of knowing it was Grandfather who had been the threat all along and not some stranger.

"The cousins say camp's fun," Beryl told him. "But Edna caught poison ivy."

"Ah, poison ivy," he said. "I remember it well. It's too bad you couldn't experience being away from home. It forces you to mix in with other kids, and you learn how to overcome homesickness. I made great friends at camp. In fact, Ned Harmon, the man we're going to meet, he's an old friend from camp."

They drove on for a while, each wrapped up in their own thoughts. "You know, I haven't thought about a certain fella for a long time," Papa told her, out of the blue. "Claude Ryder was one of my best friends at camp. He fell out of a tree and ended up paralyzed. They took the poor kid to Homewood Sanitarium and I made Dad drive me up there. I felt miserable because Claude couldn't move from the neck down. He died a few months later—pneumonia got him. Pop claimed it was just as well."

"Homewood Sanitarium—where's that?"

"Guelph. Not far from Toronto."

"Why didn't Aunt Franny go there?"

"She wanted to see California. She said if she had to live away from home, it may as well be someplace beautiful and exotic."

"California's kind of far away, when she could have stayed closer."

"If it was a matter of staying close to home, she'd have gone to Battle Creek. I hear the facilities are something else, quite posh. The Kellogg's founded the place—the *cereal* Kellogg's."

"Auntie should have gone there!"

"It was odd, Franny really wanted to go to the west coast. We all thought that was too far away and were all shocked when Pop gave in and let her go."

"I'm fascinated by sanitariums."

Papa grimaced. "What the dickens? Why?"

"I don't know, just curious I guess."

"Full of people who don't feel good for one reason or another, trying to feel better. Believe me—you'd rather be at camp. Fresh air, activities, exercise—that's all good for what ails you."

"Still…someday I'd like to visit one."

"If you ever do visit, I hope it's only to look around. I hate to think you'd ever need to stay in such a place."

They met Ned Harmon in North Bay. "You'll stay for dinner and the night," he insisted. "We'll set out for camp in the morning."

"Oh, we can't impose," Papa said. "We'll stay in town."

"My old friend's finally come to visit and I'm not about to let him stay in a hotel," Ned replied.

Once they got to the house, Kitty, Ned's sweet wife, got right down to business. "Set the table, won't you?" she asked Beryl. "Eight place settings. My sister's coming with her kids."

Kitty opened the doors to the sideboard, and then rushed back into the kitchen to check on the roast. Beryl was pleased that Ma had taught her the proper placement, so she knew exactly where each dish and glass belonged, and where the knives and spoons and forks went. Beryl would represent the Quinn family admirably. Ma would be proud.

"Hope you like moose meat," Kitty called.

She'd never eaten moose. Should she confess, or say she liked it fine?

"Well, do you like it?" Kitty asked, as she added candles to the candleholders.

"Sure I do," Beryl said. While Kitty fussed with the matches, she was reminded how her mother didn't go in for candles, except for those at church. Nicole couldn't understand why anyone would spend money on something that could burn the house down, something that melted into nothingness and had the potential to stain the tablecloth. Not when they had the convenience of electricity, anyway.

"My sister's kids won't eat anything but beef and chicken," Kitty said, "so they'll make do with potatoes and gravy and salad. Pickiest eaters you've ever seen."

The door flew open. Twin girls and a woman who looked very much like Kitty—although she was a tad bit heavier and had a wider nose—charged into the entry hall.

"Sorry I'm late," the woman said. "I forgot the bread you asked me to bring and had to turn around and go back for it."

"Beryl, meet my sister Ellenmary. We're twins—but I suppose that's obvious."

"And," Ellenmary said, "These are my twins, Betsy and Patsy."

The girls looked to be about eight or nine, and they smiled broadly. An older boy, a *handsome* boy, entered the room but didn't require any prompting. He walked straight over to where Beryl stood and extended his hand. "Ryan," he said. "Pleased to meet you."

His eyes were brown with flecks of gold and matched his hair perfectly. When Beryl took Ryan's cold hand in hers, she suddenly had another reason to be pleased about coming along with Papa.

"Ryan's my son," Kitty told Beryl. Then she turned to him. "Please, take the kids down to the basement while we get supper squared away."

Beryl followed them all downstairs. Betsy turned on the radio. Patsy picked up a jump rope and began to skip.

"Where are you from?" Ryan wanted to know.

"Detroit," Beryl answered, feeling shy.

"A Yank."

"Huh?"

"A Yankee. An American."

"Oh, yeah. Sorry, I didn't understand what you meant at first."

"We've been to Detroit," Patsy said. "To the zoo."

"I like Toronto better," Betsy added.

"Don't be rude," Ryan scolded.

"That's not rude."

"Was too," he said. "After someone says they're from a place and you have to go and say another place is better."

Patsy stopped skipping rope, rolled it up, and looped it over a nearby hook. "Don't mind them, Beryl. They're always arguing."

"That's okay."

"Have you been to Chicago?" Ryan asked.

"Yes," Beryl answered. "My grandmother's from Chicago."

"I'm dying to go there," Ryan said. "And New York City, of course."

Betsy frowned. "What for?" she asked him.

Ryan rolled his eyes. "Don't worry about it," he said. "Quit interrupting me."

"My father says New York is the most exciting city in the world," Beryl offered, "with Paris, France coming in a close second."

"Damn frogs," Ryan replied.

"Uh-oh," Patsy said. "You cussed, I'm telling."

"Shut up, squirt."

"My mother's French," Beryl said, feeling insulted by Ryan's use of the derogatory term *frog* in reference to the French.

"She's from France?"

"No, she's from here. Canada."

"Well, that's a different story. I hate French people who come from France."

"You *hate* them? Hate's a pretty strong word."

"Let's change the subject, why don't we, before someone gets all riled up."

"I see London, I see France, I see a lady's underpants," Patsy cried, and the twins were soon giggling uncontrollably.

"Jesus Christ," Ryan said. "You two are a pain in my ass."

Kitty's voice bellowed down the rickety stairs. "Wash your hands, it's time to eat."

They crowded around a porcelain sink adjacent to the washing machine. Beryl reluctantly took a turn before the twins, after Ryan absolutely insisted she wash up before anyone else.

Upstairs, the dining room smelled wonderful. "I don't want to hear any complaints about the moose," Ellenmary told her children. "You're guests in Auntie Kitty's home, and there'll be no bellyaching. There's plenty to eat besides."

The twins gave each other a look, as if to say, *yuck*.

"You know, kids," Kitty said. "Beryl likes moose."

Patrick's eyes widened. "You do? I didn't know you'd ever even eaten any."

Beryl was mortified. Surely her face was as red as the tablecloth. "At Grandmother's," she lied.

Patrick looked puzzled. He knew his mother didn't cook wild game, but he let it go.

Luckily, Beryl did enjoy the moose. It was tender, and Kitty's gravy was delectable.

When they finished with dinner, the twins went into the living room to color. Beryl and Ryan washed and dried dishes while the adults began a game of cards. The men started in on the whiskey. Beryl hoped Papa wouldn't get plastered.

"You go to Catholic school?" Ryan asked.

Beryl had to wash because he'd rather dry. "Yes. What made you ask me that?"

"Our dads went to Catholic camp together, so I figured. I go to Catholic school, too."

She nodded.

"I hate school," he said. "I planned on becoming a hunting guide. But Dad's selling the camp, and it'll be hard to convince him to let me quit school now."

"Why's he selling?"

Ryan leaned against the kitchen counter. "He's getting into the international trading business."

"Trading what?"

"You got me."

"It's probably best to finish school anyway, even if you want to be a hunting guide."

Ryan groaned. "That's what everybody tells me."

"School's important," Beryl reminded him, feeling very wise.

"Hey, maybe I can work for your dad, if he buys the camp from my dad."

Beryl could see that the boy had his heart set on being a hunting guide. "Maybe."

"Do you want him to?"

"I suppose, if it makes him happy."

"A man doesn't make business decisions based on happiness."

"Says who?"

"Everybody knows that—business is about making money."

"It seems to me that you want to be a hunting guide because that's what makes you happy. Am I wrong?"

Ryan stroked his chin, as if he were deep in thought. "Happy might not be the right word. I'm good at it. It suits me."

"I see," Beryl said, but she didn't agree with him. Not really.

"What are you good at?"

"I don't know."

"Maybe you'll be a good wife and mom."

"Maybe."

"You're very pretty," he said, softly. "But you already know that. You don't need me to tell you that."

She blushed for the second time that night.

"I think you're the prettiest girl I've ever seen in person, so that's worth mentioning. That's something."

"Thanks," she said. But it seemed odd to thank someone for complimenting her on being attractive, because it wasn't as if she had done anything to earn it. She'd simply been lucky to be born better-looking than most.

Kitty came into the kitchen. "Beryl, will you help me serve the pie?" she asked. "Ryan can finish up in here."

"Yes Ma'am," Beryl answered, as she followed Kitty into the other room.

They set out for the camp bright and early. Ned gave Papa and Beryl a grand tour when they arrived. There was a main house and eight cabins, and over two-hundred-and-fifty feet of waterfront property.

"My father built these cabins," Ned said. "They need updating, I won't lie to you. And he hated trees—I'm afraid he cleared away far too many. I've made a concerted effort to replant. My mother said a tree must have scared my grandmother when she was carrying my father, because he viewed them as personal enemies. Of course, this place was thick and overrun back in the day, as you can imagine."

Beryl grew bored and returned to the main house. She sat with the cook, who insisted on feeding her a bowl of stew she didn't want. They'd stopped for breakfast on the way, so she wasn't the least bit hungry.

Once they were alone again and on their way home back to Detroit, Papa talked nonstop. It was unusual for him to share his thoughts in such a straightforward manner, and she felt privileged to listen.

"I hope Pop will give me the dough," he said. "I hate to ask him, but I've never had any money of my own. I've been under his thumb my whole damn life. It's time I built something for myself, for us— for *our* family. I'll pay him back, naturally, with interest. I sure hope the old man doesn't dash this plan. He's always dashing my plans."

"Why wouldn't Grandfather lend you the money?" Beryl asked. "You'll pay him back, won't you?"

"It's hard to say with him. Pop likes things the way they are. He likes having me under his thumb, holding me down, watching me squirm. But where else am I to get that kind of capital? I've never built up any credit. He claims I'm heir to his fortune, but he won't share it. He bought me the house, but it stays in his name. The situation I'm in, well, it's my own fault. I know that. I should have broken away from him ages ago. He doesn't respect me. That's the long and the short of it."

How overbearing Grandfather could be. She hated him so much. If he didn't give Papa the money, she would hate him forever. She would hate him even more than she already did.

"I want this so bad I can taste it," Papa said. His eyes were all ablaze with promise and hope for the future. She wanted things to work out for him this time. She was excited to see her father so fired up.

Grandfather was invited over to the house the following night and, after dinner, Nicole sent Beryl to her room. But Beryl snuck out, hid away on the staircase, and eavesdropped. Papa made his proposal and he did a good job, too. The three grownups sat stock-still when he finished. Beryl held her breath.

James turned to Nicole. "What do *you* think?" he asked, breaking the silence.

"I don't understand," she replied. "I don't know why Patrick wants this."

Beryl bit her lip. She couldn't believe it. Her very own mother was a traitor!

"I don't either," James said. "Son, you have no experience. The depression isn't over, and a recreational-based business relies on prosperity and disposable income. I can't fund this harebrained pipe dream in good conscience. I know you don't understand now, but one day you will."

Patrick had never raised his voice at James. Or at least Beryl had never heard him do so. But he raised his voice that night.

"I'm a grown man!" he yelled at his father. "You've always treated me like a child. A blundering idiot! I don't know why I even asked you. I should have known you would say no. And you, Nicole. What *kind* of a wife are you, anyway?"

Beryl crept back upstairs. She didn't have the heart to wait around to hear Ma's reply. How could Ma act like that? Why couldn't she support her husband? Beryl hated her, and she hated Grandfather, too. Poor Papa. The camp had been lovely with its blue lake, the dock, and those rustic log cabins. It broke her heart in two to think that a brutish, greedy pervert with more money than principles had dashed her sweet father's dreams. Beryl even woke up in the middle of the night because she'd been crying in her sleep. Somehow she knew Papa would take the rejection hard, and that he would never be the same.

She stopped by Swifty's the next day. "He's in his office," Papa's new assistant told her, "but go on home. You shouldn't be here, kid."

Beryl stubbornly ignored the assistant's advice and knocked on the office door. When Papa didn't answer, she entered anyway. And there he was, slumped over, stone cold drunk, half-in and half-out of his big leather chair.

"Oh, Papa," she said, as she gave him a good shake. He opened one bloodshot eye.

"Hey," he said. "Where'd you come from?"

"Come on," she said. "Get up. Let's get a cup of hot coffee in you."

But he wasn't interested in coffee. He reached down for his bottle of Seagram's and took a long, awkward pull. His hand shook so uncontrollably Beryl thought Papa would drop the bottle for sure. Whiskey trickled out of the corner of his slack mouth and she saw it run down his neck and under his soiled collar.

"Please, no," she whined. "You're soused to the gills. Ma will be fuming. And what if Grandfather shows up?"

"Fuck 'em," he bellowed. Beryl was shocked—she'd never heard her father use *that* word. "And fuck yer mutha too!" he cried. "Fuck 'em for gangin' up on me. The pair of 'em can rot in hell. Now, get out. Go on home!"

Hurt to the quick, she scurried away. At the house, Ma stood at the kitchen sink. Beryl debated whether or not to tell her about Papa's drunkenness and how he was plastered in his office, for all the employees of Swifty's to see and ridicule.

"Where'd you go?" Ma asked, as she sharpened her favorite knife.

"Swifty's."

"How's your father doing?"

"Not good."

"It'll take him some time to rally round."

She had to tell her. "He's drunk as a skunk."

Ma turned around and the look in her eyes was cold as could be. "At work? Drunk at work?"

"Yeah, Ma. Plastered! I tried to get some coffee in him, but he wouldn't. He called you and Grandfather bad names and told me to scram."

"For the love of God, how much more can I take?"

Beryl felt brave. She went on ahead and asked the question that begged to be asked. "Ma," she said, "why didn't you back Papa up? He needs your support."

Nicole winced. "That hunting camp? What a lark! He would've spent all his time up there, and we would've been alone in this big old house. Your father is no captain of industry, that's for certain. The hunting camp would've have been a financial disaster. Surely you can see that."

"You can't see the future. I hate you! Fuck you and Grandfather for ganging up on him."

Ma moved quickly—her slap came fast and hard. Beryl's cheek stung madly as she fled up the back staircase.

"You will not end up like that father of yours!" Ma called up the stairwell. "Not if I have anything to say about it!"

Beryl stayed in bed until after the sun went down. No one had come for her. Her stomach growled something fierce, but she wouldn't beg. She wouldn't give her mother the satisfaction. She'd never eat again if it came to that. Instead, she turned on the light and tried to read for a while. The foul language had been transgression enough, but she'd also told her mother she hated her—a big no-no. A familiar dread washed over Beryl as memories surfaced. She had always felt bad after one of Grandfather's sessions, and bad girls know when they're bad. They might not like the shame misbehaving triggers but by the time the shame sets in it's too late to go back.

Beryl waited and waited. But still, not a peep.

She snuck downstairs but couldn't find a soul. Where on earth was Opal? She tiptoed over to the fridge and pulled out a chicken leg and a hunk of cheddar. She hurried back upstairs and half-heartedly nibbled her meager fare while perched on the wobbly Chippendale chair near the window. A taxi stopped and Papa climbed out. He nearly fell off the curb, but he managed to straighten up and stumble down the walk. Beryl opened her bedroom door. She intended to go to him but overheard Ma's voice call out when the front door opened.

"Oh, so here you are. Eight o'clock at night. I suppose you expect me to feed you now. I suppose you expect me to feel sorry for you. How can you entertain thoughts about James giving you that amount of money when you can't even be counted on to manage the drug store? When you can't even stay sober?"

"Leave me be, woman!" he cried. "I don't have to listen to this. I've had it with your nagging."

"Why come home then? Tell me why, Patrick."

"You got me. I should do like other fellas do and keep a girl."

"That's it! You aren't sleeping in my bed!"

"I'll sleep in my own bed, if I choose to. You can't kick me out of my own bed."

"You're a dog, a dirty dog. I rue the day I married you."

"That makes two of us. I shoulda married Irene Closky."

"Your mother hated her!"

"My mother wasn't crazy—let me rephrase that—my mother *isn't* crazy about you either!"

"As if I give a hoot—you think I care one iota about that old bat's opinion of me? Then you've got another think coming."

"Leave me be, woman."

It sounded bad between them—worse than ever before. Beryl worried they would never make up.

"Where are you going?" Ma sounded panicky.

"Leaving."

"Stop! You're in no shape. Come with me. I'll warm a bowl of soup. You can't go out like that."

Their voices grew fainter and fainter as they made their way to the kitchen. Beryl returned to the third floor. She was afraid for her parents. If only Ma would bend a little. If only she wasn't always full of opinions. If she could be just a little more sympathetic to Papa's plight. If only she had his back. A wife should have her husband's back.

Patrick Quinn died a few days later. Beryl knew the ulcers weren't what killed her papa. He had died of a broken heart.

SIXTEEN
1956

Javier was celebrating his sixtieth birthday. The old bachelor took over the party room at the Elk's Club and all his favorite poker buddies gathered for an all-night tournament. He even hired a couple of broads to work as barmaids, and they dressed in costume, wearing red velvet bustiers with exposed garter belts and fishnet stockings. Reg got a kick out of the naughty costumes. But what red-blooded male wouldn't?

Javier held a glass of beer and already had a glow on, but he made a half-assed vow to pace himself. "No tequila tonight," he told Reg. "Don't need to get shit-faced and miss out on my own party."

Reg, on the other hand, accepted two rounds of shots from his old friend Hector Santos. The two men went all the way back to grade school. Hector was the first friend Reg made when he'd arrived in California. These days, Hector installed commercial air conditioning units for a living. It was a very lucrative racket, of which Hector saw fit to inform Reg every time they ran into each other.

"I'm doing better than I ever thought I would," Hector said that night. "Of course," he added, "I'm not involved in nothing as interesting as what you do."

Reg knew most of his old friends thought he spent his days knee-deep in thrilling intrigue, but that was hardly the case. "I sit in the car much of the time," he admitted. "I lurk."

"Hey, good news," Hector told him. "I'm about to be a father again. Angelina says this is the last one, though."

"Jesus, Hector, what is that? Four kids already?"

"Five, *but who's counting*? I want more, but she's shutting the baby factory down."

"At least one of you has good sense."

"I like a big family."

Hector had two brothers and four sisters. Reg used to hang out at his house because his big sisters were good-looking exhibitionists. As young as nine years old, Reg would spend the night and watch them parade around in their baby-doll nighties, and in summer—better yet—bathing suits. He had fond memories of the Santos household for varied reasons. Hector's mother had always rustled up tasty meals in her outdoor kitchen. She rarely cooked inside the house.

"You'd better slow down," Reg warned. "You'll wear that pretty wife of yours out."

"Oh, hell no," Hector said, and then he winked. "She gets more beautiful with each baby. And she's a real good mother. But like I said, she's pulling the plug. I won't get my half-dozen."

The sexiest barmaid bounced over, her ample cleavage on full display. Reg and Hector were mesmerized by her bounty, and she seemed to enjoy the attention. As she moseyed off to fetch their order, Reg noticed her ass was kind of flat. All her padding was located up front, way up firm and high.

Hector pointed at the barmaid as she walked away. "You ought to break off a piece of that tonight."

Reg poked his old friend. "You can't have her, so I should, huh?"

"If I was single, you bet I'd be all over that cha-cha like stink on shit."

"How do you know she's not married, or a prude?"

"Come on!" his old friend chided. "You've got to be kidding, man. She's wagging those titties around like there's no tomorrow. No, that one's no prude. And if she's married, she's not *married-married*, if you get my drift. No sweet bride dresses like that."

Reg was ready for action. He'd been celibate ever since Eve's departure from the scene, except for his one-nighter with Wendy. June Gordon had him tied up in knots. The blonde had him worked up to be sure, but he wasn't about to take advantage of her, not in her delicate frame of mind. A tryst with the barmaid would provide a welcome release. When she returned with the drinks, Reg turned on the charm and joked around. Then he joined Hector at one of the many tables. That bully, Chuy—the one who had threatened Reg a while back for leaving a game while he'd been ahead—was holding court with some idiots he kept under his thumb. The group included some obnoxious guy named Mario, whose hair had turned white virtually overnight when he'd been very young, making him a curiosity in the community.

"Hey Reg," Mario said, his crooked grin on display. "How's the rent-a-cop business?"

"He's not a security guard," Hector snapped. "He's a private investigator."

Reg smiled back at Mario. "How's the cleaning business?" he asked, snidely. "It must be exciting and full of adventure, huh?"

Mario frowned.

"Let's play poker," Chuy said. "That's what I came here for." That son-of-a-bitch had the meanest eyes Reg had ever seen.

They began to play a game. It wasn't long before Reg was on a roll. He won four hands in a row. Then he got up to go to the bathroom.

"Where do you think you're going?" Chuy asked him. It was a threat, and Reg didn't like threats.

"Any damn place I want to," Reg told him. He turned to Hector. "Off to choke the chicken."

Another player—Javier's next-door neighbor named Sam-something-or-other—laughed a nervous laugh. "The man's gotta use the head," he told Chuy, peevishly. "He's coming back."

Reg felt a mean streak brewing in his roiling gut. Liquor could do this to him—upset his constitution and infect his brain with foul thoughts. That's why Reg rarely drank straight-up liquor anymore. Unfortunately, that night he felt his resolve slipping away. He was in a rowdy, reckless mood. Maybe Chuy brought out the worst in him—it was hard to say.

Back in his seat at the table, Reg asked the sexy barmaid for a shot of tequila and a beer to wash it down. "Don't forget the lime this time," he reminded her.

She brought his drink and he tipped her generously. Her dancing black eyes sent a come-hither message.

Chuy grimaced at the exchange. Reg wondered if the old pachuco had his eye on the girl.

They played another round and Hector took the pot. "This will buy baby food and milk." He laughed goodheartedly.

"You ought to buy yourself some rubbers," Mario said, "that's what you ought to buy."

"Speak for yourself," Hector told him. "If I were you, I wouldn't want to make any more little gray-haired Marios."

Mario gave him the finger. "My genetics are beyond my control, asshole."

Reg sprang up. "I need a break," he said. He walked down the long hallway that led to the alley, in search of fresh air. But outside, the stench from the dumpster overwhelmed him and sent him back inside.

The detective ran into the barmaid as she came out of the ladies' room. "Hi there," she said, flashing her pearly whites. They were standing close to each other when she reached over and opened the door to her left. She shoved Reg inside, shut the door, turned the lock, and flipped the light switch to reveal a storage room. "Want to play around?" she whispered.

The barmaid didn't have to ask twice. Reg fell back against a giant cardboard box and pulled her towards him. She was petite, and her opulent cleavage was astoundingly easy to reach. Reg undid a few clasps at the back of her revealing costume, and her breasts tumbled free. Eagerly, he caressed her perfectly shaped mounds. He hated to pull one hand away from her erect nipple to fumble with his belt buckle. Luckily, his hand got back to business in no time flat, because she deftly took over the job. Soon his pants were down around his ankles, and her garter and black fishnet stockings strewn on the floor. The panting barmaid was completely naked and rode his cock like there was no tomorrow. It was a wham, bam, thank you ma'am affair. She was a screamer, and Reg worried that

someone would hear, but he was in the throes of passion and pow-
erless to quiet her. Afterwards, she slipped off, got dressed, squared
her shoulders, and asked if he would refasten her top.

"I wouldn't tell my Dad you fucked me," she advised. "He don't
like you, anyways."

"*Dad*?" Reg asked. Why did she think he'd know who her father was?

"You're playing poker with him." She reached up to fluff her
plentiful black mane. "Chuy Carnejo."

No way. The old pachuco was her father?

She opened the door and disappeared. Seconds later, Reg vacated
the storage room. He decided it would be best if he made a hasty
exit through the back alley. He would apologize to the old bachelor
for leaving his party early, but he'd do it mañana. He had no way
of knowing what the barmaid's motives were, and that made him
nervous as hell. The detective had no desire for his name to rise to
the top of Chuy Carnejo's shit list.

✢ ✢ ✢

Reg was unfamiliar with head-shrinkers and their ways, so when
June told him she was seeing a psychiatrist, he couldn't see the harm
in encouraging her. He thought it might be a good idea. Besides
waiting tables at Pago Pago, she also worked weekdays spraying
perfume on ladies' wrists at Macy's, to bring in extra money. He
hoped staying busy and seeing a professional would keep her from
becoming so desperate as to resort to something like blackmail ever
again. He also hoped she would never become so depressed as to
want to end her life, either.

Doris thought Reg had been bewitched when he confided to her
that he thought he wanted to see more of June Gordon.

The bossy secretary narrowed her eyes. She couldn't contain her
anger, and spoke her mind. "That conniving, blackmailing blonde
has put you under her spell! Keep in mind, leopards don't change
their spots."

"Maybe I like her spots—maybe her spots just need a little
rearranging."

"You men never learn."

He didn't even try to explain. How could he explain? Doris had no way of knowing how unhappy he was. Besides, she had never even met June. It felt good to care about someone, and that was enough for Reg. He had decided to put his old ways behind him.

Whenever he thought about the quickie with the old pachuco's daughter, he felt like a letch all over again.

Doris vigorously wiped down the counter. "I hired another assistant. This time I'm giving a fella a try. I haven't had such good luck with the girls."

"Not a bad idea," Reg said.

"His name's Ricky. He's a college student."

"Good luck with Ricky," the detective said. "Hope he works out. I'm off to Orange County. See you tomorrow."

"Does this have to do with that phone call that came in this morning, and that haughty Mrs. Sheridan?"

"The wealthy widow? Yep, she's chomping at the bit to find out who's been stealing miscellaneous stuff from around the house. She's got six kids and several servants, and hasn't been able to determine if there are one or many more light-fingered culprits. The last P.I. she hired didn't pan out. She's convinced I'm the man for the job."

"What's gone missing?"

"All kinds of stuff, miscellaneous jewelry, books, and artwork."

"That would be maddening," Doris said. "I get upset when those sticky-fingered movers run off with my stapler or tape dispenser."

"She keeps most valuables in a safe. But you can't put the big stuff in a safe. No surprise, the cops haven't gotten anywhere. The rich broad's at the end of her rope." He reached for the door handle. "I'd better get out there."

✠ ✠ ✠

After visiting Mrs. Sheridan in Santa Ana, the detective returned to the office and paused at the counter to ask Doris for messages, like he almost always did. But she was busy showing her new assistant how to balance the books properly. Ricky couldn't seem to get the hang of it. His shiny, pimply brow was deeply furrowed and he looked as if he might break out in tears. It was clear to Reg that frustration with the numbers had overwhelmed the poor kid.

Doris broke away and finally handed over Reg's messages. "What's this?" she asked, reaching for the list he'd left on the counter.

"Mrs. Sheridan's list. Those are the missing books from the study, which belonged to her husband."

"Do you mind if I go over these?"

"Not at all. If you can make any sense out of what's missing, that's fine by me. Any clues would be helpful. Her house is crawling with people. She's got a slew of kids and servants, and the kids have friends. Throw aunties and uncles into the mix and that place is a zoo."

"The thief could be leaving clues," she mused. "I need a detailed list of each missing item."

Reg nodded. "Can do, I'll call her right away. Thanks, Doris."

"This is fun stuff." She tilted her head in Ricky's direction. The assistant was hunched over the books, his pale face perplexed and tortured. "Lord only knows that I welcome the distraction," she said, offering a quick wink.

After calling Mrs. Sheridan, Reg returned and handed Doris the list of missing items. She sat across from him and began to read aloud, as if he didn't already know the contents. But Reg didn't stop her. She was awfully excited, why squelch her enthusiasm?

"Mmm, how interesting," she said. "A dog leash. A Bundt pan. A worthless old brooch. Two of her children's birth certificates. A cake server with a marble handle. Four bars of lavender soap. Several jars of smoked salmon. A brass desk lamp." She paused. "This list does go on and on, doesn't it? This is going take me a while. I'll spend some time on it and see if anything rings a bell or correlates."

"You've got more patience than I do, Toots."

✛ ✛ ✛

Doris came to the conclusion that the culprit was the maid. She claimed the Brit was obviously fooling around with Mrs. Sheridan's oldest son, the one attending law school.

Reg shrugged his shoulders. "You don't have to explain yourself to me. I've solved many a case on nothing but a hunch. It's creepy, but I just know things sometimes."

"Nah, no hunch. I deduced it, plain and simple. The maid left clues, you see. Criminals like to leave clues. Sometimes intentionally — sometimes subconsciously."

And Doris had it figured right. The son crumbled when confronted. The maid had hidden most of the stolen items in an apartment off Harbor Boulevard.

"See?" the bossy secretary said, after it had been determined she'd solved the case. "I ought to write mysteries. I have a knack."

"No kidding," Reg replied, as he handed her a check for her trouble. "You'd better get busy, Toots. Write that novel. Soon you'll be able to kiss Caravan Moving and Storage, and hopeless assistants, goodbye."

SEVENTEEN
1956

Marilyn showed up to Hartman's office unexpectedly one sunny afternoon. "I need something else from you," she told the detective.

"You bet," Hartman said. "Anything."

"Maybe you can locate my mother?" She handed him a sheet of paper. "That's her name and last known address. And the other name belongs to an old friend I used to know in Hawaii. She's from Bean Station, Tennessee. Maybe you can locate her as well."

"I'll do my best to find both of them, and this one's on the house."

"I would never expect you to do that. I intend to pay you."

"Can't a guy do a girl a favor?"

"I suppose so, but why should you?"

"Any friend of June's is a friend of mine," he said. What a sucker he was for June! Marilyn accepted his offer. She'd find a way to make it up to overly generous detective, somehow.

She would've liked to have Hartman search for Opal too, but couldn't recall her last name, if she had ever known it at all.

⊹ ⊹ ⊹

True to his word, detective Hartman managed to locate not only Marilyn's mother, Nicole, but also Loretta Cahill, the whore with a heart of gold. Loretta had been so kind to Marilyn back in the brothel. Once she had her address, Marilyn immediately wrote to her old friend, who now went by Loretta Jenkins, and asked if she would like to meet. Loretta soon wrote back, thrilled at the prospect.

Marilyn had plenty of time to think during the long road trip out from California. By the time she finally crossed the Tennessee border, she had grown tired of her own company and looked forward to interacting with someone for longer than it took to say *fill it up* or *another cup of coffee, please.*

She rented a room at the first decent hotel she came across in Knoxville. Down in the lobby, she used a pay phone to call Loretta.

"Lordy mercy!" Loretta exclaimed. "I often wondered what happened to you, Beryl. Oh, I'm sorry, you go by Marilyn now, don't y'all? I sure was surprised to get that letter you sent. Drive your butt over to my place tonight. I'm gonna make you fried chicken like you've never tasted!"

"Sounds delightful," Marilyn told her.

"You got my address? You need directions?"

"I've got it all plotted out on my handy map."

Loretta had attended cosmetic school. She dyed, permed, and cut women's hair for a living in a neighborhood beauty parlor. Her own hairdo had changed substantially; she wore it in a pouf high atop her head, bright as a copper penny. Loretta lived in a Queen Anne two-story house on the outskirts of town with her husband, Clyde, and their two daughters. He was a big man, at least six-four, and must have weighed in at over three-hundred pounds.

Loretta bragged about her husband's plumbing business. "Clyde's got four trucks out there at all times," she said. "Day in and day out, drains get clogged up, toilets leak, and hot water heaters stop working at all hours. When folks need a damn plumber, they need a damn plumber."

Marilyn wondered how Clyde fit in tight spaces, how he wedged his girth underneath sinks and behind toilets. She decided he must hire subordinates to do all the dirty work.

Clyde's mother, Maybelline, had joined them for dinner. She turned to Marilyn. "I told him when he was a wee little feller—I said, be a doctor or be a plumber. He chose plumber, and he chose right."

Loretta had set the table in the formal dining room with her best china. "These dishes are a gift from Clyde," she said. "I was raised in an itty-bitty place. We didn't have running water and barely scraped by. I guess I can't get over my good luck at meeting this wonderful man and how blessed I am."

"I'm so happy for you," Marilyn told her long-lost friend.

Clyde slammed his fleshy palms on the table, sending floral teacups clattering in their saucers. "Sweetheart," he bellowed, "this fried chicken's so good, my tongue liked to have reached up and slapped my face silly!"

Their daughter, Selma—whom Marilyn happened to know was conceived while Loretta worked in the brothel and was most likely fathered by a three-minute man—was squat and thick and dark and hairy and homely, unlike her pretty, birdlike sister. Selma boldly spoke up. "Now, you always say that, Daddy. But what's it mean?"

"It means your Mama's a good cook," Clyde said, sweetly.

"If the chicken is so dang good, why would your tongue wanna slap your face? Wouldn't your tongue wanna *lick* your face?"

"Semantics, child," Clyde explained.

Selma's face went sour. "Sayings ought to make sense."

"Mind your manners, young lady," Loretta scolded.

The girl pressed on foolishly, angering her parents further. "Seems to me, we eat too much fattening food. Fried chicken, fried okra, fried this and fried that. I'm too fat. If we had salad for supper, I might get skinny."

For some reason, the girl looked straight at Marilyn, as if she expected support.

Loretta's eyebrows lowered and her lips pressed together to form a thin pink line. If she'd been a cartoon character, clouds of smoke would have shot out of her ears.

Selma stood up, and before her mother had a chance to respond, she shouted, "There are only five calories in a dill pickle—only five. From now on, I'll have nothing but a pickle for supper!"

"Lordy, Selma, you can't live on dill pickles," Loretta said. "Even if Maybelline puts up the best for miles around."

Maybelline reached up and patted Selma's broad, hairy forearm. "It's all about portions," she told her. "You just take a little bit of this and a little bit of that, and you'll thin right out."

"My friend Lindy's as skinny as Marilyn, and she eats nothing but a dill pickle for lunch *and* dinner."

"I never starve myself," Marilyn told the girl, setting the record straight. "You can see I helped myself to mashed potatoes, a chicken breast, green beans, and one of your mama's biscuits. If you try to live on dill pickles, you won't be healthy."

"I don't believe that silly friend of yours for a minute," Clyde said. "No one can get by on pickles. Did this friend teach you this fattening talk?"

"Yes she did, and it's true!" Selma insisted. "Every single day during lunch, all she does is suck on a fat pickle while the rest of us eat our sandwiches and cupcakes."

"Bag of bones," Loretta commented

"I'm two inches shorter and *way* fatter," the girl said, with tears in her eyes.

"One a' my ladies has a daughter that ate nothing but caramel corn for two weeks straight, and that foolish girl ended up in the hospital with bowel troubles," Loretta warned. She wagged her finger to emphasize her point. "That friend of yours will turn into a pickle if she don't mend her ways."

Selma sighed and sat down, defeated.

Marilyn made up her mind to stay out of it and keep her mouth shut. She'd said enough as it was.

Once the table was cleared and the dishes were done and put away, Loretta suggested Marilyn ride along to the grocery store, *as they oughta have some vanilla ice cream to go with the peach cobbler.*

"I was lookin' for an excuse to get outta there so we could talk alone," Loretta said, as she backed out of the driveway. "We don't have much time. Do your best and catch me up."

They sat in the car outside the Piggly Wiggly and Marilyn supplied Loretta with the highlights of what had happened since they'd last seen each other.

Loretta gently touched Marilyn's hand. "I hope you don't mind hearin' this, but you have lived one crazy life!"

"It's true."

"Sometimes, I get to feeling guilty," Loretta said. "I'm keeping this secret about where Selma came from and what I used to be and all. But shoot, what you've been through. I can't believe it. I can't."

"Me neither."

"I better get my butt in that store and fetch that ice cream, hadn't I? They're all gonna wonder where the heck we went off to. I hope Mother Maybelline's been able to keep Clyde from digging into that cobbler."

"Sorry I kept you so long," Marilyn said. "But you did ask, and there's so much to tell."

"I sure did. Didn't I?"

Loretta dashed off and disappeared inside the supermarket. Marilyn considered all the heartbreak she'd swept under the rug. She had dealt with the pain of the past by burying it and forgetting about it. Those three-minute liaisons that had taken place on Hotel Street had been so repugnant, and nothing but an ugly reflection of what unfettered lust and greed and misdirected good intentions could yield. Surely it was patriotic to obliterate the truth. That chapter of history would be better forgotten, she was sure of it.

On the way home, Marilyn thanked Loretta for being her friend back in the brothel.

"Anybody could see you didn't belong there," Loretta said. "I'm glad you kicked that dope habit. I don't think you know how often you came close to death. I used to worry myself sick, but you weren't in your right mind. You just couldn't listen to reason."

"You didn't belong there any more than I did. Nobody belongs in a place like that, doing the things we did. But, we both got away. That's what counts. And we both got out before the bombing. We were lucky. Some of those boys we were with, they weren't so lucky. Some of them died, and some were maimed."

"Yeah, I think about that."

"I suppose we wouldn't be human if we didn't," Marilyn said.

"We swapped body fluids with them." Loretta's voice dropped to a near whisper. "In a way they're still with us, I reckon." She shuddered, as if to shake away the sudden gloom. "I guess we did our part. We gave them what they needed when they needed it most."

"Does Clyde know about Hotel Street?"

"Oh Lordy, no, I never told a soul. Hank thinks my soldier husband died of pneumonia. And everybody thinks Clyde is Selma's daddy. We thought it best. But no matter how good he is to Selma, deep down, I just know that girl senses she ain't his."

Well, Marilyn thought, Selma didn't look one bit like Loretta either, and Loretta was her mother.

Loretta leaned forward. "Tell me, what ran through your mind when you first heard the war had finally ended?"

"Like everybody else, I was relieved. But, selfishly, I couldn't help but wonder why Wesley had to die. I loved him and we had such a short time together."

"Why, that's not selfish. Not at all."

"What were you thinking about?"

"I gave a little prayer. I asked God to take care of all those boys who didn't make it."

"See?" Marilyn said. "You are so much more selfless—and such a better person than I am!"

Loretta pulled the car over abruptly, and one tire slammed against the curb. The two women lurched forward. "No way—in fact, I know that's not so!" Loretta cried. "Stop it! You are a wonderful woman. The little sister I always wanted." Tears fell from Loretta's eyes and she gave Marilyn a squeeze. "Now, let's put times gone by behind us. No more hurtful talk!"

Loretta pulled back into traffic and drove back to the house. She urged Marilyn to stay for dessert, and Marilyn agreed.

Selma had evidently forgotten or abandoned the dill pickle diet, because when the cobbler was served, she helped herself to two heaping servings, with plenty of ice cream.

Marilyn didn't sleep a wink. She was planning to head for Florida first thing in the morning, and all she could think about was how it would feel to see Ma again.

☩ ☩ ☩

Sadly, Marilyn would never see Mémère again. Her grandmother had passed away in '49 from heart disease.

Nicole Quinn had later become Nicole Turner when she married Walt, the chiropractor she'd fornicated with on River Road, so long ago. They'd moved south after the war.

How ironic. Marilyn had lied to Gary when she'd told him she was from Florida, and now her mother lived there. It still made her angry to think that Doc had known she wasn't an orphan all along.

When Marilyn pulled up in front of the house, Nicole was standing out on the lawn, watering dense shrubbery with a spray hose, still as trim as the last time Marilyn had seen her. But, with her hair peppered and pulled back in a matronly bun, her mother looked haggard. Marilyn felt responsible. If she hadn't put the poor woman through so much, surely Nicole would appear prettier, healthier, and much happier.

As soon as Nicole saw Marilyn's car, she reached over, turned off the spigot, and rolled up the hose. Marilyn briefly shut her eyes, took in a deep breath, and willed herself to stay calm. During her trip out east, she'd had plenty of time to think, and plenty of time to plan. She intended to repair the damage of her past foolish decisions, to make it all up to her mother. They most certainly would feel like strangers to one another, but surely their mother-daughter bond and the history they shared would carry them through the reconciliation process. Marilyn opened her eyes and let go of the steering wheel, realizing how tightly she'd been holding on. Nicole waited on the sidewalk.

"This is it," Marilyn whispered to herself. "This is really happening. You can do this." She got out of the car and approached her mother.

"You didn't bring the baby?" Nicole asked. She didn't resist the light hug Marilyn offered, but didn't hug back either. Marilyn pulled away and studied her mother's face. Was she angry, disillusioned, frustrated, or all of the above? It seemed impossible to know.

"No, I didn't," Marilyn said.

"I wanted to meet Lilly."

"I know. And you will."

"Come with me," Nicole said. "Walt's not here, that gives us time alone."

Marilyn followed her inside where they sat across from one another in the kitchen. Her mother poured two glasses of sweet iced tea. In California, they drank their tea unsweetened. Marilyn didn't care for the syrupy, cloying beverage her mother served, but sipped politely.

"Are Grandfather and Grandmother Quinn still alive?" Marilyn asked, seeking to fill the awkward silence.

"That old bat's still going strong," Ma said. "And James is now as senile as they come, he doesn't even know his own name. They left

Michigan. They're in Savannah, Georgia now, and you bet Anne's in her element, running the show without James to answer to. She grew tired of Michigan winters and chose Savannah over Florida. She sent me a picture of the house, if you want to call it a house. It's just another palatial mansion. I wonder what she would think of this dump?"

"It's not bad here," Marilyn lied. Her mother's place was a shack, bleak and completely devoid of character. It was hard to believe her once-stylish mother lived in such a hovel.

"We're only renting. It's small and stuffy. It gets so hot down here in the summer. Oppressive. You have no idea what happens when you couple extreme heat with extreme humidity. Walt still has the practice, but he only works two or three days a week, so we barely scrape by. And when he's not working, he's fishing. I'm alone much of the time."

"Whatever became of Opal?" Marilyn remembered to ask, "I would love to know."

Nicole drew back. "The nanny? I have no idea, somewhere in the south, I think. She never wrote us after she went back home."

"What was her last name?"

"I don't think I recall…wait," Nicole leaned forward. "All those years ago, my old brain is straining. Let me see…maybe Boone, or Booker? Her name started with a B, or was it an R?"

"I'd like to find her."

"She's likely married. She wouldn't even have the same name."

Marilyn decided not to bother Hartman with the task, slim chance he'd even be able to locate Opal anyway.

Her mother reached up and brushed a lock of gray hair from her forehead. Remembering what Kika had said, Marilyn realized the light had gone from her mother's eyes. Her hands were nervous and always searching for something to do. They were two very different people, still mother and daughter, but separated by a vast amount of time. They were disconnected and reserved and foreign to one another.

On the spot, Marilyn made up her mind not to tell her mother about all the terrible things she had done. It seemed pointless. The past was gone now. They called it the past for a reason. It was time to forge a new relationship. That's all she knew how to do.

"Ma," she said, "I'd like for you and Walt to come out to California for a visit. I'll pay for plane tickets. Lilly's too young to travel so far, but she's your granddaughter and you ought to know each other. You don't have to answer me now." Marilyn reached for her purse. "I brought pictures," she added.

The front door slammed. Walt was home. When he entered the kitchen, Marilyn saw that the chiropractor had withered. His brown hair had turned a soiled-looking gray, and his cheeks were extremely hollow. Had he lost his molars? His long earlobes and big nose had grown at an accelerated rate. Walt hadn't been a handsome man in his youth, but he hadn't been bad-looking.

"Look at you—you're all grown up," he said, as if he were surprised she hadn't stayed a teenager.

Marilyn offered her hand. She wasn't ready to hug him, if she ever would be.

Walt proffered a puny handshake.

"Catch anything?" Nicole asked.

He let go of Marilyn's hand, went to the fridge, took out a beer, rummaged around in the drawer for an opener, and took a long gulp before answering. "Not to speak of," he said.

"Marilyn offered to pay for us to fly out to California," Nicole told him.

Walt looked at Marilyn, and his mouth went all crooked. "Oh... yeah...I forgot. You're not Beryl anymore." He turned to Nicole. "California?" he exclaimed. "I can't go to California!"

Nicole rubbed her vein-ridden, too-bony hands together. "But," she offered meekly, "I have a granddaughter. Naturally, I want to see her."

"Must be nice," Walt said. "If my son was here, I might have myself a slew of grandbabies."

"Where is Bobby?" Marilyn foolishly asked.

"Dead as a doornail," Walt said, in a bitter voice. He turned away from them and stared out the cracked window above the old-fashioned stand-alone sink.

"I'm so sorry to hear that," Marilyn mumbled.

"Battle of the Bulge," Walt said. "He was shot in the gut and froze in a snow bank. It was hard on me, losing my son. But what you did to your mother—that was worse, so much worse. You know, she's never been the same. Not knowing whether you were alive or dead just about did her in."

"Now Walt," Nicole said, "let's not do this."

Marilyn stormed off to the bathroom, fighting back guilty tears. Walt was right. She knew he was.

"Goddammit!" she heard him shout. The walls in that shack were as thin as the walls in the casitas back at the Garden of Allah. "You are *not* going to California!"

"What's to keep me here?" Nicole fired back.

"Me!"

"*You*? That's all? Well, Mister, that's not enough. I do nothing but clean and watch soap operas all day. You're never here."

"So," he hissed, "You think Beryl—oh wait, I mean *Marilyn*—is gonna want some old bag around on a full-time basis? Walk outta here and you're on your own."

Marilyn flew out of the bathroom, down the dark narrow hallway, and back into the kitchen. "Yes!" she said. "I do want her around on a full-time basis. If Ma wants to go back with me, she's welcome to! And she isn't an old bag, and she won't be on her own!"

Walt got right up in Marilyn's face. "Be careful what you wish for," he said.

Marilyn wasn't practiced at snarling, but gave it her best shot. "Step aside," she warned. "I'm taking her out of here, now."

"Stop it, Walt!" Nicole cried. "Why put up such a fuss? You know damn well there's nothing left between us. You took all the money I got from the sale of the house on River Road, and you squandered every last penny. And now I resent you for what you did, and myself for letting you do it. And you resent me because I'm a constant reminder of your failure. It's over between us. You've known that for a long time. Isn't that why you took up with Nadine Witherspoon?"

"You leave Nadine out of this."

Nicole pursed her lips. "Very well," she said, after a brief silence. Walt stormed out of the house.

Marilyn sat back down in the chair across from her mother and looked into her weary eyes. "When do you want to leave, Ma?"

"Right now," she answered. "My bag's already packed. It's been packed and ready for months. I was leaving, one damn way or another. I just needed a little motivation, that's all."

"Consider me your motivation," Marilyn said.

✤ ✤ ✤

That night, in a motel room a hundred or so miles away, Marilyn laid next to her mother. "You asleep?" she asked.

"No, not yet."

"I'm only going to say this once. I want you to know, I stayed away because I was ashamed of myself. It had nothing to do with you."

"I know I could've been a better mother."

"No," Marilyn insisted. "I'm completely responsible. You were a good mother. My leaving had nothing to do with you."

Nicole took in a ragged breath and let it out. "I know about James and what he did to you."

Marilyn gulped air before responding. "How did you find out?"

"He'd been a little too attentive and my suspicions were eating away at me. That's why I put an end to his coming around for you. It was Opal's wariness that first raised a red flag. I just up and asked James one day. That's when he broke down and admitted he had molested you."

"Opal knew," Marilyn said. "I swear she knew. She didn't like Grandfather one bit. Besides the fact that he was a bigot, she had him figured out. I've thought about her often. I'm sure she wanted to say or do something to stop him, but she couldn't go up against James Quinn. Is that why you quit working for him?"

"I mustered up the courage to ask him, and he didn't even try to lie. Imagine how shocked I was!"

"Oh, Mama!" Marilyn took her hand, but Nicole looked away with glassy eyes.

"I told him I didn't want one more dime from him. That's when I took in the boarders. I was bound and determined that we would make a go of it without James Quinn's contribution."

"And I thought he'd made a pass at you," Marilyn said.

Nicole squeezed her daughter's fingers. "Don't think he wasn't testing those waters," she said. "I had a sneaking suspicion he was considering it."

At the time June had arranged the bribe, Ma had already known what Grandfather had done. But, he hadn't wanted his wife and children to know, so he had paid up. "What a beast he is."

"He's helpless now," Nicole replied.

"It's all water under the bridge," Marilyn said, because that's the kind of thing people said when they were anxious to put the past behind them.

"I knew what he'd done, and I didn't try to talk to you about it. I didn't know what to say. I felt so guilty—responsible. And after you saw me with Walt, I thought I'd die a thousand deaths. Good mothers don't behave the way I have, they don't. I'm sure of it."

Marilyn wanted to offer reassurance, but she was in shock and fresh out of words. Side by side as still as could be, they both fell asleep on that lumpy hotel mattress. She had decided not to tell her mother about how June had come up with the idea to black-mail Grandfather and how she'd gone along with it. And she wasn't about to change her mind, either.

✂ ✂ ✂

Freya finally found the courage to move in with her girlfriend, Gladys. And Marilyn, Nicole, and little Lilly moved in to the house on Nepeta. Marilyn insisted Kika stay put.

"This is your home," she assured her.

Freya was grateful, as she was convinced her mother would never accept her homosexuality. Kika was still waiting in vain for her daughter to marry a man.

Lilly's crib sat next to Marilyn's bed for the time being. Marilyn decided to call in several different contractors to bid on a bed-room addition. She stood shivering in the side yard as one of the more obnoxious candidates told her it would be foolishly expen-sive to add onto the house. She had to wonder, didn't the idiot want work?

Nicole stuck her head out the back door and called Marilyn to the phone. Hartman was on the line.

"Can I swing by and pick you up?" he asked, in an anxious voice. "I have an emergency on my hands, and I think you might be able to help."

Since the detective had located her mother and Loretta free of charge, Marilyn couldn't very well say no. She waited for Hartman by the window. As soon as he pulled up, she hurried out and slipped into his car. "June called," he said. "She's planning to end her life."

"Oh, for crap's sake," Marilyn cried. "And I suppose you believe her?"

"I do, I really do. We've got to do something!"

Marilyn had tired of dealing with her old friend and her never-ending antics, and she most certainly would have turned the detective down had she known the reason for his call.

"She's only out for attention," Marilyn insisted.

"No, she's not!" he roared. The wind seemed to go out of his sails, and he mumbled, "She called to say goodbye."

Marilyn felt sorry for being so crass. "Where'd she call from?"

"She wouldn't say. But I have an idea."

"What's that?"

"I think June might jump off the Arroyo Seco Bridge."

"Technically it's the Colorado Street Bridge. It just happens to run above and across the Arroyo Seco wash."

"Whichever. I think she might be headed there."

"What's got you convinced?"

Reg rapped on the dashboard. "She told me she stood on the Golden Gate once and contemplated suicide. And an image came to mind. I saw her standing on a bridge."

"She's bluffing."

Hartman smacked the seat next to him with the palm of his strong hand. "Dammit, woman, listen to me! I don't think she's bluffing."

Marilyn pictured her old friend plummeting into the Arroyo Seco. She flinched. "Fat chance June would do something like that. She's a survivor."

"I need to take her threats seriously."

A recollection caused a sudden change of heart. "Come to think of it," Marilyn told Hartman, "I once read that it's quite common for children of suicidal people to follow in their parents' footsteps."

"Precisely," Hartman said. "And, the Arroyo Seco *is* called Suicide Bridge."

"I know, I know," she replied. A few seconds passed and she added, "I've heard the stories. Back in the '30s, a crazy woman threw her child off the edge and then jumped. The woman died, but the child fell into tree branches below and miraculously lived, as if an angel were looking out for the poor little thing." Marilyn shuddered to think a mother could commit such a horrible deed. How desperate she must have felt. "Let's say June's serious. How are we gonna stop her?"

"I'll abduct her if that's what it takes to stop her," the detective said.

"How does June manage do this, to make people care for her?"

Hartman gripped the steering wheel so tight his knuckles turned white. "What happened in Hawaii? Is what you two are hiding all that terrible?"

"Lay off, why don't you?" Marilyn snapped. "I don't want to talk about Hawaii."

"You should come clean, for June's sake."

"Fine, I'll tell you, but not for *her* sake." Marilyn sighed, pushed a lock of hair behind her pretty ear, and proceeded with her revelation. "You see, we were up in San Francisco when June decided we should go to Honolulu to entertain servicemen. She claimed to know two women who would get us work. Like a ninny, I listened to her silly pleading and agreed. It wasn't the first time I had gone along with her harebrained plans, either. We got on the boat with those two tricksters. I was pretty indifferent about the whole trip, and what the heck, they seemed nice enough. I was told they were promoters. As soon as we landed, we were brought to a house in the hills and I was taken into a room where they drugged me and got me hooked on morphine. Then they sold me into a life of prostitution on Hotel Street. Believe it or not, I never heard from or saw June again. Not until the day Gary died."

"June set you up for prostitution?"

"I guess so."

"But you're not sure?"

"I heard she was working in a brothel on another island and I wrote to her repeatedly. But she never answered."

"Maybe they wouldn't let her contact you?"

"Who can say? But the thing is, she came back to L.A., she knew I was working at the studio, and she didn't even try to get in touch with me. She must have a guilty conscience. Don't you think?"

"I'll tell you one thing," he said. "She's one mixed-up kid. Maybe she doesn't *think*."

"Oh, she *thinks* all right," Marilyn assured the detective. "She's diabolical. She blackmailed my grandfather long before she ever decided to do the same to me!"

Reg wore an expression of disbelief. "You two are something else," he said. "I can't keep up. What did June have over your grandfather?"

"He molested me for years. The money we got from him brought us out to California."

"The depravity of man rarely shocks me anymore," Reg said. "But this sort of perversion is nothing short of disgraceful. Any grandfather who could do something like that over and over to his own young and innocent flesh and blood ought to be hanged, drawn, and quartered." Reg shook his head from side to side in disgust. "Sounds like the old bastard had it coming," he concluded. "You know, the hush-hush nature of the relationship between you girls is coming into sharper focus."

"Hardly the point," Marilyn said. "How many seventeen-year-old girls do you know who could cook up a blackmail scheme?"

"Do I look like a guy who keeps company with seventeen-year-old girls? Do I seem like someone who would know how they operate?"

"I suppose not. Listen, what will you do if June's not on or near that bridge?"

"Drive to her house, I guess."

They got stuck in a traffic jam and the detective began to lose his cool. Marilyn realized what they were up against. Finding June would be a long shot. If Junesy planned to end her own life, the probability that they would arrive at precisely the right moment to prevent her from jumping was highly unlikely.

"Sonofabitch of a sonofabitch!" Hartman cried, as they crawled along at a snail's pace.

"Make a right up ahead," Marilyn told him. "I know a shortcut."

Incredibly enough, just as the detective had predicted, they found June. She was sprinting madly across that bridge, practically blind and deaf with intention. Hartman honked, but June didn't even look up.

Marilyn rolled down the window. "Junesy!" she screamed, at the top of her lungs. Only then did June turn to face them.

Hartman stopped the car, hopped out, and rushed towards June. Marilyn followed suit. He didn't care if his abandoned car was blocking oncoming traffic; a woman's life was at stake.

June took off, and she ran fast.

"Catch her!" Marilyn cried.

June stopped in her tracks, then whirled around. "What the hell are you doing here?" she demanded.

"Junesy," Marilyn pleaded. "Don't jump!"

Hartman slowed down and inched closer. Obnoxious drivers, anxious to get a move-on and unaware as to what the three were up to, laid on their horns. The detective waved them off.

Addressing Marilyn, June shrieked, "You must despise me! And I don't blame you. I know I hated you. I thought Gary was the love of my life. What a fool."

"Gary's not worth killing yourself over," Marilyn said.

"But I hate myself!"

Hartman pounced, grabbing June in a bear hug. He heaved her over his shoulder and headed for the car. "You drive," he called to Marilyn over his shoulder.

After a considerable tussle, Hartman and June were settled in the backseat. But Hartman did not release her.

"Damn it, I can't breathe," she told him.

"Drive," Reg told Marilyn. And drive she did. Soon, the bridge receded in the rearview mirror.

"Think you could let me go now?" June asked Hartman.

"No," he said. "Not yet."

"I'm not sure I could've gone through with it anyway," June admitted. "I think it must have been easier for my mother, because her bridge was over so much water, and she had the big old Detroit River beckoning."

Reg was still breathing heavily. Marilyn felt bad for the detective; she'd gotten him involved in her messy life.

"Honestly," June pleaded, "you can let go now."

"Uh-uh," he grunted.

Marilyn could see the detective's red-splotched face in the rearview mirror. "Junesy," she said, "I do believe Hartman's in love with you."

"Fat chance," June answered.

"Where to, detective?" Marilyn asked, suddenly feeling giddy and a bit off-balance.

"Let's head for my place," Hartman said.

"I have no idea where that is," Marilyn reminded him.

"Just head west."

Marilyn did as she was told.

Marilyn wasn't sure just what a detective's place ought to look like. Once they were inside the bare-bones apartment, she took in the long room with two windows at one end and a small kitchenette with a hexagon window over the sink at the other. She snuck a quick peak at the closet-sized bathroom.

Reg didn't let go of June. He led her inside, as if he thought she still might bolt. She broke away and plopped down in a tattered easy chair. The sleeper sofa was still a bed, and Reg hastily folded it up.

"What do you have to eat around here?" June asked.

"You're hungry?" Reg said. "You're *never* hungry."

"I suppose chronic anxiety and the prospect of impending death sparked an appetite."

Reg opened a metal cupboard and pulled out a box of crackers. He sliced up cheese and salami and set the plate down on the coffee table.

"Eat up," he said. "Milk or juice?"

"What kind of juice?" June asked, as she reached for a piece of cheddar.

"Orange."

"That'll do."

"And you?" Reg asked Marilyn.

"I'm good," she said. "Nothing for me, thanks."

"I've got Fig Newtons, too," Reg offered.

"Bring 'em on," June told the detective. "I love 'em." She turned to Marilyn. "Remember how we used to devour the whole package and your mom would get so bent out of shape?"

"Oh goodness, we did do that, didn't we?" Marilyn recalled wolfing cookies with June in her mother's kitchen. One of Lillian's weird desserts came to mind. Her mother-in-law would break Fig Newtons into pieces and layer them in dessert dishes with Hershey's chocolate sauce and whipped cream.

"I also remember how crazy you used to be about Vernors, too," June told Marilyn, as Reg handed her the package.

Marilyn smiled. "I can't find any out here."

"What's Vernors, Marilyn?" Reg asked.

"Only the best ginger ale in the world," she replied.

"I can't get used to calling you Marilyn." June said. "I keep wanting to say *Berylyn*."

Berylyn? Only Junesy would come up with that.

Reg took a cookie, but Marilyn didn't dare. She had to watch everything she ate. When it had been substantiated that she'd indeed been poisoned—albeit in small doses for an undetermined amount of time—the doctors had immediately checked her into the hospital for treatment. The nutritionist had asked Marilyn to adhere to a bland diet and had instructed her to give up cigarettes, asserting that smoking introduced even more toxins into her already compromised system.

"Why did you change your name, anyway?" June asked.

"I wanted to separate myself from what went on in Hawaii," Marilyn said. "I went into a sanitarium to recover from the morphine addiction, and I met my first husband there. When I told him I wanted to change my name, he came up with Marilyn."

June's eyes flew wide open, and she gasped. "You mean you were married once before?"

"I sure was."

"Holy smokes. Gary didn't know—did he?"

"Nope, I never told him."

"You are a clever keeper of secrets."

Marilyn nervously ran her hands through her hair.

"It's no wonder, though," June said, "with all you've been through. I think the real trouble started with the rape."

"Rape?" Reg asked.

How could the detective keep up? Marilyn frowned. "I don't go around telling people!"

"Maybe you should," June advised.

"Why would I?"

"So you can move on, I suppose."

"I'm not about to take advice from a girl who only a few short minutes ago thought it made sense to jump off a bridge!"

June laughed uncontrollably, dropped the cookies, and rolled around in the chair, in an out-and-out giggle fit.

Reg stood up and looked on, worriedly.

"Valid point," June sputtered, when she finally settled down. "You know..." she took in a deep breath, "that was funny. And you're absolutely right. Why should you take advice from me? What the hell do I know about mental health?"

Marilyn addressed Reg. "Have you ever heard of the San Francisco Exposition?"

"The World's Fair, right?"

"Yes. Well, we worked there. June performed in Sally Rand's burlesque show, and I modeled on the Gayway."

Reg took a seat. "Why am I surprised? You girls and your capers, I can't keep up."

Marilyn held up her hand. "I'm afraid it gets worse. One night a man grabbed me just after I'd gotten off work, dragged me into the bushes and raped me and beat me to a pulp. I was hospitalized. My jaw was broken in two places."

"Dirty, dirty bastard," Reg said. "Marilyn, I hope I'm not insulting you when I say your life resembles one of my mother's favorite old-time serials, *The Perils of Pauline*. Poor Pauline was constantly terrorized by villains of all sorts, but she always managed to bounce back. Just like you!"

"Hey Berylyn," June said, "he's on the money."

Marilyn smiled. "I remember *The Perils of Pauline.*"

"Listen up," June told Reg. "There's more. She barely got a chance to heal up and so what did I do? I talked her into getting on a boat with two maniacs—that's what kind of friend I am."

"The boat to Hawaii," Reg said.

June nodded. "Yep, the boat to Hawaii."

"There's something I need to know," Marilyn said to June. "Did you know what was going on with Alberta?"

"That we were to be whores?" June responded. "No, absolutely not. They wouldn't let me see you once we got to that house in the hills, and then they forcibly took me off to Maui the following morning. I was kicking and screaming, I can tell you that."

"Were you on morphine, too?"

June nodded. "For a short time. It made me sicker than a dog, though. I couldn't hack it."

"Did you get my letters?"

"I did. I heard through the brothel's grapevine that you were all strung out. They told me you were a junkie. Can you imagine how awful I felt? By the time I got up the courage to go see you, they'd already shipped you back to the States. I had no way of knowing where you went."

The detective's face registered complete and utter disbelief. He sat there listening to them talk, speechless.

"I became involved with a man on Hotel Street," June said. "The old guy was one of my regulars, and he fell in love with me. I got pregnant and made him take me to a butcher where I had a botched abortion. That's why I'm unable to have children. I got so sick. He used his money and clout and pulled strings, managed to get me out of the brothels, and moved me into a nice little house outside of town. And he took good care of me. When he got cancer and died, his adult children came over from the mainland. They inherited the house and his business interests. Naturally, they kicked me out. I returned to California and started modeling at Bullocks. That's where I met Gary. He was shopping with his girlfriend, a thick-ankled nurse named Candy."

"Aren't we a pair to draw to?" Marilyn said.

June began to pace the floor. "You were thriving, working at MGM, and I didn't have the guts to look you up. Somehow I felt as if all I'd done was to lead you from one bad situation to another, and I didn't think you'd want to see me, anyway. Gary showed up at the store one day and asked me out. I fell for him, hard, and it became my goal to get him to break up with that nurse. His mother was crazy about her so it wasn't easy. He finally ditched the nurse and popped the question, but I had to open my big mouth and tell him I couldn't have babies. What a monumental mistake on my part. He put on the brakes and I was out of the picture. He was so clinical about dumping me, too. I guess I don't have to tell you, Marilyn, Gary Palmer could be as cold as ice."

"Man, what an understatement," Reg said. "He poisoned his own wife. Talk about cold."

"Looking back," Marilyn said, "I see how he was, as opposed to how I wanted him to be. He adored Lilly, though, and I tried to make that enough. Obviously, Gary never did love me."

"That freak didn't know how to love," June said. "His mother spoiled the hell right out of him."

"I don't blame Lillian," Marilyn said. "She's a good woman. And yes, she did spoil Gary, but she didn't raise a murderer. She's sick with guilt. I feel sorry for the old girl."

"You honestly feel sorry for Lillian Palmer? I sure don't. Those Palmers *did* raise a murderer. You'd be dead if he'd had his way! I don't profess to know exactly how his parents contributed to his twisted psyche, but I know they did."

But Marilyn did feel sorry for Lillian, and she didn't blame the woman for her son's madness.

"What happens now?" Reg asked June. "You were despondent—you wanted to die. Why?"

"Oh gee whiz, I can't imagine why I'm so cracked! Could it have anything to do with how I decided to blackmail an old friend of mine by using something from her past against her—something that happened because of me? Or could it be because I met this nice guy named Stephen and I thought maybe, just maybe, he might be the one to care for me the way I've always wanted to be cared for? You see," she said sadly, "I saw something in Stephen's eyes."

She hugged herself and continued. "Or am I ashamed because I intended to take the money I extorted from my old friend to leave town and put an end to the sick relationship I had going with her husband? Or maybe I felt somehow responsible after my married lover told me he was poisoning his wife and doing it all for me. Or maybe it was enough to send me over the edge when I found out Stephen was simply spying on me, for my old friend. I'd been duped, again."

"You do it to yourself," Marilyn said. She paused, recalling one of the threatening letters. "Hey, how did you know I wore a red dress to the Valentine's gala?"

June frowned. "Gary told me. He said you looked gorgeous. I was so jealous, I could have socked him in the face!"

"What an asshole," Reg said.

June fell back onto the sofa. "I'm a mess and I have been for some time. I've been taking these pep pills," she said. "They make me feel like shit. But they keep me from eating, and wind me up like a top, and I can go, go, go."

"Well, I'm going to force you flush them down the toilet," Reg told her.

"I'll blame you if I get fat."

"Junesy," Marilyn touched her arm. "I shouldn't have said what I did."

"I deserved it."

"Still, I don't want you to jump off a bridge, or overdose on pills. Promise you'll stick around."

June sighed. "I'm not going anywhere. I got overwhelmed, that's all. I felt bad about all the wrong things I've done. Like I told you guys, I don't think I'm brave enough to end my own life."

"It's a lot easier to take pills than it is to throw yourself off a damn bridge," Reg reminded her.

"If I was going to overdose, I guess I would have done it a long time ago," she said. She sat straight up and pointed towards the window. "What the hell was that? It ran up the trunk of that palm tree! Was that a fat cat?"

"Not a cat," Reg said. "A rat. They live up in the treetops and hide in the fronds."

"That thing was huge."

"Let's not change the subject. What do we have to do to ensure you don't try to harm yourself again?"

June stared at the palm tree, waiting for the rat to reappear. "I'm okay now. I'll be fine."

"I was a rifleman in the war," Reg said. "I fought alongside the bravest, most courageous guys in the world. We were in Anzio, Italy, and one of my buddies blew his head off in the middle of the night. He just couldn't take it anymore. I've seen how a human being can be pushed into doing something they might not do if the circumstances were different."

"You make me feel like a self-involved fool," June said. "My problems are so insignificant in the overall scope of things. I'm pathetic."

"Don't get down on yourself," Reg said. "You've been through a lot. I don't think you two girls realize. Neither one of you has come to terms with how crazy your stories are. Forced into prostitution? That's nuts."

"I screwed so many servicemen," June said. "I often wonder how many didn't make it through."

"Me too," Marilyn added. "I dream about them."

"I left my house and drove down those crazy streets to go help after the Japs bombed Pearl Harbor," June said. "It was insanity. At first I thought the planes would never stop coming. I thought we'd all die. I thought the Japs were gonna blow the whole damn island to smithereens. I had no other choice but to get down to where they needed help and make myself useful."

"I can't imagine what it must've been like," Marilyn said.

"It's all a blur," June answered. "I remember giving blood. I see the burned faces and body parts. I see the chaos."

"I feel the same way. I remember the war in snippets, especially the worst of it," Reg said. "Horrible images pop in and out of my mind at the damnedest times."

"I know exactly what you mean," June said.

"There was this little girl," Reg told them, his eyes glazing over with the painful memory. "She materialized during a firefight, and she was hobbling down the road in shoes at least two sizes too small, wailing at the top of her lungs, holding a bloodied pillow and cradling the bodies of three dead kittens.

"There was nothing I could do to convince her to put those bloody kittens down. I tried my best to drag her to shelter, but she pulled away from me and took off running. Seconds later, there was another explosion, and she was as dead as those kittens."

June bolted up. "What a horrible story, just horrible."

"The girl was dead and I was still alive. Sometimes I can't believe I made it out."

Marilyn felt compelled to share her own horrible story. She couldn't stop herself. "After the beating and the rape, I woke up in so much pain with my jaw wired shut, and I remember thinking, this is the end of the line, kiddo, you're not going to make it. The second go-round, after the fed-up madam put me on the boat and I went into withdrawal, I was positive I wouldn't live long enough to get to shore. And then there was the third incident. As I lay in the hospital with bleeding ulcers, irritated by Gary's poison, it sure did feel as if I was on my way out. I guess you could say I've managed to cheat death a few times."

"You sure have! I'll never threaten to kill myself again," June said, tearfully.

Reg reached for June, and soon she was resting across the detective's lap as he whispered words Marilyn could not, and did not want to overhear. She quietly picked up the phone and called a cab. Outside on the street, she stood and waited for her ride, all the while ignoring catcalls and whistles.

EIGHTEEN
1956

June wore pink, and pink suited her just fine. Reg had never seen her look better. "This is our first official date," she announced.

"Official—yes, I suppose it is," Reg agreed.

"Between June and Reg, and not phony old Stephen."

"Where should we go?"

"I haven't the vaguest. I always call the shots. This time it's your turn."

"You like Italian?"

"Love it."

"How about linguini with clams?"

"Sounds yummy."

"Then we'll go to Napoli."

Once they were seated in a booth, June asked the old waiter for his suggestion, and he recommended the ravioli with Italian bacon and fresh basil. "It's a wonderful dish," he said, with a grin. Reg had never seen the old guy smile before, but he smiled at June.

"I like this place," she told Reg. "It's cozy. The Chianti is wonderful."

"I always get a bottle of red to start, and then a bottle of white with the food."

"That's a lot of wine."

"Yeah, but you don't pay for what you don't drink here, a good policy. You pay by the glass."

June tore off a piece of bread. "Yummy," she said, happily. "So fresh and warm."

"It is, isn't it? I try not to eat too much, though."

"My bowl of cereal from breakfast is long gone."

"You aren't taking those diet pills again, are you?"

"No pills. I forget to eat sometimes, that's all. I'm starving now, though."

"Chow down kid, everything's great here."

She lowered her eyes. "Reg, can I ask you something?"

"Anything—anything at all."

"How'd you come up with *tire salesman*?"

"Oh that?" He chuckled. "Made it up on the spot."

June thrust her slight hands upwards. "Because," she said, "when I thought you were Stephen, and legitimate, I looked into it. Seems the tire business is booming and on the upswing."

"You don't say."

"Turns out, peddling rubber can be very lucrative."

"News to me."

"Anyway, I've been meaning to tell you that. It is a piece of interesting trivia." The music kicked in. Not opera, but Frank Sinatra. "Nice," June said. "Real nice. Romantic."

"That it is," Reg said.

"Are we going for it tonight?" she asked. "I think we've waited long enough."

June's directness appealed to Reg. "Yes," he said, "since you're twisting my arm."

She smiled, her blue eyes dancing in the candlelight. "We'll break the bed, I'm sure of it."

NINETEEN
1956

Marilyn returned to MGM. It was good to be back. One day, as she stood over her worktable toiling over a set of drawings and loving every minute of it, someone lightly tapped her shoulder. She turned around to see none other than her old friends, Woody and Lydia.

"Look at you," Lydia said. "Miss Talent Incorporated!"

They embraced. "I hardly recognized you!" Marilyn cried. Lydia's hair was more honey blonde than platinum, and cut short in the latest style. She was at least thirty-five pounds lighter, and she wore a trendy frock, which showed off her trim figure. Woody was as handsome as ever.

"The new me," Lydia declared, as she spread her arms open wide. "Well, well, Marilyn, you haven't changed one little bit."

"I'll say," Woody chimed in. "Pretty as a picture."

"We're married now," Lydia told Marilyn, turning her dainty hand this way and that to display a hefty diamond.

"My wife passed away," Woody interjected.

Marilyn wasn't sure how to respond. If she congratulated them, that wouldn't sound proper. And if she offered condolences, that wouldn't sound proper, either.

Thankfully, Lydia didn't give her time to respond. "We dropped by to invite you to the show," she said. "Believe it or not, I've got a gig at the Coconut Grove tomorrow night. There'll be two tickets waiting."

"What a treat!" Marilyn said. "And tell me, what are you two up to this evening?"

"No plans," Lydia answered. "We got into town just this morning. We're staying at The Beverly Hills Hotel."

"I'm not far away. Why don't you drop by my place for drinks, say around eight?"

"Sounds like a plan," Lydia said. "We'll catch up. It's been a long time."

On the way home, Marilyn thought about the second ticket, and what friend she might ask to accompany her to the Coconut Grove. Freya wasn't one for nightclubs. Her mother and Kika weren't keen on leaving the house, save for trips to the store or the hairdresser. June—she could ask Junesy! The two friends had made up when Marilyn decided to let bygones be bygones, and it was wonderful to have June back in her life. Nobody else would get as big a kick out of seeing Lydia sing. But she couldn't very well bring June along under the circumstances. There was that history with Woody, so inviting her was out of the question. There must be someone else.

✚ ✚ ✚

Woody graciously placed a bouquet in Marilyn's arms. "Thanks," she said. "They're lovely."

Kika took the crimson roses and went in search of a vase. After she met Nicole, Lydia insisted on a tour of the house. When they were at last seated in the living room, Marilyn prepared cocktails.

"Nothing for the two of you?" Lydia asked, when she saw that Marilyn and Nicole did not take a drink.

"I've been ordered not to smoke or drink," Marilyn answered. "Got ulcers."

"You always did have a sensitive stomach," Lydia remembered.

"I abhor alcohol," Nicole said, interrupting them. She pointed at her daughter. "Her father was a drinker—his ulcers bled out and killed him."

"You don't say?" Lydia's stunned expression caused Marilyn to scowl at her mother. Why did she have to be so blunt? Her acerbic ways often made people feel awkward.

Woody hesitated to light the cigarette he'd only just pulled out. "Go on ahead," Marilyn told him. He proceeded to strike a match, light up, inhale, and let the smoke out slowly. Marilyn could almost taste the tobacco. She sure did miss the comfort a cigarette offered, especially in social situations. "How's your son, Woody?" she asked.

He let out a ragged, telltale sigh. "Holding up. He's in Oakland, with Mother. We travel all the time. No use disrupting him. He's been through enough, losing his mother and all."

Lydia shook her head. "And the kid's not exactly warming up to me," she confided. "For the time being, we feel he's better off with his grandma."

"I see," Marilyn replied. She was sorry she had asked. It was easy to see the boy was a sore issue. How difficult it must have been for Lydia to care for another woman's boy when her child was dead and buried. In the end, Woody's son was probably better off with his grandmother.

"How's June?" Lydia asked. It was easy to tell by her bright inquisitive expression that Lydia didn't have a clue about the affair between Woody and June.

Woody looked at Marilyn, and Marilyn quickly answered. "Junesy's fine."

"Where is she, and what's that girl up to?"

"Living in San Pedro. Waitressing."

"June's a *waitress*?" Woody said, aghast.

"She's recovering from a divorce," Marilyn added.

"A *divorce*?" he said.

Lydia threw her husband a strange look. "Jeez, Sweetie. Why are you so surprised?"

"I can't imagine June waiting on tables," he said. "That's all."

"Why not? It's an honest living."

"I know that," he replied, apologetically.

"She's dating a private detective," Marilyn interjected. "I introduced them."

Woody's eyebrows arched wildly. "A *detective*?"

His over-the-top response alarmed Marilyn. He'd raise suspicion with Lydia for sure.

A short while later, they found themselves alone, and Woody whispered in Marilyn's ear. "Just in case you're privy, and I'm sure June told you, Lydia doesn't have a clue about our time together."

"Figured that much," she whispered back. "Does that mean I can bring June with me to the show tomorrow?"

He grimaced. "I don't know…"

"Come on, why not?"

"Okay," he said. "But you gotta promise me there won't be a scene."

"Throw in a third ticket, so she can bring the detective along. If her beau's on her arm, she's sure to stay in line. I know Junesy would love to see Lydia perform."

"I can swing it," he said. "One more ticket, then."

Lydia strolled into the room, balancing a tray on one arm. "*One more ticket?*"

"Marilyn's bringing June and her detective boyfriend," Woody said.

"Fabulous," Lydia exclaimed. "I can't wait to see that little spitfire!"

✜ ✜ ✜

They all went to Chinatown in downtown Los Angeles after the show for chop suey, in honor of the old days. Woody hit it off with Reg instantly. The two men discussed baseball trivia over glasses of beer.

"Hey," June said to Marilyn, once they were alone in the ladies' room. "Seeing Woody again isn't as difficult as I figured it would be. Reg is even more handsome than Woody, don't you think?"

"It's a close contest," Marilyn told her. She had trouble deciding which man was better-looking.

June laughed out loud. "Oh, come on, say what I want to hear. Tell me my guy's tops!"

"Okay, Hartman's a real dreamboat," Marilyn said. "How's that?"

"Better." Junesy launched into an impromptu tap dance routine on the honeycomb tile, while Marilyn powdered her nose and reapplied her lipstick. "That girl sang her ass off," June said. "Can you imagine—we're gonna be able to buy her records soon. Sweet Lydia playing on the phonograph in our living room!"

"It is exciting," Marilyn admitted.

"*What a night, what a night!*" Junesy sang out. She stared at Marilyn's reflection in the mirror. "Ah...I swear, things work out sometimes. I'm glad Woody dumped me. Those two were meant for each other."

TWENTY
1957-1961

Quitting detective work to open a tire store in Torrance was the best decision Reg had ever made. June, who was also his wife and book-keeper, had dreamt up the name—The Tire Detective. People liked the idea of a *tire* detective. Their business logo depicted a man in silhouette examining a tire with a magnifying glass. It didn't matter if the concept made sense or not, the place was hopping from day one. People often asked Reg if he missed being a sleuthhound. He wasn't inclined to explain how he had grown tired of the seedy side of life, following cheating spouses and double-crossers all over hell and gone. Besides, his eventful career as a private detective hadn't grossed a significant enough income for a married fella. No, tires were much more profitable than snooping, and the hours were better suited to a happy home life.

The store did so well, Reg puzzled over whether or not he should open another location in West Hollywood. Marilyn drove all the way out to Torrance to buy tires, and many of her friends did, too. They claimed it was difficult to find an establishment as reliable and affordable as Reg's shop out in their neck of the woods. June worked out the numbers and made it very clear—they ought to bite the bullet and go for it. In her estimation, a second location was just good business. But Reg wasn't sure he welcomed double the money, double the work.

During the war, tires had been rationed. But with the '50s in full swing, drivers began to replace their rubber at the first sign of wear. The American public adored their automobiles, that much was certain. Reg was no different. He owned a burgundy Chrysler DeSoto and bought a Ford Country Squire for June because she needed a station wagon to carry the plants, manure, and landscaping paraphernalia she was always lugging home. In the backyard of the San Pedro house, she cultivated a considerable garden rivaling those of the surrounding neighbors. Javier had spent a good deal of time schooling June, and she was now as enthusiastic about mucking around in the dirt as the old bachelor.

Reg's good friend and former employee, Danni Lopez Weaver, had taken over The Western Detective Agency. She kept the name and kept in touch. "Hey," he had been known to ask the female detective with the butch haircut. "Haven't seen you in the shop lately. You aren't driving on bald tires, *are you*?"

✛ ✛ ✛

Reg entered the kitchen and found June stirring a concoction in a giant kettle. "What is that, some kind of witch's brew?" he asked.

"No, silly goose," she said. "This is Kika's recipe. I'm cooking up plants and roots, and once it's all strained and chilled, I'm supposed to drink several glasses a day. In good time, my buggered-up reproductive system will heal, and I'll conceive and carry a child to term."

Reg wasn't sure June should drink the stuff. He didn't want to see his wife let down and disappointed. "I don't know, Junesy," he said, cautiously. "How do you know it's safe to drink?" He thought of what poison had done to Marilyn's system.

"Red raspberry leaves and other herbs? Silly, it's safe as can be. Kika knows her stuff. Her recipe comes from the old country. You'll see, we're gonna have a baby soon."

"If she guarantees it's safe…but, what if it doesn't work? You'll get blue, and what'll I do?"

"No, honestly, I won't let the doldrums take hold. I'll throw in the towel if this potion doesn't do the trick, and we'll adopt. But it *will* work," she insisted, swept away by a blind conviction that nearly broke Reg's heart in two.

"I hope so," he murmured.

June brewed the herbal mixture up by the gallons and drank it faithfully for six months. And then one rainy morning she barfed up her breakfast. The next day some poor unsuspecting rabbit died in a nearby medical lab, proof they truly were expecting a child.

"See?" June declared. "I told you!"

The baby was a healthy six-pound-nine-ounce-boy, and they named him Stephen.

By proxy, Javier became the boy's grandfather. He would often remark that if the child's blood grandfathers were indeed still alive and kicking, then they had to be ignoramuses of the highest order and deserved to miss out on all their remarkable grandson had to offer. Of course, such matters were never discussed with the child in the room. Little Stephen believed Javier was his Poppy. He had no reason not to.

Stephen's best friend in the whole world was Lilly Palmer. He was only four years old, but he already knew his heart belonged to Lilly. She was older than he was, had the good fortune to attend school, and liked to bring along books checked out from the school library whenever she visited.

"You know, kids," Reg told the children one day, as they sat on a blanket in the front yard while he read to them, "I know an author." The ocean breeze tempered the heat from the sun, but he still felt hot and the words swam on the stark white pages that bright Sunday.

"What's an author, Daddy?" Stephen asked.

"That's who writes the books," Lilly answered, proud of herself.

"That's right," Reg said.

"Which author do you know?" Lilly asked.

"Her name is Doris Louise Wilson, and she wrote a famous mystery called *Milk of Death*, about a man who poisoned his wife. Like the evil stepmother in Snow White."

"But the man put poison in milk instead of an apple?" puzzled Lilly.

"Something like that. It's a very grown-up book." Reg realized he probably shouldn't discuss his one-time secretary's bestselling mystery novel, considering the subject matter and to whom he was speaking.

Lilly frowned. "When I get bigger, I'm going to write books," she declared. "But not grown-up books. I'll write about princesses and horses and Ferris wheels."

"I'm going to be a cowboy and a fireman when I grow up," Stephen said, with conviction.

The week before, Lilly had brought over an art book. "This painting's called *Guernica*," the little girl had told the little boy, pointing at a picture that took up two pages. "Picasso painted this. Picasso was very sad about the war. People and animals suffered. That's why the painting's so gray." Reg had wondered if her mother had taught her this, or if she'd learned it from a teacher.

The great work was dismal and the children studied it for quite a while, enrapt. Reg fought the instinct to slam the damn book shut, to offer a distraction from the gloomy image of war, which was one he knew well. But he knew bright children often had an innate awareness and seemed to instinctively know the world was a dangerous place. It troubled him to think of all the heartache and sadness Stephen and Lilly might encounter. If there were any way to shield the two of them from harm, from cruelty, he would surely do it. But he knew he would not always be able to. The world would have its way with his son and Lilly eventually, in one appalling way or another. He hoped he could live up to the job ahead of him. He hoped he could be the kind of father Stephen could rely on and admire.

June emerged from the front door with a tray of cookies in hand. "You going to help or what?" she asked. She was eight months pregnant, and she gripped the rail firmly with her free hand.

Reg hopped to his wife's assistance. "Lilly's going to be an author," he announced. "And Stephen's going to be a cowboy *and* a fireman."

June's mind was elsewhere as she carefully made her way down the steps with Reg at her elbow. "I'm looking down the barrel at nine months," she said, "and it's almost over. I've been such a good girl. I drink milk, eat liver, take my vitamins, and mind my step."

The kids dug into the cookies, while June carefully lowered herself into the pink garden chair with the shell-shaped back that Reg had placed in the shade under the Chinese elm. "My ankles are so swollen," she lamented. "I told you, Reg. I knew you'd do it. I knew you'd make me fat one day."

"You're not fat, Mrs. Hartman," Lilly said, kindly.

"No, Mommy," Stephen echoed, "'cause there's a baby in your tummy."

"Thanks sweetie, but Mommy feels like a whale."

"You aren't a whale," the boy said. "You're a lady."

June's nesting instincts compelled her focus to drift to getting the household in order before the arrival of the new baby. She dismissively patted her son's head and smiled, then turned to her husband. "When will they start on the garage?" she asked.

They'd bought the house from June's landlord, and the place had needed plenty of renovation. The most problematic repairs had been finished. But Reg wanted a proper garage. The other work, he had done personally. He'd refinished the wood floors, added a closet in the baby's nursery, and put a new roof on the patio. But he wasn't about to take on the task of building a garage from scratch.

"Monday," Reg said, responding to June's question.

He had hired a contractor to tear down the rickety carport and to build a detached garage at the back of the property. They would have an actual driveway, instead of the two measly strips of cement that led to the cracked pad under the existing structure.

"Did you tell the guy I want a potting shed attached?" June asked. "After I squirt out this kid, I want to get back to gardening in a big way."

"Yes, I told him about your garden shed."

"Did you tell him I want a hand sink in there?"

"I did."

"Did you tell him I want a window that opens?"

"Of course. I told him *everything*."

They watched the children scramble off the blanket to run and hide in the dense hibiscus plants by the wall that bordered their yard. June sighed. "I know how busy you are, and you forget stuff, that's all."

"I didn't forget anything. He's drawing up plans."

"Come over here," she said.

Reg crawled on his knees over to June's pink chair.

"Look what you've done." She pointed to the grass stains on his trousers.

"Uh-oh."

"Give me your hand," she demanded. He did, and she placed it on the ever-growing expanse of her midsection. "Rambunctious kid you have here."

He felt the baby roll around. Reg couldn't imagine how it must feel, to grow a human being inside your own body, and he marveled at how forceful the fetus's movements were.

"Yikes," he said. "Does that hurt, Junesy?"

"Not exactly," she answered. "It can get uncomfortable at times, but I wouldn't say it hurts."

"I don't remember Stephen being this active."

"He wasn't this big, that's for sure."

Reg let his hand rest on top of her belly for a while. "What are those two up to over there?" he asked.

"Lilly's telling Stephen stories—she's always telling him stories. Their legs are probably covered in ants, but neither one of them will notice, they're *so* intent."

Reg had once believed he would never marry, but his determination to remain single dissolved when he fell for June. In his bachelor days he was afraid of emotion, of unmanageable feelings. Just the thought of having children to care for had caused him misery. What if he was a low-down snake like his old man? What if he didn't have it in him to parent? Monogamy had frightened Reg. What if his capacity to love a woman was bottomless? He had feared falling into a well of desire and devotion so deep he could drown helplessly.

June had a theory—she believed Reg chose her because she needed him more than all those other women he'd kept company with. But, he didn't go along with his wife's premise. To Reg's way of thinking, many factors caused him to love her like no other. June's physicality certainly appealed to him—those blonde curls, merry blue eyes, high cheekbones and adorable little ears. Her arms and legs were shapely but slight, her body a delicate miracle in his big, hairy arms. But it was more than mere attraction. He saw beyond the reckless behavior and sensed a great strength at June's core. What a wonder steadfast commitment and happy marriage had turned out to be.

Similar difficult childhood experiences provided a strong bond of understanding between him and June. They empathized with each other's struggles and related well. Their respective fathers had deserted them. Reg's mother used to say his old man went out for a loaf of bread when Reg was two months old and didn't come back until the poor kid was in the first grade. Then the lout expected Reg to fawn all over him, a complete stranger. And, when Reg had remained reserved towards his father, the man had the audacity to turn nasty and vindictive. Equally as traumatizing, June's father made many promises and didn't keep a one.

Both their mothers had taken their own lives. Reg's mother had killed herself in a slow, deliberate fashion. Despite having emphysema, she'd smoked like a haystack. Breathless and weak, she hadn't had the energy to puff, but had held a cigarette between two feeble fingers and longingly watched it burn. In the end, she'd keeled over and died—fell right out of her chair onto the floor. Ruben had come back into the room and quickly stomped out the cigarette butt. But in his haste, he hadn't stamped it out completely, and it had burnt a hole through the Oriental rug, right down to the wood floor.

On the other hand, June's mother had grown despondent when her husband left her alone with a daughter to care for. After years of nonstop drinking, she'd taken a bus into the city and had jumped off the Ambassador Bridge. According to all reports, the young woman had met death willingly in the waters of the Detroit River.

Reg and June were a perfect fit. Or, depending on how one looked at such things, a not-so-perfect fit. She claimed their neuroses matched. Either way, he didn't reckon it made a difference why. He wanted to cherish and protect June, and that's how it was.

The baby began to kick Reg's hand rhythmically. "I do believe she's saying hi," he said.

"Or *he*," June said.

"He or she—she or he—whichever. Does it really matter?"

"Stephen will be happy if it's a boy. He says he doesn't need a sister because he has Lilly."

Reg peered over at the bushes and spied four little feet shuffling around. "What are those two doing?" he asked again.

"I'm telling you, Lilly's a storyteller, and he hangs on her every word."

"What sort of stories does she tell him?"

"She talks about how it's going to be when they grow up and get married."

"*What?*"

"They have no idea what it all means. They're just playing house."
Reg looked deep into his wife's eyes. "What if we had met back
when we were kids?"

"Oh, that would've been awful."

Reg jerked away, miffed by his wife's response. "Why's that?"

"I thought I was a regular Shirley Temple and so very special
and cute. I would have behaved terribly. You wouldn't have liked
me at all. I was a smartass and you probably would have punched
me in the arm. And if we had met when I was older, when I still
believed I was destined to be a famous movie star, well that would
have been worse. I was a horrible girl—just horrible—self-centered
and ambitious and cold-hearted. I would have slept with you and
then moved on." June put her hand to Reg's cheek. "Believe me,"
she said, softly, "we were supposed to meet exactly when we met,
otherwise we wouldn't have been ready to belong to each other."

Reg could accept that. He saw the wisdom in his wife's words.
"Why didn't you become an actress? I don't understand why it
didn't work out. You've got the looks and personality. What went
wrong, Junesy?"

Her eyes got all blinky, the way they often did whenever she grew
fretful. "I never speak about this," she said. "I went for a screen test
once and the director told me that I was effervescent, affable, and
appealing. He said the camera liked my face and all, but he went
on to tell me I couldn't act my way out of a wet paper bag. I was
devastated. His assistant claimed she could get me in to see him
again. I believed her, and she used my desire for another screen test
to bait me into what turned out to be a trap. I never told you this but
that assistant was Kay Rennick—the lesbian who held me hostage
and beat the hell out of me. I was terrified beyond reason because I
believed she would do it again, so I talked Marilyn into going to San
Francisco. I was too young and too stupid to see that what I needed
was acting lessons, and that I didn't need Kay Rennick or anyone
else to get me in the door. I was worried everyone would assume
I was homosexual, so I refused to call the cops, but I should have
turned that crazy bitch in."

June sighed and looked down at Reg. "I suppose, if I'd been
serious, none of that would have stopped me from working in
Hollywood. But looking back, I recognize I didn't have the kind of

fierce confidence you need to make it in that cutthroat business. I can't take rejection and I probably wasn't as ambitious as I imagined."

"If you had become a big star, I'd be all alone," Reg noted. "And Stephen wouldn't be here."

"That's right," she said. "Things worked out fine in the long run, didn't they?"

The children scampered out from behind the hibiscus. Stephen stood before his parents with a leaf tucked behind his ear. He pointed back to where he had come from. "Our hiding place is down in there," he told them, "and it's green and secret and fun."

"Yes it is," Lilly agreed. She wore a sly smile and a red flower. "We can disappear from the world, because Stephen and me are magic."

TWENTY-ONE
1957...

Marilyn stood in the aisle at the supermarket, scanning the list of ingredients in Lilly's favorite breakfast cereal. She nearly dropped the box when she felt a tap on her shoulder.

"Howdy hey!"

Her head snapped up in surprise at the sound of Chet Rove's voice.

"Oh my, is it really you?" Marilyn asked.

"In the flesh," he declared.

One discussion led to another, and neither one of them made a move to break away. When the singing cowboy suggested they go for coffee, she returned the box to the grocer's shelf and took his arm.

Chet filled Marilyn in on his past. While he was overseas, his wife had taken up with a much older college professor. While her husband had trudged through jungles and had risked his life in the Philippines, she'd carried on a torrid affair. Marilyn then shared her story with Chet.

"Good God, my dear," he said. "So much has happened to you since I saw you at the Hollywood Canteen."

They dated for a few short months then wed at city hall, anxious to get on with their new life together. Chet had known all along that Marilyn was *the one*, and would have most certainly asked her to be his wife all those long years ago if only she hadn't taken off with June, leaving him with no way of locating her.

Add a man into a household full of women and the dynamics changed radically. Clearly, they needed more room. Marilyn searched and searched for a property that would satisfy everyone's needs—no easy feat.

Kika longed for a kitchen with a built-in butcher block for rolling dough and general preparation. And Nicole didn't want to hear screeching tires on pavement anymore; she admitted to being sensitive to the constant din of traffic, not to mention the sirens and jet planes that flew overhead daily. Lilly had plenty of opinions, too, and pictured a two-story house with a big porch. Chet desired acreage and stables for his horses, which were currently being housed at a friend's ranch.

Chet landed a starring role, playing the father of temperamental twelve-year-old wonder-rider Virginia Huntington (played by the equally temperamental child actress, Susan Doolittle), in the hit television show, *Horseshoes and Ribbons*. The popular duet of the same name that played during the opening credits was written and performed by the singing cowboy, along with Marilyn's old friend, Lydia Lark. Much to Chet's surprise, the soundtrack went gold, a testimony to what a huge television audience could do to spur record sales.

Chet's character, fittingly named *Chet* Huntington, was continually schooling his willful daughter, doing his utmost to improve her performance and attitude. As a successful breeder of thoroughbreds and a loving father and experienced rider, Mr. Huntington had the task during each episode to wisely and affectionately instruct his daughter how to care for and ride her champion horse properly.

As the head designer in charge of costumes for the popular series, Marilyn, along with her husband and the rest of the cast and crew, had to deal with the wants, needs, and extreme mood swings of the spoiled Miss Doolittle. Chet and Marilyn formed a we-detest-Suzy-Doolittle-club, and commiserated nightly.

✛ ✛ ✛

On a day trip, Chet and Marilyn finally discovered a suitable piece of land for their new home. It was out in the San Fernando Valley, in

Chatsworth, a town in the foothills of the Santa Susana Mountains. It took time to find an architect who shared the couple's vision. It took even more time to draw up plans they would ultimately approve, and yet even more time to finally break ground and commence building.

Meanwhile, Marilyn became pregnant. The need for the completion of the project increased with each passing day, along with the circumference of her belly. But the completion was delayed and she gave birth to little Wyatt while they were still in residence on Nepeta.

As Marilyn followed the contractor through the newly-built, nearly-completed, rambling country house, she considered all her places of residence up to that point. In her relatively short time on Earth, she had grown up in a grand house on River Road in Detroit, begun life in Hollywood at the Studio Club, stayed briefly in the Garden of Allah, spent a few months in Lydia's apartment in San Francisco, endured the ghastly brothel on Hotel Street, undergone treatment at Monte Bahia Sanitarium, moved with Wesley into the house on Nepeta Road, resided with Gary Palmer in Pasadena, and then returned to the Nepeta property.

Her self-imposed prison had been painstakingly dismantled, bit by bit, over time. Chet knew every detail of her past, and he didn't hold a sliver of it against her. Marilyn surveyed the green pasture with the stony Santa Susana Mountains beyond, grateful to have nothing to hide and not one secret to keep.

When at last the new house was ready, each family member had what they wanted and needed. Kika adored the country kitchen with double-ovens, a massive island, a two-bowl sink with a built-in garbage disposal, and best of all—an automatic dishwasher machine. Nicole looked forward to moving into her bedroom on the ground floor, as her knees were shot and she couldn't climb stairs. Lilly flipped when she saw her third floor suite, complete with a playroom and murals depicting unicorns, princes and princesses, and an enormous floor-to-ceiling Ferris wheel.

✥ ✥ ✥

The baby was four months old when Kika and Nicole asked Marilyn to sit down when she got home from the studio one afternoon.

"Something's not quite right with little Wyatt," Kika announced. Marilyn's heart raced. "What are you talking about?" Nicole leaned forward and took Marilyn's hand. "He can't see us." "No, Ma!" Marilyn said. "Babies can't focus for the first few months; it says so in all the parenting books."

"You must listen to what we have to say," Kika said. "They do see shapes and light, but little Wyatt cannot."

Marilyn and Chet's baby son was in the pediatrician's office bright and early the next morning. The days and weeks that followed were a blur of specialists, hospitals, and the shocking diagnosis. Wyatt had been born blind. Their sweet baby boy couldn't see a thing.

Marilyn dealt with the blow by doing her best to create a nurturing environment. Chet offered reassurance at every turn.

"Don't you worry," he told her. "I'll be there for our son at all times. Blindness is not the end of the world. All God's creatures have their limitations."

Marilyn interviewed candidates she deemed capable of tending to Wyatt's special needs. Not so much a conventional nanny, since with both Kika and Nicole in house, willing caretakers were in abundance. She searched for a teacher who had extensive experience with blind children—someone to assist in her son's development and advancement. She chose a woman that happened to be not only a teacher but also a trained nurse. Her name was Catherine Duxbury, and she was the child of a blind mother. Catherine's mother had lived through a horrendously nightmarish childhood. Knowing this, Catherine had made it her mission in life to help other blind children avoid similar experiences. She would live-in—little Wyatt would be in good hands.

The move went smoothly. The only casualty was Wesley's Jaguar. It was being towed, and while en route to the new house, the old car was sideswiped by an out-of-control truck and smashed to smithereens. It seemed a miracle that nobody was significantly hurt in the accident. Only the stylish old car expired.

Late that night, little Wyatt was sound asleep in his crib with Catherine close at hand. Kika and Nicole had retired to their respective rooms. Lilly, upstairs in her lair, secretly read a book with a flashlight under the covers. Chet savored a much-needed nightcap and watched his wife organize her spice cupboard.

Marilyn smiled at her husband. "I'm pleased I hired that interior decorator, even though it cost a fortune. She sure set us up in style. Working so hard on the show, I'm far too swamped to worry about such things. At least the house is furnished and put together, right down to my sewing room. All I have to do is organize this kitchen, the toiletries, and our closets."

"Uh-huh," Chet replied, displaying little interest in such domestic affairs. She knew his thoughts were wrapped around the stables, where his beloved horses would soon arrive.

"Tomorrow the horses are coming, aren't they?"

His eyes lit up. "First thing in the morning."

"We should turn in early, Rover. We've had a long day." Rover was just one of the few pet names Marilyn used for her singing cowboy. Whenever he was in a talkative mood, she called him Chitchat. On the set, she called him Hunt (short for his character's name). And when he was amorous—thankfully, quite often—she called him Buck.

Not long after Chet's prized mare successfully foaled in the wee hours, Marilyn left the stables. She made her way down the gravel path just as the rising sun illuminated their country home. The radiant sight stopped her dead in her tracks, triggering a thunderbolt realization—they were all housed together for a reason. With the exception of happy-go-lucky-Chet, each and every person residing under that shimmering roof suffered from incurable maladies of one sort or another. Her own were simply too numerous to count. Kika was scarred from brutality suffered in the old country, and the loss of family and homeland. Ma carried all that guilt about Grandfather and long-gone Beryl. Lilly would always be the child of a man who tried in vain to kill her mother and then took his own life. Catherine was haunted by her mother's nightmarish childhood experiences. And little Wyatt couldn't see a thing.

Marilyn recognized the entire population of the world—every man, woman, and child—were incurable; every one set on a collision course with mortality from day one. She thought to herself: *We enter this life and can never know what wonderful or terrible thing might*

strike next. What just happened is gone forever and all we have to hold onto
is what happens next. Each moment presents an opportunity for renewed
existence. Time and time again, we reinvent ourselves, for good or for bad.
Mortal as we might be, we reject or repeat or revise or repair our lot. We
are nothing more than what we leave behind in our wake.

Just the day before, Hartman, June, and their boys, Stephen and
Spencer, had come all the way from San Pedro to Chatsworth for
a visit.

"Berylyn, are you afraid to get old?" Junesy asked.

The two friends were shelling peas that June brought from her
garden and were watching the children play croquet on the lawn
with Chet, Hartman, and Catherine. Kika and Nicole relaxed in
wicker chairs and took turns holding little Wyatt. Stephen carelessly
swung his mallet and accidentally whacked his little brother in the
shin. Spencer began to scream at the top of his lungs, and June flew
down the steps in a mad dash to tend to his hurt. As her friend con-
soled her youngest, Marilyn finished with the peas, mulling over a
potential answer to June's question. No, she'd decided at last, she
wasn't afraid to grow old. The general consensus among the doctors
had been unanimous — miraculously, she hadn't suffered any apparent long-term effects from the poison. Her first instinct had been to
rush to judgment and blame Gary for Wyatt's blindness. But the
doctors said her son's birth defect was unrelated to the poisoning.

At the age of seventy-six, Marilyn would go on to win an Oscar
for costume design for a blockbuster movie, paying loving tribute
to Mémère in her acceptance speech. Growing old had diminished
her beauty. Even the brightest star pales and burns out one day.
Despite her notoriety and accomplishment, she was free to stroll
down the street, sip coffee in a sidewalk cafe, or sit on a park bench
and delight in the invisibility old age afforded, appreciating the
benefits of being unimportant and of no consequence to passing
strangers. Sheltered by that reassuring cloak of anonymity, Beryl
Quinn, aka Marilyn Walsh Murray Palmer Rove, would live out her
days in serenity and grace.

ACKNOWLEDGMENTS

The first person I ever told I wanted to be writer when I grew up was my paternal grandmother, Emma Farmer Moore. She was so pleased, she bought me a notebook and encouraged me to "stick with it." Thanks, Emma! I filled that notebook and many more.

I can't thank you enough, Bradley John (best husband in the world and most excellent cover designer), Elaine Moore (best sister in the world and tech assistant/social media guru), and Michael Philcox, for carefully reading the manuscript in all its various stages. You guys are my indentured assistants and cheerleaders, and without you I'd be a lost little lamb. I promise to cook food you love and feed every one of you till your belts won't buckle anymore.

I'm also incredibly indebted to my beta readers, Dan Moore, Disa Ostrom-Jaye, and Meg Oberti. You guys rock.

To my publisher, Booktrope, you wonderful creation, when you accepted INCURABLE, I could hardly believe my luck. Finally, many thanks and a big hug to a beyond stellar Booktrope dream team, Annelle Willard, Jennifer Farwell and Rachel Miller, for first polishing and then launching my fiction baby into the marketplace.

ABOUT THE AUTHOR

When E.C. Moore's not writing feverishly, you will find her out walking or sightseeing. She's wild about coffee, books, cooking, good wine, Cairn Terriers, miniature ponies, historical houses, and witty people.

She resides in a fifties bungalow in Southern California, with her creative-director husband, a yappy blonde dog, and one feisty Chihuahua.

✥ ✥ ✥

Your review means everything to me! If you enjoyed this story please rate and review it on the website of your choice.

A Preview of
INSATIABLE
(*Incurable Saga Part II*)
by E.C. Moore

ONE

The receiver hit the cradle with a thud. "Trouble found me," Doris Wilson told herself. The author of the two best-selling mystery novels, Milk, and Knife, had thought a bit of poking around couldn't hurt. Evidently, she'd ruffled the wrong feathers. Pacing the floor to clear her head, she passed the window. The black Mercury still loomed across the street. The late model car was new to the neighborhood. Could the owner be linked to the threatening phone call she'd just received? On impulse, she hurried next door to the Dunkel's. Karl answered the bell. "Doris," he said, "What brings you out this evening?" She tipped her head towards the Mercury. "That black car, any idea who that belongs to?"

"Nope, why?"

"It's been there all day."

"No law against parking on a city street." Making no effort to hide his annoyance, Karl bristled. "Look, The Rifleman just started, if that's all..."

"Walk over there with me, won't you?" Doris asked before he could slam the door. "It's getting dark."

Before her impatient neighbor could refuse her request, his wife rushed into the foyer. "What's going on?" Barb asked.

Doris pointed across the street. "I was wondering about that Mercury."

Barb pushed her husband aside to join Doris on the stoop, "That black one? I noticed it earlier. The Baxter's drive a Chevy, and they always park in the garage."

"For crying out loud," Karl snapped. "You two hash this out. I've got a show to watch."

Barb's tick kicked in, and both eyes commenced to blink uncontrollably. "The house is dark but for the porch light. Looks like nobody's home over there."

"A person wouldn't park clear down here in front of the Baxter's if they were visiting the Greenbaum's up the hill," Doris noted. "And the house next door to me is still empty."

"You have such an inquisitive mind. Guess that's why your mysteries are so darned good." Barb looped her doughy arm through Doris's bony one and gave her a tug, "Let's go snooping!" Doris allowed herself to be pulled down the steps and across the street. As they approached the car, they spotted a glowing cigarette belonging to a shadowy figure behind the wheel. Barb stopped short, gasped, and squeezed her neighbor with such might Doris let out an involuntary yelp. Doris didn't need the diversion as she was busy trying to memorize the license plate number. "Sorry," Barb whispered.

The Mercury started and sped up and over the hill. "ZKA 891," Doris said. She breathlessly repeated the license plate number over and over as they hurried back to her house.

Barb stood next to Doris and watched her furiously scribble down the license plate number. "Who was that man?" she asked.

"I have no idea," Doris told her, "but I'm pretty sure he's following me. I may have bitten off a bit more than I can chew."

To be notified when *Insatiable* is released, please go to http://www.ecmooreauthor.com/#!insatiable/c1evz

MORE GREAT READS
FROM BOOKTROPE

A Decent Woman **by Eleanor Parker Sapia** (Historical Fiction) Set against the combustive backdrop of a chauvinistic society, A Decent Woman is the provocative story of two women as they battle for their dignity and for love against the pain of betrayal and social change.

Op-Dec: Operation Deceit **by K. Williams** (Historical Fiction) A shadowy past becomes a sinister future in this intense historical thriller where treason, betrayal, and chaos sweep innocent and guilty alike into the path of WWII.

Paradigm Shift **by Bill Ellis** (Historical Fiction) A rich blend of social history, drama, love, passion and determination, Ellis delivers a powerful page-turner about the struggles and perseverance to overcome all odds.

Revontuli **by Andrew Eddy** (Historical Fiction) Inspired by true events, Revontuli depicts one of the last untold stories of World War II: the burning of the Finnmark. Marit, a strong-willed Sami, comes of age and shares a forbidden romance with the German soldier occupying her home.

The Summer of Long Knives **by Jim Snowden** (Historical Thriller) Kommissar Rolf Wundt must solve a brutal murder, but in Nazi Germany in the summer of 1936, justice is non-existent. Can he crack the case while protecting his wife and himself from the Gestapo's cruel corruption?

Discover more books and learn about our
new approach to publishing at **www.booktrope.com**.